CW00448783

FOX HALT
FARM

Celia Moore

'Emotional and heartfelt moments along with plenty of drama...'
Other books by Celia Moore ~ Culmfield Cuckoo

Copyright

Contact Celia

Website Celiascosmos.com
Facebook Celia Moore Books

Dedication

Fox Halt Farm is in memory of two wonderful people – my father who only ever wanted me to be happy, and my friend Ronnie for all the love she left behind.

I want to recognise the endless support and encouragement of my mother, Peter and Tracey (who championed my story from the start).

This novel is dedicated to my incredible husband Paul, for all he has put up with while I wrote – it is for all my family, all my crazy mixed-up friends and all those I have ever worked with. Without each one of these special people, and without our times together – the sad and sometimes hare-brained moments, the sorrow and the laughter, Fox Halt Farm would never have been written.

Celia Moore

PART ONE

Chapter 1

PAROS, GREECE
SATURDAY 12 JULY 1986
RICHARD MARCFENN

Janette stares up at the steep climb to our honeymoon hotel. She doesn't grumble but I'm sure she wishes she wasn't still wearing her million-dollar heels never intended for this terrain. I'm exhausted too, the journey here was so much longer than we expected, and leaving straight from our wedding was a mistake.

'Did you see that?' I look back at her.

'No. What, Richard?' she replies, her focus still on the ground.

'Something, or someone just fell off that cliff.' I point to a jagged headland a little distance away. 'I've got to see,' I say, already charging ahead.

On the cliff edge, I scan the unfamiliar shoreline far below, but all I see is sand and sea. I am sure I saw something fall from here.

A haunting laugh? My eyes search again, desperately hunting the source of the ghostly sound. As I make out an indistinct shape on the beach, my pulse quickens. My heart pumps blood too fast around my body, and then I mouth a horrified question to myself. 'Is it a child?'

Looking up, I see Janette is now standing on the veranda with two others. She stares back at me, swiping away loose strands of hair from her face. Her companions are either side of my petite wife; one is a much taller European woman with a pregnant bump, and the other a young man, probably an islander. I shout at them, but they don't hear.

When they do understand me, the man nods towards a steep path leading to the beach. 'I come with you,' he barks before yelling at Janette. 'Get someone with boat there.'

'Okay, Kostas,' the pregnant woman replies quickly. Her tone making me suspect she is upset with him.

Janette comes towards me. 'Richard, the path looks precarious,' she says, her doe eyes widening.

'Stay,' I tell her. 'I'll be back soon, I just need to see if someone needs help down there.'

'Be careful, love.'

'I'll be fine.' I kiss her on the cheek. 'I love you.'

BILLY MAY

*A*s a girl, my earliest memory is snuggling into the warm, scratchy folds of my grandfather's worn-out jumper while he told me magical tales about the curious creatures that lived on Fox Halt Farm. He knows so much about nature that he wove strands of truth into the wondrous adventures.

I remember how Grandad explained why the villainous goblin known around the world as the *Butterfly Catcher*, found it hard to capture his victims. He said it was because insects see things differently to humans. It was all about their time perception. Grandad explained how scientists had a theory called 'Flicker Frequency,' which said the eyes of tiny creatures can process more flickers of light than humans so they see in slow motion. The butterflies of Fox Halt Farm always escaped the hobgoblin, no matter how carefully he crept up on them.

As usual, the clever man made his explanation fun. He would have been a brilliant teacher or an artist. Grandad explained using a flick book that he made me, one where he drew on each page, a slightly different image of a horse, its rider and a jump. When he let me flick the book, I saw the horse and rider go over the jump. My grandfather said that if he had made a special flick book for a butterfly then it would have required loads more pages with tinier differences to make the movement realistic for the wary insect.

I have developed Grandad's theory through eighteen years of experiments; unintentional study because it involves falling off ponies mainly, and have concluded that in times of peril, humans see in slow motion too. We don't realise this because we have such cushy lives these days. I believe humans evolved with this same flickering time perception and this is why Homo sapiens survived. For example, if a starving sabre-toothed tiger pounced on one of our cave-dwelling ancestors they would have had time to dodge its greedy grasp, and this survival instinct is still buried deep in us all today.

I think this because when I have fallen off my horse or accidentally crashed off the top of the hay stacked high in the barn, and for example, when I did a parachute jump with Tom last year, everything slowed down. Each second for an onlooker would be a whole minute for me. I have experienced lots of moments of danger and they've all been in slow motion. Time to think and time to plan.

Dad says if I nose-dive off my horse I must try to land in a forward roll, so I won't hurt myself, and when I fall, I usually have plenty of time to curl up in a ball. I have only injured myself badly a couple of times. The occasion I remember most is nearly winning the open show jumping at Okehampton Show, but I came off after the last fence; just before the timing clock, losing the cup to Tom's older sister. I broke my collarbone that time. Nonetheless, I'm sure, when your life is threatened, time slows. People say your life flashes before you, don't they?

This will be my last experiment and it is following my reasoning. Time ticks by as I plummet down the cliff, and my brain processes every detail. I see each piece of gravelly rock pass slowly upwards. I pick out tiny flowers surviving in crevices. Now I imagine the rich summer grass at Fox Halt

Farm and my favourite cow, Deidre, wrapping her long pink tongue around the succulent stems. I see my hardworking mother encouraging the greedy animal to stop munching because she needs to get her, and the rest of our black and white Friesian herd, into fresh pasture. Mum will have another twenty jobs to do after this.

I watch a dark shape on the sand below me grow bigger. The shape morphs into a partial rowing boat, some of its timbers buried in the sand. The half-sunken wreck was once vibrant yellow but now most of the original colour has flaked off and its frame is holey. Inside, I make out a messy tangle of nets and ropes.

I won't prepare for this landing, content with my flat seagull-like approach. I will land face down on the boat and that will be fine.

Thud!

Thoughts and senses jam.

Twisting. Tearing.

Pain screams through my body and bile spews from my mouth.

Torturous pain in my ankle, leg and stomach.

Overwhelming taste of blood.

Shivering.

Silence.

An orange glow fills my vision. I'm happy… but now I realise I am seeing through the skirt of my tangerine coloured dress. I laugh, realising how the bright light they say you see when you are dying is a myth after all, because I'm sure I am about to die.

My eyes shut.

We are naked in the waves, the two of us laughing together in a sea of flickering diamonds.

Chapter 2

RICHARD

*R*unning towards her, I see the young woman's long tanned legs, then her pants and her naked back. All exposed where her dress was forced upwards as she fell. Her body is slumped over and quite still. Her shoulders and head are shrouded by the skirt of her dress. Just one sandal survived the fall. Her bare foot has a little silver toe-ring, and I flinch as I realise her ankle is at ninety degrees from where it should be.

Kostas wrenches the orange veil away. The girl is pretty, maybe eighteen years old. Her long straw-coloured hair is damp, and her skin, sickeningly white. She looks like she is sleeping, unaware her lips shine with blood from a cut on her cheek.

'Bella, Bella,' Kostas cries.

'You know her?' I check.

'She works as waitress in Atekia, she English like you. Here for the summer, I think.' The girl blinks.

'She lives?' Kostas searches my face to confirm that I saw the tiny movement. His eyes well up. This is not what I expect from him, he seemed so manful before. But now, Kostas notices something behind me and he regains his composure. I turn around. Ten shadowy figures have crept out of small boats, which are rocking in the shallows. The fishermen stand watching us. I think how we might look like a composition in a painting by Renoir – the men wasted no time getting here, but now it seems, they don't know what to do.

'We take her to the surgeon,' Kostas commands. Immediately, three of them move forward.

At first, we can't lift the girl. She is around five foot nine inches tall and heavy.

'Her speared,' a fisherman calls out. This man was further back, so he could see underneath Bella as we raised her slightly. It seems the collapsing of the rotting timbers, and the cushioning netting and ropes inside it, probably saved the girl but she is injured, her stomach skewered by a huge wooden splinter from the boat.

I can't understand their language, but I guess Kostas is discussing how to pull her free with the other men.

'No!' I scream at them, remembering how my best friend once told me you should leave the blade of a knife from a stabbing in place to cap blood flow until you get the casualty to hospital, otherwise they could bleed to death.

'Break it. Don't take it out,' I shout, and they listen, carefully breaking the timber spear away from the boat, and leaving it stuck out of the girl's skinny stomach. I know it's crass, but Bella reminds me of a cocktail sausage on a short stick as we carry her to one of the waiting boats.

We gently lower her onto blankets which Kostas lays out, and I cover her with a spare one. I am sure we all believe this is hopeless, we are simply trying to make the dying woman as comfortable as possible.

Kostas ushers me into the boat with the unconscious girl, and as I perch on the hull, my hand is sticky. I'm sitting in the residual scum from an earlier haul of fish.

It's just me with Bella as we are towed along by one of the larger boats. 'Bella, you'll be okay,' I say, trying to convince myself. It is hard making my voice heard over the grumbling engine, but I keep telling her, she *will* be alright.

The boat Kostas is in, comes alongside mine. 'Where are we going?' I shout at him.

'The surgeon,' he replies, pointing into the empty blackness. I assume he doesn't know the English word for hospital but, when we draw up against a small jetty, I realise that we have arrived at a private house. Only its white walls make it stand out, there are no lights on.

If the hospital was not what I expected, the surgeon is more of a surprise. He answers our furious knocking in a flower-patterned shirt that only just covers his naked genitals.

It isn't his nudity that shocks me, it is his shovel hands and fat sausage fingers, unsuited to dexterity or precision.

'What do you want?' The meaty-fingered man speaks English with a thick German accent, which sounds too high for his handle-bar-moustached mouth.

'Girl.' Kostas points to Bella. 'She fell from cliff. She land on…' He pauses and touches the spear of wood in Bella's stomach. 'You take out,' he says.

'I cannot help you.' The surgeon turns to go back inside.

'*Können Sie mir helfen.*' I pause trying to recall the German word for emergency. '*Notfall,*' I say at last, watching the surgeon, hoping I have used the right phrase.

'No time. Help her, please,' Kostas calls out, as the surgeon looks back at us.

Kostas repeats, 'Help her, please,' three more times – each plea more despairing than the last, until the surgeon relents. 'Okay, put her on my kitchen table,' he says. Kostas and his friends waste no time carrying Bella inside, and then they disappear, leaving me and the girl behind in the kitchen; their coordinated movement reminds me of a wave washing in and washing out again, leaving driftwood stranded on the shore.

I see there is another man now. The stranger holds a cloth, which he has used to polish the kitchen table ready for Bella to be placed on it. He is younger than the surgeon, Asian or African, it's hard to tell, with sloping eyes and a nest of curly hair.

'This is Ulrich,' the surgeon introduces the man to me.

'I'm Richard MarcFenn and this is Bella,' I say, placing my hand gently on her shoulder.

'Rainard Becker,' the surgeon says, in a manner which makes me think he expects me to recognise his name. 'Ulrich and I worked together in the Munich Hospital.'

'I was his theatre nurse,' Ulrich quickly explains, 'before we retired and came here.' I think they mean to reassure me Bella is in safe hands, but I suddenly want to laugh, not out of desperation, but because the 'YMCA' pop video jumps into my mind. I feel like I am in the actual presence of the Village People's biker and cop, as the lyric '*Young man, there's no need to feel down…*' starts to play in my head.

'Please wait in the next room, Mr MarcFenn. You will be of little help to us in here.' Ulrich's voice cuts across my song.

'Yes, of course,' I reply, looking around me to see where he wants me to wait.

'Here, please.' Ulrich shows me into a small sitting room. All I can do is wait. I test out the four black leather settees in turn to find the most comfortable one…

'We have finished.' The surgeon wakes me, and I see how he is forcing his eyes to stay open.

'Bella, she is in our guest room. Please come,' he says. 'It is good, you brought her here so fast.'

'*You* saved her life,' I reply. 'I only helped to rescue her.'

The guest room is enormous with Impressionist paintings all around its walls. This large space is strikingly out of proportion to the other rooms I have seen so far, and the surgeon notes my surprise.

'We had this room, and the one above it, built on when we got here. We wanted a bit of luxury,' he tells me.

'It is magnificent,' I say. 'I love the high ceiling.'

'Yes, we like it very much.' Rainard smiles.

I see the girl is asleep. 'Anaesthetic. She will be,' Ulrich pauses, and trying to think of the English words to use, 'out of it for a while.'

'Fifty per cent chance,' the surgeon says, as he stands next to me. I want to say fifty-fifty is rubbish, and I want to ask what he did, but the man must have done what he could. I can't quiz him, I see he is exhausted.

Rainard looks at me, leaning his head on one side and closing his eyes for a moment. '*Kaputt*,' he says.

I nod at him. 'I can see you are worn out,' I say. 'Thank you, both.'

'We will go and have a lie down, for a while,' Ulrich tells me, and as I sit in a chair next to the bed, they leave.

'You will be fine; as good as new,' I tell Bella, directing my words at her closed eyes, and thinking how I ought to keep talking. I have remembered my best friend Saffi Sanders again, and more of his advice. He told me once about what it had been like for him, when he was in a coma. Saffi said even when he couldn't move, he still heard things happening around him. He explained talking to unconscious patients is comforting, even if you don't see any reaction.

There are so many things I have learnt from Saffi, not all of them good. We were inseparable at primary school. He led me into all sorts of scrapes; mainly involving blowing things up. Saffi's army father is English but his mother was Mauritian, so he's bilingual. My school friend taught me French just so we had a secret language to plot in. When he moved to a new school in Germany, I was devastated. We lost touch, until I heard he'd been injured in the Falklands War. He was in a coma when I first saw him again, and I sat by his bed for many hours hoping he'd recover.

Saffi slowly got better, and now I find it hard to believe we are both only twenty-five years old, he has so many tales about the things he's done. I'm never sure his accounts are wholly true, I think he embellishes them just to make me laugh. Saffi said while he was in the coma, he had nightmares – one I remember him telling me about was particularly horrendous; 'I was in a meat processing plant and all my friends were lined up by enemy soldiers,' Saffi said. 'One by one, I saw my companions being pushed into a mincing machine, and then I was shoved in too.' He described how he felt a blade running through his kneecaps, his spine and then his neck, until –

'I was just a severed head and I had to roll away to escape,' he said.

I hope talking to her will stop Bella's unconscious mind conjuring up wretched demons like the ones that tormented Saffi. I don't know what to talk about, so I decide to ramble on about me, well, Janette and me.

'My wife, she's called Janette,' I tell her, trying to make my voice upbeat. 'She always wanted a fairy-tale wedding, and I have to say that yesterday –' I pause, wondering if it was only yesterday, that we were married, I feel so tired and so much has happened since, that I'm not sure. I decide it doesn't matter and carry on, ' – she looked more beautiful than I have ever seen before. I love her so very much.'

Fatigue makes my brain feel unreliable, so I'm not certain if I just sensed movement in her face. I watch closely but she is completely still. I consider the percentage figure the surgeon quoted and hope that keeping her company increases her chances.

'I have just taken over my family's property company, MarcFenn. It's pretty big with offices in London, Paris, Brussels and Berlin, and we're opening in New York soon,' I say, feeling a bit odd talking out loud like this to a stranger. 'Everything is selling so easily that the company is swimming in commissions. We just can't go wrong at the moment.' I stop and consider what else I could talk about, but my mind isn't up to discussing interesting topics of conversation, so I carry on about Janette, thinking how proud I am of her. 'My lovely Janette,' I say, 'is the only reason I have been able to take over the business from my father so easily. I'm just a newly qualified surveyor, but Janette knows MarcFenns inside out. She started there as a filing clerk when she was sixteen, and she's been my father's personal assistant for years.'

Bella isn't moving and I dread that she has died; *bored to death,* I think, placing the back of my hand up to her mouth, and then reassured as her breath warms my skin.

'Janette asks questions all the time. My father's nickname for her is his 'Mersey Magnus' after Magnus Magnusson, the host of *Mastermind*. She's amazing at her job. While we are here on honeymoon, my father is back in charge. I don't think Father will miss me much, he will miss my new wife though; I don't think he appreciates how much she does.'

The word 'honeymoon,' has triggered thoughts of Janette waiting for me back at the hotel. This isn't fair on her, or me. I should be having lots of fantastic sex now, not stuck here. I hope Rainard or Ulrich will take me back to our hotel as soon as they have had some rest.

I take hold of Bella's hand and massage her fingers, 'You are going to be alright,' I say, not knowing what else to say. 'When I took over the business from Father, he insisted on replacing the old letters which spell out 'MarcFenn' across the front of our head office in Berkeley Square. Father said that the weather-beaten name was letting down our prestigious frontage and they had to go, but the replacement letters are slightly smaller than the original ones, so you can still see the outlines of the old characters. This is like my father and me because he is still in the background of everything I do. My father still comes into the office for a short while each day, and I still check all the big decisions with him.'

I scan my eyes over the girl, but there is no change. 'Maybe I should tell you something funny. Laughter is the best medicine, they say. I'll tell you about the first day I met Janette.' I watch closely, but still, she doesn't move. 'I was just fifteen years old and I had gone into London with my father. We travelled on his commuter train from our house in Amersham in Buckinghamshire. My father was taking me to the dentist. It was the only time he did anything domestic, leaving everything else to my mother. Our family dentist was five minutes from the company's office, and the routine was always the same. We went to the dentist and afterwards, we called into the office so my father could deal with anything requiring his urgent attention.

'Back then, my own impression of me was that I was Mr Tickle, one of Roger Hargreaves' Mr Men characters with long skinny arms unbalancing every step on my spindly legs. My clothes never fitted either, because I kept growing out of them.'

I think she just blinked again. *No, she didn't* – 'I looked like messy Mr Tickle when my father and I went into the office that day, my face numb, from an injection. I still recall the shock of seeing Janette for the first time. She was eighteen, and the most beautiful girl I had ever seen. She stepped into Father's office wearing a cream coloured top with gold buttons and a tight navy skirt, so sophisticated, I thought.

'Hey, it's good to meet you, Richard,' she said, smiling at me. I turn to Bella. 'In case you haven't realised, she's from Liverpool, I can't do accents.'

There is no response.

'Then Janette said, 'You'll be taking over MarcFenn one day, so you better know, that since I can't run off with your dad, I am going to marry you instead. When you are old enough, that is.' I went to an all-boys school; I knew nothing about girls and I felt like the most unattractive being on the planet, I couldn't believe this stunning young woman wanted to marry me. I tried replying that it was nice to meet her too, but all that came out of my deadened mouth was an unintelligible mess of noise and dribble. That was probably my most embarrassing moment ever.

'When I saw Janette again, I had been at university for a while, Mr Tickle had been replaced by Mr Cool – I was still pretty lanky but I'd spent time in the gym preparing for my next encounter with my father's personal assistant.

'I went into MarcFenn's offices, all guns blazing with a toy ring in my pocket ready to call Janette's bluff. It was hopeless though, she just told me she was sorry, but she was expecting a full one-carat diamond. I stayed calm, telling her I would get something more to her liking.

'The following afternoon I was back, and Janette laughed. 'Have you got it then?'

'I need to ask you to marry me, first,' I replied.

'Janette badgered me. 'Come on, you've kept me waiting long enough – it was years ago, I told you I would marry you, one day.'

'I remember that day all too well,' I said, reaching for a drink. I swigged some water and made the best repeat of the dribble and noises I made years earlier. As Janette cuffed me around my ears, I produced a new ring. 'Will this do?' I asked her. It seemed ages before she said, 'Yes.'

'Afterwards, my father asked how I had paid for the ring, and I explained, I sold the Cosworth car he'd just bought me. 'Good thinking, Richard,' he said. 'Janette is wonderful, I'll get the dealer's number, they'll give me a good price for a second one, I'm sure.

'We do love each other, you know. We waited nearly four years after that day, to get married. I know we will be happy.'

It's late afternoon, when I find Janette in a shaded corner of the hotel veranda.

'Hi, love,' she says, looking up from her book. 'You're back, then.' Janette's smile makes me think how lucky I am.

'Sorry, darling,' I tell her, as I kiss her neck.

'Is the girl okay?' she asks.

I frown, confused by the question.

'Kostas filled me in,' she explains quickly, 'his wife owns this place.'

'Oh, I see.'

'He was pretty drunk when he got back, he'd been drinking with the fishermen who helped you.'

'Did he tell you about the surgeon?' I ask

She nods at me. 'Yes – and he said he'd been talking to someone in the bar, who'd seen the girl on the cliffs taking photographs. She told them she wanted to get some good pictures for her parents to see when she got home.'

'So, she must have slipped,' I say, trying to remember if I had seen a camera at the bottom of the cliff.

'And is she alright?' Janette asks again.

'I think so,' I reply but in truth, I am apprehensive. Bella hadn't woken up when I left.

'Richard.'

'Yes.'

'You look terrible, have a bath and a lie down.' Janette's concerned face turns into a smile. 'You look way too tired for me to jump on you right now.'

'I wish you would,' I laugh, but I'm not joking, I am frantic for her. 'I can't believe I have waited so long already,' I say.

'Have a bath, then come and find me.' She picks up her book again. I know my wife had a rough time with her family growing up, and she doesn't want to repeat her mother's mistakes, but waiting until we were married has been maddening. I'm glad Janette wants six kids because I foresee a lot of making up for lost time.

I turn to go, thinking maybe I am too young to settle down, but this is all Janette wanted, total commitment and marriage – nothing less. I do understand her. I realise that it's all down to the way her mother has treated her. That damn woman doesn't value her daughter at all. Her mother tells everyone she only got pregnant to glue her and Janette's father together, not that it worked. Janette says, 'I was one unhappy mistake.' That's why she left home at sixteen and went to London and that's why she wanted to be sure that I was her 'forever man,' determined her children would have two loving parents.

My eyes take time to adjust to the darkness in the hotel lobby, so it takes a second for me to see the woman who was with Janette yesterday.

'Mr MarcFenn,' she says. Her accent makes me think she is from Liverpool too. 'Welcome to the Ariadne Crescent.' The woman holds out her hand. 'Shall I show you your room?'

'Thank you.'

'You booked our best room, Mr MarcFenn,' she tells me, stepping onto the wooden stairs.

'Richard,' I say, 'call me Richard.'

'I'm Zara,' she replies.

She opens the door onto a small room. 'Is there a bath?' I ask.

'Yeah,' she replies but the only item I can see is a bed. Zara walks into the room, crossing to the window. She stares through the dusty glass. 'Look at that view,' she says, 'it's so beautiful.'

I don't notice the seascape at first, because my gaze is fixed on the cramped concrete terrace with two chairs, which look like they are held together with paint. I lift my eyes slowly to the horizon and now I see the faint silhouettes of distant islands. The woman is right, it *is* beautiful.

On the far left, there is a small town, and I wonder if this was where Kostas was last night, and if it might also have been the place where Bella worked? I think about checking the name of the town, but then instead, I ask, 'Where is the bath?'

'Just along the hall, I'll show you.' I follow her, thinking how Janette would have been disappointed when she saw this room last night. I insisted I would book our honeymoon. Janette had done everything for the wedding; 'it's only fair,' I said but I didn't research this place properly. It looked so much better in the glossy brochure. Janette would have checked. She would have had them send her room measurements, photos and a menu, at the very least.

Poor Janette, I think, remembering the terrible journey to get here, I didn't research that either. The travel article boasted, '*Paros, a remote island paradise.*' It sounded romantic to me. I had no idea we would have to travel for hours; flight, ferry, frightening bus ride and then the ferocious climb. I think how I disappeared as soon as we arrived, and how Janette was here in this forlorn room, all alone on the very first night of our honeymoon.

'Have a bath then get some sleep, you look like you need it,' Zara tells me before heading back downstairs.

I smell like I need it too, I think, suddenly aware of my odour. It's from the sticky goo in the rescue boat. I feel even guiltier now; having eventually got back to my abandoned wife, I stink of rotting fish.

I say it again to myself, *my wife,* and as rusty water trickles into my bath, I run our wonderful wedding through my mind. The bridesmaids laughing with my father. Saffi, as my best man, chatting up one of my managers, Vanessa, who is also best friends with Janette. The cake my mother made; it all took some planning, didn't it?

I think back to the cake. Of course, my mother didn't make it. It was eight tiers high and Sharpie was far too busy with all her other commitments to make it. My mother is not just chairman of her local Women's Institute, she is also rushed off her feet as 'a person of significance,' in many other societies around Buckinghamshire.

I remember Sharpie's phone call to me in the office; 'Darling, your cake is 'sorted', so tell Janette not to worry.' It turned out that my mother had simply put our wedding cake on the agenda of her WI meeting with a request for help. She informed me, 'I have fifteen volunteers, ask Janette to invite them all.'

'What about these ladies' husbands, shouldn't we invite them too?' I asked.

'No, Richard, don't be silly, my ladies will have more fun without their partners being there,' she replied, giving further instructions. 'You're having tables of eight at the reception, so Janette should allocate three tables to me.'

'Sharpie, from my calculations,' I said, 'fifteen people would need just two tables.'

'No, darling, my gardening club are doing the flowers, and the extra places are for any additional volunteers I discover I need, nearer the time.' Sharpie decides what will happen and it's done. My dear mother says she will stand down from her committees once her grandchildren come along. She wants to be a 'hands-on granny' and she wasn't even put off when Janette said she wanted six. She's taken it for granted we will have babies straight away – she can't wait.

I need to find my wife, I want her so much. The only person I find downstairs is Kostas, who looks worse for wear.

'Janette gone to call your office about important letter she forgotten to post to Mr Around?' he tells me. 'Sit with me.' He waves at the chair next to him.

'Sorry, where is my wife?' I check, ignoring his suggestion to sit down.

'She look worried. The phone here broken so I tell her to walk down to Atekia. There is a phone box there she can use.'

'My wife has gone to phone my father?'

'Yes, your wife say she must phone him about a letter she forgot to post to Mr Around. She telephoning him to say she forgot letter. She tell me to say to you, she will be back.' He looks at his watch. 'In an hour.'

I know about the forgotten letter. I drafted it last week and Father was making minor changes to it. The letter is to our biggest client, Michael O'Rowde, and the right outcome to it should complete another major deal for MarcFenn.

Janette was run ragged with final arrangements for our wedding, while making sure everything runs smoothly during our absence from the office. It is no wonder she forgot; I should have helped out more.

Chapter 3
THURSDAY 17 JULY
BILLY

I think back to 'Day 1' and opening my eyes as soon as Richard MarcFenn left my room. I remember blinking hard against the sunshine boomeranging off the cream walls.

I had been listening to Richard for hours, fully conscious before he even came in – but I didn't want to be conscious. I didn't want to live. I wanted to be in the glittering water, laughing. I loathed him from the moment I heard his voice, talking to Rainard about how he had rescued me and discussing the room. *Bloody* surveyor, is that all he thinks about? Well, obviously not, because then all he talked about was how rich he is and how he's married the most wonderful woman in the world. Loathing became hatred. He has no idea what it's like to have no money and to lose the only person you will ever love.

It's Day 5 today. Ulrich is setting up two flipcharts next to my bed. 'Right, Fräulein,' he says; he's been calling me *Fräulein*, ever since I told him my name wasn't Bella.

'It's Billy,' I said.

'Not Bella?'

'No, Billy,' I repeated.

'I can't be bothered with all your different names, you will be Fräulein now to me.'

I shrugged. 'Okay,' I agreed, quite happy with my new name because Bella hurts; that's what he called me, his 'Lovely Bella.'

'You still mad about everything?' Ulrich asks.

'I'm sorry,' I reply because I am sorry, upset I am still alive and in so much pain.

'Fräulein, you can't keep all this anger inside, I am going to make you talk.' He springs to his feet and leaps towards the flipcharts. His action reminds me of the cats at home pouncing on a mouse; an accurate explosion of energy. Ulrich folds over the front covers of the flipcharts, exposing pristine blank paper.

'I'm not playing Pictionary,' I say remembering the new board-game I played at home last Christmas. I used to love Christmas Day. It was the only day when Dad and Grandad would stay indoors rather than doing something outside on the farm. Of course, the cows have to be milked every morning and every evening, but Christmas Day is special and once the milking is done, they will stay inside. Grandad can draw very well so I insisted on being on his team, and we won every game. 'I don't want to play games,' I say.

'Not dictionary,' Ulrich says. He hasn't heard of the new game, he wouldn't have, stuck here on this island.

My nurse writes 'Ulrich' in red ink on the first flipchart, drawing a heart underneath his name. He swaps to a black pen, moving to the second chart. This time he writes 'Richard,' and draws a skull and crossbones beneath. I think how much better Grandad would have drawn the skull. 'You have to give me ten good reasons why you love me, and ten why you hate Mr MarcFenn,' he says.

I do like Ulrich, he has been kind and thoughtful. I asked Ulrich to make sure that Richard didn't visit me, so on 'Day 2,' he went to his hotel to speak to him, and his *amazingly fantastic* wife. Ulrich said they were still in bed, so he left a message that I was fine but still weak, saying it would be best if no-one came to see me. The lady at the hotel told Ulrich that I had slipped off the cliff while I was taking photos, so he asked me if this was right, but I haven't answered him.

Ulrich also offered to ring my mother, but I asked him not to. I spoke to Mum on the morning before my fall and I agreed to call her every two weeks. Mum doesn't need to know yet. She will only worry, and she has so much else to be anxious about. I want her to think that I'm having a brilliant time.

My nurse fetched my things from the place where I was working, and put it all away for me. Mum would never imagine me with such a tidy room.

'Number one, handsome,' Ulrich says, writing this under the red heart on *his* flipchart. He swaps to the black pen and moves across to the second flipchart with Richard's name on it.

'Come on, I have started. I need good reasons.'

'Ulrich, this is silly.'

'No, you are silly, you need to think about this and stop hating. You won't get better with hate.'

I think how I don't want to get better but I can see he is determined, and, in a way, I want to tell him how I feel. I don't know what to say first because there are so many reasons why I loathe my rescuer.

Ulrich thinks he still needs to persuade me and writes '1.' on Richard's chart. I know this tactic from debating competitions at the Young Farmer's Club. Tom told me, 'If you write down the sequential number of the next bullet point then your audience will know you are waiting for a comment and, generally, they'll supply one. It'll keep the debate going.' I am thinking of Tom now, dependable Tom, my best friend from always, who may love me but who is too shy to say anything. Growing up on the next farm. First day at school together, both working to get the straw or hay in from the fields, dancing at Young Farmers' discos. I even got him to ride my horse a couple of times, but I don't love him. I never thought about love before. Ponies then horses and exams, that is all I ever thought about until I came to Paros.

'Stinking rich!' I spit the words at Ulrich with such force, he flinches. The neatly sewn wound in my stomach pulls and hurts.

'You need to justify what you are saying. Explain please?' Ulrich says.

'That man has never had to worry about anything. Richard Marc-La-de-da ought to see my parents and my grandfather slogging their guts out every day. Getting up at five o'clock in the morning to milk the cows. Mum fawning away to her bed and breakfast guests, finding time she doesn't have to make homemade jam and cream for them. Growing all those vegetables, picking fruit and everything for such a tiny reward. He should see my mother lying awake at night hoping we can pay the mortgage. Every day, worrying where we find the next penny to keep our farm.'

I picture the lovely cows, imagining them waiting to go into the milking parlour. No instructions and no force. The cows just know it's milking time and queue quietly, always in the same order. My great-great-grandfather started the herd, and my family have kept the bloodlines going, breeding them to introduce tougher genes and increase milk yields. I love the shiny black and white cows in our fields at Fox Halt Farm. It's not good grazing on the edge of Dartmoor, but with years of experience, we know how to make the best of it.

Ulrich writes 'Money' on the flipchart under Richard's name, not 'Stinking rich.' He turns to face me.

'Okay, so he has no money worries, but I don't think you should hate him for that.' Below his name Ulrich writes, '2. Gay and Gorgeous.' On the other chart, the number two. He waits for me.

'Self-obsessed,' I say, launching into a tirade. 'He can't stop talking about how wonderful he is. On, and bloody on, about himself and his posh family.' Ulrich writes neatly in black ink, 'Talks a lot,' and now, in red, 'Listens.'

I want him to scrub that out because I don't feel Ulrich *is* listening. Okay, maybe his English isn't that good and perhaps he doesn't know '*self-obsessed*.' No, Ulrich's English is excellent. He is just not listening. He has listened the last few days when I complained how much I hurt. He helped me to the toilet and gave me painkillers. He was sympathetic about how awful I was feeling. I decide to get his attention – he will *listen* to this.

'Number three is spineless,' I tell him. 'I have plenty of reasons. Can you believe that his wife told him she wanted to marry him, and he said yes? 'Yes.' Just like that. He didn't even know her. They'd met twice. She only wants his money. His father too, he just does everything to please his dad. He's a wimp.'

Ulrich actually writes 'Spineless,' and then a red 'Thoughtful.'

'He stinks,' I say.

'Is this point four?' Ulrich raises one eyebrow and tilts his head. He stares at me. I can see that he thinks I'm running out of steam, but I'm not.

'Yes.' I am defiant. 'You have to agree with me, Richard stank.' I am remembering being stupid enough to think that if

I held my breath, I could make the horrible man believe I was dead so he'd leave but, instead, he put his hand right up to my mouth. I felt him touch my lips and I almost gagged at the stench.

Ulrich writes 'Smells' in black, and then 'Smells divine thanks to Giorgio' in red under his name. Ulrich is right this time; he does smell divine. I assume Giorgio is an expensive cologne.

'You do smell nice,' I tell him. 'Five. Not funny,' I say, retelling what Richard said about his marriage proposal. 'Is that funny?' I ask.

'Yes, it is amusing,' Ulrich replies but he does allow me to have Richard's lack of humour as a point. There is a pattern beginning to form, and he writes in red, 'Funny – makes me laugh.'

I can tell making people happy is important to Ulrich, and I recall Tom again, he always wanted to make me laugh too.

'What now, Fräulein?' Ulrich writes '6' in black.

'Spoilt. His dad buys him an expensive car which he sells to pay for a stupid ring, and then he gets a new one just like that with bells and whistles on it too, I expect,' I say. Ulrich frowns.

'What do you mean bells and whistles?' he asks and I explain, pleased he is not questioning me about being spoilt, because I have been spoilt by Dad and Grandad all my life. All the ponies and horses they've bought me, all the riding equipment, the keep and everything – as a boy, my grandfather used heavy horses on the farm and he misses them. He loves horses more than cows, and horses certainly don't make money – they cost a fortune and it is all money we don't have.

They bought me a Shetland-cross-Dartmoor foal a week after I was born, from a local pony sale, on the way to picking up Mum and me from hospital. Dad collected us with Grandad and the scruffy brown and white pony they named 'Banjo,' squashed in the back of his van. I've always had ponies, two or three at a time. I rode them before school. I reckon in lessons, I must have reeked of them. I only hope the other farming kids smelt too, all blissfully unaware of our animal scent. Every day was full of ponies for me, looking after them, or training them. One of my favourite tricks for Banjo was teaching him to climb steps. Now I'm too big to ride him, Grandad has made him a little cart to pull.

My grandfather has given me all the encouragement in the world. He took me to my first gymkhana and I remember Banjo with his bridle held together with orange baler cord. I was so embarrassed about our appearance when everyone else seemed so well turned out. I must have looked like the local gypsy. Of course, Grandad realised how inadequate I felt, and each birthday or Christmas after that, he would find a new piece of riding kit for me. He and Dad loved it when I started winning rosettes. They loved me winning as much as I did. There was no spare money for anything but somehow, they always scraped enough together for riding.

I got a Saturday job at the local O'Rowdes' supermarket, to help, but it was never adequate to meet the costs. Dad and Grandad built homemade jumps, so I could practise. The ponies that they bought were always really good too. Yes, I was spoilt like Richard.

I am confused. I still hate him, yet thinking about the farm makes me think that I need to get better. But now I remember Kostas laughing at me. 'Stupid Bella, you so naive. You have to see I never leave my wife.' Weeks of him telling me how much he loved me, all that amazing time together, and not once did I guess he was married. No confession until now about his wife and their imminent baby.

I tried to throw my arms around him, but he fought me off. I was wracked with hateful rejection. I remember the anguish as my body folded over with disbelief he'd lied and used me. My lungs emptied. Hollowness. Then my insides froze. A thick block of ice like the one Mum tips out of the hen's bucket on frosted mornings so she can refill the container with the warm water. Nothing will melt my heart. The ice is still there, spikey and hard.

Kostas was exciting. His charcoal eyes smouldering when he insisted, he'd love me forever. Swimming together in the shadowy night. The gritty beach. Cool water lapping our entangled legs. Soft kisses on my neck and then the forceful pressure on my willing mouth. My need for him. The caring concern when I told him I'd never been with anyone before. The fire. Pain. Joy. Utter devotion. 'My Beautiful Bella. I am in Wonderland,' that's what he said.

Harrowing hurt as he shoved me away. Then everything turned grey. His grey silhouette marching towards his wife. My grey skin and my glacier heart trembling. My vision steaming with boiling tears. No life without him.

The cliff edge.

I am falling…

I yell at Ulrich, 'He rescued me. I don't want to be rescued, I want to die!'

Chapter 4

BERKELEY SQUARE, LONDON
MONDAY 15 SEPTEMBER
RICHARD

'*My daughter is lost.*' These words reverberate around my brain – the four words are from a letter I received this morning. It said,

'The girl who came back to Fox Halt Farm is not the same. The loving girl who left to be a waitress on a faraway island between school exams and starting university is gone. Billy had a fire in her belly. She and I used to talk about everything. We used to laugh. The outside of my beautiful daughter looks just as it did. Maybe skinnier. The scar is healing well, but inside – all her joy and fighting spirit have died.'

So, Kostas was wrong when he said the girl at the bottom of the cliff was called 'Bella,' she is Billy. It is a shame, 'Billy' just doesn't seem to do her justice. Bella was better.

'We had a week before she went off to her London university, but I couldn't get her to open up. Billy said she was fine, saying it was probably delayed shock after the terrible fall. She wouldn't see any of her friends. She didn't even see her horse, saying he was okay because her grandfather is looking after him now.'

It seems as though her mother wrote her thoughts down as they came into her head.

'Billy's dad and her grandfather couldn't deal with her, so they kept pretending they needed to sort things outside. My daughter used to help me all the time. She used to say I had too much to do with the cows and everything else, but she didn't notice how busy I was.'

I hope she will be okay. I wrote to her this morning, sending all our love, to a tiny bedsit she's rented, and then decided to contact you to see if you can tell me anything about what happened.

Please write back - Anything will help. Thank you, Daniella May.'

There's a postscript, which says Billy only mentioned my name once. Mrs May said it took her ages to find me, and she hoped I was the person who rescued her daughter. She says thank you again and apologises for troubling me. As the phone starts to ring, I put the letter down.

'Yes, Shannon?'

'Richard, Mr Sanders is on the line for you.'

'Saffi,' I say.

'Hello, Richard, I need some help…'

'What is it this time? Someone else you want me to tell you were with me?'

The line is quiet. 'Err, something like that,' he replies eventually.

'Saffi, why do you have to have such a complicated life?' I say. 'It's a good job I love you because I don't like lying for you. Always some prank or other. Won't you ever change?'

BALHAM, LONDON
THURSDAY 16 FEBRUARY 1989
BILLY

I stare at the letter heading 'MarcFenn' and the logo of a pineapple, embossed in gold. The name agitates me, taking me back more than three years. Some of my desolation rises to the surface – the feelings I dropped into a deep grave and covered over with the lonely distraction of my degree. All my focus on achieving first class honours. No socialising, no drinking, and no student parties, just study. I want these memories to remain interred. *Go away!*

I don't understand. I am not expecting this correspondence. One scan is usually all it takes. I am always reading these days, and the quicker I find the important parts the better.

My eyes skim over the words. *'Hello Billy, I am Richard MarcFenn, I helped rescue you in Paros.'*

Sweat under my armpits. Anger. My head is thumping. *'My wife, Janette has always sent a Christmas card to your mother, and your mum always writes back telling us how well you are doing.'*

A new uncomfortable recollection comes into my mind. I'm home, at Fox Halt Farm with the MarcFenns' framed wedding photograph on the sideboard. This picture 'of the happy couple' my mother always explains to her bed and breakfast guests, telling them how her family is indebted to the man because he rescued her daughter after a serious accident when she fell off a cliff trying to take a snap shot of the sea – I haven't said I fell, but it is easier to let her believe that. Whenever I can, I hide the odious picture behind an ornament, but it soon returns to the front again. This is a wordless war between Mum and me.

Every year, my mother reads me the paragraph of news in Janette's Christmas card. I want her words to wash over me but they stick like drool, so I know that the couple have twin girls who must be nearly two.

I put the letter down to make a mug of tea, and I return to 'The Major Design Project' that Tom's sister lent me. Charlotte was highly commended for this assignment which she completed for her architectural degree, and the way she has presented it is helping me with my own final dissertation.

My flatmate Simon Arkly comes in, picking up the hateful letter.

'What's this?' he asks.

'I don't know,' I reply.

He glances at the envelope. 'It's for you – is it a reply from another company about their tax regime?'

I shrug at him.

'Are you sure it's not for your study paper?' he checks again.

'No,' I say firmly.

He moves a couple of paces to the sink. 'Do you want another drink?' he asks and I hold out my mug to indicate that I do.

'How did your neuroscience presentation go?' I ask as he takes the cup.

'The prof liked it a lot,' he replies. We don't ask questions about anything other than our studies. Nothing personal is ever discussed. He's studying psychology and I am completing a business studies degree. We are in the same year at the same university, and we will achieve top honours in June, because all Simon and I do is study.

We live in this tiny room and have our home computers side by side on one cramped wall, sharing a sofa-bed because that's all that fits in the space we have; making it up into a bed at exactly ten o'clock each night. We sleep beside each other but never touch. We eat our meals together and we talk, but only about our study subjects, arguing differing points of view, discussing the minutest details and sometimes, I feel we take opposite stands just to make our conversations last longer. I think we could get a degree in each other's subjects. It's been like this since we met. His demons and mine locked away in the deepest recesses of our lonely minds.

Simon picks up my letter and waves it at me. I have been vague, and he is used to me responding with facts and figures. He thinks it must be something to do with a questionnaire I sent out to a hundred businesses, part of my research for my degree.

'Is this not going to be useful?' he asks me.

'It's just a circular, throw it away please.'

'Is it?' He frowns.

'Yes,' I reply, getting up and snatching the letter. We don't behave like this. We are always polite to each other.

'Sorry,' I say quickly. 'I haven't read it properly, but I don't think it's important.'

'Okay,' Simon says as he sits down at his computer. I have the letter in my hand and I start to read from where I stopped before. '*I will keep this to the point. I am hoping that you will come and work for MarcFenn when you graduate. We need people like you, offering a highly competitive salary for the right people.*'

I am sweating again; it's February and it's freezing in the bedsit, yet I feel stifled. My mouth is dry. I move my tongue in a wide slow circle to moisten my lips and to stop me from crying. '*MarcFenn takes on three graduates each year. We don't employ anyone with property related degrees because we have found that the skills they believe they have mastered at college and their over-confidence are unhelpful. We would also like to offer your friend, Simon Ackly, a place too.'*

The incorrect spelling of Simon's surname immediately rings alarm bells in my mind. I'm suspicious now that Mum has some involvement in this strange offer. She asked me what Simon's surname was in one of her letters last month. She said that she had guests staying and their son was called Simon and he was studying psychology at university. 'I wonder if they're your Simon's family?' she asked.

I expect my carelessly scrawled reply was difficult to read. Mum writes to me every three or four days. So many letters that, most of the time, I don't even read them. I know what they will say; it will be trivia about every silly detail of the life on the farm, which cow has mastitis, how many lambs were born the night before, even when the dog hasn't eaten his dinner. I write back occasionally when there is something a little different that I can comment on. We speak on the phone every other Sunday, when I go to the phone box down the road. Simon and I can't afford a phone, we wouldn't want one either. I never have much to say other than we are studying and doing well. Mum likes it that Simon is here, even though she has never met him. I like it too.

My scar burns as I finish reading. *'I hope everything is going well for you. Please let me, or my personal assistant, Shannon Xavier, know by the end of March, if you would like to discuss these job offers. Richard.'*

Simon stares at me. He must see that I'm upset.

'It's a job offer for you,' I say, my voice cracking as I pass him the letter. 'I have to get some air,' I explain and I walk out of the flat. I wonder why Richard MarcFenn doesn't know how much I hate him and his wife. I should be dead now and at peace but I'm not dead – I'm a distrustful angry mess.

I wander around the local streets trying to focus on positive thoughts, such as when I met Simon: It was in the first week of university when I noticed him in the refectory. Something drew me to him right away. He was out of place, like an illustrated textbook on the mechanics of steam engines in the romance section of a small bookshop.

He was alone reading a dog-eared pamphlet. I could see he was tall and thin but the most noticeable thing for me was his hair. His black hair had no shine. I thought it was dyed and crimped. None of the males I had met up to then dyed their hair. His hair was like fur.

I took my lunch over to him and sat down. He ignored me. It felt refreshing because all the other new students asked the same questions like, where are you from? What course are you doing? Where are you staying? Not listening, just speaking about themselves and handing out invitations to parties.

I ate my sandwich and then left to go to my class. The next two days, I sat with him again and still no words. But the following day, he held out his hand.

'Simon Arkly.' He didn't look up, but I took hold of his bony fingers.

'Billy May,' I replied, noticing his purple nail varnish. It was another week before I saw his eyes. That day, he closed his book.

'Where do you live, Billy?' he asked. I thought it was nice to hear his voice again

'I've got a tiny bedsit in Balham.'

'Can I stay there for a few days?'

I shook my head, thinking there was hardly enough room for me.

'I argued with my sister this morning, I can't stay at her flat any longer. She's pregnant. I hate all her moods.'

'Okay,' I said, assuming it would be a day or two but all this time later, we are still together yet not together. I guessed the first time I saw Simon, all dressed in black in the furthest corner of the room, that he was hiding. I felt an empathy. The day he became an uncle he was quite emotional and started to tell me about how he was relentlessly bullied at school. I couldn't deal with his misery, and I quickly closed the difficult subject down. This has been the only mention of our past lives.

Simon wears wonderful eye make-up and nail varnish and I don't wear either because I want to be invisible. I am avoiding being hurt again. This isn't helping, painful memories are stirring, even my ankle is agonising and it hasn't ached for years.

When I get back to the bedsit, Simon is lying in his half of the sofa-bed. 'Are you okay?' he asks.

I nod.

His voice is gentle. 'It's a job offer for both of us, we could work together, Billy.'

'No.' My reply is too loud, this is not the way I should be responding. 'Who offers a job without an interview?' I ask as calmly as I can. 'Richard MarcFenn doesn't know me. He may think he helped me, but I don't have to accept his stupid job offer.'

'Billy, I'm sorry, I didn't mean to upset you.' Simon sits up. 'But what can anyone suss from an interview anyway? This chap must know we're top of our respective classes. This could be fun.'

The word fun shocks me. We never say anything is fun. We use words like helpful and interesting. *When did we have fun?*

'I can't,' I reply. 'Sorry, but I just can't.'

'Billy, it will be alright. We can look after each other.' I see how Simon is scared too. 'Okay, I'll think about it,' I say, attempting to make him feel better, 'but let's not talk about this now, I've got to get up early to finish another questionnaire before I send it out.'

'Do you want to run it through with me in the morning?' Simon asks. 'I don't need to be in college till eleven.'

'Yes please, that would be useful,' I say.

Chapter 5

BERKELEY SQUARE
MONDAY 29 MAY 1989
RICHARD

*I*t has been years since I received Daniella's first letter. I wrote back straight away, explaining that I hadn't seen Billy after we took her to the surgeon, regretting that I couldn't help her.

A second letter arrived. Daniella apologised again for being a bother. She said how hard it was without Billy at home, and that her father was saying, 'Even that 'orse of 'ers is looking all melancholy.'

Daniella wrote about how they had been helping get the last of the straw in on their neighbour's farm and that it was all behind this year because the rain hadn't let up for days. She then immediately, added some good news, happy that they had managed to get in enough logs for the winter for her Rayburn stove in her kitchen and for the open fire in the guests' sitting room. She explained they were mainly oak logs, and the logs would be wetter than she would have liked, but it would be easier than running out in January, like they had the previous year, when she had sent her husband, Jack, to chainsaw down a tree. The ground was too sodden to drive the tractor on – its tyre tracks would mess up the pasture – so they had to make several trips, carrying the logs in sacks on their backs. I replied, saying I had never been on a farm in my life but her letter had painted vivid pictures of a 'bit of Devon'. I signed off saying she mustn't worry about bothering me because I was genuinely pleased she had written.

The next week she wrote again, inviting Janette and me to stay for bed and breakfast, saying she wouldn't charge us ten pounds a night per person, like she normally did, it was the least she could do for saving her daughter's life. I thanked her, commenting she was charging too little, and we just continued to write.

I feel I know Daniella so well, and she knows me better than anyone else in the world, even Janette and Saffi. Her letters arrive on Mondays, making me smile when I recognise her writing on the envelopes headed up. 'STRICTLY PRIVATE – ADDRESSEE ONLY.' I always reply immediately using a brown envelope, because Daniella said it was best if they look like bills, 'then no-one will be suspicious,' she said. She made me laugh suggesting this, but now our secret correspondence makes me feel more confident about the things I write.

We pour our hearts out; her to me about her worries for Billy, her husband, her father, the cows and everything else. I write to her about my sad and lonely life. I feel guilty because I shouldn't be sad or lonely. I love Janette, and Ariadne and Cressida, our twins named after our honeymoon hotel, 'The Ariadne Crest,' but I never imagined how Janette would change after they were born.

It was a difficult pregnancy and a traumatic birth and, at first, I thought my wife was exhausted, but tiredness developed into hopeless depression. I can't do anything right now and I can't seem to make her happy anymore. I throw myself into work because it is the only place, I feel like I matter, helping pay for all the things Janette wants. My mother is great with the girls but I don't think she's helping Janette either when she tells her to 'pull herself together'. Father is properly retired now and loves his grandchildren as much as Sharpie, but like my mother and me, he can't cheer Janette up either.

Daniella's letters are my precious escape. She tells me all about the farm, in every little detail, enclosing photographs too sometimes; she says an extra set of prints is only seventy-nine pence, so she doesn't feel bad about the expense. I'm now aware of each season going by. I know when it's lambing time, when they are harvesting and when the ice and snow makes their tough lives even harder. I am there with her on the worn-out tractor, and I understand her worry about unplanned costs when things break down.

I imagine myself feeding the hens with Fly, their Border collie sheepdog, watching on and I know that her hens stop laying sometime around Halloween, not laying again until Valentine's Day. I understand about the extra housekeeping money from selling the eggs. Although I've not been there, I feel I know Fox Halt Farm like I know my own house in Jordans, maybe better.

Her letter today complains how hot it's been. It's funny, I haven't noticed the weather but to Daniella it is critical. She says their sixty white-faced Dartmoor sheep were struggling because of their thick fleeces. It was a relief that their neighbour's son, Tom, helped Jack to shear them. Daniella says she took photos before and after for me. She has described the animals before with their long curly coats and white faces and explained how both their ewes and rams have horns. She told me the rams have magnificent spiralled horns, so it will be good to see if the pictures in my head match her photographs when they come.

Her descriptions take me away to the farm nestled below the tors on Dartmoor. I tell Daniella it feels like she is talking to me because she writes just as she speaks – but she says if she was speaking to me, her Devonian accent and her dialect words would be tricky. She says she learnt to write well at school but 'they' teachers couldn't change the way she spoke, a way of speaking that harks back to a past 'closed in' time. 'Just like me vather, and his vather afore him,' she said.

Her letter continues. 'I'm so pleased I went to see Billy. It was almost like it was before her accident. As you know, she said, 'No' to my trip to London at first, but I'm glad I persisted.

I have been putting five pounds away each week since she went to university, something to fall back on, if she ever told me she needed anything, but Billy never has, living within her student grant, sharing that tiny room with Simon, never putting the heating on, never going out, no phone… I wish she'd get a phone, it would make me happier if I could get hold of her if I needed to. I often think, 'What would happen if Father was taken into hospital?'

It wasn't until last month, that Billy told me she's going to work for you. I despair of her sometimes - she just told me on the telephone, in an 'off hand' comment, 'Simon and I start work at MarcFenn on July 4th, Independence Day. Nice easy date to remember.' Not another word about it since. I gave up waiting for her to say anything more, and last week, I told her I was coming up to London to buy her something to wear for her new job.

I explained I had saved some money for her but she wouldn't accept anything, until she eventually agreed that I could spend half on her if I spent the rest on me. (I've already used my share on a vet's bill for sewing up that gash down the side of the new bull and the injections he needed, plus I paid off some of the previous debt that's been owing for far too long).

As the coach drew into London Victoria, I saw Billy propped against a wall reading a book. She was so thin and pale, wearing the usual jumper with threads hanging out all over it, and her hair wasn't even brushed. I thought how I wanted to give that old sweater to Lily, the new Border collie puppy to sleep on.

I wanted Billy to let me stay at the bedsit but she said there was no room, and she was too busy revising. So, I caught the seven-fifteen bus back in the evening. Dear Tom was waiting for me when I got back to Exeter coach station - another different girl with him; Melissa, she's from Plymouth, I only spoke to her briefly whilst Tom drove us back to the farm. The girl insisted I sit in the front of his Land Rover while she climbed in the back with his two dogs. That vehicle is so rattley, it was difficult to talk to her.

When Billy suggested we could find her something from the charity shops in Balham, I sighed inside because everything is so hard to say to her. I have to anticipate how my touchy daughter will react, and work out the exact sentence to persuade her about anything these days. 'But I've never been to Oxford Street,' I said. 'I am looking forward to it.' Luckily, she still has some sense of pleasing people and she agreed in the end.

I miss us laughing together. I am sad that every time I mention her name to Jack, or to her grandad, I see sorrow in their faces. The day she went to Paros was the last time I heard her laugh. I remember the vivacious happy child that I used to congratulate myself that I had brought up on my own. Yes, her grandfather and Jack gave her everything she wanted and told Billy how fabulous she was, but they didn't encourage her to succeed in her exams or push her towards university. All I wanted for my daughter was a life without being terrified of the postman and the bills he delivers. Not a life like mine, working so hard and worrying everyday if her family can afford to keep their animals and their home.

I do feel guilty though because if I hadn't argued with Jack about letting Billy go to Paros then we would be happy now. If I *hadn't encouraged her towards a well-paid career, she might have married Tom and I might even be a grandma by now.*

Sorry Richard, my fruitcake needs to come out of the oven. I will try to stay focused on how amazing Billy looked when I got her to try on a fantastic red suit - I can't wait for you to see her in it.

What did Janette think about you two, leaving the children with Sharpie, and coming to stay for a weekend this year? I so want to meet you both at last. Love Daniella x'

I wonder why Daniella doesn't tell her family that she writes to me, but then, I only told Janette about her first two letters, and my ever-efficient wife immediately put Mr and Mrs May of Fox Halt Farm on our Christmas card list. Janette doesn't know that Daniella already has all the information that she writes in the expensive card she sends. I choose to keep it secret too, Daniella's words are my magic carpet ride to another world and if anyone knew, I fear it could break the spell.

I used to talk to Saffi like this, I suppose, but I haven't seen him for about four months. With Janette struggling, it didn't seem right to be spending the evening drinking with my friend, so Saffi and I started phoning every couple of weeks instead. His new business is doing well, with many large corporations asking him to provide key staff for them as well as war veterans to work for them. Like me, he doesn't get much spare time either. I miss him. The last occasion I saw Saffi, I fetched him from Oxford because he'd been locked out of his hotel, with no wallet and no trousers. It was good to have an excuse to see him, he always makes me smile.

Chapter 6

BERKELEY SQUARE
TUESDAY 4 JULY 1989
BILLY

*T*he woman behind the reception desk looks like Princess Diana, she is immaculate, exuding expensive perfume. For once, I am glad I listened to my mother and I think I *almost* look as nice as she does.

I remember my feelings of inferiority at my first gymkhana with my scruffy pony; it's nice to hold my head up high here. Maybe a little higher than I used to thanks to my new haircut. I am not sure about my hair, it feels strange.

Perhaps I shouldn't have been so rash? When she came to see me, Mum had insisted we had time and money left for the hairdressers. I am uncertain why I had it cut; maybe I was making a stand after I had given in to all Mum's choices of new clothes. We had laughed a little when I tried on things that looked awful. Splashes of warmth between us, but I just longed for the solitude of the bedsit, not someone messing with my hair. Yet, instead of fighting, I followed my mother into the salon. It was posh inside and smelt of newly picked strawberries. There was a glamorous looking folder with possible hairstyles in it and one caught my eye, short with the back cut into a sharp uniform step. As I was staring at it, the stylist said, 'That would be radical,' and I thought how shocked Richard would be if I walked into his office looking like the girl in the photo. 'Go for it,' I said.

I watched Mum as my long tresses fell onto the floor. I could see she wasn't impressed, but she didn't say anything. Afterwards, she said I looked incredible, trying to make me feel good, just like she always does. I wish I could feel happy again.

I may not be sure about my hair, but my new suit is definitely boosting me a little, as Simon and I stride up the grand staircase on our way to Richard's office.

RICHARD

I don't recognise Billy as she walks in, but Simon is more of a shock, in a black jumper, tight black jeans and old boots, looking as though he has just walked off stage, reminiscent of Marc Almond and the band Soft Cell. I console myself I don't see piercings or lipstick.

Their demeanour reminds me of how I used to feel when Saffi and I were hauled in front of our headmaster at primary school, heads down, wondering what sanction would follow after the trouble we had caused. I don't want to be that kind of chilling figure, so I hold my hand out to Billy and smile. She doesn't look at me as she sits down quickly with her red-suited shoulders hunched up.

'So glad you are both joining us,' I say, as the pop star shakes my hand. There is no reply. 'Sorry about the smell, Vanessa, one of my managers, was in here just before you and she has taken to smoking a cigar.' I open the window just to find something to do. I want to appear relaxed. 'Has anyone offered you a tea or coffee?'

'Thank you but we are not thirsty,' Simon replies.

'Right,' I say, trying to be upbeat. 'We'll start with a tour of the building.' Quietly, my new recruits follow me out of my office.

BILLY

Richard is just like Mum's photo which sits on the sideboard at Fox Halt Farm; seeming no older, and equally smart in his three-piece suit and wide-striped shirt with a button-down collar. There is no whiff of the rotten fish from the last time I was near him, instead I inhale drifts of vanilla as he opens a door to another room.

'This is your office; it's just for the two of you.' He waves his arm into a room no bigger than a large cupboard. 'Sorry.' Richard says, sounding embarrassed. 'This was the only place we could find for you. We haven't taken on a third graduate because we couldn't find any more space to accommodate them.'

'Isn't this an eight-storey building?' Simon asks, sounding as surprised as I feel; there isn't even a window.

'No, nine, but the business keeps expanding. We are taking on two floors in the building next door. We should have the extra space by Christmas, so I promise you more luxury then.'

In our 'office' two small desks with a computer on each, are jammed tight together. There is just one phone, which either of us could reach at a stretch. I wonder what we'll be expected to do? 'I'll show you the rest of the place.' Richard turns away, expecting us to follow.

There are people in every nook and cranny. Cigarette smoke swirls up behind low partitions, and the racket from each member of staff trying to make themselves heard above their neighbours, or shouting out of self-importance, makes me suddenly relieved we have our cupboard to hide in. Everyone greets us enthusiastically, laughing loudly with crass quips like 'Welcome to the madhouse,' and 'You will love it here.'

There is no warmth in the final department we enter. The large open-plan room occupies more than half a floor and it is as though all its occupants immediately hate us. 'This is the typing pool. These 'lovely ladies' will type all your letters for you,' Richard says. I can't believe we won't be able to do our own typing. I wish we could because this is not a typing pool, it is more like a lagoon of insidious alligators.

'I'll introduce you to Chantelle, she has started here today too.' Richard walks up to a Chinese looking girl who is about our age.

'I am not new to MarcFenn,' she explains, 'this is a transfer for me.' She speaks with a soft French accent.

'Oh,' Simon says. I notice he has grown an inch in height and how he has set his shoulders back.

'Yes.' Chantelle smiles at him. 'I requested a move here for three months from the Paris office. I wanted to improve my English.' I think Chantelle doesn't need to improve her language skills, and I think that Simon has fallen in love in an instant.

'I'm Simon,' he tells her, holding out his hand. 'This is Billy.' His voice sounds posher than I've ever heard it before.

'Pleased to meet you.' Chantelle raises a perfectly shaped eyebrow a fraction, and I see how she squeezes his hand gently. She is beautiful; her long black hair has red highlights and dark make-up emphasises her black eyes. The tilt of her head and dimpled smile make it look like she is up to mischief, *God help you, Simon.* I think.

Richard interrupts my thoughts. 'We'll go back to my office now,' he says. 'We can discuss what I have in mind for you both to do.' It sounds like we may have options.

RICHARD

The pair remind me of my twins, always looking out for each other. Seeming to move only once they have the other's telepathic approval. I hope they will be alright when I tell them I plan to put them in different departments.

I can't tie Billy up with the girl in Paros. It may be that her skin is so alabaster now, or the formal red trouser suit, or it might be that her golden hair has been chopped, and what is left of her lovely blonde mane has stark white highlights in it. I am pleased I don't connect her with the helpless girl, it should make it easier for me. Daniella has always been grateful that I rescued her daughter, but Billy has never thought to thank me.

After all the grief she has caused her family, I'm not sure I like her.

'Have a seat,' I say, pointing to two chairs that Shannon, my personal assistant, has placed next to a low coffee table in the corner of my room. They sit down at the same time, crossing their legs and folding their arms simultaneously.

BILLY

Richard has purposely put us here instead of in front of his enormous desk. He's done it to break down barriers. I know this from Simon's psychology studies. He wants to make us feel comfortable, so Simon and I use our legs and arms as our means of defence.

There are piles of paper everywhere, journals are stacked high on the floor and plans lie half-open on top of stuffed bookcases. I think the coffee table was covered too until recently, because there is so much on Richard's desk that I can't imagine how he could work there.

'I've asked Shannon to get us a selection of sandwiches and drinks, I hope you don't mind if we eat while we talk,' Richard says. 'I have to leave at two o'clock for another meeting, so I won't get any lunch otherwise.'

'That will be fine,' Simon replies. I check my watch, it's half past one already. I am glad because this meeting won't be long. Richard's voice sounds friendly as he asks another question. 'Have you heard the story about the woodcutters and their boss?'

Simon, and I shake our heads.

'Well, the story goes that the woodcutters are in a forest cutting down trees. They have been chopping for a week. The hardworking men are planning to go home early because they were told it would take two weeks to clear the trees and they've nearly finished, but then their boss turns up.

'The manager has come to see how his workers are getting on, and the woodcutters can't understand why he is angry with them. 'I couldn't find you guys anywhere, why are you here?' their boss asks, looking around. Then he shouts at them, 'Wrong forest'.' Richard looks at me. 'Billy, the job I have for you, is to see if we are cutting down the wrong forest, as it were. My manager, Vanessa Majors, the one who smokes cigars, is looking at the value of everything MarcFenn is doing. She is examining all the work of all the different departments in every one of our offices. She has two other people working for her, but she needs someone else to help. I think you'll be ideal, and it will be a good opportunity for you to find out all about the business. I need Vanessa's report just before our Christmas break.'

I think that sounds like a long time for a report to take but it does sound like a massive undertaking. It could keep me busy and I wouldn't be working directly with Richard.

Shannon brings in a tray laden with sandwiches, cake, cups, glasses, pots and jugs. Richard thanks her.

'Help yourself please,' he tells us. 'Don't worry, if you can't finish it all off before two o'clock because Vanessa will come in here with you after that. She will be able to give you any more information you need. There's plenty of time to eat and drink what you like.'

My heart sinks because we will be detained here for a while. I decide not to ask questions about the proposed job for me because I want to know what he has planned for Simon.

A two-minute silence, while we busy ourselves with the sandwiches. Eventually, I ask, 'What about Simon?' This is the first time I have spoken to Richard, I don't want to say anything else.

'Simon, I need you to go undercover.' Richard says this as though he is talking to a child, trying to encourage them into a game they have already said they don't want to play. He talks quickly, without pausing, so he can present all the reasons to join in. 'There's one man in my residential team, head and shoulders above the rest of the department. He is called Stefan Schwartz and he's selling twice the number of houses and achieving four times the margins of anyone else. It's a team of ten, who have been working together for years. I want you to report back to me in a fortnight's time pinpointing the five most important things that Stefan is doing differently from his colleagues. I need to get the rest of the team performing too, and I want to direct them in a tangible way.

'I haven't told Stefan about you or my plan, because I don't want him doing anything differently, and I don't want him worrying that the other guys will steal the bonus I give him each month for achieving his top seller ranking.'

'So how exactly do you expect me to infiltrate this team?' Simon is intrigued.

'Easy.' Richard sits back in his chair and has a gulp of tea. 'Yesterday, I bollocksed Mr Schwartz about his paperwork. I told him I was getting complaints. This isn't a lie; Stefan is hopeless when it comes to filling in forms. I told him I had found someone to help him out. I said the proposed assistant was excellent with administration but knew nothing about property so they wouldn't interfere with his work.'

'Was he pleased?'

'He asked me what her name was, and I told him he'd meet them today. I also said it wouldn't be a girl because of his awful reputation with so many women here already.'

'So, he *was* okay about it?' Simon checks.

'Well, other than you being male, Stefan is thrilled with the idea.' Richard has taken a large piece of Battenberg cake from the coffee table hoard. My mother's Battenbergs are my favourite. She makes them whenever I am home. I steal large amounts of her cake because she leaves it unguarded, always busy doing something else. This is another of our secret silent wars. Mum pretends to be cross when all her wonderful cake has vanished but then she bakes another one for me. I am relieved that there are still two more slices left. Richard's face says it's his favourite too.

'Listen, you two.' Richard has finished eating. He is smiling. 'You won't have to stay with your respective teams all the time, you know? You can just say you need some quiet to get your work done and retreat to your office. It's hellishly noisy in this building. The open-plan system is a pain some-times. I'm glad I have my own space here to hide in – I'm sorry your room is so small but at least you can escape there too.'

And that's it. I can't think of any real objections to the job he outlined with this Vanessa woman, and Simon was hooked by Richard as soon as he said, 'undercover.' I think about Simon all dressed in black as the company's new secret agent. Richard certainly got lucky there, *what would he know about subterfuge?*

Chapter 7

MAYFAIR, LONDON
RICHARD

I am late. I didn't want to be; it was Vanessa's fault. She came into my office just before two o'clock and kept me talking. She knew I had an appointment and I could tell she was doing it deliberately. The more I tried to excuse myself, the more questions she fired at me, determined to try and impress the new recruits.

As I enter the exclusive and fashionable foyer of the Fitzclaine Mayfair Hotel, I search the room for the woman I am meeting. We haven't met before, but I know she will be anxious if she is here on her own. I feel upset because I intended to get here first.

I see her, recognising her from the photos she sent me. Her tanned skin and rose cheeks are familiar. She is wearing a black trouser suit, which I know she has just bought in Marks and Spencer's. I know this because she said she had nothing to wear so I sent her the money to buy something she felt was right for the occasion.

I walk up to her and kiss her on the cheek. 'Daniella,' I say, watching her blue eyes light up.

'Tis me,' she replies in a soft West Country accent. I notice her trembling hands, which are clutching the carrier bag with her previous outfit in. I catch hold of them, feeling her rough and dry skin.

Daniella's hair is a surprise, it is the same gold shade as I remember Billy's, but there are many grey streaks amongst her soft curls. I also notice the wrinkles around her eyes. Now

I am angry, thinking how the grey hair and lines on her face were probably caused by the daughter who doesn't take after her. Daniella is open and loving – her miserable daughter, cold and selfish. 'Shall we find our table?' I ask, trying to put her at ease. 'I have booked a private side lounge for us.'

'Can't believe I'm 'ere.' She gets up quickly from the red leather armchair and a uniformed concierge approaches us. 'Sorry,' I say to him, 'Would you give us a minute please?'

'Certainly, sir.'

I have noticed some magazines and journals on an exquisite Louis XVI gilded table. I pick up *The Lady* magazine from the top of the pile and skim to the classified section. 'Look, Daniella.'

'What am I supposed to be looking at?' she asks.

'Here.' I point to a page. 'It's an advert for bed and breakfast, and farm stays at Fox Halt Farm,' I explain. She looks carefully at the small printed box with a cartoon cow in one corner. 'I paid for a weekly advert in here for the next year,' I say. 'I hope it brings in more business.'

Daniella has turned down every offer I have made to help her. If I'd asked if I could do this small thing, she would have said *'No'* to that too. My companion is now sobbing so hard that I wish I could take back the last few minutes. This was supposed to be a celebration and I have ruined it. The concierge returns, and he puts a white gloved hand on Daniella's shoulder. 'Madam, would you like to freshen up?' he asks gently. 'I'll show you where the washroom is.'

'Yes please.' Daniella goes with him.

After five minutes, she returns, looking as though nothing happened. 'You are too kind, Richard,' she says, kissing me happily on the cheek. 'The advert should help a lot – since the new bypass has opened, I've been getting fewer guests.'

I nod. 'Yes, I hope it helps,' I say

'Thank you so much.' Daniella make it sound like I have given her the keys to a mansion.

'We have booked afternoon tea,' I tell the kind concierge.

'Yes, what is the name please, sir?'

'MarcFenn,' I say, and he indicates for us to follow him. Instinctively, I hold Daniella's hand.

I see how she is impressed by the sumptuous room. I smile contentedly as Daniella drinks everything in. I imagine that she has been thinking about this trip for days. I can't believe I persuaded her to come. I know she has lied to her husband, and her father. Daniella has told them she was coming to see Billy. It is wonderful to meet her at last. She clamps the linen tablecloth between her chapped thumb and her blackened index finger, which was injured by a calf pushing at a metal bucket once it had finished drinking the warm milk inside. Its abrupt action squeezed Daniella's finger between the empty container and the wooden frame of the calf pen. She said it was hard to write last week because it hurt so much.

She picks up her empty cup and examines their delicate forget-me-not design, pressing her fingers on the impossibly thin edges. I wonder if Daniella is thinking about the table she lays out for her guests at home? In my imagination, her table setting is as lovely as this. I know she uses her grandmother's bone china to serve tea to the ones who arrive early because she has told me when pieces have been broken. Each clumsy breakage means more money to find and a little more of Daniella's heritage chipped away.

'So how did it go then?' she smiles.

'Very good, I think.' Daniella seems to relax as I continue. 'Your daughter and her friend are certainly a couple of characters, but your insider knowledge worked well,' I say.

'What do you mean, Richard?'

'I've put them both in good places, and you never know, I may make some money out of them.'

Daniella laughs because she knows I don't need to make any money out of Billy and Simon. She was so happy that I agreed to her idea of offering them both jobs. She insisted that the only way she could see Billy accepting the employment was for me to find Simon a role too. She warned me how Billy would behave and that I would have to present her with a fait accompli. She said if I gave Billy enough information she wouldn't be inclined to argue. Her mother had joked that the only other way she could bribe her daughter into anything was with Battenberg cake. 'She has loved that yellow and pink cake since she was two years old,' she said.

Daniella asked me whether the twins had a favourite cake too, but I had to confess that I didn't know, I am always working, and Janette and Sharpie sort out the meals at home. I love the way Daniella asks me about my life too. The caring woman never just talks about herself. She always wants to check that I am alright.

I sent Billy's mother my proposed offer letter before I sent it to her daughter, and it was her idea to say we were taking on three graduates, like we did the same every year. MarcFenn has never had a policy of taking on university leavers.

Daniella's final comment had stumped me at first. 'They will need a hiding place,' she wrote.

'Hiding place?' I queried. She explained what she meant, and I described the stationery store. Daniella thought it was perfect. I only arranged for the store to be cleared out yesterday and was relieved that the two desks could be squeezed in.

Until my twins were born, I didn't understand the bond a parent feels for their children, and the way we will do anything to keep them safe and happy. I wish Billy could see how her family are grieving over their lost child. Sometimes, I think the Mays' anguish would have been less if I hadn't rescued Billy. Her family would have had good memories instead of the forlorn hope that the bright and sparky daughter and granddaughter might re-emerge one day.

'Richard, this reminds me of how I felt when I first met Jack,' Daniella says.

I frown. 'Why?'

'Jack makes me feel special like this.' she smiles. 'Thank you so much for this afternoon.'

'Jack's from Slough, isn't he?'

'Yes, that's right, he says I ran out my golden web to tie him to the farm forever.'

'Go on, you haven't told me this story.'

'It's a long one. Are you sure?' she asks.

'We have all the time in the world,' I say. 'You can save some ink, because if you don't tell me now, I'll get you to relate the whole saga in your next letter,' I wish we did have all the time in the world. This is lovely.

Daniella leans forward.

'When Mother died, Father and I were flat broke. We feared we'd lose the farm. So, I thought of offering bed and breakfast at the farm to get some money to help us. Father told me this was a 'castle-in-the-air' notion because of the state of the house, and because he didn't think visitors would find Fox Halt. On top of this, I already had enough to do. He said even if it did bring in a bit of cash, we'd still have to beg the bank for a big loan to keep us afloat. The thing was, Richard, his resistance made me even more determined to give it a go.

'Without spending a penny, and with a bit of help from family and friends I got the place spruced up. It wasn't grand but the thatched roof and thick cob walls gave it a country charm. Sorry, Richard, I've gone off track a bit.'

'It doesn't matter, Daniella. Please go on,' I say.

'Fox Halt Farm is two and a half miles from the main A30, that's the main road to Cornwall. Two and a half miles, that is, if you don't get lost in the lanes. Every Friday and Saturday night, the A30 was choked up with hundreds of grockles, and I was determined to divert some of the holidaymakers to the farm. I painted up about twenty marker signs to point the way. Father didn't offer a scrap of help but on the day I put up my markers, he surprised me.'

'How?' I smile, aware she is dying to tell me.

'With a whacking great sign, that's how. It said. '*Fox Halt Farm, Bed and Breakfast*.' He'd secretly painted it, hiding it in the barn. His sign had the farm cottage on it and different animals all around the edges. He even asked Pat, our neighbour, if I could stick it up on his land, which was next to the main road.

'This bleedin' sign was the reason my Jack came to Fox Halt Farm in the first place.' Daniella's face fills with delight as she mentions her husband's name. She sips some tea quickly, so she can tell me the next part of the story.

'Jack was supposed to be going to a wedding in Penzance the day we met. Some distant cousin of his was gettin' married. None of the rest of Jack's family wanted to go to this wedding, so he decided to go on his own. Jack hadn't even left Slough before. He even had to borrow a car. Well, the long and short of it, is he was early, he saw Father's sign and thought he'd have a quick nosey. He turned up just as I finished milking – he must have thought I was a walking scarecrow. I had cow shit all down my front and Father's boots on because mine leaked. I happily stomped over to him to see if he wanted bed and breakfast and he just stared at me. Then, after a bit of an awkward silence, he said no thanks, but he asked me if I'd mind showing him around.'

Daniella's face seems to lose its wrinkles as she remembers this meeting from years before. 'You know, Richard, we ended up walking round all the fields. I told him the name of every cow. I opened every shed, and when he was holding one of the sheepdog puppies, my Jack said he wanted to stay after all, so he could help with the morning milking. Jack said I bewitched him with my love of life. I was thirty-nine years old, and I thought it would be Father and me on our own for good. I never expected that after we said goodbye, he'd turn up the next Friday, and each one after that. Six months later we were married in Hamsgate church; on my birthday.'

'You are amazing, Daniella, I see why Jack was hooked.'

All too soon, we are back at the coach station, and I feel like I've known this wonderful woman all my life.

'Richard, I didn't tell you this, but Jack's surname was Anderson. He took my name when we married. He said the Mays had always been at Fox Halt Farm, and he wanted it to stay that way.'

As I smile at her, she hands me a carrier bag with a nearly new black trouser suit inside. 'Richard, these clothes certainly made me feel like a Lady Who Lunches. Thank you again for being so thoughtful,' she says.

'Keep them, please,' I tell her.

'I can't. Sorry. How would I explain to Jack?'

'Alright, I'll keep your lovely outfit safe for next time,' but as Daniella thanks me and steps on the bus, I know there won't be a next time; she found it too hard to lie to her husband.

TUESDAY 11 JULY 1989

BILLY

Vanessa is alright, she doesn't waste time with small talk. She tells me what she wants and gives me a deadline. She doesn't interfere.

Chapter 8
BALHAM, LONDON
SATURDAY 9 SEPTEMBER 1989
BILLY

Two months on, everything is working out well, especially when I watch Simon and Stefan together. Simon completed a deal for Stefan yesterday, and his boss was so pleased that he marched him off to the wine bar across the road to celebrate. They stayed there all afternoon, and I think he may be out with Stefan now.

At first, I thought that Simon was faking the camaraderie to win Stefan's trust. To me, the two men seemed total opposites with Stefan in his designer suits, brimming with self-confidence compared to Simon all buttoned up in his matt black tube. But every time Simon came into our 'office-cupboard,' or home to our bedsit, it was clear he was smitten with Richard's top residential agent. It was always, 'Stefan did this' or 'Stefan said that.'

The top agent introduced Simon to his clients straight away, saying how helpful it was to have someone working with him. He pressed Richard to extend Simon's time with him, and afterwards even shared his bonus, saying he couldn't have achieved the prize without Simon's assistance. This was untrue because Stefan would have outstripped the rest of the office anyway, but I saw how good it made my friend feel.

Richard was pleased too; Simon presented him with five pointers with reasoned arguments. Number one on his list was 'builds a rapport.' I am happy for Simon, it is great to see others appreciating him like I do.

There has been another surprise, and that's my feelings towards Richard. I keep thinking how insightful he was, finding perfect roles for Simon and me, and every time I creep into our office-cupboard I am glad he gave us a sanctuary. Our safety hole is so vital to me, reminding me of the dens I used to build as a child with Mum's clothes-airer and crocheted blankets. I used to force our old sheepdog to hide with me. In the gloom, I would bore that poor deaf dog to death with my horsey dreams for the future. At MarcFenn, I think the ice inside my heart defrosts a little as each day passes, and Simon is changing too.

From the first day here, he took his dictation tapes to Chantelle. Any excuse and Simon said it needed typing up. My friend was supposed to put his tapes in a designated place in the alligator nest, clearly marked. *'ALL Typing here. TYPING will be done in strict rotation - NO EXCEPTIONS.'* Simon pretended he hadn't seen the bossy notice but the alligator commandant, Allison Cummins, caught him out on day three. Simon apologised, saying he was unaware of the correct procedure, but since then, he has marked his little cassettes with a discreet red cross – Chantelle picks these marked tapes out of the communal tray, so he doesn't have to wait for his work. Chantelle doesn't appreciate the constraints of the reptile ruler either, she likes to misbehave and I think she likes Simon too.

It wasn't until we were on the tube train, on the morning of day six, that I realised there was something odd about my flat mate; he was wearing a suit. It wasn't even black; it was dark grey. He still had the black polo-neck and scruffy boots, but even so? 'Stefan suggested I should smarten myself up a bit,' he laughed. The next day, my friend had brogue style shoes, and the following morning, I found him trying to iron a brand new white shirt. I ended up doing it for him, along with another five he had bought.

When the shirts arrived, his eyeliner and nail varnish left. Simon's transformation has been gradual enough for me not to feel like I'm living with a stranger, but a man has just let himself into our bedsit who I don't recognise. His smile takes over his entire face and his hair is now so stylish that I cannot believe it is really Simon. My friend who left this morning had a hood of hair which I had to look under to see his eyes. This new man has eyes I can stare into easily. 'What do you think?' he asks.

'I like it.' I nod and smile.

'Chantelle said she couldn't bear looking at me any longer so she took me to an amazing barber in Camden.'

'Really, she took you?'

'Yes.'

'How great,' I say, shocked now, at both his new image and that he has been out with Chantelle. I walk over to him and squeeze his hands; only the second time I've ever touched him. *What a difference from the scared boy in the refectory, when he first told me his name.*

SOUTHWARK, LONDON
FRIDAY 3 NOVEMBER 1989
BILLY

I wish I hadn't let my mother talk me into this. I am standing in a long queue in Southwark Cathedral wrapped in a stupid gown with a mortar board stuck on my head, waiting for someone who I have never heard of, to present me with a rolled-up paper with nothing written on it – how ridiculous is this? I already have my degree certificate, this is all for show. Simon isn't even here because his psychology course has its graduation ceremony in the Main Hall today.

As each person's name is called out everyone claps. It will be ages before it's my turn. I smile at Mum and Tom because they are grinning at me and I think I should.

What is Tom wearing? To me, he looks as though he has just come out of prison, and someone has given him back his regular clothes from ten years before. I suppose with me living and working in London, the latest styles have been absorbed into my head subconsciously. The *Evening Standard* newspaper, which I pick up each night, is crammed with fashion articles. The billboards and the people I see in the expensive part of London where I work have gradually influenced my sense of what looks good, and Tom does *not* look good to me.

If I was at the farm now, then Tom might seem well-dressed, especially as I am only used to seeing him in his blue mechanics overalls. His shirt is like a Romany dancer's, bright white and billowy. His dark hair and deep tanned face only add to this impression. He probably looks worse because Mum is wearing a lovely dress, and she has dyed out the grey in her hair. She looks incredibly smart. I love it when she wears make-up, it adds so much to her appearance. I feel proud of her. The man on the other side of Tom looks like he just stepped off the front page of *Vogue* magazine, but thankfully Tom seems blissfully unaware of his unfashionable attire.

I am disappointed that Tom is here. It was supposed to be Dad in the place where he is sitting. That's why I agreed to this, I wanted Dad to be here proud of me again, like he used to be with my horse riding.

Mum persuaded Dad to come. She said we could go out for a nice meal afterwards and when I told her my crazy salary, she agreed I could pay for it all. I have booked a posh restaurant that Chantelle recommended nearby. I was looking forward to a lovely day for us to remember, and as today drew closer, Mum even managed to get my father to agree to stay overnight, saying, 'Dear Tom will look after everything with Grandad,' and I found a smart hotel for them, moving my posh restaurant booking to the restaurant in the same hotel.

In hindsight, I should have smelt a rat because I know Dad wouldn't have left the farm that long. My parents have not had a holiday since their honeymoon, when Dad took Mum to Cornwall for four days. It is funny to think that my father grew up in the middle of a city but when he met Mum, the farm cast a spell on him and he has not wanted to leave since. Other than Dad's accent, you would think he had been a farmer all his life, that he was born to it and farming was in his blood.

I should have guessed that Dad would find an excuse not to come, and that's just what happened – I don't know how he managed to rustle up a difficult calving, and the cow he couldn't leave because he was too worried that she might lose her precious baby, but he did. I wonder if Mum actually checked. *Did she see the cow?* I can't ask her.

I was so gullible. I even booked myself a room in the same hotel, thinking it would be nice if I didn't have to go back to the bedsit. I planned breakfast with my parents before they left to go home. Dad wouldn't have had to disappear to see to the animals and Mum wouldn't have had her guests to look after.

Tom, and a girl called Samantha who I haven't heard of before, were at Fox Halt this morning, so that my parents could set off early, and when Dad said he couldn't leave, Tom offered to accompany my mother, quickly volunteering his new girlfriend to take them to the train station. He said it would be nice to have a trip to London, especially as he'd freed up the time from his own farm anyway.

At last, I reach the end of the line and I stand in front of the chancellor of the university. Everyone claps as my name is read out, and the woman hands me a scroll. Her assistant says, 'BA Honours, First Class.' More applause. Tom photographs the moment and I smile at him. And now I have to wait for the interminable speeches to end.

Four o'clock, and we are outside the cathedral. Tom takes more photographs and I do more smiling, but I can't help wishing that Dad was holding the camera. Our table isn't booked until seven so I suggest walking to Buckingham Palace and around Trafalgar Square. Neither Mum nor Tom have seen either before. It will be nice, but I still keep thinking of Dad. It's been years since I missed him like this. I feel easy with Tom. We have known each other all our lives. He is funny and good company but he is not my lovely father.

Tonight, the meal is amazing. There are two lovely girls who are waiting on us like we are royalty, probably because Tom is chatting them up all the time. We laugh too loudly for the exclusive surroundings we are in. Laughing as we recall lots of things that Tom, his sister Charlotte, and I got up to when we were young. There is too much wine because Tom keeps refilling our glasses when we aren't looking. A relaxed and happy time.

'Gonna have to sleep with you tonight, Bills,' Tom tells me as he returns from the hotel's reception area. He looks like the cat who has got the cream, his eyes are dazzling.

'What do you mean?' I ask him, frowning hard.

'They haven't got any more rooms.' Tom seems delighted. This isn't the boy I remember from our childhood. This is a confident man.

It's been more than three years since I left to go to Paros and Tom has grown up. I know from Mum's letters that 'Dear Tom,' as she always seems to call him, has apparently had a different girlfriend every month since I left. He is a good catch. He is gradually taking over his father's farm, which is six times the size of ours, and of an acreage that makes it economically viable. He's good looking and probably, most important of all, he is now chairman of the local Young Farmers Club. I know how I used to fawn at our old chairman's feet when I was younger, he seemed so unattainable and gorgeous. Tom is clever too, winning most of the young farmers' debating and public speaking competitions.

To me though, he is just Tom, my best friend, who I grew up with. We are also related, he is a cousin of some kind to me. His grandmother and my great-grandmother were sisters. I can't work this out, but it is so common at home. My grandfather was the eldest of eleven children and his wife, Annie, was one of ten so it seems we are related to everyone in some way. It makes you careful about what you say about your neighbours, because they are probably distant family, but it also makes you feel connected to everyone around you, giving a sense of belonging to the place.

Tom's confidence is reminding me of Kostas. His powerful muscular frame and his self-assurance are frightening me. 'No, Tom,' I tell him. 'I won't share a room with you. I'll get a taxi back to Balham, thank you.'

'Suit yourself. Just let me know when, and I will call you a cab.'

'Thank you,' I reply.

'So, you really want to go back to that dingy place you live in?'

'Yes. Now would be great,' I say. 'I'll just say bye to Mum.' I am definitely tipsy because I hug my mother harder than I ever remember and tell her how much I love her, asking her to give Dad and Grandad a massive hug from me too.

There are tears in Mum's eyes. I feel my eyes begin to water too but neither of us will cry in front of the other. She gathers up her enormous handbag.

'I'm going to bed, it's been a wonderful day, Billy,' she says. Tom hears and asks the girl on the reception desk for Mum's room key. He hands the key to my mother and she kisses his cheek.

'Dear Tom,' she says, 'thank you for being here today, taking Jack's place, you're a good lad.'

'I've had a great time. Thanks for letting me come with you.'

Mum nods; I suspect she is wishing Dad was here now, *maybe as much as I am?*

'Mrs May, I'm in room…' Tom checks his key. 'Room ten. Please, Mrs May, there's a phone in your room – so would you ring me in the morning, just to make sure I'm awake?' The receptionist hands my mother a piece of paper with Tom's room number on it. She has noticed that we are all a little drunk, and doesn't believe Mum will remember. My mother gets in the lift. 'Love you, Billy,' she says as the doors slide shut.

'I haven't booked a taxi.' Tom's voice is softer now. He sees I am upset, putting an arm around my shoulder. I am suddenly back on the farm, it's late, and we've just managed to get the last of the hay loaded up before it rains. I stop the tractor, which is towing the trailer stacked high with hay bales. Mum is sitting on top of the load, and I watch as she catches a rope, which Tom has thrown up to her to secure the load so the bales can't fall off. The stripped field glows in the sunset and we're all exhausted. Tom insists Dad takes over the tractor driving so that I can walk with him back to the farmhouse. 'We'll unload in the morning,' Dad says. 'I'll just park the trailer in the barn for now.'

Tom and I traipse wearily across the field with our arms over each other's shoulders. It's uncomfortable but we are comrades and will get home together. When we have walked along the hotel corridor and Tom has opened the door to the room, he says, 'It is okay, Bills.' I don't reply, I am taking in the room. It is stunning. I went mad when I made the booking. I have more money than I know what to do with at the moment, and Mum still refuses to let me help out the farm. She keeps saying, 'You enjoy it, darling,' or 'leave it another year, then we'll see.' I booked the best rooms in the place because I wanted to spoil her and Dad, they wouldn't have been away together for more than twenty years.

The first thing I notice is the magnificent golden chandelier. The ceiling reminds me of my mother's impossibly smooth Christmas cake icing. I notice, too, a gilded ornate mirror stretching across the width of the room. The bed is so big that it looks like three beds pushed together. 'Christ. You've booked Buckingham Palace.' Tom stares at the scarlet floor rugs. He looks up, his eyes meeting mine. He whispers, 'I care about you, Bills. I really do care about you. You know that?' His thoughtful words flow deep inside me – I feel ice cracking.

'No, Tom.' He ignores my hesitancy and moves towards me. Our lips gently touch, like the light rain that started as we crossed the bare hayfield together.

A shrill noise suddenly cuts through the moment. 'The blasted phone is ringing.' Tom lets go of me.

'Leave it,' I say.

'No, it might be your ma.' He answers the call, and I hear my mother. She is upset because she has spoken to Dad and he has let some guests stay. The couple turned up late and Dad said he couldn't turn them away. My father plans on making them breakfast but Mum says he doesn't even know where the frying pan is. I laugh because I can't imagine my father cooking either. Mum hears me. 'Dear Tom, is someone with you?'

'No, Mrs May,' he replies. 'What do you want to do? Do you want to go home?' Tom shakes his head at me and mouths, *'Noooo.'* He makes me laugh again.

'Tom – there *is* someone with you, is it one of those waitresses? Is it the blonde one?'

'No,' – but he can't help himself, 'it's actually both of them.'

'Dear Tom,' she says – I can't believe she doesn't sound shocked. 'Look, I'm sorry, but I'd like to go home please. Can you meet me downstairs in five minutes? There's a late train, and Jack said he'll pick us up from Exeter.'

Tom jokes again, 'But there are two of them, Mrs May – can't you give me six minutes?'

'See you downstairs, lad.' Mum is gone.

As Tom leaves, he turns to me. 'Bills, you are very special to me, please understand.'

I have sobered up. 'Tom, this was a mistake. You and I are on different paths now,' I tell him.

Chapter 9
BERKELEY SQUARE
MONDAY 8 JANUARY 1990
RICHARD

I search out the special envelope from the mountain of mail that has been dumped on my desk, and as I start to read, I am transported to Devon. It feels as though I am about to sit at her kitchen table. Daniella will stop working for a while, sit down beside me and we will chat. I imagine her voice.

'*Dearest Richard,*

Jack and I loved the card from you and Janette. I missed not writing last week but you were on your Christmas break.

Sid and Harry (I still can't believe your mother has shortened Cressida's and Ariadne's beautiful names to these, but I suppose when she was dealing with the terrible two's, nick-names were easier) Your girls will be old enough now, to know what Christmas is all about, and I'm sure you had a lovely time.

I keep seeing pretty outfits in one of the small shops in Okehampton when I do my weekly shop, and I wish there was a way to buy them and send them to you. I keep imagining your daughters in them. I could never get Billy into dresses. She was always charging around in wellies and trousers.

It's snowing outside, big fat flakes that make everything look so romantic. If you have the snow in Jordans, the twins must love it. Of course, I hate it; everything takes so long - defrosting pipes, carrying buckets of hot water to melt the ice in the animals' water troughs. The blimmin' snow blows in everywhere, so we are struggling to keep the lambs warm.

There is a new-born live lamb now in the bottom warming cupboard of my Rayburn cooker. I hope it won't die. The poor little mite was so cold. I hope he'll warm up, and I can get some warm milk in him. We lost his mother, a ewe we'd had for seven years, my favourite because she was an orphan lamb too, one that Billy looked after years ago. It was a difficult lambing because the lamb was the wrong way around and big too, being a single. I took too long trying to help - the ewe was weak when we found her. She had taken herself off into the copse at the edge of the field. As you know, we call it 'nesting,' and we usually see the signs and get the heavily pregnant mothers in before they lamb, but this old girl was almost completely covered in snow when we discovered her. Poor creature.

This Christmas, I decided not to have any bed and breakfast guests, even though I had four separate enquiries, thanks to your kind advert. You didn't tell me you put it in the Sunday Times too - one of the guests told me they had found Fox Halt Farm in there. I loved the advert with the animals around the edge, and the picture of the farmhouse in the middle, it reminded me of Dad's old sign, which rotted away a long while back. These days, we have Jack's old van parked where the sign used to be, and Father painted the side of that. It's helpful, but not as nice as the old sign. Richard, thank you again.

The extra money from the Christmas guests would have paid a bit towards the barn roof that finally gave in yesterday under the weight of the snow, but with Billy here it was nice to have more time for her.

She seems so much better, she said how she wished her Dad had been at her graduation, and she helped with the milking. Billy insisted on delivering a Christmas card to the Westcotts (Tom's parents) and she did it on horseback. You know, she hasn't bothered with old Sultan since she left for university. My poor father was crying his eyes out as she rode out the gate. She only rode once, but that's a start, isn't it? She even suggested playing a board game on Christmas Day, and it felt like old times - until Simon Arkly rang. He and Chantelle are engaged.

Simon asked Chantelle to marry him while he was staying with her parents in a chateau just outside Paris. Sounded lovely. Hit Billy like a bombshell though. I'm worried that he wants to move to Paris right away to be with his fiancée. Billy said Simon is going to persuade you to give him a transfer. She pretended to be pleased for him but you know how close those two are - a step forward and now two back - but I won't ask you to stop Simon from going. I'm happy for him.

Dear Tom has just left. He has yet another new girlfriend, Martha with a nose ring and short blonde cropped hair that's dyed pink in patches. She looks too young to be a vet. She seems kind-hearted. Tom and Martha were here when Simon rang, they both tried hard to cheer Billy up - Dear Tom is such a great lad, but I don't know if he has any bed post left with the notches that must be on it - I don't know why none of his relationships last? Yes, I'll say it again, sometimes I wish he would get together with Billy. I do think those two could be happy together.

Anyway, I have a funny thing to tell you. You know how much Fly, our sheepdog, likes riding in the Land Rover. Well, yesterday, Fly was eating her breakfast when Jack started the vehicle up. He sat in the Land Rover waiting for the windscreen to de-ice. Fly heard the familiar engine, and as usual she was off, desperate to go with him.

The front gate was slightly open, and the dog headed for the narrow gap but the gate was still loosely tied up. Poor Fly became stuck half way through the gap. She was off the floor with her feet galloping in the air. I tried to rescue her but the more she pushed, the harder it was to loosen the tie. I yelled at Jack to help. I was worried she'd break ribs but Jack just laughed, saying he would sort her out. He turned the engine off and Fly was switched off too. Her legs stopped racing and she backed out of the gap as though nothing had happened. She was fine...

BALHAM
WEDNESDAY 14 FEBRUARY 1990
BILLY

*T*wo red envelopes lie on my doormat, I recognise the writing on the first, it is a Valentine's card from Fox Halt Farm, saying how they all miss me and they love me. The second has a little Republique Française postage stamp. I tear it open. It's another card, this one, from Simon and Chantelle – they miss me and love me too.

Simon moved out at the end of last month. He's working with Chantelle in MarcFenn's Paris office now. I'm uncertain what upset Stefan the most, losing his friend or having to face the alligators again to get his typing done. By the time Simon left, he had his own separate client list and was competing with Stefan to be the top seller. In France, Simon will be learning about the different French property tenure and land systems, as well as a foreign language, but I reassure myself that he didn't know anything about the English property market six months ago, and he soon got the hang of that.

The bedsit is empty without him. I am throwing myself into work, avoiding being here. I'm staying late at the office, arriving early and working weekends too.

BERKELEY SQUARE
THURSDAY 15 FEBRUARY 1990

*E*ven my little office seems empty without Simon. Today, we finally move into the space next door. The new accommodation is lovely with large partitioned offices, and wiring hidden away in conduits rather than having electric cable extension leads snaked around the floors as trip hazards. It took a month for the surveyors just to work out the differences in floor levels, but it has been finished well and now the second and third floors run smoothly across the two buildings.

I pick up the phone, feeling sad. Simon answers straight away.

'Billy, wasting company resources again?' he laughs.

'I couldn't help myself.'

'What do you mean? Are you okay?'

'I've just finished clearing out our cupboard-office and I was about to disconnect the phone to take it to my new room. I just wanted to say hi.'

'Hi, Billy,' he plays along.

'Do you know, Simon, I can hear Vanessa with Richard down the corridor.'

'Really? From there?'

'Yes, it sounds like she is having a massive argument with him. She wants the biggest of the new offices for herself, but Richard wants it too. I can't hear their exact words, but she's been screeching at him for a couple of minutes already.'

'Up to her normal tricks, then?'

I nod, even though Simon can't see me. 'Richard should have the new one – it's bigger and much nicer than that tired old office he's in now, but you know Vanessa…'

'You mean Manipulative Vanessa? The Always Get My Own Way Vanessa? That one?' he checks.

'Yes, she'll keep on at Richard until he eventually gives in to her whining.'

'Sorry, Billy,' Simon says. 'I'm going to have to hang up, there is someone here who needs me to sign something. Good luck with it all. Ring me tomorrow.'

'Okay, I'd better take everything down to my new office anyway. Take care – love to Chantelle. Thank…'

He's gone.

While Stefan and Simon became best buddies, Vanessa and I have deteriorated into adversaries. We clashed as I began to see our fundamental differences.

From our brief cigar-smoked conversations, I have gleaned that she joined the company at the same time as Janette, and they became good friends. They still are, but I have a strong suspicion that Vanessa is jealous of Richard's wife. I notice the subtle stiffening in her body when she talks about her '*friend.*' She said when Janette left to have the twins, she was the obvious choice to take over as Richard's personal assistant. She boasted that straight away he promoted her to manage a special new team he'd set up, looking at company strategy.

Vanessa uses long words and complicated sentences to befuddle people and I find myself watching her, rather than listening to her. She is a sham. I can't believe Richard thinks so highly of her. Vanessa steals my ideas, pretending my reports are hers and she always blames her mistakes on me. I find my manager quite fascinating though. I see how she flirts to get her own way, and I love the way she squirms when she's lied, and someone's found her out. The biggest reason I put up with her behaviour is that I'm enjoying what I am doing, it's challenging and fulfilling.

MarcFenn has grown organically. It seems that where someone saw an opportunity to make money, they went for it, and no-one has ever revalued these once money-making avenues to see if they remain profitable or could be developed. I enjoy examining all the varied work the company does.

As I plonk everything down on my new desk, a thunderous bang shakes the floor. I am scared, thinking it might be an IRA bomb, the Irish Republican Army campaign has come close to here a couple of times. Their Semtex attacks are happening occasionally in central London, but now I realise it wasn't a terrorist detonation, it was Vanessa slamming the door of Richard's office.

She storms towards me, her face scarlet. 'I am out of here!' she yells at me, as she pushes past. 'That fricking man...' She strides into the office she wanted and scoops up a large box marked 'VANESSA - PERSONAL.' It's too heavy for her to manage but her adrenaline enables her to carry it. The box charges by me, and then it's quiet.

I imagine many other members of MarcFenn's staff watch with me, from various of the head office's windows overlooking the square – we see a taxi pull up and watch as Vanessa and her whopping great box disappear inside. I suspect that quite a few, like me, are happy to see her go.

I turn away from the window and see Richard is next to me. He is still staring out. 'Thank God for that,' he whispers. 'I never thought I'd get rid of that woman.' He touches my arm. 'Sorry, Billy, I know it's been hard for you. I am well aware you are the one producing all those useful facts and figures that keep landing on my desk with Miss Major's name on. It's great work. I hope we can have a meeting tomorrow, once you have sorted out your new office.' He is pointing to the room Vanessa wanted.

'I thought that one would be yours now?' I frown.

'No, I like it where I am. My office is fine. I just hoped that I could rile her enough to force her to resign over it. I know she expected me to concede. She really believed I couldn't do without her. I only promoted the woman and created your department, so I didn't have to put up with her as my personal assistant.'

'Then you don't need me either, if my role is just a charade?'

'Billy, I *do* need you.'

'Are you sure?' I ask.

'Yes, I am. Your reports have been very useful to the company. MarcFenn needs your expertise, I just didn't need your boss.'

'So, you planned all this?' My next sentence is out of my mouth before I engage my brain. 'You are more cunning than I thought, Mr MarcFenn.'

He smiles. 'She'll be heading off to see my wife, saying how unreasonable I was. She will tell Janette that I'll phone her tomorrow, begging her to come back but I won't be ringing, and there is a certain friend I have, a head-hunter, who'll ensure Vanessa receives an unbelievable offer from our main business rival, Taylorsons, this evening.'

I step into my new office with its incredible view of Berkeley Square, and I wonder, *how much have I got wrong?*

Chapter 10
BERKELEY SQUARE
FRIDAY 1 FEBRUARY 1991
BILLY

Richard walks in. It's almost a year since I was allocated this office, and he has never stepped in here before. I meet my boss in *his* office – each Wednesday at half past nine. We have coffee and Battenberg cake, and it's an easy two hours, discussing whatever Richard has asked me to investigate. We are relaxed in each other's company, respecting and appreciating each other's knowledge and skills. I enjoy our short time together and, if I'm honest, Wednesday mornings have become the highlight of my week.

It's not Wednesday and Richard is in my office, and I haven't invited him.

'Billy, I need you in the boardroom. Now.' No explanation, no asking if I am busy. This is an order.

'Okay,' I say, standing up. 'Do I need anything?'

'Just you. Hurry up please.' He spins around and I follow.

As we enter the boardroom, Richard points at a seat.

'Sit down there, please, Billy,' he says.

I sit.

I don't know why it's called the boardroom because MarcFenn is a partnership. Richard runs everything as the majority partner with his father owning just a small remainder, so there is no board as such. I have only been in this room three times before, but I know Richard uses it frequently because there are few clients that he would let see the chaos of his office.

The boardroom is amazing. I love the comfortable smell when I walk in the door; years of beeswax polish blended with centuries of dust, it reminds me of the front room at Fox Halt.

The impressive polished-oak room is hung with portraits of Richard and the men who have run the company since 1777. They stretch back to Richard's many-times-over great-grandfather, Frederick Fen, who supposedly won the beginnings of the MarcFenn fortune in a bet over a pineapple. I am sceptical of the story, but I like it, and the gold chalice in the room that always holds a single fresh pineapple in reverence to the company's founder.

I am sitting next to a man I don't know. Richard walks around to the other side of the long table and stops directly opposite us. 'Billy, I don't think you have met Michael O'Rowde,' he says. The stranger nods at me.

'Hello, Mr O'Rowde,' I say, interested to meet him. I have heard his name many times before. He owns, amongst other things, an ever-expanding supermarket chain and I know he has just bought out a large pharmaceutical company. I'm aware, too, that five of our staff are working full time on the viability of a scheme to develop an old power station, which he is thinking of buying. He is the company's biggest client but he looks different from the smart businessman I imagined. His expensive suit is so creased that I think he might have slept in it.

Michael O'Rowde is thirty-three years old. I remember this from an article in last week's *Property Gazette* about O'Rowde developing the tallest office tower in London's Docklands. I remember wondering how such a relatively young man was so successful.

As I stare, I decide his sad eyes look kind. I expected his features to be shrewder befitting the man I had previously built up in my mind. He extends a hand to me.

'Call me, Michael, please, Billy,' he smiles. 'I hope you can talk sense into this man. I just made him the offer of a lifetime and he has, stupidly, turned me down.'

'I only work for Richard, Mr O'Rowde,' I reply. 'I don't have any influence over him. If Mr MarcFenn has said, 'No' to you then he will have a good reason.'

'I said to call me Michael. I hope it's okay to call you Billy.' He sits back in his chair. 'Well, Richard must be using you as a smokescreen, Billy. My old friend is just trying to buy himself time perhaps?' He looks at Richard, lifting his eyebrows.

I like Michael's frankness. He could be right. I have no idea why I am here. I look at Richard but his face is expressionless. I fill the awkward silence with a question to Michael. 'So, please can you tell me about your proposal.' He sits forward and thumps a large hand on the table, making me jump.

'I want this building, Billy. I've offered my friend over thirty million pounds for it, which is a lot more than it's worth,' he replies. 'How much do *you* think it's worth?'

I don't reply.

Michael continues to question me. 'Do you believe MarcFenn could operate from another head office somewhere else? Relocate, I mean.'

I saw a valuation figure a couple of months ago, but I don't remember it exactly. I trusted the sum was right, assuming it was a fixed business expense, I haven't studied whether this is the best place for the company to be, it just seemed set. I play for time, adopting the tactics that Vanessa would have used.

'Well, Michael, I think it would be worth a much greater figure than that, taking into account the logistics, the legals, the administration, and everything else. We'd have to chew over the appropriateness and suitability of any new site for MarcFenn. We would need to locate and acquire another prestigious building in a desirable and central neck of the woods, you know?' I ramble on. 'Is it possible to give me, say, two weeks to answer your questions? So, I can properly examine it all in detail? I do understand you wanted to come in with a figure to start negotiations, but we would need time to see if there is even a negligible chance we could move. MarcFenn only have a lease of the extended parts on floors two, and three. We are just talking about a valuation of the freehold of this building, aren't we?'

'Yes, Billy,' he smiles at me again. 'Two weeks will be fine.' Michael looks back at my boss. 'Same time in a fortnight, Richard?' The man sitting next to me slaps me on the shoulder.

He looks thrilled as he searches out a small diary from inside his crumpled jacket. I watch as he thumbs through the book with his tongue between his lips. Michael O'Rowde looks like he wants to record his moving-in date.

'Okay, see you then, but the answer will still be *no*,' Richard says as he stands up.

'Yes, we'll discuss it again then.' Michael gets up too, and turns to me. 'Nice to meet you, Billy,' he says. 'I look forward to meeting you again.'

I shake his hand and then he leaves. I sit back down opposite Richard, waiting for him to say something.

RICHARD

*T*hat wasn't fair on Billy, Michael was right. I was using her as a diversion. Michael is our best client. I enjoy working with him and I consider him a friend too, so I didn't want to disappoint him.

Poor Billy, I can see she doesn't know what to do next. Michael out-foxed me; I wasn't prepared for that trick at the end of our weekly meeting. I know the approach he used – adding 'just one last thing,' when everything else has been agreed, calling it a 'little extra point,' that the other party will concede while they're caught up in the moment.

'Please forgive me, Billy,' I say. 'I shouldn't have got you involved in this. Putting you on the spot like that, was wrong of me. I'm sorry.'

Looking back now, I know I should have apologised to her, but I didn't, this is what really happens...

Rage makes my blood pump hard around my body. I thought Billy knew I'd never sell this building. I expected her to understand my connection with this place. This head office has been in my family for generations like Fox Halt Farm has been in hers. I only fetched her into my meeting with Michael, to make a pause while I thought through an acceptable way to explain why I will never leave Berkeley Square; for once in his life Michael isn't going to get what he wanted.

Billy is looking down at the table with no clue about what she has just done.

'You have given him false hope, Billy.' My jowls vibrate and my face reddens. 'And *now* it is only going to be harder to disappoint him.' I am sweating. The last time I remember shouting at anyone like this was years ago, yelling at my father when he said it was great, I wouldn't be seeing Saffi anymore. I have never lost my temper like that again. I am usually careful with what I say, but this place is in my heart.

'Michael is a businessman, Richard.' Her response is calm. 'If we provide a proper account of all the reasons why we have to stay here, he will have to back down.' I stare at her, trying to even out my breathing. 'Listen,' she says. 'I've only got two weeks, so you had better let me get on with all the fact finding.'

Billy stands up, her eyes on mine. 'Please don't worry,' she says.

As she softly closes the door behind her, I scoop up the fresh pineapple fruit beside me and crush it. Juice runs through my fingers while the spiny peel pierces my skin – I need to calm down.

The boardroom phone rings. I ignore it.

The ringing goes on–

When I can no longer bear its persistence, I pick it up.

'Yes,' I say, still angry.

'Richard, it's Janette… I'm sorry.' She is crying.

'What is wrong Darling?'

'It's Sharpie, she had a massive heart attack. Your mum has died…'

'No, no, no. *Oh God. No...*'

BILLY

I have never spoken to Richard with such determination before; I had wanted to scream at him years ago, when he was sitting by my bed at the surgeon's house. 'How dare you? You've ruined everything – I wanted to die!' but instead, I pretended to be unconscious, staying silent so he would give up on me and leave, but he didn't.

Just before Ulrich took him home, he held my hand and started to cry. Hopeless sobs. He was exhausted from talking to me for hours. I pitied him crying, but still I felt no gratitude, only hatred. Hate I should have directed at another man, someone so different from caring and gentle Richard.

Everything has changed. I know Richard must be crying again and I feel desperately sorry for him. He says he will be back at work tomorrow, but I know I couldn't face work so quickly if my mother died. Sharpie's death has made me see how phenomenal my mum is. I love her so much. Poor, poor man.

I understood straight away why Richard yelled at me in the boardroom. He couldn't bear to lose his head office. I was not upset. I simply decided, there and then, to make my report to Michael the best I've ever produced, and as I think about my wonderful boss grieving for his mother, I am convinced that MarcFenn will never leave Berkeley Square.

Chapter 11

FOX HALT FARM, HAMSGATE, DEVON,
SATURDAY 23 NOVEMBER 1991
BILLY

My feet don't seem to have touched the ground in the ten months since I met Michael O'Rowde, so it feels good to be at the farm for the weekend. I am reading a property magazine, and Mum has just passed me a mug of tea.

'Billy, don't you ever stop working?' she asks.

'Not really, but I do enjoy it, Mum,' I reply quickly, taking the drink from her.

'Darling–' She pauses, and I know she wants something.

'What, Mum?' I ask, smiling at her, thinking how much she cares about me.

'Would you mind finding that article, and please could you read it out again, I was so busy getting everyone's breakfast before, I didn't hear it all.' She sits down next to me while I find the page in *The Architects' Journal.* It is well-thumbed from being looked at a few times already. I read it out to her slowly.

'*A FRUITFUL MOVE: London based staff and clients of MarcFenn, property agents and surveyors, will be looking out of new diamond-shaped windows soon:*

'*The company, who employ over two thousand staff in London, Paris, Berlin, Brussels, Prague, and New York has just confirmed rumours that they are increasing their presence in the property market still further by moving their long-established*

London headquarters from Berkeley Square to one of London's most striking new landmarks, 'The Pineappli 1,' in London's Docklands.

'The futuristic pineapple-shaped building was the brainchild of up and coming architect Charlotte Westcott of Architects Rose & Rose, who came up with the state-of-the-art concept in her final degree project at Edinburgh University; she told us she was delighted to develop her design to 'fruition.'

'Richard MarcFenn says he is looking forward to the proposed new move. He said, 'Everything changes so fast in property and we are moving to keep pace. Since the year 1777, MarcFenn has had the emblem of a pineapple as its company logo, and Miss Westcott's revolutionary new building seemed like it was created especially for us. MarcFenn always strives to develop the best opportunities for its clients and this move is a part of our ongoing strategy for continuous improvement.'

'The iconic building that we have all watched rise up out of the London Dockland's skyline has earned its nickname 'The 'Pineappli 1' from the sculptured external envelope of jagged hardwood panels and its expansive tinted triple-glazed windows which bring a pineapple instantly to mind, and of course, its address at Number One, Columbus Wharf.

'The dramatic design and the unique detailing have, no doubt, led to Charlotte Westcott; who grew up on a farm in Devon, being nominated for the prestigious Architect of the Year Award.'

'I'm so proud of you girls,' Mum says. 'Leave me that magazine, will you? So, I can show everyone.'

'Mum, it's all down to you really. All your encouragement telling me I could win at anything.'

She shakes her head. 'No, you and Charlotte, you are so much cleverer than me–' She pauses and checks the clock. 'Sorry, sweetheart, I've got some guests due in a minute. I need to make up their beds.'

'Can I help you?' I put down the magazine.

'No, stay there, you need a break. I'm fine.'

My attention is on the rhythmic ticking of the kitchen clock, and my mind slowly drifts, thinking through how this happened.

There seems to be a tacit understanding amongst farming families that the eldest son will take on the farm. It is like the mist that hangs in some valleys and not in others, it's just the way it is. This was why my mother was so upset when I was born. She knew she was having a boy. Apparently, everyone knew, all the signs confirmed it; she was 'carrying low,' suffered no morning sickness *and* when she dangled her wedding ring on a length of cotton thread over her bump it swung from side to side, this definitely foretold a boy, it was science. She named her bump William Daniel, like her dad and her younger brother; tragically, her brother died in a farm accident when he was only two. Mum was with him when a plough toppled over, crushing him to death. My mother never talks about it, I only know because my grandad always uses the terrible incident as the reason why children mustn't play on farm machinery.

Mum was over forty when she gave birth to me, she thought she was too old to have more children, so she was pretty disappointed when her bump turned out to be a girl. She called me, 'the baby,' as though I didn't belong to her. It was Dad and Grandad who named me. The pair couldn't agree on my middle name, so I am plain Billy, not even the feminine version Billie, because the men didn't know there was an alternative spelling. Mum's expected baby boy would never have gone to university, he would have inherited whatever was left of Fox Halt Farm and that would have been that.

The invisible wisp of convention pushed Tom's sister, Charlotte, away from her roots too, and because of this shared choice of a professional career over farming, she and I found an affinity with our degree studies. This was why she lent me her final year design project to help with my dissertation, and this loan, in the long run, is why Richard is moving out of Berkeley Square.

I think back to the days before the crucial meeting with Michael. My report for MarcFenn remaining in Berkeley Square seemed O'Rowde-proof. I was ready to present all my evidence to Richard first, so that we had time to close any chinks that he saw in our armour; however, this was when things turned upside down.

I had carefully considered all the counter-arguments that Michael might use. I had churned everything over for days and I was shattered. Three o'clock in the morning was the worst time, because in the early hours, my wild ideas about what our adversary might do became plausible.

One particular early morning, I remembered the futuristic building Charlotte had designed for her university project. It was actually being built and was nearly finished. I knew her building inside and out because I had read my friend's presentation from cover to cover. My reckless brain began to think what it might be like if MarcFenn moved into Charlotte's spectacular creation.

In my mind, her tall oval shaped building mutated into a giant pineapple, the MarcFenn logo. The timber cladding and the windows were already in a diamond formation just like the peel of a pineapple, and I thought the profile of the roof could be modified slightly to form the outline of the fruit's spiky crown.

It was still early, when I rang Charlotte, who confirmed the developer had no tenants lined up, and then I reconsidered everything about relocating.

Hours later, Richard agreed to meet me in the wine bar opposite MarcFenn's offices. I think he expected us to talk about his mum dying. This was all we had discussed since he had returned to work. So, he was unprepared for my sudden change of heart. To me, my idea was perfect though to Richard, it was his worst nightmare, but I finally made him admit that the fundamental reason he couldn't leave Berkeley Square was the boardroom and all the history there. It wasn't the costs or the logistics of the move. His argument boiled down to nine portraits and a perpetual pineapple fruit in a precious cup.

I offered to recreate the room, moving its treasured contents lock, stock and barrel. I wore poor Richard down. I was frantic and he was helpless, not just from my frenzied enthusiasm, but also from the sapping fatigue of his mother's death. He was heartbroken, hardly up to deciding anything. His mind wasn't focused on my proposal, but I took no notice of his despair, certain it was the best thing for the company's future. I would try and comfort him later, but at that moment, I needed him to see all the advantages.

When Richard did agree to consider the move, I was allowed to use all the staff I required to check every detail.

'Just triple everything,' Richard told me.

I shook my head, not understanding.

'Triple all the sums you come up with,' he explained. 'And triple the time it will take to move to the new address too.'

'But Michael won't agree to that.'

'He can take it or leave it,' Richard said and I'm sure he hoped Michael would walk away.

Michael 'took it' without a single negotiated word. He even said he had people lined up to copy the portraits, to replicate the golden chalice and someone guaranteeing him endless pineapples. He wanted the boardroom to stay just as it was. There was of course, one last thing. 'I need you out by Christmas,' he said.

Now, we have exactly a month before the move. I'll be back in London early on Monday morning. There is still so much to sort out, but it feels good to be trusted to manage such an important project.

Chapter 12

BEECHWOOD, BUCKINGHAMSHIRE
SATURDAY 23 NOVEMBER 1991
RICHARD

At home in my bathroom, brushing my teeth at my own sink in this palace of a house, I can't stop thinking about my mother.

I am flying to Paris later, to attend the christening of Simon and Chantelle's baby. This is definitely out of a duty to Simon. I felt I had to accept the invitation, even without Janette, who is staying behind to look after the twins.

I do like Simon and he is my top residential seller in Paris. Actually, the others there might as well pack up and leave. If it wasn't for Monsieur Arkly, I would have Billy closing down the French residential side of the business. I just wish Janette was coming with me.

She knew I loved her, didn't she? This single question won't leave me alone, wherever I am, it's there: It came to me first at the hospital. I had answers to how? When? Where? But as my tired and troubled mind absorbed these facts, *It* arrived, the unanswerable question. *Did Sharpie know I loved her?*

I understand my mother isn't around anymore. Sharpie won't be there when I get home from work, conspiring with Janette, whispering to my wife, knowing I can hear, 'How can we get him to agree to this?' or 'Have you told him yet?' It was just my mother's way of keeping me up to date with events that I had missed with my family. I think about the way Sharpie used to pick up Sid and Harry, lifting them high in the air so she could see them properly, smiling at them as if her heart would break. Always in turn. Always giving them exactly the same amount of her adored attention. She knew the twins loved her. Janette and my father showed how they felt. They hugged her and held her hand. They talked to Sharpie about their feelings, but to me, Sharpie was just there. I was a bystander, watching her as she threw herself into all she did. I recognised every amazing thing she accomplished but I can't recall ever telling her how much I loved her.

My father, Janette and Billy, tell me that my mother knew my love for her, but I am not reassured.

'I'll look after the twins.' I can hear Sharpie's words. 'You two go. It will be good for you to have some time away together.'

'Yes,' Janette replied, staring hard at me. 'My dear husband is always at work these days. We can have time to talk for once, it *would* be nice, do you mind, Sharpie?'

'Not at all, I'll cope.' My mother wouldn't have just coped, she would have arranged the most exciting treats for her granddaughters – the twins wouldn't have missed us for one tiny moment.

Like me always working, Janette is preoccupied too, looking after the girls, and busy with her Quaker Meeting House friends. Sharpie was right, it would have been nice to have a little time together.

It was Daniella who suggested that I went with Janette to the Quaker Meeting House in our village. Billy's mother told me how she'd found out the group was open to anyone, and we wouldn't be expected to join in, if we didn't want to. Janette and I could just sit and listen. We did go and it wasn't really for me, but something clicked with my unhappy wife. I was shocked when Janette told the whole meeting how overwhelming it was with two babies, and how useless she felt. She wouldn't talk to me, but she opened up to the strangers, explaining her anxiety without a moment's hesitation. I was hurt at first, but it was the beginning of her getting better.

I don't get involved with her new friends, but I am grateful they helped pull my wife out of her misery. She is like the old Janette now. Organising me, the house, the girls, my father, and most of the village all at once. She has packed my suitcase for my overnight stay, booked my tickets, sorted a hire car and found me a room in the chateau where the christening is going to be held. I am so lucky how she arranges everything, but it would have been good if she was coming with me today. Sharpie would have loved having sole charge of Harry and Sid.

Did she know I loved her?

JUST OUTSIDE PARIS
BILLY

The christening is over. I sit next to Simon and while he drives, I think about how things change. Charlotte is probably my best friend now. Since I suggested taking on her building, we have been talking on the phone a lot, and not always about the move. We just chat sometimes. It's nice.

When we were little, Charlotte to me was just Tom's older sister, an annoyance who would 'snitch' on us, telling how we had gone fishing in the trout pond on the big country estate next to our farms, or informing her mother we had stolen the warm cakes that were supposed to be for our tea.

I envied Charlotte too, for all the rosettes she won. Then, during the time we were both in pony club together, I would sometimes come first in the competitions. These were always my most satisfying victories – my pony beating her bigger and more expensive one.

While Charlotte was at university, we didn't see each other except when she came home during the holidays, but later on, when I was at college, she always tried to help me by sharing her experiences. I'm sure I feel closer to her now than Tom. I never imagined someone could replace Simon, but in a way, Charlotte is more of a friend to me than he ever was. I actually talk to her about my feelings. I feel I can confide in her.

'You and Richard are both the same. Couldn't come last night. Always working,' Simon laughs. I've never seen him so happy. He has been talking nonstop since the ceremony at the town hall. 'Nearly everyone else arrived last night.'

'I'm sorry, but you know how busy I am.'

'Well, you missed a good night, that's all I'm saying.' It's not all he says. 'It would have been even better with you there too.'

'Look, I'm really sorry, it's just work. I'm here now and we have all afternoon left together.' I am feeling a little defensive now, there are so many reasons why I wasn't keen to be here. Firstly, I am not sociable, and then there is the fact that I am not into babies. I hate how the whole office comes to a halt when doting parents bring their little 'bundles of joy' into work. I can't see what all the fuss is about. Aren't they all the same? Clawing, needy, screechy things. *'Sick and poo machines,'* crying all the time, Yuck! I am certainly not godmother material, but Simon wouldn't take no for an answer. 'Surely you can imagine how busy it's been trying to sort the move out. You know I would have loved to have been here last night.'

'And you can't stay late either?'

'Sorry again, but it is Mum's birthday tomorrow and Mum and Dad's wedding anniversary,' I explain. 'There's a family meal planned.'

'Okay.' He doesn't sound convinced.

'Simon, I am trying to make up for the grief I caused over the years. I have to be there.'

'I know, I just haven't seen you in ages.' He smiles, making me feel guilty.

'You have booked me a taxi for later, haven't you?'

'Yes, don't you trust me?'

'Of course, I do but you and Chantelle must have been busy organising everything, it might have been overlooked.'

'Here you are, this is the taxi firm's card just in case they are late, and you want to chase them. Chantelle has written the time on the back. She said it would help if you've drunk too much champagne by then.' He knows I won't be drinking, I will have one glass to toast the baby, or whatever you do at these events.

'Thank you,' I say, checking the business card. The cab is booked for six o'clock just as I asked.

'We're here.' He stops the car. 'Billy, let's not get cross with each other, please.' We have arrived at a chateau, and we climb out of the vehicle to go inside to find the rest of the guests. 'Sorry,' I tell Simon. 'I'm just tired and crotchety. It's been a great day, I am so pleased to be Anouk's godmother – such an honour for me, thank you.'

This is the place where Simon and Chantelle were staying when Simon proposed. I suddenly recall that awful moment when Simon told me he wanted to move to France. It was that Christmas when I first tried to fix some of the hurt, I had caused at home. Attempting to bring back the person my family waved off to Paros. I shiver, only slightly, but Simon notices. 'Are you okay, Billy?' he asks.

'Yes, fine, thanks, just a bit cold.' I am chilly in the dress I am wearing. The dress my mother said I ought to wear because it would be nice for the photos. She said to get my hair tidied up a bit too. I wear trouser suits at work, and I am missing the extra layers. It's cold in the chateau, I don't think there is any heating on.

Château Filbert looks splendid from the outside. It has expansive lawns and box-hedged borders. I had imagined that in the summertime, the borders would have been full of roses but now that I am inside, I reconsider my first impression. I now think the flower beds will be overrun with weeds. The chateau's fairy-tale redbrick turrets are a façade because indoors everything is worn out as though there is no money for upkeep anymore. The place was obviously elegant once but now the faded red rugs are ragged on the parquet flooring, which lost its lustre long ago. The silk wallpaper is water-stained, the paintwork is peeling and the once cardinal red velvet curtains are pink and paper-thin. Dampness hovers in the air. In a way, it feels like me, externally all tarted up but a big let-down inside.

'Here, Billy. You haven't held your little goddaughter yet.' Chantelle smiles, and I remember the first time we met in the alligator pool at Berkeley Square – she still looks mischievous.

'I'm okay,' I reply, but the proud mother assumes I am just being English and polite. She virtually dumps the baby into my arms, and I have no option but to cradle the child.

'Anouk,' I say, looking into her trusting black eyes and noticing her delicate lashes. The baby smiles a cheeky smile – switching on something unexpected deep inside me. I am shocked at the bond I feel. Anouk warms my cold body. I want to hold her tight and never let her go. I recall the orphan lambs at Fox Halt, remembering how I used to cuddle those poor motherless babies for hours. I can't believe I am holding Simon's baby. She is gorgeous. Anouk giggles at me, and I – like some infatuated schoolgirl – giggle back at her.

RICHARD

I make a snap decision as soon as I step inside Château Filbert, deciding that Saffi's apartment in Paris would be a hundred times nicer than the room Janette has booked for me here. I ask at the reception if there is a phone I can use.

When I ring Saffi's number. There is an answer machine message. First in French, and then in English – he's away for the weekend. I am disappointed. I would have loved to have seen him. I could use my key – he never minds me staying – but if he's not around, then I'll go home this evening.

'That's a lovely picture,' I say, as I spy Billy in the next room. She smiles at me and then looks back at the baby in her arms. I keep staring. I haven't seen Billy in a dress since she was lying at the bottom of the cliff, but that's not something that I want to think about, however my mind whirrs; picturing the striking girl she was, even then, more than six years ago. I recall too the young woman who walked into my office in 1989, and how her mother had told me how to handle her. Billy's thick hair just skims her shoulders now. She looks happy and sure of herself.

'She is lovely. Look.' Billy lifts her face from the baby, and for a fleeting moment, my body is stirred up. I am not sure why.

'She is beautiful,' I agree, but I am not talking about the child. I know I am excited to see Billy, and it is not because I got horribly lost trying to find this dump of a chateau, and it is not because she is one of the few familiar faces in the room. It is just standing next to her. I smell essence of coconut in her hair and sense the warmth from her neck. But this is wrong. *Stop.*

'Can I hold her?' I ask.

'We were beginning to think you weren't coming,' she says, as she passes me the baby. I am aware of Billy's hands touching mine. She hands over the little girl in the same way that Janette used to, when she needed to 'change twins,' as she called it. This is better, I am thinking about my wife now.

'You are late,' Billy says.

'I don't think so.' I frown at her.

'You are, Richard. You've missed the actual civil baptism. That happened earlier at the local town hall.' The baby starts to wriggle and Billy quickly holds her hands out, wanting her back. 'The ceremony was presided over by the local mayor, I assure you, Richard, you *have* missed the christening.'

'What's all this then?' I ask, looking around at all the guests here.

'Can I have Anouk please?' Billy asks.

'Yes, of course,' I say, sliding the little girl back into her arms.

'It's just a buffet and some champagne, that's all.' She is engrossed in the baby again. I check my invitation as Billy walks away to speak to Chantelle. I notice how her dress hugs the contours of her body and my eyes fix on her bare shoulders and neck as she moves. *I have to get out of here.* I am an emotional wreck since Sharpie died. I am tired from worrying about the office move, unable to think clearly. I will have a few words with Simon and Chantelle, and then organise my flight home.

They are approaching me. Simon looks sheepish, and Billy is coming over too. *Has she held that baby all day?* Seeing Billy with Simon's child makes me think of my mother – *did she know I loved her…?*

'-you see, Richard, they want to move closer to Chantelle's Mum and Dad. They've found a business they want to buy.' I wonder why Billy is telling me this. She is looking at me with those same eyes she did in the wine bar, when she wanted me to consider leaving Berkeley Square. I realised then that Billy has a way of getting to me. I am beginning to feel like she is the one calling the shots in the office these days. I seem to agree with everything she suggests.

What has really touched me lately, is her concern. She understands my desperation about my mother's death. Billy seems to be the only one concerned that I am alright. Janette is in pieces about Sharpie and she expects me to help her with her grief. My wife doesn't see that I miss my mother too. Janette is propping up my father, and Father is being all 'stiff upper lip' about the whole thing, trying not to show how lost he is.

Billy is the only one who has wanted to know if I am coping. She listens. I am so pleased to have that from her. I remember how I yelled at her in the boardroom. She should have been mad at me, but she sent the most incredible card when Sharpie died with a wonderful sympathetic message. Her thoughtful words were like a balm on an open wound.

'Richard. Are you listening?' Billy asks.

I haven't heard it all, it was something about Antibes in south-east France. There were other words in my mind. Words that they can't hear. *Sharpie knew I loved her, didn't she?*

'Sorry, Simon,' I say. 'Could we talk about this on Monday? I will ring you if that's okay?'

'Yes, that's fine,' he replies.

'Thank you for letting me know face to face,' I say to both him and Chantelle. 'I am sorry but I need to go outside, I need some air.' *Did I tell her?*

BILLY

I stand next to Richard as he stares into a dark pool surrounding an old fountain, which must have been breath-taking once. He hasn't looked up but I'm sure he knows I am here. 'Are you thinking about Sharpie?' I ask.

He doesn't move.

'She knew, Richard, just like my mother knew that I loved her despite everything I put her through,' I say, and I must strike a chord because his hazel eyes look up at me. He seems so lost and I want to put my arms around him to provide some comfort. Until now, this man has always been so strong; he has always done his best for me, but since his mother's heart attack, I feel that the tables have turned, and he needs me now.

I am sure that I am the only one who is looking out for my boss. Janette and his dad have no idea of the guilt that is consuming him. We have had so many conversations recently where he has talked for hours about his mother. It is really all he can think about.

I shiver and consider how it might be nice to steal some heat from his body. I move closer, slipping my arm around his waist. Richard moves his face towards mine; our lips meet.

This is a total surprise. This is wrong. This is amazing. His arms are around me, making me feel safe.

'Billy, I need you so much.'

'I want you too.'

The only thing I can think about is his tongue in my mouth. The taste and the fury. My whole being reacts. As I press myself into him, I feel his body hard against mine. Excitement. *What is happening?* I want to get closer. I don't care if Simon or Chantelle observe us together. I don't care if the other people from the Paris office notice – they don't see – all I want is this.

'Could we spend tonight together, Billy – just tonight?' he whispers.

'Yes. Please. Just tonight.' I stare into his eyes, as he takes my hand, intertwining our fingers, before bringing our hands up to my face. The back of his fingers stroke my mouth and I sniff, remembering the stink of fish when he last touched my lips. He smells gorgeous now; I laugh.

'What's funny?'

'Nothing really, I can't believe this is happening. I want to be with you so much, but I can't see us tiptoeing through all the people inside the chateau to get up to your room.'

He laughs too. 'Billy, please don't think for one minute I'm sleeping in there. We would be eaten alive by bed bugs. No, my lovely Billy, I am thinking of whisking you off to my friend's apartment in central Paris. It's twenty minutes from here and he's away.'

'Did you have this planned?' I ask. He looks hurt.

'No, Billy, I just need you – please don't tease me.'

'Sorry, I'm nervous.' He kisses me again, and I know I have to go with him. 'So, you just happen to have a key to your friend's apartment?'

'Yes, he doesn't live there all the time; Saffi spends half his time in London, in his apartment there. I use the place sometimes when I am working at the Paris office. You will love it there.'

'Where is your car?' I check, as he pulls me towards the car park. Reckless and mad. But all I want is him.

Richard keeps one hand on my knee as he drives. It is as though he is scared that if he lets go of me, I will float away. I lean towards him with my head on his shoulder. I don't think either of us wants to stop being in contact. It feels like the most obvious thing to do in the world.

We are nearly at the apartment, when all these new feelings coursing around my body, force the last vestiges of truth out of me. 'It wasn't an accident, I wanted to die.' I don't think he has heard, so I say it again, more quickly this time.

Richard stops the car on the pavement. 'You didn't fall?'

'No, not exactly.'

He doesn't understand. I see it in his eyes. 'Sorry,' I say. 'I can't let you think that anymore.' No tears. No pain. Just relief that I have told someone.

'Billy, you said it was an accident.'

'I never said it was, I just let everyone believe that I slipped – That terrible day, I was upset – I couldn't think clearly – but I was aware of the edge of the cliff. I think I could have stopped myself from falling off, but I wanted to die.'

He folds his hand under his chin. 'Why are you telling me this now?'

'I want you to have the truth, Richard, and there is something else I have to say, I know you will never leave your wife, and I don't want you to.'

He seems to draw back, and I think he is going to return me to the chateau but instead he moves his hand and lifts my hair from my forehead. His fingers run through my hair, reminding me of Mum tidying me up before she allowed me to go to school. It's reassuring.

'Look, Billy, this is not a game I am playing with you. I have no idea what I am doing here. All I do know is that I want to be with you for the whole night and wake up next to you. No false promises. Let us have just tonight together. I want us to forget about everything else in the world for now.' He pauses for a moment. 'Listen, my sweetheart, if you want to talk about what happened in Paros then we can. I won't judge you. Tell me everything in your own time. I will listen.'

I don't want to talk about Kostas now. I have something else I need to say. I know this will shock him too, but I want him to understand. 'This isn't just a bit of fun for me either, Richard. It's a longing for you. Ever since Vanessa left and you gave me my lovely office, I have slowly loved you more each day. I can't wait for our Wednesday meetings. Every morning I try to time my arrival at the office with you, just so I can say a quick hello. I have been trying to find extra questions that seem urgent enough to phone you. I think about you before I go to sleep, and my mind is full of you as soon as I open my eyes again in the morning.'

'Yet you know I will never leave Janette or the twins?'

'I know, but it doesn't stop me feeling like this.'

We sit in silence. Again, I don't know whether he will turn back or go on to the apartment.

He starts up the car again but neither of us says anything.

Richard drives into the private basement parking of a massive Regency style residential building, which must be twelve storeys high.

A security cage automatically surrounds the car as we walk towards the lift. He holds my hand. Richard presses the number twelve and still in silence, we go up in the lift.

When he unlocks the apartment, we step into the most amazing room I have ever seen. It is as though we have entered a department store with everything you could ever imagine you wanted to buy laid out before you, all your dreams and all at once.

Richard lets go of my hand so he can pick up a phone in the corner of the room. He is dialling. He may be phoning Janette. He is. I try not to listen, but I do. 'Hello, darling, just to let you know I am staying at Saff's tonight, it wasn't much fun without you. The chateau was a bit of a dump. Lots to tell you. See you tomorrow. Love to the girls.'

Two of the walls of the huge apartment have full height classical style murals of naked men and women, with their beautiful bodies extending over the ceiling. There are candles and candelabras on every surface. Massive gold and silver chandeliers hang from the gold painted high ceiling. There is black and white marble and fake zebra skin rugs.

I watch, as Richard goes into what may be his friend's Saffi's bedroom and in seconds, and he comes out again with a box of condoms. He waves the box at me, smiling. I should be embarrassed, but I am not. I just feel like this is what we both want to do, and he is just making it happen.

Richard speaks at last. 'Please come with me.'

We are in another room, as wildly exotic, but totally out of keeping with the rest of the apartment. If there was a theme in the other rooms then it was perhaps classical, but this bedroom is wholly romantic. The four-poster brass bed is dramatically draped with the finest lace and heaped with delicate silk pillows. He is no longer gentle, kissing me and pushing me back onto the bed. I try to lift my head so I can kiss him harder, but all his weight is on me. He pulls at my dress while I tear at the buttons on his shirt. Lace and silk and our souls are abandoned. Intoxicating.

SUNDAY 24 NOVEMBER 1991
RICHARD

'*Oh la la, mon ami. Oh la la, Monsieur MarcFenn. Ce n'est pas ta femme, si je ne me trompe pas. Tu es un très mauvais garçon.*'

My God. It's Saffi. He is not away. I check the cuckoo clock on the wall and it's twenty past eleven. We didn't close the shutters and the sunshine highlights his features. My friend loves to make an entrance. It's easy for him. He stands out in any room, like a coiled spring ready to fly. His dark brown skin stretched over his gigantic arm muscles, his dreadlocked hair rolled through multi-coloured beads and his innovative wheelchair, which he manoeuvres with ease, all add to his presence. There is a smoky aura of pure joy that radiates from him. He seems like a giant of a man.

My lungs vibrate as I sit up on the bed. *Is it worse that I will miss my flight or that Saffi is here?* Billy is stretched out, face down and uncovered. She turns her head towards Saffi but this is the only movement she makes. She looks terrible. I must look the same because we were still awake at five o'clock this morning.

Saffi has a grin on his face. '*Vous avez faim? Je peux vous préparer un petit déjeuner?*'

My brain is fogged and my translating skills are reduced, but so far, I have understood that Saffi sees I am not with my wife, which from his tone, he is delighted about – probably because he's usually the one in trouble – and he has organised some breakfast for us. I can smell expensive coffee.

'*Saff*, will you please speak English?'

'Will you introduce me to your lovely femme fatale?' he replies.

'Billy, this is my friend Saffi, it would seem he is not away.' I think what to do next. Saffi has read my mind.

'Perhaps you would like to ring your wife to tell her you will be late,' he says, waving my plane ticket at me. 'Sorry, you both looked so comfortable; I didn't have the heart to wake you earlier.'

'You are enjoying this.'

'If you mean the foot being on the other shoe, then yes, very much.' I have been his alibi too often – he is pleased that he has caught me out. The only time lately that I have asked him for a favour was getting Vanessa off my hands. Saffi should have woken me as soon as he came in, I want to be cross with him, but it's difficult when he is looking so happy. We see each other so rarely these days, and somehow everything always feels better when he is around. He calls it his 'bubble.' His world is ruled on the basis of living for now. There is no past and no future in the *bubble*.

'What am I going to do, Saffi?' I am so tired I can't think.

'Simply find a good reason for you to not get back until this evening. I have booked us all a late lunch at Chez Ambages, it's my favourite place at the moment. I have taken you there before, Rich, the restaurant in Saint Germain, you remember?'

'Yes, it's very nice but I should be at the airport *now*, not discussing top bistros in Paris with you.'

Saffi ignores me. 'I am paying Émilie an awful lot of extra francs to stay open after two o'clock just for us. It will be good to have a proper catch up and this lovely lady can tell me what she sees in you.'

He surveys Billy's body. She still isn't moving, like she is in a trance. Saffi turns back to me. 'Come on, Richard, find a reason why you have to stay.'

Billy sits up, doing nothing to stop Saffi seeing the rest of her. She doesn't seem embarrassed. 'Tell Janette that you need to talk to your friend about a replacement for Simon,' she suggests.

'Clever, as well as beautiful to look at,' Saffi smiles as he stares at her. 'She is right,' he says, 'tell Janette we need to talk about Simon?' He looks back at me. 'Is that his name?'

As Billy heads for the bathroom, Saffi holds out her dress. 'I ironed this for you earlier,' he tells her, 'such a shame crumpling it up on the floor like that.' She laughs, takes the dress from him, and leaves.

I want to hit him, but at the same time, I want to hug him too. It is as though the years we spent apart have evaporated. His paralysed legs are the only change from when we were four years old, and he is so adept with his chair that I rarely notice that difference anymore. He is still my adorable crazy friend.

'Saffi, this isn't–'

'Isn't what I think it is.' He finishes my sentence. 'Come on, Richard, I know you are cut up about Sharpie, and the pressure you are under moving the business. You have found someone to take your mind off it all for a while. I am no saint either. Look, you better use the phone.' He wheels backwards so I can pass him to ring Janette. *Will my wife even be at home?*

BILLY

*H*ot water runs over my sore body but it's not reviving me. Mentally and physically I am not here. I can't think how this has happened. It's like a dream come to life. I am in another world in this extraordinary apartment, and with Richard. I love Saffi, how he has made it possible to dream on. Even the thought of contacting Mum to tell her I am going to miss her special meal feels ethereal.

Two hours later, we are in a small room at the end of a sequence of small rooms. It seems too far for the friendly waiters and waitresses to come when we are the only customers. It was tricky for Saffi to get his wheelchair in as far as he did, but he was determined, saying it would be more secluded for us.

Saffi tells us the history of each of the classic French dishes on offer, and explains which ones he likes the most, but he wants us to choose for ourselves. 'I am sorry,' I say. 'I'm too tired to choose.'

'Okay, on this *first* occasion, I'll order for you.' He makes it seem like we will do this again, but I know we won't. This is blissful, so much happy conversation and so much love.

BERKELEY SQUARE
MONDAY 25 NOVEMBER 1991

*I*n the office my phone rings. 'Hi, Billy, our meeting on Wednesday–' Richard pauses.

'What about it?' I ask.

Well, we've only got the move to discuss and we both know the schedule for that inside out, so I don't see the need to meet up this week.'

My heart seems to stop. 'Okay,' I reply.

'And I've told Shannon that Wednesday mornings are free in my diary for other appointments for now.'

No! Please no! my mind shouts but I ask him calmly, 'Have you spoken to Simon?'

'He rang first thing; saying he can give me four months' notice. So, we can postpone considering the options for Paris until after the head office move.'

'That's good,' I say holding my voice steady.

'Yes, it is. The move is taking up so much time at the moment. Keeping our clients happy during the transition is hard enough, without thinking about replacing him.'

'True,' I reply, trying to think of another reason to see my boss, but I can't.

'Look, Billy, please ring me if you need to speak to me about work.'

'Yes. I will. Thanks for freeing up Wednesday mornings, I have loads to do, so that will give me a bit of extra time.'

'That's what I thought,' he replies quickly.

'Alright, then,' I say. 'Sorry, Richard, there's someone waiting outside my office, I think they want to see me – I'd better go.'

'Okay, bye for now.'

'Bye,' I reply, choking up my disappointment. I signal for the boy outside my room to come in.

'Hello?' I say. I don't recognise my visitor, he's tall but I guess just sixteen years old. 'Can I help?'

'I'm Ed Mackintosh – Mr MarcFenn sent me.'

I shake my head. 'Why?' I frown, hoping this is not for work experience, I have enough to do without being shadowed and finding pointless things for him to do that I will have to supervise closely.

'He said you needed help with the move.'

'So, what exactly do you think you are going to help me with?' I snap.

The boy sits down in the chair opposite me. He places his hands on my desk and leans forward, fixing his blue eyes on me. 'Look, Miss May, I left school in September, and I've contacted all the major companies asking them to take me on. As I told Mr MarcFenn, I don't want to take any more school exams because I think I'll learn more working in the real world. Starting at the bottom and earning my way to the top. So, I'm sat here with you now, keen to learn and ready to do anything you want me to do. I assure you I will listen to your instructions, and carry out whatever you ask me to do, to the best of my ability, as quickly as I can.' I am suddenly reminded of me at sixteen. I thought I could do anything back then.

'So, how long are you planning on helping me?' I check.

'A month at least, but Mr MarcFenn said three, if you agree to extend the time.'

'Right, Ed Mackintosh, I've got a list here,' I say, holding up a folder. 'Get me a coffee while I find something for you to tackle.'

'How do you like it, Miss May?' he smiles.

'Strong and black, no sugar. Get one for yourself too.'

'No problem,' he says, and leaves.

I am going to focus on making sure MarcFenn moves on as smoothly as possible. I will be resilient. Yes, I agreed to just one night, but it felt so special and I was confident Richard would change his mind. I hoped I was *not* simply a temporary diversion from his grief, but it seems I was.

Chapter 13

BERKELEY SQUARE
THURSDAY 19 DECEMBER 1991
BILLY

$\mathcal{A}$ phone resting on the empty floor still rings in Berkeley Square, and I wish I had arranged for the phones to be transferred to Pineappli 1 earlier. All the furniture is gone. Not even a scrap of paper remains. There are just dust patterns and stains where everything used to be.

All the staff mucked in, helping with the clear-out but now they are busy at Columbus Wharf making their desks ready so that they can get away for the two-week Christmas break.

Ed Mackintosh is beside me, as I check my watch. 'Fifteen seconds, and someone will shove a telecom switch somewhere and MarcFenn will be disconnected from here for good,' I tell him. 'I'll just check to see if it happens – so, Ed, what's your plan after this? Have you spoken to Richard about your next placement?'

'Thanks for the report you sent him about me,' he says.

'I only told him the truth,' I reply. 'You *are* astute and I do like you. Every time I've turned around lately, you've been there, asking what to do next. I really appreciate what you've done to help.'

'Thank you, though – I know you weren't keen on having me hanging around to start with. As for what's next for me? Well, I love sport, I might just leave altogether to join an expedition to climb Mount Everest. Or maybe find some work with the scientists at the South Pole.' His face is earnest, so I don't know if he is joking.

'Everything is one big adventure to you, isn't it?' I laugh, as I pick up the phone to see if it's dead.

It is just Ed and me in the building, it's as though all the hustle and bustle that was always here before is something I imagined. It's ghostly quiet. You can no longer walk through the adjoining buildings. The neighbouring offices are separated again with a solid barrier rebuilt between my side and Richard's. The lease on the extra space is surrendered and MarcFenn have no interest here anymore.

PINEAPPLI 1, DOCKLANDS, LONDON
FRIDAY 20 DECEMBER 1991
BILLY

*I*nside Pineappli 1 this morning, the new ceiling lights are like twinkling constellations. They are all on now because it's so overcast today. The pretty lights make me think of the stars in the clear night skies over Fox Halt Farm.

The whole building is breath-taking, enhanced with the futuristic furniture that Charlotte and I chose for it. It is airy inside with so much glass and pine. So spacious, that it makes me feel happy just walking around it.

By eight o'clock last night, almost everything seemed in order. There were one or two, small things to sort out, for example, no-one had realised the wastepaper bins were still on a pallet in the basement. Ed left at half past ten, when I assured him I couldn't think of anything more he could do. I just wanted to go over my notes for the interview later this morning with the BBC about our new high-tech headquarters. Charlotte will be here too, and I can't wait to see her, she will be as pleased as I am to have her special building fully occupied.

I had been up since six, so by nearly midnight my brain was fried, and it took me ages to memorise all the facts and figures I wanted to discuss in the television interview. Afterwards, I made a last check on the new boardroom, which is where I am now, waiting for a meeting to start. This informal get-together will be for all the departmental heads so we can discuss any unexpected problems.

I am so pleased with this room. Every last detail of the boardroom in Berkeley Square has been reproduced to the millimetre, but in the early hours, just as I was about to leave, I saw that the MarcFenn portraits were in the wrong order. I have only just finished repositioning them. I think I may have fallen asleep for an hour but other than that, I haven't stopped, and now people are beginning to arrive for the meeting.

Richard walks in. The last time we were together was on the return flight from Paris.

I flip inside as I see him. All I do is look at him, incapable of thinking. My eyes are closing. *Stay awake*. I pinch the sensitive skin on the back of my hand, hoping the pain will keep me alert. As I shut my eyes again, Richard must see me. 'Billy, have you been here all night? You are exhausted, you need to go home,' he tells me. 'Please just hand me your notes for the BBC. I will deal with everything. No arguments.'

'But…'

'No buts, Billy, I'll get someone to drive you home.'

'I'll get a taxi, thank you,' I reply, as I stand up to leave the room.

Although I desperately want to, I can't look back.

BALHAM

A swift rap on the door stirs me out of my stupor, I am lying fully clothed on my sofa-bed in Balham. Instinctively, I check the clock. It's three in the afternoon. I am not fully awake, as I open the door.

'Gosh, Billy, you took so long to answer that I thought you might have left for the farm already.'

I laugh. 'Way too tired to do anything like that.' I rub my eyes.

'I didn't get a chance to say what an amazing job you've done.'

'It's great, isn't it?' I say.

I smile at him and he smiles back at me. Eventually he speaks. 'You're killing me, Billy.'

'Do you want to come in?' I ask.

'I have to.' He kisses me and I kiss him back…

ℱOX ℋALT ℱARM
SUNDAY 29 DECEMBER 1991

At Fox Halt Farm, Mum knows something is up. She keeps asking questions, which I either ignore or avoid. She has noticed that ever since I got here, the phone rings at exactly the same time every day, and how I am always waiting to pick it up. Poor Mum, I know she is struggling to leave me alone in the hallway, allowing me to have a private conversation. She is desperate to find out who I'm talking to.

She watches me at the kitchen table while I daydream instead of eating – and arguing, which is what I normally do now at mealtimes here. I love firing Dad up about farming issues. He is an avid member of the National Farmers' Union, keeping himself abreast with everything agriculture related. I make sure I read the *Farmers Weekly*, so I am well informed too, and we have debates about all sorts of topics. Our discussions are light-hearted with lots of laughter. It feels good. But while I've grown close to Dad again, poor Grandad is further away from me. He has become forgetful and confused, losing interest in the farm and now all he wants to know is that our sheepdog, Fly, is alright.

Grandad wants Fly with him all the time, and this causes problems. Dad needs the dog to help him with the animals, and in turn, Fly wants to be with my father or in the Land Rover. There is a new pup called Barney who's intended to replace Fly, and Dad parks his Land Rover at the bottom of the lane now, so Fly can't hear it start up. Dad's second dog, Lily, and the new puppy are having all the fun while poor Fly is kept indoors – Grandad's early signs of dementia are hard for the sheepdog, just as they are for all of us.

I finish my dinner which I expect was delicious, but I haven't tasted it. My mind is elsewhere.

'I have something I need to say to you, Billy.' Mum waits for me to reply, making sure that I am listening to her before she starts.

'What, Mum?' I say at last.

'Darling, you are definitely coming home for your dad's sixtieth birthday party, aren't you?'

'Yes.'

'But you missed my birthday and our anniversary meal.'

'I've explained about that, something critical came up at work. I'm sorry I let you down.'

'You've not missed it before. Family's important.'

'Yes, I know,' I reply. 'I'm definitely down again, after work on the Thursday before. I'll help you all day on Friday with all the preparations for Saturday – it's all booked in my diary.'

'And invite this new person, whoever they are?'

'Thank you but I won't be doing that. The date's sorted, believe me,' I say as firmly as I can. My eyes now focus on Dad who is crossing the farmyard, heading for the house, and I rush outside to meet him.

'What do you think?' I ask him.

'You should call the vet, Billy. You were right. There's something not right with Banjo. Sultan keeps pushing up against him, flaring his nostrils.'

'Poor Banjo,' I reply. 'It was just that he didn't touch his breakfast, that's all. He looks bright and happy, and he whinnied when I walked into his stable this morning. But I'm not su…'

'Yep, you go and call the vet. Best to get their opinion. Better safe than sorry.' Dad pats me on my shoulder. Mum is on the doorstep. 'Make sure you ask for Martha, Billy,' she says.

'Why?' I frown.

'Pat Westcott swears by her. Tanya too; she said, her horse weren't right for ages but that Martha Lewis, she saw what were wrong with her animal straight away. Everyone's saying she's very good, and her's gentle.'

I turn to Dad. 'Would you phone the vet for me, please? I want to go to the stable, to stay with Banjo until the vet gets here.'

PINEAPPLI 1
WEDNESDAY 1 JANUARY 1992
RICHARD

*I*t is peaceful in my office. MarcFenn is closed for a Christmas break, so there are just a few essential staff around. All the paraphernalia that was strewn around my old office has been dumped in the middle of my new room. This fresh beginning is a perfect opportunity to have a tidy up. I have a mountain of flat-packed archive boxes ready to be made up and filled but there is something else I have to do first. I pick up my pen.

Dearest Daniella,

I am sorry, but this will be my last letter. Please don't write again. Circumstances have changed for me. At the moment, I can't tell what will happen but please be assured that I am happy. Sorry I can't explain.

I am so glad that your recent letters have been full of positivity about Billy. She certainly seems the happiest I have seen her. It was a shame that you didn't get to see her on the television news report about our new building. We had to send her home that day because she had worked all night to get everything just right. You have a fantastic daughter and I can see why you never wanted to give up on her.

If you need ANYTHING, however small, please get in touch again. I know you have never accepted any money from me, but it will always be available if you need it.

I wish you and your wonderful family every happiness for the future.

Love Richard x

Just one more thing before I start on the boxes, I open my new 1992 diary, to enter an appointment. *'Meeting Developer - Exeter.'*

I make up the first box and place all Daniella's precious letters inside. I couldn't bear to throw any away. I will get on with this. It will keep my mind occupied until I ring Billy at twenty past four.

FOX HALT FARM
FRIDAY 10 JANUARY 1992
RICHARD

*D*aniella opens the front door. 'Richard! I saw your car and thought you were a bed and breakfast guest. I can't believe you're here.'

'You recognized me from the photo my wife sent all those years ago?' I ask quickly.

She pauses. 'Yes, your lovely wedding photo is on our sideboard in the lounge – you saved my daughter's life, how could I not remember your face?'

I smile and she grins back at me. 'I had a meeting in Exeter this morning,' I say, 'but I received a call on my car-phone just as I got to the outskirts of the city, cancelling it, so I thought it would be nice to see Fox Halt Farm. Billy has mentioned this place occasionally, during our work meetings.'

'Well, it is nice to meet you,' she smiles again.

'And you too, Mrs May.'

'Come in, love, come in.' Daniella virtually pushes me through the door of the farmhouse.

I feel overdressed. I have never seen such a mess of individuals. Everyone, including Billy, has on tatty work clothes. They are enjoying their breakfast together around a scrubbed pine table. Cats curl up on every easy chair and a dog is outstretched by an old man's feet. I know the old man and the dog. I know the kitchen and the kettle sitting on the stove, always ready to make more tea. I feel I have come home.

Daniella tells everyone about my cancelled meeting, as Billy gets up. 'This is great, Richard,' she says. 'I can show you around the farm. You…'

Her mother interrupts. 'Let the man get some breakfast inside him first.' She clears a space at the table 'Sit down, Mr MarcFenn.'

Billy's grandad stares at me, unable to grasp who I am, and Billy tries to explain, as Daniella fills a plate with breakfast for me.

Jack sits opposite. 'Hello, Mr May,' I say, reaching across the table to shake his hand. 'I wish I had got here earlier because I have missed the cows being milked, I expect?' I say, trying to sound unfamiliar with his daily routine.

'Call me Jack, boy. Yes, 'fraid you're much too late for milking, but Billy's got some lambs to bottle feed after breakfast. Maybe you can go out with her then. How long are you staying?'

'Two hours perhaps, I don't have another deadline today, but aren't you busy organising tomorrow's big celebration?' I ask, handing him an envelope. 'I stopped off just now to get you this. Billy told me it's your sixtieth tomorrow. That's why she needed the time off from work.' The birthday card took me ages to find. I've been in several shops the last few days, trying to find the right one. It has a photo of a horse on the front, which looks just like Billy's horse Sultan. I can picture the animal because Daniella has sent me photographs, but I am still desperate to see him.

The little pony Banjo has died. This sad news was in the last letter I received from Daniella, it crossed with my letter which said our correspondence had to stop. She wrote how upset she was about the pony, but relieved that Billy was there when it happened. Her daughter had stayed up all night with him. She said how they would all miss Banjo, except Billy's grandfather who is not interested anymore. The letter was even more heart-breaking, because I knew there would be no more farm reports. Daniella told me her eyes keep welling up every time she sees the little cart her father made, not because Billy's first pony has gone, but because her father is lost too.

Jack places the envelope on the table. 'Will open it tomorrow, boy. Thank you.' He smiles at me, and then stabs a large sausage with his fork. The breakfasts look good. I take a deep breath, desperate to remember this smell forever. Daniella's letters have not provided the aroma of the place, and I note the scent of the fried bacon mixed with essence of farmyard.

Billy's mother is standing by the kitchen window, looking outside. 'Dear Tom is here,' she announces.

Jack frowns. 'But I told him last night, I still haven't found the part we need for the tractor.'

'No, Jack,' Daniella says. 'He's going to help you set up the tables in the village hall for the party.'

'My do isn't till tomorrow so why's he here now?'

'I told you, darling, the hall isn't being used today, so we can sort it all out early. I don't want a mad panic just before seven o'clock tomorrow night.'

'Well, missus, the boy can have a cup of tea first.' Jack won't be rushed.

The new visitor walks straight into the kitchen without an invitation. He stops when he sees me, his eyes widening.

'Tom, this is Billy's boss, Richard MarcFenn – the man who rescued her when she fell off the cliff,' Daniella tells him.

'Hello, Mr MarcFenn. I'm Tom Westcott, I live on the next farm. Billy and I grew up together – we went to school together.'

'Pleased to meet you, Tom,' I say, holding out my hand to him.

'Get Billy to show you around Fox Halt, you'll find it a bit different around here, especially after that fancy place my sister has designed for you.'

'Have you seen it, Tom, Pineappli 1, I mean?'

'Not yet.'

'Well, if you ever come up to London, I'll take you round it. Your sister is a clever woman. It is very impressive.'

'I just might one day, Charlotte keeps going on about it.' Tom takes the mug of tea Daniella has made for him, and I turn to Billy. 'Do you think you have time to show me around the farm? It would be interesting to see it.' I try to sound offhand.

'Yes, of course,' Billy replies casually but I hope she is dying to be outside with me. I can't wait to hold her again.

'I have a spare pair of wellies in my pick–' Tom stops and holds his breath, looking shocked. 'Sugar, I've forgotten Louise! I'll bring her in, if that's okay, Mrs May?'

Daniella smiles, 'Of course.'

I imagine he has left a sheepdog in his farm vehicle, but it turns out to be a pretty girl, about twenty years old with auburn springy hair.

'This is Louise, everyone, she's from Hatherleigh, I'm afraid, but don't hold that against her.' Tom laughs as they walk back into the kitchen.

The girl clips his ear. 'I met this chap last weekend at the Young Farmers' rally. He seemed alright then.'

Tom puts his arm around her. 'I was joking, you're quite lovely really–' he pauses and smiles '–even if you *are* from Hatherleigh.'

Louise ignores him, speaking to Daniella instead. 'Tom said you might need a hand today. I wasn't doing anything in particular, so I am all yours, if you want me to help with preparations for the big party.' She looks back at Tom. 'Tom said I might get an invite to the celebration too?'

Daniella answers straight away. 'Yes, sweetheart. I could do with all the help I can get, and yes, you are welcome to come to Jack's party.'

Billy stands up. 'Richard, why don't you try on the boots Tom has brought in for you?'

'It's okay,' I reply. 'I have a change of clothes and boots in the car.'

'Oh?' Billy raises her eyebrows.

'Yes, I thought I might need them. The development site I came to see has a river running through the middle of it. The seller warned me there'd be mud and brambles. I brought wellingtons and some old clothes just in case.'

She smiles knowingly. 'Get them, and I'll show you where you can change. Just a shame you can't stay for Dad's party too.'

I feel, in a way, Daniella should be showing me around the farm. Afterall, I am only here because of her wonderful letters but I have a suspicion that Billy's ever-knowing mother sees what's going on here. 'Show Mr MarcFenn, everything, Billy,' she says. 'He looks like he could do with some country air in his lungs. Louise is here to help me now, so take your time.'

As we step outside, Billy punches my shoulder. 'Why didn't you tell me you were coming?'

'I couldn't,' I say. 'You know what it's like in the office at the moment. I wasn't sure I'd get away. I didn't want to get your hopes up.'

BILLY

Richard's car pulls away and I sit down heavily on the front step. I can't believe he was here. He stayed for tea in the end, and I sent him off with half a Battenberg cake. 'I keep telling you, my mother's homemade cake is a hundred times better than the one we have on Wednesdays, so here's your chance to try it,' I said, wanting to kiss him but I couldn't because Mum and Louise were in the kitchen too.

We walked the whole boundary of our land with the puppy, Barney, running in circles around us. Right up to the highest point on the farm, gazing across at Dartmoor. The tops of Yes Tor and High Willhays were speckled with snow like someone had dusted them in icing sugar. 'I can almost smell the primroses,' Richard said, and I frowned slightly, thinking his comment was odd. At the place we were standing there will be masses of the spring flowers, but there wasn't a trace of them today.

My unexpected guest was plastered in hair and grease by the time we got back to the house. The muck was from Sultan's coat, and from the few cows who allow people to stroke them.

Richard was disappointed that we only had three lambs to feed. He insisted on making up their warm milk and cuddled the little orphans afterwards too. I checked his car before he left, in case he had taken one home. He loved it here. It was funny seeing my boss out of his city suit and marching around in boots; he didn't stop smiling.

Mum made me take him all around the house so I could show him what his family are missing by not coming to stay. We kissed so many times it took forty minutes to get back to the kitchen, and then he wanted to go outside again in case he had missed anything.

I was amazed how comfortable he seemed. It's hard to believe he has never been on a farm before. It was like being back in Paris all over again. A dream.

We talked about his family. We talked about Grandad and the things I used to do with him when I was little. He was sad about my pony dying, he understood how much Banjo meant to me, and I am sure he was nearly crying when I showed him the cart that my grandfather built.

He wanted to see Sultan. Like Banjo, my horse is getting old too, but he didn't mind Richard sitting on his back for a little while. We collected the eggs, and before he left, he asked Dad lots of sensible questions about Grandad's old tractor which he is restoring with Tom's help.

I think back to the moment when we were sitting on a hay bale in Sultan's stable and I told him all about my grandad. I wanted him to understand the person he used to be. He listened carefully, holding my hand, just letting me explain all about my grandparents. 'I never knew my grandmother, Annie. She was born the same year as Grandad, in 1910, in a small cottage on Dartmoor. Grandad said it was a desolate home, high up in the hills and hunkered down in a granite-strewn valley. The cottage was made chillier by icy spray from a moorland stream that almost tumbled through its thick grey walls.

'In 1926, my grandfather found Annie's isolated home by chance, when he got lost on the moor. He was riding one of his family's carthorses, returning home from Widecombe Fair with two live geese he'd bought, in sacks slung across his horse's back. His story about meeting my gran is that he rode home four days later with empty sacks and a wife. Grandad always tells me he swapped the geese for Annie. I will never know if it's true. He loves reciting tall tales.

'I think my grandparents were happy until my mum's brother, little William, died in a tragic farm accident. After that Annie was quite ill, suffering badly with rheumatism until she passed away when she was only fifty-three.

'Grandad still tells me about his life but now he focusses on the time between when he was sixteen and twenty-two years old. His mind seems stuck here, when the farmhouse was crammed full with his parents and his younger brothers and sisters. Three or four to a bed, sleeping head to toe. Years when his authoritarian father gave his children their own specific chores around the farm. Grandad's duties included looking after their precious sheepdog. Now Grandad looks after Fly, and he calls me Annie sometimes. I can't bear to tell him I'm not her.' Richard could see I was about to cry, and he smiled. 'You are lucky he is still here, Billy. You must always treasure that and all the years your grandfather was here with your Mum and Dad while you were growing up.'

'Like I treasure you being at Fox Halt today,' I said. 'It's so precious because we both know this is another snatched moment, don't we?'

'It feels like we're on a magic carpet ride,' Richard laughed before he kissed me again.

I get up and go back indoors. Mum is ironing some tablecloths, and she looks up at me.

'Billy, I've been thinking?' she says.

'About what?'

'About this chap who keeps ringing you.'

'So, it's a chap then?' I reply.

'Yes, it's this Ed Mackintosh fella, isn't it?'

I stare at her in disbelief and shake my head. 'Don't deny it, Billy, these last few weeks, whenever you have talked about the move, it's been Ed this and Ed that. You haven't stopped going on about him. I am your mother, just tell me the truth, please.' I shrug my shoulders, not confirming or denying what she has guessed – hoping she will continue to believe I am seeing Ed. In the same way I allow her to think I fell accidentally from the cliff in Paros, it will be easier this way.

Chapter 14

PINEAPPLI 1
MONDAY 13 JANUARY 1992
BILLY

I notice Richard has an envelope in his hand as he knocks on my office door and steps inside. Straightaway he reads out loud the name of the file lying on my desk. 'Operation Foxglove? What's that got to do with Simon?'

I point to a framed picture of a foxglove standing on my desk. 'Because of this,' I reply. 'This is the first card Simon ever gave me. It was such a surprise, I didn't realise he knew it was my birthday. I framed the actual card he gave me and it always reminds me of him.'

'Good name. I like it.' Richard nods thoughtfully.

This new project will concern Simon's successor, or perhaps the closing down of the residential team in Paris. I have used code names since I started with MarcFenn. I set up my secret filing system because of Simon – he was getting on my nerves when he kept referring to his mission to infiltrate Stefan's team. His cloak and dagger comments irritated me, so after a while, I said I was working on 'Operation Alligator,' and I explained it was a secret mission of my own to find a way to break up the terrifying typing pool. I could see the typists were causing hell for everyone. Nobody liked taking anything to be typed. We hated asking for corrections and we couldn't get anything completed urgently. The senior managers had their own personal assistants, so they didn't see what was happening.

I worked on Operation Alligator behind Vanessa's back. Doing this was satisfying because I felt I could actually own this work and my manager wouldn't be able to claim it as hers. When Simon left to go to Paris, I gave my notes to Stefan to present to Richard and miraculously, the chief alligator, Allison, retired early, and then a number of secretaries, 'pet crocodiles', were assigned to each department depending on workload. The secretaries actually sat with the people they typed for. The new arrangement was a success. Everyone was happier, not just Stefan and me.

Most of the work I do is confidential because it can affect people's jobs or create uncertainty, so when Richard gave me Vanessa's role, I started giving my projects code names. My cryptic titles have tenuous links with whatever I am investigating.

'This feels strange, Richard,' I tell him. 'I never imagined I would be collecting data about my friend, nor that I'd be looking for someone to replace him.'

'So, you'd prefer me to send someone else to France today?'

'No.' I frown at him. 'I am looking forward to seeing Simon.' I open the envelope Richard has now given me and find only an airline ticket inside. 'What hotel am I staying in, isn't it booked?'

'L'appartement de Saffi.'

I stare at him for a moment. 'I'm staying at Saffi's, are you sure he doesn't mind?'

'He insisted.'

'Wow! That's nice of him. Your friend reminds me of Tom Westcott, the way he tries to make people laugh all the time.' Richard makes no comment about Tom. He has his work head on, intent on maintaining a professional relationship between us in the office. 'I've employed Saffi to help you too. MarcFenn has subcontracted him so he can help you with translation, and at the same time, he'll look at Simon's role and draw up a short list for a potential replacement.'

'Well, with Saffi and me on the case we'll have Operation Foxglove done and dusted very quickly then.'

'I hope so.' He steps back out of my office. 'Have a good trip, Billy,' he calls back at me from the corridor.

$\mathcal{P}ARIS$

Saffi has delicate tableware laid out when I arrive. There is cut crystal and lit candles. He has decided that I would like roast beef because I grew up on a farm, and is busy in his kitchen preparing everything. He won't let me help, and insists instead that I choose something to read from the bookcase, which stretches floor to ceiling right the way along one wall of the room.

'I have read each and every one of these. They are all my favourites,' Saffi says before he shoots back into the kitchen.

'It smells delicious – just like one of my mother's wonderful roast dinners,' I call after him.

'That's the plan,' he says, reappearing in the doorway. 'Now go and find yourself a book and sit down please.'

I haven't read fiction for years, I did as a child, but when I started university, I only had time for factual study, and now I only read information for work, or the *Farmers Weekly*. It will be a treat to sit here and immerse myself in a good story while someone cooks dinner for me.

As I pull out a bright orange tome with red writing on its spine, Saffi returns and sees the book. '*Prince Sunshine* by Marc Tirrello, there's an inspired choice,' he says.

I have never read this classic and I don't know much about it, but the book feels solid and comfortable in my hand and its musty scent reminds me of the fresh wood shavings I used to put down for the horses to lie on. 'I think so too,' I reply, thinking how my choice inspired by the book's cover; the way it feels and its smell is an appropriate way to select a book, in this madly decorated apartment owned by Richard's crazy friend.

I start to leaf through the pages. 'Are all your books first editions?' I ask Saffi, but he isn't listening, too busy choosing a CD.

'Hope this will be okay?' he says, but he is back in the kitchen before The Three Tenors start to sing.

I have just noticed that part of the classical mural has gone and now half of one wall of Saffi's apartment looks like a small glade of trees with sunlight pouring through. I am shocked, from this top floor flat I can see the Eiffel Tower lit up, and yet Saffi wants the walls to be interesting too. I wonder if he is happy with his new woodland scene and I wonder at the clever perspective the artist has used to make you feel you are lying on the ground looking up through the trees.

'Right, it is ready.' Saffi has dashed back in. I expect us to serve ourselves from the top of the oven like at home, where we load our plates straight from hot saucepans.

'Please take a seat at the table now.' Saffi directs me to where he wants me to sit. He is opposite, sliding himself from his wheelchair onto a high-backed chair. I am confused; *where is our meal?*

'Billy, the jewelled cowbell in front of you. Would you ring it?' I am bewildered but I do as he asks. Straight away, the head chef from Chez Ambages walks in from the kitchen with a domed platter.

I laugh. I can't believe what Saffi has been up to. A waiter follows the female chef and he pours wine for us both.

'I wanted to make it special for you,' Saffi says.

'Thank you,' I reply, feeling overwhelmed with everything.

'It's a pleasure.'

I look behind Saffi, at the woodland glade. 'The new painting is quite stunning,' I say. He keeps his gaze on me. 'Oh, I just wanted a bit of a change.'

'The artist is very talented.'

'Yes, he is. Grégoire Laurent, he'll be famous one day – he hadn't got any commissions booked, so I nabbed him quickly. I thought the old place needed brightening up, and I just let my friend create what he felt like – I love it, don't you?'

'It's incredible. Your home is amazing and you're amazing too.'

'It's just down to my friends really, I have another pal who's a fashion photographer, and another who deals with the props at the Palais Garnier – they find me bits and pieces, or inspire me into buying something new for the place.'

'Sorry, a palace?' I frown at him.

'No, the Palais Garnier, the Paris Opera House.'

'I have never been to the opera,' I tell him. 'Growing up on a small farm in Devon, there wasn't much call for such grand things. I could go in London, but I work all the time.'

'That's a shame, Billy.'

'Do *you* go?' I ask.

'It's my favourite thing to do in the evenings, when I am not entertaining lovely ladies. Maybe I can take you there one day? That would be the best of both worlds.'

I laugh, thinking I need to change the subject. I feel a little vulnerable now, aware of Saffi's reputation. I hope he is not trying to chat me up, he should know I only want to be with Richard. 'Sorry,' I say. 'I interrupted what you were saying about your friends, the photographer and the chap from the opera house.'

'Yes, I never know what they will turn up with next, you'd be quite shocked by what comes and goes out of here. I can't wait for you to see your bedroom.'

I move to go and look at the room, but Saffi presses my hand onto the table. 'No. Not yet, Billy, I shouldn't have said anything, I wanted to surprise you again, please let's enjoy this meal first. It's great to have you here.'

I feel nervous again. I was brazen when he saw me before. *Does he think I am an easy target?* He must read my mind because he releases my hand instantly. 'No, don't worry Billy, I am not trying to steal you from my best friend.' He laughs. 'Talking of surprises, you must look inside that centrepiece.' He points at the middle of the table. I had noticed the large ornament before but only because it was out of place. Everything around it was exquisite and expensive, but this item looked clumsy and cheap. It is made up of three ceramic pineapples stacked on top of each other. The top crown is vibrant green, and then the three different coloured fruit below are red, white and blue. Its starkness is jarring.

'Please pass Billy the top pineapple,' Saffi asks the waiter.

'Mademoiselle.' The waiter passes me the pineapple and when I lift the china crown, I see there are two tickets for the opera for tomorrow night. I feel like Saffi is a magician, and I hold the white rabbit from his hat. He is looking at me. 'I plan on getting you something ravishing to wear,' Saffi says. 'Do you mind if we go shopping after we finish in the office tomorrow?'

'That would be fantastic,' I tell him, wondering which chic places he will take me to. Shopping with him will be fun.

'Saffi, is headhunting lucrative then?' I ask him. I feel at ease with this man, so I feel comfortable probing. Everything I have witnessed so far about Saffi seems extravagant.

'No, Billy, no not on this scale, I have a hefty allowance from my grandmother's estate, I'm her only grandchild. I never wanted her money, but I am rather enjoying it, I'm afraid. Since my injury I have revalued everything in my life, and I believe family and friends are far more important than money.'

Saffi takes his eyes off me, telling me that the waiter is holding the second pineapple. I open it and find another opera ticket. He reads my mind again, 'No, it's not for Richard,' he says. 'This spare one is for a woman who is very special to me, her name is Ella. You'll get on like a house on fire, I know. She has just moved to Paris and I've invited her to join us tomorrow night.'

The last pineapple is in front of me. I have given up speculating, as I pick out a small gold envelope, but I do find a fourth ticket inside, and this one has *'Richard MarcFenn'* written in neat writing across the top. I look at Saffi.

'He's coming, Billy. He'll be here tomorrow evening and should be staying for a day or two. I will stay with Ella; you'll have this place to yourselves. By the way, I have already sorted the Simon problem.'

'What are you talking about? Have you been into the office and seen it's hopeless? Is Richard closing it down?'

'No, far from it, I have found someone to take on Simon's role. The contracts are signed. We will take the woman I've found to meet Simon tomorrow morning. Genevieve Dubois is excellent, I assure you. You will be shocked though, when you find out the salary Richard has agreed to pay her. She is a tough biscuit to negotiate with.'

'So, are you telling me Richard is coming to Paris for no reason? You have already employed a replacement. Why am I here then?'

Saffi sits back in his chair. 'My devious friend Rich thought that the Simon problem was a good excuse for you two to be together here, in *le gai Paris* and I agree with him – it does sound like a *very* good excuse.'

'You two have been scheming behind my back?' I frown in mock disgust but then I can't help smiling.

Everything is cleared away, and Saffi and I are both reading while opera music drifts through the candlelight.

'Eleven o'clock, that's my bedtime,' Saffi says. 'Is there anything you need?' I look up and shake my head.

'Hey, Billy. Before I crash, I'd like to show you the bit that means most to me in that book. There should be a bookmark on the page.' He grabs my book and stabs a finger at a single paragraph.

'Look this is it. You must read it all.' Saffi waits for me to finish reading. 'Do you see, Billy, Prince Sunshine, that's who I want to be. I love to bring joy into everybody's life.' He waves his hand excitedly around the room.

'You are my Prince Sunshine, Saffi, you are great.' I laugh at his enthusiasm, but there was something else in the special paragraph, which has resonance for me. It read, '*The shadows fill you up until their blackness overwhelms you.*' I think how you don't know what has happened in people's lives, and how they can look good on the outside but inside they are about to break. I remember the pain I felt when Richard was by my bed at Ulrich and Rainard's house, and how he had no idea of my shredded heart. I think how no-one really knows anyone, *do they?*

Saffi watches my face and he is soon ready to cheer me up again, 'Keep the book, Billy. Come on, you haven't seen your bedroom yet.'

'I will treasure your book, thank you so much. So, I am allowed to see the room now?' I am on my feet in a second and as I open the bedroom door, I am horrified, but in the same moment, my revulsion vanishes, I adore it. The bedroom is reinvented. There is a beach, sea, and sky. On the horizon are islands or mountains. The doorway is the bottom of a cliff. It must be Grégoire's work because it's wholly brilliant.

Saffi wheels into the room and lowers himself onto the single piece of furniture, a rowing boat that has been sliced down the middle to widen it. It's made up into a bed. There are oars, old rope, and netting. It is mad. It should be filling me with disgust, but I don't feel hurt. My only emotion is happiness, I feel my demons are banished and this couldn't be better.

'I hope I have recreated the place you two met. I imagined it from what you told me when you were here before.'

I sit down next to Saffi and hug him. 'You, Mr Sanders, are the most thoughtful person I know. You are awesome. Did your friend Grégoire create this too? If he did, he must have been here ever since we left.'

Saffi nods. 'He did, and it *did* take ages. He let me help though, I paint a little, you know? Not the way he can, nowhere near that well. It was fun doing it. Grégoire said he was letting me do the colouring in.' He laughs. 'And I helped to get the old furniture out too. I passed it all on to my photographer friend. I wouldn't be surprised if we don't see a famous model draped over that old brass bed soon, maybe in *Marie Claire* magazine. She won't be as lovely as you were though.'

I ignore this comment, and I am pleased that he changes the subject. 'Billy, how did a girl from a little farm in Devon end up on the island of Paros anyway? You had a job, didn't you?'

I look across the beautiful room to the false sea and I think back. It was, I suppose, because I wanted new leather riding boots. That was the start of it all. I don't say this to Saffi because I want to tell him the whole thing. I am not keen on this magical evening ending. I enjoy his company. It is nice being with someone who doesn't take life seriously. I have forgotten how this feels. All this began when I was like that too, back when everything was fun.

'Our family doctor had a Greek wife who he met in Athens; she was exotic, extraordinary, and always laughing,' I say.

'Like me then.'

'Yes, just like you, my dearest Saffi, but her name was Marina.'

'Like the car?'

'I think so.'

'Billy, go on, it doesn't matter, just tell me the rest.'

'I was fifteen years old, and Grandad told me he had spoken to his doctor about how he was trying to get some money together to buy me some new riding boots. It was his doctor who suggested I ought to get a Saturday job to help pay for all my horsey things.'

'The doctor wasn't keen on you being spoilt?' Saffi teases me.

'Yes, I expect he did think I was spoilt. Any rate, Doctor Hale's wife – Marina – worked in the supermarket in Okehampton, the town, near where I lived. She managed the delicatessen counter, and she needed someone to help on busy Saturdays. Working with Marina led me to Paros.'

Saffi moves to lie out flat on the boat-bed and as I watch him, he grins at me. 'Please continue.'

'Marina used to pick me up from the farm and we spent all day serving and chatting. She told me about the island where she grew up. All her family were still there and she described every inch of the faraway place. I was enthralled with her tales of her childhood, so different from my farming one. I asked her why she didn't have a holiday and see her family again.

'Eventually, she booked the trip, but this happened at about the same time as they found she had a brain tumour. I didn't think she would die, I thought her husband would sort it out.' My voice falters, remembering how my friend was determined to beat the disease, losing so much weight, she looked like a staggering skeleton. But she fought hard. 'Saffi, I can't talk about her death, I'll go on a bit.' He sits up and clasps my hands in his. 'Billy, I didn't mean to stir up bad memories. Don't tell me any more, I am sorry, I asked you.'

'No, it's fine. I'll just tell you what happened after she died – I took Marina's ticket because I was desperate to see the island she had described so beautifully. Doctor Hale didn't want to go, but he suggested that I should write to her family to see if I could meet them while I was there.

'The letter that I received from Marina's parents was warm like her. They suggested staying for the whole summer holiday, and working in their nephew's bar. They said it would be good to have someone English there. So, I went on my own.' I expect my heart to quicken, as I start to think about the next bit, but it doesn't. 'As I got off the ferry, a young man helped me with my bags, and he knew the place I needed to go. He carried my luggage, he came into the bar where I worked nearly every night, and he offered to show me the secret places that Marina had talked about so vividly.

'I was by myself in a foreign country with someone who was warm, kind and Greek; just like my dead friend. Kostas was perfect to me. It was weeks later that one of the bar staff told me he was married. I was devastated by the news.' I stop because Saffi knows the rest. I am sad about Marina but I realise Kostas is not bothering me at all. I now see him as a phoney, everything he said was lies, but Marina was incredible. She was like Saffi, a person who only wanted to bring sunshine into people's lives. I want to talk about something else. 'I can't believe this is the same room,' I say.

'I didn't want you to see it until you knew about Richard. Do you like this crazy bed?' He makes us rock.

'Yes it's brilliant.' I yawn and realise how tired I am. Saffi pulls his wheelchair towards him, so he can get back on it. 'I'll see you in the morning,' he says, 'but I'm making breakfast, so please don't expect it to be as good as our dinner tonight.' I laugh, wondering what he will surprise me with next.

I lie down on the boat-bed, and the painted sky is full of stars.

TUESDAY 14 JANUARY 1992

At eight o'clock, Saffi pulls up his chair beside the boat and we laugh our way through coffee and warm chocolate croissants.

'What shall we do today, Billy?' he asks.

'Have you forgotten we are going into MarcFenn's offices?'

'Look, I assure you Genevieve is perfect, we could go shopping straight away instead.'

'I know she'll be perfect, I believe you, but...'

'But nothing.'

'But I want to see Simon and I want to see the way things are being run there.' Reluctantly, he agrees.

Just before midday, Saffi crashes into me wearing a tall top hat he might have stolen from the Mad Hatter in *Alice in Wonderland*.

'Come on,' he says. 'We are going to be late. We're finished here, I have a table booked at Chez Ambages.' I laugh, which is obviously his intention.

'What's the hat about?' I ask.

'Sometimes it's nice to give people something else to notice rather than Mr Wheelie and my paralysed legs,' he smiles. 'Let's go.'

He refuses to take the hat off the whole afternoon, even on the Champs Élysées, and he keeps it on in the swanky boutiques on the Avenue Montaigne. It's fun. Saffi keeps on referring to me as his beautiful wife, finding the most expensive dresses for me to try on. He reminds me of Mum in Oxford Street, but this is a search for just one outfit, and Saffi's budget is unlimited. The fortune he spends on my 'out of this world' dress could have fixed the barn roof that collapsed two years ago. Actually, it could have bought a whole new barn.

We have the best seats at the opera. It feels surreal as Richard arrives and sits down next to me.

Everyone knows Saffi, and we meet lots of his equally mad friends. He introduces us to most of the performers and all of the backstage crew. Saffi is right about Ella; we hit it off straight away. It is a very late night with nothing but laughter.

WEDNESDAY 15 JANUARY 1992

Richard and I visit the Paris office because there were procedures I saw yesterday that I didn't understand. Everything turns out to be fine, it is simply because property law is different in France. Afterwards, we spend the rest of the day at the Musée d'Orsay. 'Can we see some of the originals of the paintings in my bedroom at Rainard and Ulrich's house?' I ask.

'Of course,' Richard replies. He lets me stand and stare as long as I like at them. He doesn't force me to move on, wrapping his arms around me, or holding my hand. We stay in front of the Édouard Manet's painting, 'A Bar at the Folies-Bergère,' for half an hour or more. The detached girl with the mirror behind her is full of questions for me. I tried to figure her out in Paros and it is no different seeing her here – I still can't work out her story.

We walk along the Seine and later we sit in the front pews of Notre Dame and I pray that I can be with Richard forever. I know I can't. He will never leave his wife, and I couldn't let him.

THURSDAY 16 JANUARY 1992

Our last morning ends with an early lunch high up in the Eiffel Tower. It is spellbinding.

'At this height, it's like we are back on our magic carpet ride,' he says.

'I feel that I have spent my entire life with you,' I tell him. 'You understand me, Richard.'

Chapter 15
PINEAPPLI 1,
MONDAY 20 JANUARY 1992
BILLY

*I*n my new Pineappli office, I close my eyes and think back over every detail of my time in France. I never want to forget any of it. Our sightseeing and the nights in Saffi's apartment. I can't stop revisiting all the moments over and over again, but I must sort out the small amount of filing I have gathered about the Paris office. I like my confidential reports to be safely secured off site. I can easily call them back from the storage depot if I need to check anything.

The archive box looks very empty but the longer I leave it here, the more it will remind me of everything I want so much and can't have. The project is finished anyway, Saffi pretty much had it sorted before it even began.

As I start to enter the file name 'Foxglove' into the archive record, the computer predicts what I am going to write. I type 'Fox' and it automatically generates 'Fox Halt Farm.' I am surprised, there can only be one place with that name – I am remembering my parents telling me how Dad teased Mum when he first arrived at the farm. He said, 'Foxes live in dens, and badgers inhabit holts. I am from Slough and even I know that.' Mum nodded at him, smiling, wondering how many times she'd heard this before. 'And what's more,' he laughed, 'even the *holt* spelling's wrong.' My mother had an explanation ready. 'The name was a mistake from the time when maps were first drawn up around here. This place was originally Fox

Hall Farm, part of the big local estate but the cartographers copied the name wrong. It just stayed that way.'

The unique name in the spreadsheet intrigues me, so I quickly order up the archive. It will be with me tomorrow.

TUESDAY 21 JANUARY 1992

As soon as the heavy filing box arrives on my desk, I dive into it. First, pulling out a black jacket with no shop tags. It looks brand new. There is a faint familiar scent. Next, I find a pair of trousers. I don't study these because of what I uncover underneath. I am opening Pandora's Box.

Hidden beneath the clothes are stacks of letters, and instantly, I recognise Mum's handwriting. I don't understand. *Has someone gathered up all the letters she has ever sent me?* But I threw mine away, if I actually opened them. This correspondence is flattened out and tied in bundles. These are cherished, and now I see who they are addressed to. There must be years of letters here, all sent to Richard.

I can't help myself. I start to read.

I cry my heart out, but I keep going; realising all the things I hadn't bothered about – I was so full of self-pity I was blind to what my mother and family were going through. I can't believe what I read. Slowly, my guilt turns to rage. My mother has told all our family history to a complete stranger. She has lied and conspired, and she has kept this all from me, and probably Dad too.

Everything I feel about Richard falls away. He was never intuitive. He probably doesn't even like Battenberg cake! I shiver, wondering if he has told my mother about our affair.

I need to get away. I won't go back to the bedsit. I can't bear to be anywhere with links to Richard. In the state I'm in, it wouldn't be safe for me to drive so I decide that there is just one person who isn't embroiled in this treachery. I pick up the phone.

'Can I stay with you for a few days?' I ask Tom, trying to hide how I am falling apart.

'Billy, what do you mean?' I imagine him frowning. 'You want to stay at ours? Why can't you go to Fox Halt?'

'I can't explain. All you need to know is I need to hide somewhere. Can you smuggle me into your bedroom, like you did when we were kids? And Tom, I'm trusting you not to tell anyone.'

'Billy...'

'Will you help me, that's all I want to know?'

'Of course, but what's wrong?'

'Can you pick me up from Saint David's in four hours' time? I can meet you in the café opposite the train station. Yes or no, Tom?'

'Yes...'

'Thank you – don't tell anyone I've phoned you. No-one, Tom, I mean it. Not my family or your parents, nor Charlotte. Not anyone.'

'Alright, I'll see you later,' he agrees.

'Thank you.'

My young assistant has just returned from lunch and I catch his attention. 'Ed.'

'Yes?'

'I have a family crisis at home, so I need to get back to Devon straight away. There is nothing pressing here but I'll need you to stand in for me at my meeting with Richard tomorrow?'

'Okay.' He doesn't sound confident.

'These are the files for tomorrow's meeting, just look through them, and discuss it all with Richard – it's self-explanatory -just the stuff we talked about on Friday.'

'Right, you are going straight away?' he checks.

'Yes. You'll be fine Ed and please, I'd rather you didn't bother me about work while I'm gone – you know it all, I'm sure you do. If you don't, I'll sort it when I get back. Okay?'

'Okay,' he agrees, still sounding unsure.

My insides churn over. All I want to do is cry and cry. I feel wholly betrayed.

Why do people I love, lie to me?

PINEAPPLE 1
WEDNESDAY 22 JANUARY 1992
RICHARD

*T*he door to my office opens at half past nine. 'Good morning, Mr MarcFenn.' Billy's young helper seems to think I am expecting him.

'Where's Billy?' I ask quickly.

'Hasn't she spoken to you?'

'No.'

'There was a crisis yesterday at the farm. She said she had to go there straight away.'

'Did she?' I check, not understanding.

'Yes.'

'Ed, I need to find out some more about this – can you come back later?'

'What time?' he asks.

'I'll get Shannon to call you to reschedule.' I stare at him.

Eventually, he gets to his feet. 'I'll wait for Shannon to call me then,' he says, walking to the door.

Why didn't she come to me? I pick up the phone to call the farm.

'Daniella, what's happened?'

'Richard, is that you?' she replies. 'Nothing's happened, why?'

'Billy. Is she there?' I ask quickly.

'No, why would she be?' I think hard, trying to work out what's going on. 'Sorry to have bothered you,' I tell Daniella. 'I had a message from her. I've obviously misunderstood what she meant. I think she must be at the bedsit. I'll send my assistant over there to see what the problem is.'

'Let me know, will you?'

'Of course, I'll call you later,' I say, ending the call, impatient to check Billy's office.

There is a box on her desk and I see immediately it's mine. *Hell! Why is this here?*

I squash down all the guilty contents and hold the lid closed, trying to keep its secrets inside, but I'm too late, the damage is done. Those little signs that made Billy think I was special, that I was the one, will all be a pretence now. I will be a rotten hateful cheat just like Kostas was. *I am the one, I am, my darling.* I get my coat from my office and leave.

BALHAM

I am relieved to see her car parked up outside as I knock and knock on the door of the bedsit. I shout at her to let me in and her neighbour is not pleased about the racket I am making.

I decide I need to use my key to get inside, terrified Billy has tried to kill herself again. She is not here. The things she might have taken are; her passport is on the side.

Saffi is my next thought, maybe she's with him in his London apartment? I grab her phone to ring my friend. Billy is not with him and she hasn't been in touch. I talk to Saffi for ages, trying to make sure he isn't lying. He and Billy seemed as thick as thieves when I arrived in Paris.

I call Daniella back. 'Yes?' she says, sounding anxious.

'I haven't found her yet, sorry, but I think she may go to the farm. Will you ring me right away, if she does, please?'

'Have you two had an argument? I know you're in some kind of relationship, and *no* I don't approve.'

'Daniella, she found your letters to me,' I tell her, avoiding the fact she has guessed about our affair and how she is not happy about it. 'She discovered every one of them, and she's probably read them all, too.'

'No.' Her disapproval turns to horror.

'I was stupid to have kept them, I just couldn't bear to throw them away.' I choke a little.

Daniella starts to cry. 'I've kept all yours too,' she sobs, 'they are hidden at the bottom of my wardrobe. It might have been your letters she found – Billy could have easily stumbled across them here. I could have caused this disaster as easily as you.'

'Shall I ring the police, the hospit…' My voice trails off. I can't tell Daniella that her daughter tried to kill herself before.

'Yes, you call them in London, and I'll phone around the police and hospital here, but, Richard…'

'What?' I cut in.

'Give me a minute please – there is somewhere else she might be. When Billy was a child and she was upset she used to sleep in the stable with her ponies. I will check around the farm before I phone the police.'

'But her car is here.'

'Sorry, I need to look. Ring me if you find her.'

'Ring me if you do, I am at the bedsit,' I say.

'She doesn't have a phone?'

'Sorry, Daniella, I made her get one. I'll give you the number…'

I sit on Billy's empty sofa-bed and cry my heart out. Two-faced, two-timing turmoil. My marriage is in trouble.

I have to find her.

I love you, Billy.

Where are you, my darling?

Chapter 16

FOXLANDS FARM, HAMSGATE
BILLY

Eight o'clock in the evening, and I am in Tom's bedroom. He has been brilliant, sneaking me over the porch roof and in through his window. I think about how many times he has done this with all his different girlfriends. If I wasn't so upset, it might have been romantic or funny.

He has given me a loaf of bread, a large bottle of water and a bucket with a lid so I can go to the loo. He says he will get sandwiches later, and has promised that as soon as his parents are out, I can use their bathroom for a shower.

Tom put a lock on his bedroom door years ago so his mother couldn't come in and tidy his room. He said if he wasn't going to get a place of his own, then at least he should have some privacy. I am locked in, so if there's a fire, I must get out through the window. I don't care about any of it. I just want to lie in his bed and never get up. Tom didn't touch me last night and best of all, he didn't ask me why I can't stop crying. I feel sick.

The door unlocks.

'I thought you were supposed to be at a Young Farmers' meeting?' I ask, as soon as Tom walks in.

'Nope,' he shakes his head and puts his hand on his stomach, bending forward in the middle. 'I've told everyone I bought a dodgy pasty at lunchtime, I've a horribly upset stomach.' He laughs. 'Even if you won't talk to me, Bills, I'm staying here with you.'

I remember coming into this room when we were small. With no brothers or sisters, I used to find Tom whenever I could. There was always a good game that we would make up, mine always involving ponies, and his, bikes, fishing rods or dens. As we grew up, Tom's dad gave him a wreck of a car which Tom and I did up. We used to race around the fields. It usually wasn't long before something would break and we both learnt a lot about car mechanics repairing that unreliable heap. Racing was best at harvest time because we made a track around the bales left in neat pyramids to dry in the sun.

'Bills, I have a confession.' He sits on the bed beside me.

I shut my eyes, breathing in slowly. 'You've told Mum.'

'I haven't, Bills. But *you* must. She is going mental. I hate seeing her like it. Let me tell her if you won't. Your mother loves you, she'd never do anything to deserve this.'

'She has, Tom. I can't tell you, but she has.' I slide off the bed to sit on the bucket. Tom stares at me. I have peed in front of him a hundred times, when we were little and on long excursions around the fields, 'Billy, we aren't children anymore. We've grown up, can't you see?' I get up and flop back down on the bed leaving a huge gap between us.

'There are wet wipes in the drawer,' he offers, and immediately, I consider why they are there.

'What do you need to confess?' I ask him, my mind travelling back in time again. We are in the barn at Fox Halt Farm. Tom won't tell me where he has hidden my pony's bridle so I can't ride, he wants me to go fishing with him instead. 'Tell me, Tom.'

'I paid them all.'

'What?' I frown at him.

'All those girls I have taken up to Fox Halt Farm. I paid them all.'

'Don't be stupid. Why are you saying this?'

'Because it's true,' he says. 'It started off because I knew your mum was writing to you. I was trying to make you jealous, so you'd come home to be with me.'

'You are making this up. Please stop it. I don't need this.'

'I love you, Billy, I have always loved you. Why won't you see? I didn't lie to any of the girls I was with, I told them upfront, I didn't want anything serious. It's only ever been you. Please understand.'

'You'll not make me fall into your arms again like this. We agreed that was a mistake.'

'No, Bills, I didn't agree. My dream is still with you.'

'Whoa. Tom. We need to go back a bit here. Are you expecting me to believe the lovely Louise, you were with at Dad's party; you paid her to come with you? I don't believe it.'

'It's true, Louise told me that her horse's stable was running with water because the automatic drinker kept sticking open. I did a deal with her to fix it, plus another three hours' work, if she came with me that Friday. I knew you would be home because your mother tells me everything. Don't you remember how she kept leaving me alone with you at the party? Surely, you don't think that was normal? I had to agree to move her dung heap to get her to come that night.'

'What about Martha who came to Fox Halt Farm with you one Christmas Day afternoon. She was so kind when I found out Simon and Chantelle had got engaged.'

'Martha, the vet?'

'Yes.'

'That's easy. She'd just moved to Hamsgate and her long-term partner from university had just dumped her. When I met Martha she was crying, and she told me how her boyfriend didn't want a long-distance relationship. She was working that Christmas and she didn't know anyone in the village, so I invited her here for Christmas dinner. Afterwards, when I described your mother's fabulous Christmas cake, she agreed to come with me to see your family. You're right, Bills, Martha is very nice, but I assure you nothing has ever happened between us.'

'Tom, all those girls just to make me jealous. You are insane.'

'It just became a habit, I suppose, and word got out if any of the local girls needed help, I was usually up for it.'

He jumps off the bed, and stands by the door with his hand on the key. 'Billy, let me ring your mother. I'll tell her you've phoned and you're safe. I could say you need a few days to get in touch with her, but she mustn't worry. Please.'

'Go on then, but get back here soon, I need to quiz you some more. What you're telling me is ridiculous. Have you got receipts?'

BEECHWOOD
RICHARD

Janette opens the door as I step out of the car. 'You're late, darling,' she says, reaching out to kiss me.

'Sorry, the damn car phone is broken again. I should've stopped and called you from a phone box, but I just wanted to get home.'

'It's okay, don't worry,' she replies. 'Your dinner is in the microwave. It'll be fine, I'm sure.' I follow her indoors.

'I'm sorry I'm so late, Michael O'Rowde rang me just as I was leaving the office, he urgently wanted to meet me, to talk about a scheme he needed to put a sealed bid on.'

'Oh, where is that?' she asks. I'm feeling wary now, my wife doesn't normally greet me at the front door, and she hasn't really asked me much about work since she left to have the children. Maybe I'm just tired and she *was* worried, ordinarily I would have called her if I was going to be late. I try to sound convincing with lots of information.

'Some ex-railway land in Redditch. Michael needs to put in his offer first thing in the morning and he was desperate for a chat. He wanted my opinion. He's going to bid twelve million for it, it seems.'

'But you could have phoned before you went to see him. I have been a little worried, and the girls wanted to know where you were, when I put them to bed.'

'I didn't think it would take so long. I met him at his house, and he's having a new state-of-the-art phone and security system installed there, so his phones haven't been working the last couple of days. I'm so sorry I worried you, I wasn't thinking. Are Sid and Harry alright?' I don't say at nine o'clock I thought I needed to get home, and I was too scared to ring my wife in case Daniella rang back, or Billy phoned, nor that just as I arrived outside the village, I stopped to take the battery out of my own car phone.

I start the microwave, even though I don't think I can eat a thing. I sit at the kitchen counter with my head in my hands.

When our home phone rings, I expect Janette to answer it – the call has to be for her, it's always someone who needs to speak to my wife. It stops, but it starts ringing again and there is still no sign of Janette. I decide to pick it up.

'Hello, Richard, I just wanted to tell you that Billy is safe.'

'Okay,' I say, realising Janette is beside me now.

'You can't talk, can you? Sorry to ring you at home but...'

'Right, tell me,' I cut in.

'She has contacted dear Tom and told him she is alright, but he said for me not to expect her to get in touch for a couple of weeks.'

'Okay, that sounds good. Good luck with your offer. Bye for now, Michael.' I want to crumple to the floor with relief, but Janette is still with me. All I can do is wait and hope. Billy is okay, that's the main thing, isn't it?

THURSDAY 23 JANUARY 1992

I must have fallen asleep eventually, because it is now half past two in the morning. Janette's side of the bed is empty. I wait ten minutes thinking she is in the bathroom, but she isn't back. I am going to find her.

In the kitchen, I see two A4 sheets of paper on the counter. It's a long handwritten note. There are quite a few sheets of crumpled paper in the bin. This must have taken Janette a long time to write.

My darling Rich,

When you read this, I will be at your dad's with the girls. I have a spare key, so I won't need to get him up. I won't return unless you come and get me but I hope with all my heart that you do.

I know about Billy and I know too that I let this happen. I always wanted our marriage to be perfect. I didn't want to end up like my mother. I wanted our kids to have a dad and a loving home but I have messed everything up. I am sorry.

Please don't lie to me about Billy. I don't think it's been going on long, has it? Was it the christening when you rang me, saying you needed to stay and speak with Saffi? You seemed distant for a few days afterwards. Then, at Christmas, when you kept taking Trixie for a walk. You said you needed some peace, to try and sort your feelings out about Sharpie. Were you calling her then? Jayne saw you in the phone box on Bad Foot Lane, she even joked, asking me if you were having an affair.

On Wednesday last week, I phoned the Paris office just to check what time you would be home on Thursday. Sid had messed around with the magnets on the fridge and the note you left had vanished. I rang but they said you weren't there, so I decided you were doing something with Saffi.

But today, I had that whizzy thing in my eye, and I thought I had a migraine coming on, so I rang the office to ask if you would pick the girls up from school. Shannon was surprised when I rang. She thought you were home already. She said you stormed past her desk and that you left without a word. 'No idea when he's coming back,' she said. Your PA remembered when Sharpie had her heart attack and she thought there was another emergency. Shannon said you always tell her where you are going, and when you'll be back, but you didn't.

Two separate days when the office have no clue where you are? And now tonight, you come home late with a cock-and-bull story about Michael which I know wasn't true because of Mrs May - she rang here before you got back, and she was crying her eyes out. She told me she had been trying to get hold of you on another number, but you weren't answering. She asked if I would give you a message. Then she sobbed her heart out while she told me her daughter was safe. I tried to calm her down but, in the end, I said you would probably be home soon, and suggested she should ring back. I had the distinct feeling she didn't want to talk to me. She wanted to speak to you.

My head was all over the place after that call, trying to piece everything together - and then, when Mrs May phoned back, you pretended she was Michael, (you had just told me he had no bloody phone!) - you said you were tired and took yourself off to bed without eating anything. I'm still down here, and pretty mad now that I have written this. I will make a cup of tea and start again - I don't want to be angry. This is my fault.

Right. I hope you're still reading this. I hope you will come and get us tomorrow/today. Look, darling; you've had a rough ride since the twins were born. I know you tried everything to get me out of that awful depression I was in but I pushed you away. I see now we have been drifting apart ever since, me at home, and you at work. I have made a mistake trying to be like Sharpie, I admired your mother so much I didn't see what she had done to you, or your dad. I thought she was marvellous the way she stormed about organising everyone *and everything. I was trying to do it all too, but I've neglected you, darling.*

You kept asking me if Sharpie knew you loved her. I was deaf. I just wanted you to help me get over her heart attack. I saw it all. I was there when she died, you weren't, and I kept thinking what I could have done to save her. I was wracked with guilt, just like you were, but I kept expecting you to help me. I haven't considered your feelings. Please, Rich, forgive me for being selfish.

I imagine Billy saw your pain. The card she sent after Sharpie died was full of sympathy and understanding. I thought her words were just for me. I didn't consider how much pain you were in too.

I want you to choose me. I don't want it to be because you think you ought to. I want to get back to where we were. Let's try for more children. I was scared after having the twins, but I can't be frightened anymore. I want to be with you. I want to try to mend us. Please don't throw us away like some worn old shoe.

I would like you at home more, and for you to do things with the girls. You are missing out on so much. I want you with me at their Nativity plays and their games days, I would like proper holidays together. Please will you talk to me and I will hold you and listen to you and not dump my problems onto you, please choose me, Rich. Let's get our family back together. Let's love each other and care about one another like we used to.

I will take the girls off school tomorrow, I will say they are both sick and I'll take them to London Zoo for the day. It will keep my mind off this letter, and what you will choose to do.

If you come, then I want us to go away together next weekend, just us two. Jayne will have the twins - her little girl, Amy, is Sid's best mate in class. Amy is always asking if the twins can stay over at her house. I am sorry I am telling you this in a letter. We have stopped talking. Sharpie was always there, and I started talking to her instead of you.

Finally, your dad is doing fine. The women from Sharpie's WI are falling over themselves making sure he is okay. Franklin is loving every minute of it. You won't have seen any of this because I can't stop you working. He's fine on his own, and we need time together.

Let's have a future with our wonderful children.

I love you,

Janette xxxx

FOXLANDS FARM
BILLY

When Tom wakes up, I am sitting on the bed. He has hardly opened his eyes, but I can't wait to talk to him. I have to say something before I lose my resolve again. 'I am pregnant. There you go, Tom, as it's confession time,' I tell him, saying the words I have been too scared to even say to myself.

'No.'

'Yes.'

'Is it that Richard bloke? Is it his?' Tom sits down beside me, putting his arm around my shoulder. 'Is your bloody boss the father? He is married.'

'Why do you think it's his?'

'I was suspicious of you two, as soon as I saw him in the kitchen at Fox Halt Farm.'

I thought I could explain our affair without crying, but I do cry. I must look disgusting. My face is burning red. I have been in the same clothes for two days. I haven't washed but still Tom pulls me close into his chest.

'Does he know?' he asks.

My sobs take up too much air. 'No and, he isn't … he isn't going to.'

'Do you want to keep it?'

'Yes, I think so.'

'If you do want to keep it, I will marry you. You know that, don't you.'

I cry and laugh at the same time. Tom sounds old-fashioned, He must realise unmarried women can have babies without shame anymore.

'What I mean, Bills, is that I love you and I want to be with you, even if you are having someone else's baby. I would love the little one as if it were mine. Please, Billy, understand what I mean.'

I've just noticed how Tom tells me things and then checks that I understand, but maybe he should check. Maybe he needs to because for years I have been unaware of his deep feelings for me. He was just Tom, the boy next door, my best friend, my confidante and comrade. He was just there. He is just here now, and I have no idea what to do. 'I believe you love me, Tom,' I tell him.

'And.'

'I love you too, but only as my forever friend who knows me inside out. I'm sorry, Tom, I never imagined that me going away hurt you so much.' I put my arm around him. 'Listen, I'm all over the place at the moment. I think I'd like to go home and talk to Mum.'

He looks disappointed. 'Do you want to go right now?'

I reconsider, and then shake my head. 'When I've tidied myself up a bit, is that okay? Will you come with me?'

'What, turning up at Fox Halt Farm with yet another girl? What will your mother think of me?'

He is making me laugh again. I recall my mother's letters to Richard. 'Dear Tom,' I say, 'if you turn up there with me, Mum will be delighted.'

BEECHWOOD
RICHARD

I have another note in my hand, and I am reading it again, making sure it truly says what I want it to convey.

Dearest Janette,

I could just say this when I see you, but I feel writing makes it more certain.

Please forgive me, darling.

I won't deny it. I have no excuse. I have hurt you and I am hurting Billy too. I never intended any of this. It sounds feeble but it 'just happened.' I promise never to lie to you again.

I'll speak to Shannon, and book off lots of days during the school holidays. Also, I will arrange to stay off work until Tuesday next week, so we can have some proper time away, just us two. I hope your friend Jayne can cope with the girls that long. I would book somewhere nice but after my honeymoon disaster, I'll let you choose.

I didn't realise about Dad. Thank you for telling me. You are right, there is so much I don't know. For example, we will be leaving our adored children with a woman I can't even picture. I haven't met any of your new friends and I'm sorry I let that happen.

This morning, I'll ask Saffi to find Billy some employment options elsewhere, and I will tell Shannon to draft a severance letter to include a good sum of money for her to leave immediately. I won't see her again.

I think we may have to start looking closely at our business. I feel it's been too good for too long so I will need a fair bit of help. Would you like to work one day each week back in the office? You could pick your hours. Sorry, I am going on about work as usual.

What I want to say is I am sorry. I would love us to have another baby and you are my only choice. Please forgive me.

All my love,

Rich xxx

Chapter 17
FOX HALT FARM
FRIDAY 24 JANUARY 1992
BILLY

*T*he prevailing winds were probably why the oak trees were allowed to get so big at the edge of the farmyard. The two-hundred-year-old trees provide much needed shelter, but in winter time, when their gnarly limbs are stripped of leaves, Mum says she can sometimes make out the ghostly silhouettes of her mother and little brother sitting on the highest branches. She is adamant that they look down on her, telling me how, through the noise of the whispering wind, she hears her mother singing nursery rhymes.

It is getting dark, as I try to spot my grandmother's ghost amongst the noisy magpies flying in to roost. I hear a car come into the yard, and turn to see the vehicle park up in front of the house. I recognise it immediately, it's the same vehicle I was so happy to see here just three weeks ago.

Tom is beside me. He slides a protective arm around me as Richard and Janette climb out of the car and begin to walk towards us. My vision blurs and all I am really aware of is my heart thumping in my ears.

'I'm sorry, Billy,' Richard says, slipping his arm around his wife, mirroring the way Tom and I are standing. 'We are on our way to stay in a hotel in Cornwall. The place overlooks the sea.'

'That sounds nice.' I mumble. I can't look at him, my eyes are filling up with tears.

'Yes, I hope so. Janette knows I've been unfaithful to her but she's willing to forgive me.' His wife smiles at him, before she turns to me.

'We are going to mend our marriage, Billy,' she says.

Tom grips my waist tightly, as my knees try to fold under me. I smile back at Janette, concentrating hard to stay upright and focus. 'That's wonderful news,' I reply and then I make a flash decision. 'I should never have left Hamsgate, these last few days have made me realise now how much Tom means to me.' Reckless words leap out of my mouth, I don't want Richard or Janette to see how much I am hurting. 'Tom has asked me to marry him, and I said yes.' I look at Tom, and his face is one big smile.

'I hope you will be happy, Billy,' Richard says, before turning to Tom. 'Look after her.'

Janette takes a step towards me. 'I need to thank you, Billy, you have made Richard and me see how we have slowly drifted apart. Here,' she says, handing me an envelope. 'You'll find a very large cheque in there, to compensate you for the immediate termination of your job with MarcFenn.'

'Thank you for all your hard work, Billy.' Richard's eyes are fixed on the envelope and he doesn't look at me.

As Janette moves back, she squeezes her husband's hand. 'Saffi will be in touch with you, Billy,' she says. 'Rich has asked him to talk to you about finding another position somewhere else.'

'Thank you,' I say, forcing the words out of my mouth and then I see her pull Richard's hand towards their car.

Tom and I stand side by side, as Richard drives out of my life without a backward glance. I will never tell him about the future son or daughter he leaves behind too.

I place my hand over my stomach, and I stare up at the magpies, who are silent now, and I'm sure I hear Annie.

One for sorrow, Two for joy,
Three for a girl, Four for a boy,
Five for silver, Six for gold,
Seven for a secret never to be told…

Eight for a wish.

PART TWO

Chapter 18

FOX HALT FARM
WEDNESDAY 26 FEBRUARY 1992
BILLY

'No!' I scream. My body is folding over, I am desperate for this to stop. I can't explain the terror of my screaming cry, it is like the shouting of yesterday but far worse. Yesterday was terrible; beyond terrible, when I realised my amazing grandfather had passed away.

Grandad was in his easy chair in the kitchen, snoozing. There were two cats lounging on his lap and Fly was at his feet. I was sitting staring out of the window, thinking about marrying Tom, trying to decide if I should backtrack out of our month-long engagement. Inside, I know it's wrong, but he loves me, and I'm certain he'll look after the baby; a secure family life for us all. Tom is so excited that we are engaged, but can I be happy when my feelings about Richard are so confused and raw?

I suddenly realised I couldn't hear my grandfather's breathing. I knew something was wrong, as I turned to him. I tried to shake him awake before I ran outside to find Mum and

Dad. We were all yelling at one another and crying and then the ambulance came and took Grandad away.

The phone didn't stop ringing – so many people wanting to say they had heard about our loss and offering their condolences.

'Eighty-two. That was a good age,' they said, as though it made a difference. Some said, 'Well, it is probably best really, what with all the dangerous machinery around the farm. He could have been knocked over by a cow. He wasn't really sure where he was anymore.' Those were the kind of consoling words I heard. Useless words. They didn't say anything about the empty chasm that is left. My longing for one more hug from my adoring grandfather. One more little joke with him. –And now, it is me struggling to find the right words, for this even deeper despair. This is worse than Grandad dying. This is diving into the blackest bottomless pit. I will never reach the bottom.

Blood everywhere. The bathroom is scarlet. I was cleaning it for the guests that Mum wouldn't let me put off. 'Best if we keep busy,' that's what she said.

There is a red puddle on the white tiled floor and crimson smears over the basin and the toilet. Somehow there are even spatters in the shower. It must stop. I *can't* lose my baby. But it's useless, he or she is pouring out of me.

ROYAL DEVON AND EXETER HOSPITAL

*I*n a hospital bed, and everyone is whispering, but I know what they are saying. They say, I have lost my baby. *I am here. I know.*

The doctor stabs me with a needle but the injection doesn't hurt. I can't feel more pain.

Isolation. My baby is gone. My only tiny bit of Richard is gone.

A man speaks to me now, bringing more pain, more sadness, and more heartbreak. More. I thought more was impossible but it's not. 'I'm sorry,' he says, 'but, Billy, you should never have got pregnant in the first place. The internal injuries you sustained from the accident, and the scar tissue have caused too much damage–' I scream again, for all the babies I will never have. A silent scream held in my throat. *No!*

Tom was enthusiastic and delighted about being a father. Making plans. It is all he's been talking about…But now, *never* a daddy. I can't do that to him.

PINEAPPLI 1
FRIDAY 17 APRIL 1992
MICHAEL O'ROWDE

Richard's face is white – like chalk. 'What is it, man? You look like hell. You are not going to tell me Brislington has fallen through after all the hours we've put in. Have we lost it?'

When the call came in, Richard asked me to leave him for a minute and as he put the receiver down, I went back into his office to continue our meeting, but now the bloke looks like he is about to cry. Men like us don't cry. 'Is it your father?' I ask.

'No, Michael, it's not my father. Do you fancy a drink?'

Here, in the Christopher Columbus pub, I am still in shock. 'Jeez, Richard,' I say. 'I thought I knew you – you and Billy May, never. I can see what you saw in her though. Great looking girl, clever and all. But…'

'Yes, Michael, you have told me already. You didn't think I was the cheating kind. Well it happened. And Janette and I are smoothing things out.'

'Things are all right between you and Janette, then?' I check.

'Yes. Yes, they are.'

'I thought so,' I nod at him and smile knowingly. 'I saw your lovely wife just before our meeting. I thought she might be pregnant. Twins like last time?'

'Michael, please don't say anything. Janette wants to get through these first critical weeks before we tell anybody. I said she looked fine this morning, and no-one would notice in that dress. We don't know if it's twins again. I hope not.'

'No, mum's the word. Whoops – I won't say anything. Don't worry. You got Billy May knocked up too. Hey, you're a bit of a stud, aren't you?'

'Will you stop joking around, please?'

'Sorry, mate.'

Richard puts his head in his hands. 'It was Billy's mother on the phone, she said she lost the baby nearly two months ago; it happened the day after her grandad died, the grandfather who had lived with her all her life. Daniella says her daughter is seriously depressed. They've seen her down before, but this is bad. Billy has called off her wedding to her childhood best friend. She won't even see him, and she just sits in her parents' sitting room every day, mourning the loss of the baby and the fact that she can never have children in the future.'

'Miscarriages can do that,' I say. 'Richard, why did her mother ring you? You said you didn't even know the girl was pregnant.'

'She asked if I'd go and see Billy. See if I could persuade her to go to the doctor and perhaps she'd get some tablets, or counselling or something. Anything. Daniella sounded desperate for me to help, if I could.'

'So, will you?' I ask. 'Go and see the girl, I mean.'

'I can't.'

'Because you don't trust yourself if you do?'

'No, Michael, that's not it. I love my wife and I have promised her there will be no more lie–'

I cut in. 'You can't tell Janette. Don't do that. She'll have all those hormones buzzing around at the moment, and that could be you out on your ear for good. Do you understand what I am saying?'

'Don't worry, I'm not planning to, but listen please, would you see Billy for me? Can you talk to her? She knows you, but you aren't too close to her. She thinks you're astute. You might get through to her.'

'I like the astute bit. You mean a cunning bastard, don't you? I do owe the girl though. Without her, you would have never sold me Berkeley Square. Look, I will be in Devon next week, checking on the new houses at Culmfield. I'll see if I can get there then. No guarantee though.'

Richard draws a deep breath, I can see he didn't think I would agree. Hell, I don't know why I did, but I do like him, and I would like to thank Billy for persuading him to move.

'I think I need another drink,' Richard says, smiling a bit now. I slap the poor man on the back. 'I'll get them,' I offer. 'We need to go over this again, anyway.'

THURSDAY 23 APRIL 1992

*T*he Culmfield houses were on track so I'd better get off to this Foxes Farm place. I wish I hadn't brought the new Bentley, I expect it's down some godforsaken potholed track, and I hate the way those Dartmoor hedges are actually granite walls masquerading as hedges. Not soft at all, they can bash your vehicles to bits. A hundred pounds last time, just for a smashed indicator on my Porsche 550 Spyder. It's not the money; I just don't like injuring my beautiful cars.

These lanes are actually a maze designed to keep foreigners out. I am sure I have been at these crossroads more than once now.

Cows. That's all I need. If they shit on my bonnet…

I am pretty sweaty now, but at least I have found the sign at the farm entrance. *Don't foxes live in dens?*

I can see buildings in the dip below. There is a pretty solid looking farmhouse with a thatched roof surrounded by a jumble of barns and sheds that all look old, but some look ancient. A roof or three need serious attention, and bits of the place need demolishing. I tell myself to stop looking at ways of developing the place to make money out of it.

'Shit! No…' *I don't believe it,* I have just run over their bleedin' cat. This is not a great start.

Chapter 19
FOX HALT FARM
BILLY

*T*hey will give up in a minute. Surely, they can't think anyone is in here. No-one would be that deaf or that slow to get to the door, it's not that big a house. I can't believe they are hammering like that. Just go away.

'Billy, I know you're in there. Open this door. Now.'

I have no idea who that voice belongs to. It sounds slightly familiar and it sounds pretty cross. I don't care anyway; I am not having visitors. There must be someone in the yard who can deal with them.

Go away please. I hear the front door open. They are through the boot store and the place where we hang up our outdoor clothes. They are here, standing in front of me. I recognise him but I don't remember his name. I am not getting up. I wonder what he is holding. It could be driving gloves. *Who the hell wears driving gloves these days?*

'Billy, look. I have run over this kitten. You need to come with me right now. I need to get him to a vet. You have to show me the way.' He pauses and then he yells at me. 'Now.'

Dad won't be pleased if we waste money on one of the farm cats, they breed like rabbits anyway. They are wild really, just keeping the numbers of mice and rats down a bit. I've now missed what the house looked like when that guy finished it. I like *Homes Under the Hammer* because it's always the same, people buy the property without looking at it, find lots of problems because they didn't do a survey or get a legal pack. The man cradles the kitten in one of his big hands as he grabs the collar of my pyjamas with the other. He tries to pull me onto my feet. I swipe him off. 'Look. Just leave me alone, will you?'

'No, Billy, I need to get this little mite to a vet, and you *will* get in my car and show me where the surgery is.'

I turn to face him, and I do remember him, it is Michael O' something or other. *What is he doing here?* I tell him what I know. 'Look, Mr ehm. That kitten will die. We have no money to pay for a vet and I won't come with you.'

'Michael. Call me Michael – and you *will* help me, Billy. Get up.'

I find I have stood up. His voice must have made me. He sounds angry. He turns around, expecting me to follow. I am in my pyjamas but I haven't noticed. I take a coat from the hooks by the door and I walk in my socks to his car. He holds the passenger door open.

As I get in, he tells me to look after the kitten, placing it gently on my knees.

The man is in the driver's seat. He locks the doors. We drive up the farm lane. It is too fast. I haven't been outside for weeks and it seems bright. The cows look happy. I wish I was happy like them.

'Billy, tell me which way?'

I don't know which way. It is not something that is important for me to remember. I know I can't have any children, that's important.

'Which way, Billy? Left, or right? And hold on to the kitten, will you? It will slide on the floor any minute.'

That is a question and an instruction. I can't remember the question, so I hold the kitten. Actually, it doesn't look too badly injured. It may be okay. The man yells again at me. 'Left or right?'

I don't know but I want the man to stop shouting at me, so I say to turn left. The kitten has moved a little bit in my hands, and it is like a little baby. Helpless. Suddenly, I know I have to save it.

'It's a baby, we need to save it.' I said that to myself, but the man has heard. He speaks softly now. 'Billy we are taking it to the vet.'

I now remember where the vet is, and I tell him to turn around. He isn't pleased. His car seems far too big for this narrow road. I look behind me and I think he is going to hit a gatepost. Yes, I was right. He hasn't sworn. I would have been swearing. Mind you, I wouldn't have hit the granite post.

The kitten is still blind. It can only be a day or two old. I think they normally open their eyes after that. Its mother must have been moving it and dropped it on the mud in front of our house. Maybe she was carrying it in her mouth to a safe place when the car hit it. I wonder if its mum is injured too? We will never find her because the cats hide in all sorts of places around the farm and they are too wild to catch.

The kitten is a light grey colour with stripy brown squiggly lines running through its soft fur. We have stopped and the man is looking at me. 'Billy.'

'Yes.'

'You want to save that little kitten, don't you?'

'Yes.'

'Then you need to tell me where I have to go.'

'It's only about a mile,' I say because I want to save the kitten and I want to help.

'A mile in which of these possible three directions, Billy? Do you think you could point to which way I need to go?'

I point and he turns the car that way. When he gets to another junction, he slows down, and he looks at me, and I point again.

He has seen the sign for the vets.

He parks the car and comes around to my side and opens the door for me. I follow him into the surgery.

The vet wants to know the kitten's name so she can put it in her computer, and when she writes the name, the kitten will be better.

'Paros, or Ross,' I say. 'It depends, if it is a girl or a boy. That is what I was going to call my baby, Paros or Ross.' The vet stares at me and I think she is sad like me because I can see she is starting to cry. I think I have seen her before. I think her name is Martha, but I can't see her name badge because my eyes are too wet.

The lady vet thinks the kitten is a boy and she says his name as she types, 'Ross May.' I tell her that would have been my little boy's name too, if I hadn't married Tom. Then, I say I am not going to marry Tom because I can't have babies.

Another lady in a white coat comes in, and she puts her arm around me, asking me to sit down. I watch the man and the vet, who I think is called Martha. She tells the man that she thinks Ross has a broken leg. It is too small to plaster but the limb should heal itself if the kitten doesn't run on it. Ross must be kept in a small cage for four weeks. Martha gets some bits together so we can feed the little chap. The clever vet knows we won't be able to find its mother and she gives the man a feeding syringe.

The lady who is with me asks if the man needs any help and he says, he'd like to go to the doctors and then he asks her for directions.

'How much do I owe you?' he asks, but the vet won't let him pay. The man gives her a fifty-pound note to put in whichever charity box she wants. Then he takes another fifty-pound note out of his wallet and gives that to her too. Mum will be upset when she gets a bill for one hundred pounds.

Little Ross is tucked into my coat and we go with Mr Michael O'Rowde. This is the name he gives the doctor's receptionist and he gives her my name too.

Michael wants Ross and me to go in with him to see the doctor. I don't know what he is scared of. Michael saved Ross. I can help him now. I follow him.

Michael lies to the doctor, but I don't say anything. He says he was the father of the baby I lost and he says too, how until now, he couldn't persuade me to get any help. Maybe I am going mad because he knows about Grandad and Tom. He tells the doctor when I lost my baby, and about the time when I slipped off the cliff and how a stake skewered me, and how I can't have any more babies with Tom. I don't think Michael should know this. Maybe Mum has told him. She tells everyone about everything I do, no matter how private it is.

I think Mum must have told Michael, but I am not sure how she has met him before.

The doctor gives me a prescription for some tablets, and he also gives me the name of a person I can see on Monday who I can talk to. I don't want to talk to anyone, but the doctor says I should, so I will go on Monday. The doctor says I can't bottle up my feelings. I need to talk. Now I remember a man called Ulrich, he said I ought to talk too.

Michael thinks we are lucky that we can get his prescription at the surgery. I'm confused *why are they asking me to sign for his tablets?*

We need to go home now because Ross is hungry. I will look after Ross because I can remember when Tom and I found a baby hedgehog and we looked after it. We had to feed it all hours of the day and night, so I stayed in Tom's bedroom and we took turns to feed it.

MICHAEL

As we arrive back at the farm, a woman rushes up to the car. I guess she is Billy's mother. She is almost in tears.

'Take the injured kitten inside, Billy, I'm sure it will be fine now we have taken it to the vet.' I speak loudly so her mother can hear. 'Your mum will find a little bed for it, and she'll bring it inside for you in a moment.' Her mother quickly grasps what is happening.

'Billy, sweetheart,' she says. 'You can take the little dear into the best room, I don't mind just this once.' Her daughter walks inside without a word.

Mrs May collapses down onto the front step. She sits, looking up at me. 'Thank goodness she's okay, I have been looking for Billy everywhere.' I sit down next to her. She continues, her eyes wide with fear. 'I had just finished checking the outbuildings in case she'd hung herself.'

'I'm so sorry,' I reply, reaching out to hold her hand. 'I didn't think to leave a note about where we'd gone – I was too concerned about getting the kitten to a vet. I ran it over when I arrived earlier.'

'It's not going to die is it? I don't think my daughter would be able to cope with that.'

'No, don't worry, the vet said it should be fine. Its leg is broken but it should mend on its own if it is rested up.'

'Thank goodness for that,' she says. 'I'm Mrs May, were you looking for somewhere to stay tonight, bed and breakfast? Is that why you were here earlier?'

'No, I am Michael O'Rowde…'

Billy's mother interrupts, looking yet more upset. 'Do we owe your company money, is that why you are here?'

'No, don't worry, I'm Richard's friend. He sent me, he asked me to talk to Billy.' Mrs May throws her arms around me. 'Thank you, Mr O'Rowde. Thank you so much for coming here.' I find I hug her back.

'Please call me Michael,' I say. 'I am sure you'll be pleased to know I got your daughter to the doctors. She has a prescription now, and the doctor has organised her a counsellor for Monday too. I do think she needs some serious help. She is so mixed up.'

Her mother nods at me. 'Michael, I was scared Billy might have gone to see her horse,' she says.

I frown at her because I don't understand why she is telling me this. Her mother tries to explain. 'Since Billy was a child, if she was upset, she would find her pony and sob into its warm neck but her old horse – he was called Sultan, died the same moment as her grandfather. With all the distress of her grandad dying, and then her miscarriage, my husband and I haven't had the courage to tell her. Billy still doesn't know.'

'Crikey, that was good then, that she hadn't gone to see the horse, I mean. I don't think your daughter could deal with much more,' I say.

'Yes, it was so strange.'

'What was?' I ask.

'Jack and I had been worried about Sultan, and we were with him when he died. It was just before we heard Billy shouting that her grandfather had passed away too.'

I move to stand up. 'Can I make us both a cup of tea?' I say.

'No, you're our guest, come inside. I'll make you one, Michael.' I put my arm out to help her up. She looks worn out with worry.

Mrs May now has her drink beside her while she calls various people to say her daughter has been to the doctor at last. The neighbours will probably know already because this seems the kind of place where you sneeze, and the vicar knows. Billy and I were quite a sight in the doctors. Me, a stranger in a posh car with Billy in her socks and pyjamas with her hair that didn't look like it had been brushed in days. Her body odour is horrendous; when we were sitting in the small consulting room, I hoped the doctor thought the bad smell was the cat. That should make a good tale in the local pub tonight.

Daniella comes into the room, where I'm sitting with Billy. 'Mrs M, do you mind me calling you that?' I ask her.

'No, Michael, go ahead, it sounds like I'm an important person in a movie. I certainly don't feel in charge of anything here anymore. I feel so helpless,' she says and then stares at Billy who appears transfixed on the kitten. 'Billy keeps saying she's fine. She just can't see how ill she is. She keeps blaming us for everything and anything. She won't see anyone; not her friends or Tom. None of us can get through to her. A real nightmare, Michael.' It's as though her mother has got so used to Billy not responding to her that she behaves as if her daughter is not in the room with us. I watch Billy for a moment or two, and decide she really is not listening, transfixed on the kitten, wholly oblivious to both me and her mother.

'Well, let's hope the medication helps her,' I say. 'By the way, Mrs M, would it be possible for me to stay tonight? I know you do bed and breakfast and I have another meeting in Launceston tomorrow afternoon. It would save me going back to Richmond tonight, and coming back down again tomorrow.'

Mrs M looks delighted. I don't know if she is happy because she can give me hospitality to thank me for what I have done – she hasn't stopped thanking me since I first met her – or whether it's a bit more money in the pot. Of course, it could just be sharing what she is going through with somebody else. Her husband, Jack, has come indoors but he is sitting in the kitchen – I'm sure he is just keeping out of the way. I suspect he's one of those people who runs away from misery.

Mrs M keeps calling this small sitting room the 'Best Room.' It is full of bits of furniture cobbled together, probably items other people were getting rid of. I can only think it's called the Best Room because the cats and dogs are normally banned from here and the family don't cross its threshold unless they have changed out of their outdoor clothes.

'Come on, Michael, I'll show you your room.'

'Thank you,' I say, getting up to follow her. Mrs M shows me every room in the farmhouse, and I wonder if she's doing this in case I know of any other potential patrons. I know now that the small sitting room is not the best room. There are much nicer rooms, but they are all reserved for guests. There is a cosy sitting room with a large granite inglenook fireplace, a smart dining area and two very comfortable looking bedrooms.

'So, there you have it, Michael, I hope you'll sleep well.'

'I'm sure I shall, Mrs M.'

'In the busier summer months, Jack and I decamp to the old caravan in the yard, giving up our bedroom for guests too. We used Billy's room as well, while she was at university and when she worked for Richard, but I keep it as though she sleeps there all the time. Look.' She pushes open the door and we step inside. The walls are smothered in rosettes. There is a whole shelf of replica trophies, ones Billy could keep when the actual cup had to be returned for the same competition the following year. Photographs and pictures of horses fill any gaps. Mrs M shows me photos of her daughter competing.

'Doesn't she look so young and skinny in her jodhpurs,' she says, making me feel even sadder for the girl. I expect Billy imagined she would teach her children to ride like her one day. Now her dreams are gone.

As we walk back out onto the landing, Mrs M points to another door. 'My father slept in that room,' she says. 'I'm afraid it's become a bit of a hidey-hole now, for useful and precious things we don't want to throw away. That's it, Michael, the grand tour.'

I do want to stay tonight, and that's why I said I had a meeting tomorrow. Actually, I've cancelled my diary for the next few days. I want to make sure Billy sees the counsellor.

Other than Billy, the rest of Fox Halt Farm seems a haven away from everything, and with my fiancée in Australia, there is nowhere else I want to be this weekend. Hopefully me being here will give Mrs M a bit of support; she's a nice lady and her daughter's hopeless depression on top of her father's recent death must be terrible for her.

I keep going hot and cold about ringing Richard. He kept banging on about being honest, but I can't tell him the truth. I know he will be desperate to hear from me though, so I'll say Billy will be fine but I sure as God don't think she will be. *Richard, if you saw what you've caused here you would be jumping off a cliff right now yourself.*

I sit with Billy all evening and help her look after Ross. Poor little blighters, both the kitten and the girl.

Chapter 20
FOX HALT FARM
FRIDAY 26 JUNE 1992
BILLY

I never expected to be looking forward to my birthday tomorrow. I will be twenty-four years old, but my body feels seventy. I can't decide if it's the drugs the doctors won't let me stop or it's my perpetual grief that's wearing me out.

Losing my baby runs constantly through my mind. I can talk about it now without crying, but I hate it when anyone refers to it as a 'miscarriage.' That is such a rubbish word, it doesn't convey my heartbreak in the way that 'lost my baby' does, and those words still don't describe it adequately, because I have lost my future babies too. It's so hard for me to accept this appalling fact.

I wish I had not held Simon's little Anouk in my arms. If I hadn't, I don't think it would be so bad. Before the christening, I didn't understand what the fuss was about, and I keep trying to think of babies as horrible 'sick and poo machines.' I try feeling sorry for the new mums in the doctors' surgery, and I try to forget that sometime around the twenty-seventh of July my little Ross, or Paros, would have been born. I would be fat now and my horrible scar would be stretched right out. Tom and I would be feeling little kicks.

The tablets help me feel less miserable, but they also stop me feeling any joy. I am looking forward to tomorrow though because Michael will be here. It's strange, he is only ten years older than me, but it seems like he is my father and I am his little girl. I have managed to push my real dad away again because he is so sad too. I think he couldn't wait to find a little foal for his grandchild; one that my son or daughter could have grown up with just like I did with Banjo.

I say I can talk about it without crying and I do most of the time. I speak more slowly than I used to and if I concentrate, I am fine. I have to think of the words as words and not let the feelings bubble up.

It is the thinking that makes my nose run and tears slip down my face. I don't want more tablets, but if there was one that could stop my tears that would be good. People could look at me then and not know how I am suffering inside.

There is some good news. Tom was devastated too, and when I wouldn't see him, he found consolation in the kind vet Martha, the lady who saved Kitten. They are seeing each other now, and Mum says they are happy. I think they will be good together.

Kitten is driving me mad running around all over the place. I can't call him Ross for two reasons, one is that he is a girl, and the other is that it hurts too much.

Michael has been here every Saturday since he took me to the doctors. He always brings me white roses and he gives Mum an even bigger bunch of yellow chrysanths. Mum says they are her favourite flowers but I think it is only because they aren't too expensive and they last a long time. She always puts hers in the sitting room for the guests to enjoy.

Usually, Michael stays Saturday nights too, and Mum cooks us one of her amazing Sunday roasts. I hope they are still amazing. I can't tell; my sense of taste disappeared with my sense of humour. I still tell her everything she cooks is delicious though, and there is nothing wrong with my appetite, the tablets are making me eat like a horse but I have banned Mum from ever making Battenberg cake, or even mentioning it again.

Michael, Mum and I are going to see *Wayne's World* at the cinema tomorrow night, which I hope will work out okay. I hope I can laugh at something in the film. Michael and Mum are also taking me to Exeter so I can get something to wear that is comfortable. I have put on nearly a stone since I started the medication. Michael kindly brought my clothes down from Balham but nothing fits me now.

The kind man emptied my London bedsit and I am no longer tied to a tenancy. He stacked all my belongings into Grandad's old room. If I say I'm worried about something, Michael fixes it. Jessie is lucky to have him. I can't believe she is staying out in Australia for another year before they get married.

Michael has shown me his new plans for Berkeley Square. In just five days' time his new head office will be open there and the name 'O'Rowdes' will be in six-foot-high lettering across the front.

When I saw an artist's impression of the new façade, I asked Michael if perhaps the apostrophe at the end of his name was in the wrong place, but he shot me down in flames, so I haven't commented much on any of the other alterations. I don't want to talk about it anyway because it brings back Richard. I try not to think about him. That is hard too.

The best thing is that Jessie and Michael met in the boardroom of our old offices and that's why he wants to keep it just as it was. Jessie had some land that she wanted to try and develop and Richard organised for her to meet Michael so they could talk through ideas. I think it was love at first sight. Michael says he never had time to think about a woman in his life before but Jessie knocked him sideways. He asked her to marry him almost straight away. He hasn't told me much but this is what I have managed to get out of him so far.

I know MarcFenn are managing Jessie's properties while she is away and also that she's on a boat in the Great Barrier Reef. She is leading a scientific study on sharks.

SATURDAY 2 JANUARY 1993
MICHAEL

At Fox Halt Farm, I have a plan. I wanted to ask Mrs M what she thought of my scheme, but I didn't want to go behind Billy's back. Her daughter trusts me and I don't want to lose her confidence.

This last month, Billy has come out of herself. She even seems to be coping with Tom and Martha being together, genuinely happy for them both. Now though, I need to stop her from festering. She is just hiding away at the farm.

There are a couple of major reasons why I must encourage her to leave; firstly, it will be the anniversary of her miscarriage soon and she will have that date fixed in her mind. Billy is obsessed about times and dates. I know depression can bring on compulsive behaviour because of my own mother's troubles.

My mum had a terrible spell with cleaning. Everything had to be spotless. Our home smelt of bleach and now the smell of cleaning products immediately takes me back to a lonely time when my poor ma wouldn't let me in the house with dirty shoes or grubby clothes. It became so bad that she would strip me naked in the doorway before I was allowed in.

It seems ironic here, on the farm, where one day drifts into the next, that Billy is fixated with time. There are few specific timescales here, other than 'tomorrow,' 'next spring,' 'this winter' or that lovely measure of time Mrs M uses called 'directly.' She says it as 'drackley,' which seems to mean sometime today, maybe tomorrow and definitely after she's completed all the other things she has to do.

Billy has to know dates and times for everything. Whenever she goes into the kitchen, she has to check the calendar. If I say we will do something, she has to know when, and then she writes it on the calendar straight away. I wonder if time to her is something that is fixed, something manageable, unlike everything else in her mind, which can wander from one subject to another with no logical connections.

Billy's mind drifts along and sometimes, we struggle to grasp what she is trying to say. The issue she is talking about can swap mid-sentence. Other times she just stops speaking, suddenly thinking about something else. She can't tell you her thoughts because it will be too painful for her. In those moments, we wait, we hold her hand or we put an arm around her shoulders. There is little we can do really, other than just be there for her.

The second reason that I need her to leave is that Martha is pregnant, and although Tom's partner is curvy anyway, it will show soon. I am scared to death of what it will do to Billy if she finds out. So, I have everything planned and I just have to get her to agree.

When I open the door, she is in bed but not asleep. She frowns at me. 'Why are you here so early, Michael?' she asks, 'it's only nine o'clock, you arrive at midday on Saturdays.'

'To help you pack,' I reply.

'What?'

'I need you back in London working for me and Jessie.'

'Michael, what are you talking about?' she snaps. 'Jessie is in Australia, and anyway, even if she's coming home to the UK, I *cannot* work for you both, or anyone else for that matter.'

I sit on the bed next to her, keeping my voice upbeat but calm. It is difficult to gauge the right tone to use. 'My gorgeous fiancée flies back this Tuesday to stay with me in Richmond. We'll have just ten days together before she heads back to Australia, so with you being there too, we can tell you what we need.' She stares at me, as I continue. 'After our ten days together, Jessie will be away until November, and we need you to sort our wedding out for us. Jessie can't do it stuck on a boat all those miles away. The date is looming so fast, and we've realised we need help. *Your* help, Billy. We need *you*.'

Billy instinctively checks the date. 'You're getting married on November fifth, aren't you?'

'Yes. You can sort out everything by then?'

'I can't!' She sounds upset now.

'Why not?'

'There's one reason for a start.' She points to the end of the bed and her sleeping cat.

'No, it isn't, I have Kitten's place sorted. She will have the most luxurious basket you ever saw in the lovely place I've arranged for you to stay. Listen, Billy, you need something to do. You know you are brilliant at organising, and we definitely need organising. We need you, Billy,' I say, scooping up the cat, and placing her gently onto my lap.

'I used to be good at managing things, but I'm not anymore.' Billy smooths the animal's head. I notice her relax a little.

'Come on,' I say. 'We'll pay handsomely. I have a flat all sorted for you too – it goes with the job. You can send loads of money back here to help your mum and dad out a bit. You could probably pay for a relief milker for them. You know it's getting harder for your dad. Maybe the extra money could help him buy one of those automatic parlours he keeps telling me about. I am talking good wages, Billy. I owe you.'

She looks a little more interested. She sees how the relentless early mornings and the tough manual work is getting to her parents. Mrs M has told me how Billy's grandfather used to work with them, but gradually he became more of a liability than a help; he'd put animals in the wrong fields and would forget to shut the gates. He'd even turned the tractor over on some steep ground that he shouldn't have been on, he might have been killed. Her parents could certainly do with some help. Billy has tried to assist them, but her dad treats her like a little broken bird, not allowing her to do anything that might be difficult. Billy finds him frustrating, but she won't say. She can't bear disagreeing with anyone.

I don't think she can find the arguments anymore. If she does, she loses track or her confidence goes. It is awful to see how this terrible thing has changed her.

'You don't owe me anything, it's the other way around: I owe you. Look at all the things you've done to help me. Every Saturday you've been here. All those kind things you do without a second thought. I am in debt to you, big time,' she says.

I laugh. 'Missie, money doesn't get you everything. Without you convincing Richard, I wouldn't have Berkeley Square. I wouldn't have moved to my fantastic new head office.'

She doesn't reply. I know this is hard for her. Billy avoids long discussions like this, preferring to go along with things. I think it's because there is nothing she really cares about anymore. She agrees with people, so she can be left alone with her thoughts. I keep talking, hoping she gives in soon.

'Billy, please understand that without you, Jessie and I won't have the dream wedding which I know you can organise for us. Look, we have the venue and the date sorted but we don't even have a bloody list of who we want to invite yet.'

'We charged you a packet for it though.' Billy is still focused on me taking over Berkeley Square.

'I would have paid Richard double that. You, young lady, will be in credit with me for a long time,' I say. 'Come on, let's get everything you want to take sorted. All you need to pack is clothes and Kitten's food. Everything else is set up ready for you. We can take your computer if you like, but if you'd prefer a new one, I'll buy it for you.' Richard explained to me how he originally got Billy to work for him so I present her with 'a done deal' with nothing to argue about.

My next strategy is to focus on dates and times. I give Billy the calendar I have taken from the kitchen. 'Jessie arrives on Tuesday, at six o'clock in the evening. Ten days later she returns to Oz. She won't be back again until two weeks before our wedding, on Friday, November fifth. We are getting married on a Friday so we can have one big party over the weekend and at the moment, none of that is organised either.'

Watching her write all this information on the calendar makes me feel more hopeful.

Next, I take an envelope out of my pocket. 'Open it,' I say and she does so, straight away. 'It's a card,' I explain, 'with a view of the Terrace Walk on Richmond Hill -this is where your new flat is.' I have written inside, *Dear Billy and Kitten, we need you so much, Love from Michael and Jessie xx*. I point at the picture. 'Look, we are not talking Balham here. My house is only a two-minute walk away. Billy. I know you'll get this sorted for us, and if you need extra people to help you, I'll find them.'

'Okay. I will,' she says.

Oh my God. I can't believe it. I still have another five arguments to use. 'Come on then,' I say, standing up and moving to the door. 'You get dressed so we can tell Mrs M.'

'She doesn't know?'

'Your mother hasn't got a clue.' Billy looks more pleased about this than anything else I have said. Her mother is wonderful but I know how Billy gets upset when her mum tells everyone everything. She thinks Mrs M interferes into her life, not appreciating that her mother is always trying to look out for her.

There doesn't seem to be any private subjects in Daniella May's mind. She loves people; she is innocent and guileless. Billy's mum lives in an older time than her daughter does, when everything was more straightforward. Maybe her mother is right. Perhaps, this is how we all should behave. Billy's ma was born in a house full of aunts and uncles who gradually left as they found husbands and wives. There was little room for privacy; they all knew each other too well, crammed into one house. Mrs M's relations moved out but they are all still connected. Nowadays in our spacious homes, we can be private and we value having our own space and our secret lives, but Billy's mother comes from a different time of sharing and knowing, openness and helping. Mrs M, in her unsophisticated old-fashioned way, hurts her daughter sometimes without meaning to.

I stand next to Billy as she tells her mother she is leaving, and I let her explain about the job and her new flat. I watch as they hug each other for ages. They are both crying as I clear my throat, to get their attention. 'I'll help Billy get her things together and then I'll have to go at half past three this afternoon,' I say.

'I can't leave that soon.' Billy lets go of her mother to stare at me, her eyes wide open in fear.

'No, Billy,' I say, trying to reassure her. 'I'm going back to Richmond on my own but I'll be back here at twelve o'clock tomorrow, in time for your ma's wonderful Sunday lunch. You and I will leave for Richmond after we've eaten.'

I expect another protest but Billy nods 'Okay,' she says.

I will miss Mrs M and Jack, and the animals too. Weekends at Fox Halt have been a special time for me. It is such a unique place.

Later on, I find Mrs M alone in the kitchen. 'Could someone else join us for lunch tomorrow?' I ask her.

'Yes, Michael, there will be plenty of food, don't worry.'

'I wanted to ask you on the quiet because I want to surprise Billy, so please don't lay an extra place at the table until they're here.'

'Is it Richard?' I see her expectant eyes and hear her searching tone; she hopes I will say yes.

'No, I am sorry, it's not.' Her face drops. Richard obviously means a lot to this lady even though her daughter wouldn't be the way she is, if they hadn't had an affair. Richard saved her daughter's life when she crashed off that cliff. Her daughter came home, that is all that matters. Richard was Mrs M's confidante too, while her daughter pushed her away. He will always be her hero.

Chapter 21
FOX HALT FARM
SUNDAY 3 JANUARY 1993
BILLY

I will never forget Dad's face when he was allowed to drive the brand-spanking-new, top of the range Rolls Royce. Michael said only twenty-two of these particular cars were made and most of them were sold to the Middle East. It is seriously stylish especially because it's so long, and the number plate, *ROWD III* finishes it off nicely.

Dad asked if his friend Pat Westcott, Tom's father, could have a go too, and Michael readily agreed. Before they set off for their driving experience of a lifetime, Dad and Pat put on their best suits, having decided they ought to be as smart as the car.

They took it in turns to try out the vehicle with Michael sitting in the back, venturing miles in the two hours they were gone. Dinner was delayed and we will be late getting to Richmond too, but it was worth it, hearing how much they loved it. I think driving the Rolls Royce Silver Spur II Touring Limousine will, I'm sure, be something Dad and his friend will be talking about for years.

I was horrible to Dad when I discovered he hadn't told me that Sultan had died. I didn't speak to him for a whole week afterwards. I would have loved to have given Sultan one last cuddle. Mum or Dad should have said they were concerned that my horse wasn't well, but my father is the horse person, in my eyes, and that is why I was so evil to him. The atmosphere between us is mending now, and this is a happy event for me to leave on.

The immaculate Rolls Royce is parked outside the farmhouse while Michael and his chauffeur Amir have dinner with us. It feels like a scene from *Upstairs Downstairs*; we are the ones downstairs of course, as no matter what Michael wears, he looks scruffy, so he fits in well.

The Rolls glides out of the farmyard so silently that being inside feels unreal. The car has been stretched behind the driver seat so there is loads of legroom. Michael is in the back with me and he has put Kitten on a cushion between us. I hope she stays curled up on it, her sharp claws could ruin the soft leather upholstery in seconds.

Kitten opens a sleepy eye and looks at me – suddenly, the cushion and the cat disappear, and I imagine a baby seat and my baby Ross beside me instead. He has such a big grin that it makes me smile just looking at him. He beats his arms up and down, showing how happy he is too. I saw my cousin Tanya's little girl make this same action two weeks ago when she was strapped into a car seat. Tanya was parked in the O'Rowdes' supermarket in Okehampton, and seeing her baby made my heart jolt.

I keep seeing the child's little face and hearing her giggling, wishing she was mine. But my baby is a boy – the Christmas card that Richard sent Mum made me decide this; the card I wasn't supposed to see, the one Mum tried to hide from me, had an additional name on it, *Freddy*. Richard and Janette have a son, and as I stared at the name in the card, I decided my baby would have been a boy too.

Christmas was so difficult. I kept thinking how it should have been, and I made things worse for myself with a torturous notion that I might have been pregnant again with Tom's child. I keep imagining what our future would have been like with Ross and Tom's son, who we would name William, running around Fox Halt Farm in their little wellies – just like Tom and I used to. I see our boys competing with each other, racing around or riding together. Little Ross and William Westcott sat at the kitchen table and my father telling them stories, like Grandad used to do with me. Michael squeezes my hand.

'Billy, it's going to be alright,' he says softly but I know he is lying. I don't reply.

I decided I would like a new computer, so the few bits I brought with me looked lost in the enormous car boot. I feel a bit lost in this car too because there is so much space. I would feel more lost though if I was skinny like I used to be. I have put on two stones in weight in less than a year; the tablets make me hungry all the time and Mum's roast dinners and cakes have done me no favours either.

At the top of the lane, I consider asking Michael if we can go via the doctors' surgery. I think what I looked like the day we took Kitten to the vet. It would be nice to give everyone something different to talk about but now, I look down on my too tight clothes and my idea skips away.

As I take in the car's silk curtains, I smile a bit inside, thinking what Jessie and Michael could get up to in the back here. I relax into the seat and start to stare at the controls for the intercom system. I try to think of something important to ask Amir just so I can use them. I want a reason too, to press the switch, which will bring the screen down between him and us. I decide I don't need an excuse and lean forward, ready to push the button.

'Please don't touch that ,' Michael says, holding my hand still.

'Sorry.' I look at Michael to see if I have upset him, but he just smiles back at me.

'It's okay,' he says, 'it's just that Amir has only just started working for me. He is not one hundred per cent familiar with this new car yet. He needs to concentrate on what he's doing.'

'Sorry,' I say again, turning away from him, and noticing other luxurious features. It makes me feel like a child again – I think about what Tom and I would have done in here when we were little. We would have pressed every button – turning the television on and off, testing all the different lights, and I would have got Tom to make drinks from the cocktail cabinet too.

I miss Tom, I think he would have made me laugh again but I couldn't let him miss out on having children. No child to take on his farm. I couldn't have done that.

RICHMOND, SURREY

*O*h gosh! If the chauffeur driven car was amazing then this is ridiculous. I am walking into what Michael just called 'your apartment.' He hasn't used that description before, he had said 'your flat,' and if he had, then I am not sure I would have agreed to come. This is overwhelming. I thought 'my flat' would be a bit bigger than my bedsit in Balham, but I could fit my old place in here fifteen times. It's beautiful too. Decorated in a soft white tone, the exact same shade as the fresh roses in the snow-white vases on the fireplaces. I head straight to one of the full height windows to stare outside.

The view is nice. I see a bridge over the river below. My geography of this part of London is not good; I suppose it must be Richmond Bridge and the Thames. On the opposite river bank there are tall trees which almost hide a line of pristine Georgian houses. From this fourth-floor window, I look straight down to a steep grassy bank and the walkway against the water's edge. I watch a nicely dressed couple walk along the embankment, holding hands and chatting. My eyes sting, remembering Richard and me sauntering along the Seine, laughing. I turn away, resolving not to look out of these windows again – I will put up voiles to shield myself from hurtful memories like these.

I have been foolish, I thought Kitten and I were Dick Whittington and his cat coming to London, not for gold though, we were running away. Michael thinks I came here for the chance to help Mum and Dad; and it'll be great if I can. But I'm not here for that. I came here because I couldn't bear to stay at Fox Halt Farm. Not now that I know. If only I hadn't heard Mum on the phone. Why does she tell everyone everything? Why didn't she check? If she had checked, she'd have realised I was back inside the house and I could overhear. Martha's pregnant.

The stabbing agony of this new discovery wells up inside again, as I remember running to the calendar to check the dates. Tom will be a dad by July. His child will always be just a year younger than the baby we might have brought up together. I thought I would never stop crying. At least I know now, and there was never going to be an easy way to find out this devastating news. I am lucky Michael and Jessie need me. I can throw myself into planning their wedding just like I did with studying for my degree. I will hide again.

'Come on, missie, tell me you like the place, I wanted to get it just right for you.'

'It's stunning, Michael, but I am very tired, do you think I could just go to bed? Will you come back tomorrow morning? I will have taken it all in by then,' I reply, then I check. 'You're not working tomorrow, are you?'

'You're right, I'm not, but are you sure you'll be alright?'

I nod, trying to look happy. 'I'll be fine,' I tell him, wishing he would just go.

'I'll be back at eleven tomorrow morning,' he says.

'Yes, great.'

'Look, missie, I'll write it on the calendar.' He points to a smart calendar hung on the wall. The January picture is a white Arab horse, just like dear Sultan. I will tear that down as soon as Michael leaves, I won't be reminded of my dead horse either. He writes the time down neatly by tomorrow's date. 'By the way you need to be ready to go out at eleven, I have something else for you.' He stares into my eyes.

'Michael,' I say in a flat voice, casting my eyes to the floor, 'thank you again. I'll see you tomorrow.' I know I haven't conveyed any appreciation of him, or excitement, but I am tired and sad. I am fed up with pretence. *Why doesn't he go?*

'Do you know, Billy,' he says. 'I've never felt like the kind of person someone would confide in. I don't think others generally trust me. I'm successful and people think it's through cunning and trickery. Richard has given me something here, asking me to help you, I mean. He's a good man and I like that he trusts me. Relied on me to keep his secrets and asked me to help you. He'd never have wanted you to suffer like you are.'

'Please don't mention Richard anymore. I can't bear it.' Tears are coming and my throat is swelling up. 'And Tom and Martha, don't talk about them either,' I say.

'Missie, I promise,' he replies quickly. 'Listen, tomorrow, you'll need jeans and those brown boots.'

At last, he is gone. I sit down heavily on my antique French sofa with its cabriole legs and carved scrolled arms, and Kitten jumps up to snuggle up close against my hips. I stroke her, close my eyes and sigh.

Chapter 22

RICHMOND
MONDAY 4 JANUARY 1993
BILLY

*I*t is evening, and Michael has just left. I sigh as I scoop cat food into a little bowl marked '*Kitten,*' wishing I was dishing up something onto a plate for little Ross instead. Wishing too that Richard was here offering to help. I think about him so often, he flashes into my mind all the time.

I force myself to remember the resolutions I made when I woke up this morning – Life will be good for me from now on – because I am going to make it so. I have a chance here and I will seize it. I will stop wallowing in my grief. Start over and value what I have; my wonderful family and now this amazing opportunity. I will shrug off the blackness. Ignore it. It won't win.

I am astounded by the apartment: it's so stylish with its hand-crafted furniture. Queen-size brass beds with crisp white bedding and thick white rugs like rafts on the sea of shiny pale oak flooring. I wonder if Saffi's friend Grégoire was consulted to get everything just so. If he wasn't then the artist would be impressed with whoever laid the place out with such attention to detail. I feel unworthy of it, as though I should cover myself up with a big white sheet and hide in a corner because my presence spoils its elegance and peacefulness.

In one area there is an exercise bike and a treadmill, and I thought for a fleeting moment that these were a hint from Michael that I should use them to lose some weight, but I know he would never suggest that, he knows it would knock any fragile confidence I have left. That said, I really should do some exercise because I hate the way my clothes stick to my repulsive fat. Maybe getting the wedding together will keep me so busy that I stop eating everything in sight, taking my mind off my hunger, and my heartache too.

Stepping over Kitten, who is purring contentedly lying flat out on the heated bathroom floor, I walk back into the kitchen. Every pot and pan imaginable is in here. The fridge is full and the cupboards are jammed with all the brands my mother normally buys – back at the farm, Mum, Michael and I would often do the food shopping on Saturday afternoons in O'Rowdes' in Okehampton, so Michael must have noted every item Mum usually chooses. I used to love it in that supermarket, where no-one knew that the *actual* Mr O'Rowde was pushing our trolley. But, then again, they probably did know, and they were being discreet because that was what Mum had asked them to do, after she told them who he was.

I guess Michael organised the contents of the fridge and the beautiful roses on Saturday when he left early, and that's when he arranged for Amir to drive the Rolls Royce too. The chauffeured car was so thoughtful, enabling us to sit together, rather than him being distracted with driving. It made it easier for me to leave the farm, with him there sitting on the back seat beside me. I didn't talk to my companion but he made me feel less alone. I expect that's what he planned. If I didn't know how much he loves Jessie, I could imagine he is trying to seduce me. I know he is not. He is broken somewhere inside too. He knows me. Michael recognises my pain, and sometime soon, I will get him to tell me why he does; when I am strong enough to help him, like he's helped me – I see it in his eyes, I know there is something. His never-ending kindness isn't a favour for his friend. I am sure there is some other secret reason behind his empathy.

I wrap myself up in the thought of my wonderful gift from Michael earlier. There were two surprises, the first tiny in comparison to the second. The smallest one was that my old car is here, parked up in my own allocated private space. Also, Michael told me that the concierge here will look after Kitten at any time, I just have to ask. I haven't even thought about my car. I don't know where it's been since I lost my baby, I had no desire to drive anyway, I couldn't even get myself out the front door – I will have to ask Michael if he will come with me when I go out in it again.

The other surprise was incredible, and I will cry over it a lot – literally weep all over it, I expect – I have a new horse. He is sixteen hands high and liveried in a stable down the road at Richmond Park. I will rename him Prince Sunshine, Prince for short. I know Saffi would agree that it's a great name because I am so happy he is mine. He must have taken some finding because he looks just like Sultan, only bigger, glassy white with a beautiful long mane and tail.

Today, I found out that Michael has never ridden before but he has always dreamt of playing polo. Not just a *spur of the moment dream*, I mean this is a big deal to him. Something he has always wanted to do, so this morning, I agreed to teach him to ride.

I wonder, was Prince really a present for me? Or was it that Michael wanted riding lessons. Was my new horse just another way of getting what he wants? He's always scheming, I don't care though, because Prince is wonderful. I will ride around Richmond Park tomorrow, while Michael sorts out everything for Jessie's arrival. I can't wait to meet her on Friday.

FRIDAY 8 JANUARY 1993

*J*essica Matilda Cambell-Drunas is not how I imagined. I expected… actually, I am not sure how I thought she'd be. I know it wasn't how she is. Perhaps that's because she was just a name before, lacking form in my mind, but now I see her.

The first thing that strikes me is that she looks like Chantelle but Jessie is Caucasian, she has sleek endless black hair and dimples too, just like Simon's wife – Jessie though, is taller, about my height. I notice how she uses her eyes to emphasise what she is saying, just like Chantelle does. They both move their eyes and you are hypnotised, however, I think it is Chantelle's dimples that give her an air of mischief, whereas with Jessie it's not just her face, it's the way she uses her whole body. When she moves, I think it is only to have fun. She is an enchantress.

I find out straight away that she is exactly the same age as me. We were born on the same day. I haven't met anyone with the same birthday as me before, let alone a person who arrived on this planet in the same year too. If you think of all the people in the world, this coincidence has to be less likely than winning the lottery. Which I don't do, so there is no chance at all.

Jessie says she comes from Barrowculme originally, a village I know quite well. It is near Exeter; about thirty-five miles away from Fox Halt Farm. I was born in a different hospital than her. I check and she tells me my mum and her mother weren't in the same maternity ward. I don't push this question hard because Jessie seems to find it difficult to talk about her family, but I have never felt so close to someone so quickly. It is as though we were always friends. Maybe it's because we are 'twins.'

We discuss the wedding and I will make a list of potential guests. Without definite numbers, I don't know where to start. Jessie gives me a folder of thoughts. It's stuffed so full, everything keeps falling out. It's crammed with scribbled notes, cut-outs from magazines and fabric samples. The spectacular wedding Jessie imagines is like her folder, an impulsive array of ingenious ideas. The only fixed details are it will be at Jessie's family home, left empty since her father died, and the date, Bonfire Night. Michael says he will go along with anything Jessie wants, and what she wants is a party no-one will forget. They don't need me, they require a miracle.

RICHMOND
SATURDAY 9 JANUARY 1993
MICHAEL

We haven't argued before, Jessie and I normally agree on everything. She likes what I like and in turn, I appreciate the things that are important to her, we have the same fundamental understanding about what matters in life; the special people in our lives.

I let her go to Australia before we got married. I didn't want her to, but I knew her father had suddenly died, leaving the whole Culmfield Estate to her, and I appreciated she felt too young and unprepared to take on the responsibility of managing the estate, and a husband too. She needed time on her own to contemplate what she wanted to do with her inheritance, and work out who she was. I saw that. I still see that, but Jessie just won't understand that these few days are precious. I have missed her so much, and wanting to go to North Wales to go climbing in our short time together has really got to me.

I am sure she loves me as much as I love her, and I know what it's like to lose a parent who was such a presence in your life that it seems like you have lost yourself when they die, but two days away is unacceptable. It might have been the best thing she did with her dad, but I won't go with her, my dread of heights is worse than not being with my beloved fiancée. She knows I can't go too.

Jessie says that when she pictures her dead father, it is always the two of them rock climbing, clambering up Flying Buttress, high up in the Llanberis Pass near Snowdon. She says she needs to go there before the wedding because her father was always happiest in the Welsh mountains. 'His spirit is there,' she says. Jess wants to stand on the top of their favourite climb and call out to her dead father, reassuring him that she is happy, laying his ghost to rest.

Ten minutes have ticked by since either of us has spoken.

'Go,' I say. 'Have a great time – leave tonight. Stay in the climbing centre in Capel Curig. Climb all day tomorrow and then come back here, straight away. Is that alright?'

'Yes, yes! Michael, thank you. Thank you for being the best man in the world, I love you so much.'

'I love you, Jessie,' I say, as she gets up.

'I'll get Billy to come,' she says. 'It'll take five hours to get there, so we can chat about the wedding all the way.'

'You can see what Billy says, but if I'm honest, I don't think you'll get her away from her new horse.' Every time I think about Billy with Prince Sunshine, it reminds me of how she was with Kitten. It is as if she can't bear to be out of his sight. My eyes start to well up as I remember Billy seeing the new horse for the first time. It was as though I had brought Sultan back to life for her. Billy flung her arms around his neck, sobbing her heart out. I cried too, but I was crying for my mother – remembering how I hugged her when I realised she might be dead, desperately hoping she would wake up and tell me everything was going to be okay.

I wouldn't be surprised if that crazy girl slept in the horse's stable the first night. She tells me Prince is 'very responsive,' whatever that means. I think she is trying to make it sound like it will be easy for me to learn to ride. I've told her we have to wait until Jessie has gone back to Australia. It will be good to have something to do again. I was worried about Billy missing the farm but the horse should be a good distraction for us both.

I watch Jessie now, as she excitedly puts her climbing gear together. I feel so lucky that this wonderful woman is mine. 'It will take you three hours to get there,' I say, 'the way you drive,' In a small way, I am glad I am not going. Jessie's driving terrifies me. *How can I let her go tonight?*

LLANBERIS PASS, NORTH WALES
SUNDAY 10 JANUARY 1993
BILLY

Jessie is definitely an enchantress. Why the hell would I be here otherwise? I have left Kitten and Prince so I can perch on the edge of a mountain.

'If you know me then you'll know what I want,' Jessie told me. She said I wouldn't be able to keep checking with her about the wedding because there wouldn't be time, and she'd be too difficult to get hold of in the middle of the Coral Sea. If I knew her well enough, I could organise everything, without wondering if she would like what I had chosen for her. That's how she persuaded me to come.

It seemed reasonable; I was worried how we would communicate. There is so much in her head about the wedding and she said it was a five-hour drive and I took a notepad with me to make notes as we chatted. The drive took three. I didn't think there would be a wedding, a couple of times. Jessie drives like roads are race tracks. We didn't talk because I didn't want to distract her. She said that Michael bought her the vibrant-red Ferrari 348 with its V8 engine, but I am sure he has never been her passenger. I certainly couldn't have written anything down anyway, I was holding on too tightly to my seat. I was so relieved when we got to the climbing centre where we stayed overnight, picking up the kit I needed for today.

We picked up an instructor too, who obviously knows Jessie well, because he borrowed a minibus from the centre to drive us here. Martin must have driven with the racing driver before. Or, of course, it could be that there were only two seats in the sleek sports car. Whatever, I am glad Martin drove. He and Jessie seem good friends. The instructor is easy-going too, just like her.

Jessie told me a little about her dad. He died three years ago, and now I know too that her mother was killed in an air crash. Her mum was advised not to fly in the fog that day, but took no notice. Jessie was just six years old when it happened and afterwards, her dad looked after her with his male partner. I think her dad died from AIDS, but Jessie found it hard to talk about it, taking in deep breaths before she started each sentence. I know how she feels because I did the same, when she asked about my baby.

I told Jessie about Richard and Tom and my 'accident.' I felt I had to because she had managed to tell me about her family. I think she was pushing the car's accelerator too hard because of all the emotion but maybe she just likes danger? Climbing seems pretty hazardous to me too.

We left the climbing centre in thick fog earlier, and I hoped that it would be so wet that Jessie would call this adventure off. But as we drove the couple of miles here, the mist cleared. A beautiful blue lake revealed itself beside the road and Martin pointed out the top of Mount Snowdon right in front of us. I am warm now from the sunshine reflecting off the rock. It seems like Jessie has bewitched the weather too.

'You weren't joking, were you? You said you were too chubby to do this.' I can't believe she has just said that to me. She may have run out of ideas, I suppose. I have been here for forty minutes trying to get more than two feet off the ground.

Jessie has given me everything; climbing shoes, helmet, harness, and I am tied by a long rope to Martin who I can see twenty feet above me. She has given me top tips on how to make it easy for myself, along with demonstrations and encouragement. What else could she do?

Her derogatory comment sounded jokey, but she is right. The climbing harness makes my rolls of fat seem even bigger and just the scramble up to the start of this climb was hard. It was all loose rock; steep and scary. I am seriously out of shape. I won't admit this to Jessie though; I will show her. I wasn't the bravest and fastest rider around the hunter trial at Powderham Castle for nothing. I am brave and I will get up this if it kills me. I may die in a horrific car crash on the way home, anyway.

I am next to Martin, relieved he is here, 'making me safe,' as he calls it, which means he is tethering me to a rock. Jessie is climbing up the part I took nearly an hour to do, in seconds, just like Martin did.

'Only five more pitches to go.' Jessie sounds so happy. She is delighted I managed to get up here. I love all her energy and joy, even if she did beguile me into this.

Finally, we are at the top. It was a struggle but as my arms got weaker, my mind grew stronger and I am thrilled with myself. I could get hooked on this sport, the adrenaline, the beauty and drama of our surroundings and my sense of achievement. The clear air and the camaraderie are exhilarating.

Martin is further along the ridge, sorting out an abseil so we can get back down. Abseiling sounds appalling but I don't have much choice. I think I am up for anything now anyway. I turn to Jessie. 'Why won't Michael do this with you? He would love it, I am sure.'

Jessie's demeanour changes. Her beautiful face was red from the wind and the exertion but now she looks pale and serious. *Have I said something stupid?*

Fox Halt Farm

'I'll explain, Billy,' she replies, 'but you mustn't tell Michael, I told you. He has never said more than a couple of sentences about it to me.'

'I won't say anything,' I assure her, 'but you don't have to explain. I am sorry, I asked you.'

'No, I'll tell you – Michael talked to me about this the first day we met and he has never mentioned it again.' Jessie is so close to me on the ledge that I feel uneasy. If she moves quickly, she could knock me off but she doesn't notice the danger. 'He can't climb with me because he has the worst fear of heights imaginable, He can barely get three feet off the ground before he starts to shake. He thinks his awful phobia stems from his mother's death. You see, Billy, his mother jumped from the twentieth floor of a high-rise. He was right next to her when she jumped. He was nine years old with no dad to look after him. Can you imagine it, Billy? His mother killing herself and knowing her little boy would be left on his own.'

'No, I can't,' I say, shaking my head – I knew there was something buried inside my rescuer but I never imagined anything as devastating as this. I catch hold of Jessie's hand. 'Sorry, Jessie, you came here to talk to your dad,' I say, 'and I have ruined it for you.'

'You haven't. I think Dad is looking over my shoulder and sees I have found a special friend in you. With Michael and you, everything is going to be okay. All three of us broken. All strong together. The Three Musketeers.'

She throws a climbing rope over her shoulder and keeps her mesmerising eyes fixed on me. 'We'll look after each other, Billy, won't we? All roped together. The three of us.'

'Yes. All for one, and one for all,' I say. 'Together we stand, divided we fall.'

Chapter 23

CULMFIELD COURT, BARROWCULME, TUESDAY 12 JANUARY 1993

BILLY

Michael parks the Bentley right in the middle of the courtyard of Jessie's family home, Culmfield Court.

As Jessie and I climb out of the back seat, all I know is this is the proposed wedding venue, and the date for the celebration.

The place was magnificent. I meant *was*, because I imagine about twenty years ago, it would have been the party capital of the South West. However, the death of Jessie's mum and the extravagance of her father and Dennis, his lover, took its toll. When Dennis died, her father became a recluse and everything on the estate has been neglected since.

Despite its rundown state, this is love at first sight for me – I adore the house, with its twisted brick chimneys and heavy oak doors. Nothing matches, every window is a slightly different shape, and each wooden gable is carved with a unique and intricate knot design. It is very grand but its lack of symmetry makes it feel friendly.

The first thing I notice is that one of the chimneys has collapsed and the resultant hole in the roof is covered up with a patchwork of torn tarpaulins.

As we step inside the formerly impressive Culmfield House, I pull my coat tight around me, as it seems colder inside than out. The external walls are just the thickness of single bricks and there is no central heating. Jessie laughs at me.

'Seeing you all huddled up like that, reminds me of growing up here. I used to stomp around these rooms with a portable heater in tow trying to keep warm.'

'Yes, this place wasn't built to keep heat in, was it?' Michael says, as he points to the beautiful granite mullioned windows. The expansive single sheets of glass let in more coldness.

'A never-ending fire in every fireplace would have been the only way to make this place warm,' Jessie laughs. 'That never happened, well, not that I remember.'

As we walk around, I sketch a plan of the rooms, making notes. We reckon we can sit twenty-five people max, in the largest room in the house, so marquees will be needed for the big day. The gardens are extensive with enormous areas of flat lawn; untidy and overgrown at the moment, but still, there is plenty of room.

'Let's see the chapel, next,' Jessie says.

I nod, happy to go outdoors again for a moment to warm up.

'Yes, come on,' Michael agrees, marching us outside. 'The chapel belongs to the house, it's just across the courtyard.'

The church is a shock. I know this is the place where Michael and Jessie want the actual marriage ceremony to be held. This building is in a much worse state than the house.

There have been leaks everywhere and some of the timbers from the rotting domed ceiling lie on the floor. We walk in paint shavings reminding me of snow, but the flakes of debris crunch under our feet like fallen leaves.

'You've got to change the venue, or at least the date,' I say, as I kick up some paint and dust. 'It will take months and months to sort this. Maybe a couple of years.'

'Not negotiable, Billy,' Jessie says, shaking her head. 'November fifth isn't just Bonfire Night, it was my mother's birthday too. She would have been fifty, this year.' I wish I had met her mum. I saw a stunning portrait of her in the house. I recognised Jessie in her face and in her expressions, but her mother had wild, curly red hair. In all the photos Jessie showed me she was up to something; riding a racehorse, or by her plane, or next to a fantastic sports car. Always with a big grin on her face. I wonder if she knew her husband was gay, and how much hurt that might have caused her.

'So, how about finding somewhere else to hold the ceremony and come back here, to the house, afterwards?'

'Culmfield is where Jessie wants to be married and that's it,' Michael says. 'I know we can get some kind of roof on the chapel by November, the domed ceiling can be restored inside afterwards.'

'Okay,' I say, feeling relieved he has something planned.

'Yes, Billy, sort that and then–' He pauses. 'Please hand me your notes.' Michael reads them quickly, and looks back up at me. 'Yes, Billy, so you need to get the rooms in the house ready for guests. The chimney rebuilt, the main roof repaired, a new heating system and a brand new kitchen.' I nod, feeling pretty nervous now. Michael laughs. 'This project should be straight forward for you, missie. After what you did in weeks, moving out of Berkeley Square, into Pineappli 1. This'll be child's play, but you enjoy arranging all this kind of stuff, don't you? Jessie and I know you'll make November fifth a day to remember.'

I smile, trying to disguise my panic. 'You don't mind paying whatever it takes to get everything finished by then?' I ask.

'I'll write the cheques – you just make sure it's all done. Our wedding will be perfect, and it will be all down to you.'

ROYAL DEVON AND EXETER HOSPITAL
SATURDAY 31 JULY 1993
BILLY

Today is a day off and I am glad I am at the hospital. I'm having to be brave, but I know this is the right thing to do. I needed to face my demons again, and this little chap in my arms is certainly no demon. He is gorgeous. I insisted that Mum and I came to see Martha and him. Tom is here too. Even the name they chose is difficult. He is named William, after

Martha's father. But still, I can see the happiness he is already bringing to his family.

Each little step, like this one, heals me slowly. There are still black days but I am busy, and I find if I cycle my exercise bike hard for a while, the adrenaline pushes the darkness away. Prince Sunshine brings light into my life too, just being near him makes me feel happier.

It takes sadness to appreciate happiness, noise to appreciate silence and absence to value presence. I read that in a book last night, I read lots these days, mainly inspirational, autobiographical books where people have overcome tragedies or fought for their lives. Ernest Shackleton is my hero. These courageous accounts help me to be brave too.

Nearly every day, I ride Prince and I spend time with Michael teaching him to ride. He mentioned his fear of heights at the beginning of my first lesson with him. He said it casually, but once he was sitting astride my horse, he said it was fine because he was seated, and Prince's neck and ears were always in front of him. He improves all the time, obviously loving it.

Getting the weight off was important to me, so I started manically using the exercise bike in my apartment and after my time with Jessie in North Wales, I persuaded Charlotte to climb with me, finding an indoor wall near her workplace. We meet up twice a week, and occasionally we see Ed, the boy who worked for me at MarcFenn, there too with a couple of his friends. His climbing companions may work for Richard's company too, I think I recognise them but I don't talk to any of them because I don't want to end up discussing their boss.

Reading, riding, cycling and climbing are my quiet times; the rest of my life is filled with all the crazy organising for the wedding. Michael keeps throwing money at me. He doesn't mind what I plan; he simply provides the finance or diverts a team of people from his company to help me. There are two things I am relieved about with the wedding, one is that Charlotte is coming, which will make the celebration more enjoyable for me. If I am run ragged, I know she will help me. The best thing, however, is that Richard and Janette have a holiday booked to Disneyland in November, so I don't have to worry about seeing Richard or little Freddy.

Michael and Jessie asked me to invite Mum and Dad to their special day. I was touched at first, but then Michael explained how much they meant to him, and how he enjoyed being with them every weekend at Fox Halt Farm. I hope Dad will actually come. He can wear the suit that my mother bought him for my graduation.

Mum is returning to Richmond with me tomorrow, and on Monday, we will shop for her outfit for the wedding. I am so looking forward to spending the time with her. I thought I might have persuaded Dad to come too so he could see Prince but I have given up on that idea now. He would not leave the farm for that long.

Dad isn't here at the hospital either, because he is collecting a young colt this morning he has bought for Martha and Tom's baby. My father says the pony will live at Fox Halt and later on William can come over whenever he likes to see him, and eventually ride him. Holding this baby, reminds me of Anouk, and how Richard and I passed her between us – and now, the fountain – God, this is difficult.

Chapter 24
CULMFIELD COURT
SATURDAY 27 MARCH 1999
BILLY

Mary is four years old. I think Michael and Jessie's daughter takes after her grandmother with her flame red hair and love of danger.

I am helping the young daredevil get her pony over a low jump. Mary has a riding lesson with me every Saturday morning and Sharmarke, her best friend, always joins us.

Sharmarke is Amir's son, and since the chauffeur and his wife, Nala, live in the Culmfield gatehouse, the little riders have grown up together. Mary has two ponies and she chooses which one she wants to ride, allowing her friend to have her cast-off for the day. I think her choice depends on which animal has the shiniest coat when she arrives in the morning, meaning it will take less time to groom. Sharmarke doesn't seem to mind, he is just happy to be able to ride.

I finish the riding lesson, and the children lead the ponies towards the stables. Michael is here watching.

Sharmarke's pony stops, ducks its head and begins to graze.

'I don't think he will ever be as good as Mary, do you?' Michael says quietly, his eyes focused on the boy.

I shake my head. 'It's a shame because he certainly tries harder than your daughter does, but he's not fearless like her.'

Michael laughs. 'I don't know, he may surprise us yet. Sharmarke may be a late starter, like me. You didn't think you would get me riding a few times, did you?'

'Because you wouldn't listen to me. You always knew better.' Michael looks hurt.

'I do have a pretty good instinct normally, missie, but you are right, these creatures need gentle coaxing rather than my heavy-handed approach. Are you nearly ready?' Michael asks.

'Two more minutes, I just want to put these jump poles back on the ground. Mary keeps sneaking them up and it's not fair on Sharmarke, she is only going to scare him more.' Mary's best friend is nearly a year older than her but she is the one who always leads the way. I remember how I put Tom off riding because I had no patience either. If I could do something then Tom could do it too, that was my philosophy.

I hope Tom's little boy is getting on alright with the pony that my dad bought him. Dad named the little animal Banjo, but he doesn't look a bit like my old brown and white pony. He is chestnut with a flaxen mane that stands on end all the time. I call him the punk pony, because no matter what you do to brush his mane, it won't lie flat, standing resolutely up. I know Martha is into horses too, so she and Tom probably have a second pony at home for William. I imagine Banjo, and the foal my father found later for William's younger sister, Grace, are really just at Fox Halt for decoration. I expect the bed and breakfast guests love the pair of equine rascals, who live in the paddock next to the farmhouse nearly as much as Dad does.

My uncertainty about what's happening at the farm is down to Mum keeping off the subject of Tom and his family when I speak to her on the phone. I have hardly been home either so I don't know if the little ponies are being ridden. The farm is so close but I never seem to book any time off. I keep thinking I must, but I don't. Jessie and I constantly shuffle between looking after her children and trying to get Culmfield Court sorted out. It's been hard work getting the estate running smoothly. It would have been easier, I suppose, if Jessie hadn't kept on producing babies; Mary, then Arthur and number three is imminent any day.

The work done over the years to Culmfield to restore it to its former glory is incredible and we hope this year, it may start paying for itself again. I know Michael checks how much everything costs but Jessie and I have managed it all within budgets and to tight timescales.

The ever-expanding O'Rowde family live in the main house. They have kept the stables for their horses and ponies, and Michael's collection of cars fill up the old coach house but now the rest of the outbuildings and all the cottages and farms that belong to the estate, have tenants in – commercial and residential.

The O'Rowdes have so much money that it wouldn't matter if Culmfield was still a money pit but Jessie has been resolute that their home must never be a millstone around their children's necks. She is determined that Culmfield will be self-sufficient.

I have a lovely room above the stables, which is good because another load of my time goes into looking after the horses and ponies. Mary, always 'helps' if she can. We adore each other, the little girl and me.

Michael waits for me, sitting on Sandringham, his immaculate, all black ex-racehorse, while holding the reins of my horse, Prince. My boy is gobbling new shoots of celandines, just starting to flower. Prince looks splendid, his coat contrasted against his ebony companion. I stare at the rider, wondering why he always looks untidy. Jessie only bought his expensive jodhpurs last week and they already look like they came from a charity shop.

Saturdays at Culmfield are special, they are nearly always the same; Michael is a creature of habit. He lives in Richmond all week but on Friday nights, he returns here, following a fixed routine. Macallan whisky in hand, he finds Jessie and me and then we run through what we have done all week. Michael asks us tons of questions but we never hear about London or his business. Then it's tea with the kids… It just the way things go and it feels comfortable and relaxed.

On Saturday mornings, once I finish my hour with Mary and Sharmarke, Michael meets me at the ménage. He rides his horse and leads Prince, all tacked up ready for me to ride. Michael and I ride round the estate land together. Jessie has never had any interest in the horses so it's just him and me. He is a competent horseman now, but he is happy with just riding around Culmfield. He has shelved the idea of playing polo, as leaning off the saddle to hit the ball would be too scary for him. He still hasn't told me the reason for his fear of heights and the time never seems right to ask him about it, but one day, I will find the right moment to talk to him about his mother, not letting on what I know already. Even now, with his wonderful life, there are odd moments when I see sorrow in his eyes. Maybe he wishes his mother was around, having fun with her grandchildren. Jessie talks to me about how she misses her parents but Michael never mentions his.

Our ride together follows the same route each time, cantering in the same places, and walking when we have to cross the river Culm, which cuts right through the middle of the estate land. The children don't ride if the weather is horrible but Michael and I always do. The weather today is drizzly, but Mary still wanted her lesson with me, so she arranged for Sharmarke to join her.

We cross the lazy river for the second and final time today, and Michael pulls up Sandringham. This is odd, we normally go straight into a gallop and race across the next two fields. After this, we will walk back through about a mile of ancient beech wood because the tree-lined path is too narrow and too low in places to do anything else. Our final walk allows our horses to cool down before we take them back in.

Michael turns so that his horse faces the flooded river. I rein Prince in, making him stand still beside Sandringham. It is nice to stop for a while to drink everything in. The air is moist and soothing but even so, I feel uneasy about why Michael hasn't galloped on.

'Serenity is good for the soul,' he tells me. This is weird too, because that isn't something Michael would say. I am not going to rush him. He muses on. 'I read that last night in that book you left on the side. I don't stop, do I, Billy? Rushing from meeting to meeting, wrapped up in business all week, and then home here and Mary and Arthur want all my attention. When do I get any peace?'

'I know what you mean,' I say, not understanding at all. He has something to tell me. This is just a warm-up, while he thinks how best to say it. I've known Michael for a long time, and I see this as a normal preamble. He will tell me in a moment what's troubling him.

I stare at the inky-black river and a trout lifts out of the water to catch an unsuspecting fly.

Eventually, Michael opens up. 'I am worried, Billy. I am not sure what I am doing at O'Rowdes' anymore.'

'What? You are not giving it up, are you? Retiring, I mean?'

I am shocked. I recall my long conversation with Charlotte last week when she told me she wanted to get off the 'gravy train,' as she called it. How she was questioning everything she had achieved and said how she should have married Sebastian, the lovely effeminate boy from our pony club days who was desperately in love with her back then.

Tom's sister and I became closer after I dragged her kicking and screaming to the climbing wall. I told Charlotte she couldn't work all the time, she should give her brain a rest. My friend protested about my climbing idea to start with, she said she would break her fingernails and complained how unflattering climbing harnesses were, but in the end she became as keen as me. We went climbing every week unless the wall was 'too busy,' and then we would head for the gallery instead to watch other people climbing while we ate fat slices of *the best carrot cake in London,* according to Charlotte, and drank mugs of hot tea always topped with a greasy film of dust from the climbing chalk. I miss her. Since I moved to Culmfield, we only speak on the phone. She is one of those people who tells a good story, always making you laugh, usually at the expense of her latest beau who just like poor Sebastian, has fallen truly, madly, deeply in love with her.

Lately, though, I feel the shine has gone off her successful single city life, and she keeps talking about what might have been if we'd stayed in Hamsgate. She is missing the green fields and the feeling of belonging in Devon where everyone knows everyone. She sees Tom and Martha and their contentment, and she is re-examining her own life and what she wants.

'No, not retire,' Michael replies. 'No, it's the company. Markets are changing and I'll be in trouble if I'm not careful. I think I am losing direction, I don't know where to take

O'Rowdes' next. Sorry, Billy, but I want you to work in Berkeley Square with me and help me figure it all out.'

'What? No way.' I flinch and Prince, sensing my unease, jerks his head up. I soothe him. 'It's okay, it's okay.'

As stroke my horse's neck, Michael continues in the same calm but persuasive tone. 'We need to move quickly. O'Rowdes' may have gotten too big. I have created a monster and I've lost control. You have to help me.' He sounds like he expects me to agree.

'You think I will make a difference? No, Michael, I won't. Get a top business analyst in, they will know far more than I do. You don't need me.'

'Billy, I need someone I trust. I want someone looking in without their own agenda. No self-interest and totally reliable. I do need you, missie.'

'Michael, I can't,' I speak slowly. 'Jessie and everything here. I can't leave Culmfield.'

'Just for twelve months, Billy; that would be enough time, I am sure. One year, that's all I want.'

'No. What about Jessie? The children, the ponies, cooking, cleaning, organising everything on the estate and making sure it all runs smoothly. I'm always working here, you know that. It's important work too. There's got to be someone else who can help you. Ask Saffi, he'll find you someone,' I reply. 'Never, Michael, I won't work in London again.'

BERKELEY SQUARE
WEDNESDAY 21 APRIL 1999

'HEARTBREAK.' 'HORRIFIC.' These are the headlines in the newspapers lying on the table next to me. Two students in an American High School in Columbine, Colorado, have murdered twelve of their fellow students and a teacher. I can't stop thinking about the shocking attack, as I sit in the wine bar opposite Michael's offices in Berkeley Square, waiting for him to finish on the phone.

We heard the dreadful news of the killing last night, when I turned on the television at Culmfield. The ten o'clock evening news had been on for a minute and we listened to the last of the report. I had only put the television on to break the silence that had been hanging between Jessie and me. I felt like a traitor. Jessie has been good about it, but I know it's not going to be easy for her either, the terrible twins have been split up. The months and years we have spent together are over. I will be working for her husband in London for now.

Michael had the whole thing worked out before he even mentioned it to me. We couldn't stop him.

He has employed Charlotte on a 'year's sabbatical,' as he called it, to look after the horses and help Jessie with the baby when it arrives. He says Charlotte will be excellent company for his wife during the week.

There was also the shock of the ever-diligent Michael readily agreeing to my suggestion that we employed Grégoire to paint the chapel ceiling for the spectacular wedding venue Jessie and I were proposing. When I mentioned Grégoire, Michael said it was a great idea and that we must get him to paint the chapel walls too; and also employ him to create a romantic interior in a neighbouring building. Initially, Saffi's friend said he had other commitments but Michael soon talked him round for us.

Up until then, Michael had examined all our spending at Culmfield so we were surprised when he didn't say Grégoire was an unnecessary extravagance. He said we should get it all sorted soon because the wedding venue was the last thing we had to finish. Now, I see the reason for all his enthusiasm, he was making sure I had no excuse to stay. His wife could manage without me and the talented artist would be company for Jessie too. At the time, Jessie and I were so happy about Michael encouraging us to commission Grégoire, but I see now he duped us both. Saffi's friend arrives at Culmfield today, but I won't be there.

Michael kept on at his wife about an impending recession and he said if he wasn't careful there would be no money to fund the private schools, the nice holidays and everything they want for their own, and their children's, future. I still didn't think Jessie would agree with me going but when she did, I really had no choice.

Heartbreak for those children and their poor parents in Columbine. Heartbreak for me, Jessie, Mary, Arthur, Prince and Kitten, all left behind. I am back in London, but this isn't running away, this is a forced march to Michael's tune. He made sure he got what he wanted again, just like he intended when he wanted to take over Richard's head office.

The only consolations are that I will return to Culmfield at weekends, and that I will be staying in Saffi's London apartment in South Kensington for now. It was Michael's suggestion; he said I had got used to being with people at Culmfield. He hinted that I should contact Saffi, to ask if I could lodge with him for a while. Michael said staying with my friend would be nicer than being on my own in the Richmond apartment. Michael knows how much I like Saffi and I think it was just another one of his strategies to convince me to leave Jessie.

Tonight, I will be seeing Saffi's special London home for the first time. In a way, I can't wait, it's been such a long time since I have seen the lovely man. I am sure he will make me laugh.

I don't want to say much about my initial meeting with Michael in his office this morning, other than to say that I fell to bits. The strain of leaving Jessie and the children was too much and, if I'm honest, I haven't got over Richard. Walking into his old office, even though it looked completely different, was awful and I started to cry. Michael gently escorted me out of the building and he brought me to the wine bar. I am here now, while he sorts another option for me.

So many thoughts of Richard, I think about him often. Wondering what might have been if I hadn't stormed off to Devon when I found the letters. I know he is a good man and I hope he is happy with Janette. I remember the emotional meeting with him here trying to get him to move from Berkeley Square. He was special. *No, he wouldn't have left his wife; I do know that.*

Michael makes several calls, finding me a new place to work from. He puts the phone down. 'Right, Billy, let me show you your new office. Someone will meet us there in a few minutes with a key. We can put the heating on, and you can start right away. It's just around the corner, so we'll walk there.'

On the way, he explains it's a spare office in a building he has recently bought in Piccadilly, near Green Park tube station. 'Well,' he says, 'it's not really an office; it was a small building society before, it should be easy to find though; our architects have already splashed the name O'Rowdes' right across the plate-glass frontage. The whole building is empty at the moment…'

'What were you planning to do with it then?' I ask.

He shrugs. 'It just seemed cheap, I haven't really looked at the options properly yet. For now, though, you can have the whole building to yourself. Later, if you need more people to work with you that'll be fine; there will be plenty of space.'

'So, what you are saying, Michael, is I don't have to come back into Berkeley Square again?'

'That's right, we can meet in your office. Everything will be set up for you in a couple of days. For now, you'll just have to ignore the workmen and delivery drivers.'

'What about files and the information I will need?'

'I've been promised you'll have a computer by this evening, and a load of files are being copied as we speak, they'll be transported over to you later.'

I don't know why I feel surprised at the speed this has been organised, I know Michael doesn't take no for an answer so everyone he has contacted must be pulling out all the stops.

By the time Michael leaves me in my new office, I know my first assignment is to grasp what this massive company is involved with. I know the main focus is the supermarket. I am also aware he develops land and he has other business interests too but I don't see how it all joins up. He says he wants to determine if they are going in the right direction because he feels markets are changing, but I don't know where I am starting from, let alone where O'Rowdes' needs to be heading.

PICCADILLY, LONDON
MONDAY 26 APRIL 1999

I twist the phone cord, while I wait for an answer. It's not because I'm nervous, it's more that this is an easy option. I am sure there are other ways but I have been thinking about this all weekend and this should be a quick solution. I stand up because that will make my voice sound more forceful and he is more likely to say yes.

'Strategy and Planning, Ed Mackintosh.' He sounds cheerful.

'Hello, Ed, it's Billy Ma–'

'Billy! This is a surprise. How can I help you? What do I owe the pleasure...'

'Ed. Look, I'm not going to say what I have been doing all this time because I'm hoping I can get you to come climbing with me this week, and we can chat then,' I say.

'I haven't seen you and Charlotte Westcott at the wall for ages.'

'Tomorrow evening, perhaps?'

'How about tonight?'

'Okay, tonight is good for me – what time? Six-thirty.'

'See you there. Bye, Billy, look forward to seeing you.'

'Bye,' I say, surprised that was so simple to organise. It will be nice to climb, especially since Saffi went back to Paris on Friday, and I'll be alone in his apartment this week. His lovely place will feel empty without him. I want to see Ed because he is still at MarcFenn's, doing my old job, and I could do with his advice about something Michael has asked me to look at. I'm way over my head at O'Rowdes'. In the last three days since I started working for Michael, I have only scuffed the edges of his complicated affairs.

MILE END, LONDON

Ed is waiting outside the climbing wall for me- he looks so young still, but he must be twenty-three, perhaps twenty-four years old, now. He is obviously fit. I remember he used to go to the gym and run too, when he was working for me. He smiles, looking confident. I'm shocked, he is different from the meek boy I remember, who was always ready to help.

'Hello, Billy. It's good to see you.' He kisses me on the cheek. How are you doing?' he asks.

'Great thanks, Ed, I hope you didn't mind me phoning you out of the blue,' I say. 'I just need your help with something.'

'Not to climb then?'

'Yes, I do, but I want to pick your brains too.'

Time rushes on, as Ed shows me new rope techniques. I love learning new things, and I am elated to be back climbing, remembering the subtle balances I need to make with my body. I had forgotten the fear of falling and how exhilarating it is. I concentrate so hard on everything Ed explains that I don't ask him anything else.

At half past nine, we walk out of the climbing wall. 'Do you want to find something to eat?' he asks.

'Yes, I am pretty hungry after all that,' I say.

In Ed's favourite Chinese restaurant in the West End, I tell him about the farm and me losing the baby, I don't say it was Richard's. I talk about Culmfield and he says how much he likes it at MarcFenns. Our easy conversation drifts into the wild adventures he still has on his list of things to do.

Later on, I drink coffee in his flat in Knightsbridge, and I still haven't asked him my burning work question.

'Ed,' I say at last.

'Yes.'

'What is MarcFenn doing about the Millennium Bug? I have been through various files at O'Rowdes' and it's niggling at me. They seem to be overlooking the possible threat.'

Ed laughs at me. 'Billy, is that your important question? You don't change, do you? Work is all you think about. Well, if you must know, we have got something major in place – it was all my idea.' He laughs again, saying he won't give me any more information unless I beat him at draughts, a game I used to play for hours with Grandad. He picks up the box and starts setting out the pieces. 'Are you up for a challenge, then?' He lifts one eyebrow and I know he expects me to say yes.

It is pretty late, so I think I should be getting back to Saffi's; beating Ed at draughts will delay me. I have a meeting with Michael first thing that will take all my concentration. I should be going but I know I would enjoy playing the game, and I know too that I will win; I always used to beat my grandfather with my fail-proof strategy. It's just the time to play and then the time it will take for Ed to tell me what

MarcFenn are doing, which concerns me. In truth, I like the idea of the game; it makes me think of my wonderful grandfather and me playing in the kitchen, while Mum busied herself around us; happy carefree times.

'Agreed,' I say but Ed has new rules; terms and conditions that I am fairly happy about because I am convinced I will win, and they won't matter. I feel a bit sorry for Ed, but it was his idea, so really, it's his lookout. This will cause him grief but then again, I can allow him to concede.

When I jump my first white counter over one of his black pieces, he quickly removes a sock, and it seems everything is going to plan. There will be no consequences for me because this will be a whitewash. Strip draughts is going to be easy for me to win.

It isn't easy. It is the most squeamish thing I have ever done; I try to get out of every obligation to remove my clothing. The more uncomfortable I become, the more pieces I lose, and Ed enjoys every moment of it.

Chapter 25

PICCADILLY
TUESDAY 27 APRIL 1999
MICHAEL

*I*n her new office, my new strategy manager looks a little ruffled this morning. I watch her rub her eyes before she looks up at me.

'We need to safeguard O'Rowdes' against the potential catastrophe of the Millennium Bug,' Billy says, holding up one of the files I handed to her last week.

'I hadn't thought of it in those terms before,' I reply. 'I admit it, Billy, I brushed that file aside. 'Millennium Bug' were just two words on a report that someone put on my desk a while back; I shoved it to one side, I'm afraid, planning to look at it later.'

'You do need to take this seriously,' she says. 'I've spoken to someone at MarcFenns. Richard has this firm of consultants working for him.' She hands me a business card. 'They are dealing with the whole thing for him.' The poor girl looks haggard, she must have been working on this all night.

'Set up a meeting with them too, then,' I reply.

'This afternoon?' she suggests. I check my diary. 'Yes, I can do half past two,' I say, 'if their head honcho is free.'

'She is.' Billy smiles.

'Well, that's the Millennium Bug sorted. What next?'

She moves her position in her chair two or three times. 'Look, Michael, I'm sorry, but I need more time to even begin to think what next. I just saw this as I skimmed through all those files you gave me. I didn't know anything about it; it just looked urgent. I haven't got to grips with any of the other issues yet. I'm sorry. I don't want to let you down.' I like the way she tells me straight. I did the right thing in getting her to help me.

'Missie, I can see from your face how hard you are working, I know you won't let me down. Let's have a full morning in here next Tuesday, and you can go through everything you have managed to do by then,' I say, standing up to go. 'By the way, Billy, I am not paying you to work all the time. Go running or climbing, or do whatever you enjoy. Work isn't everything, have some fun too, you deserve it.'

BILLY

Michael knows! That damn man knows me far too well. I can't believe it. *How could he tell?* I was in on time, I had all the information he needed. I was efficient. I was immaculately dressed. Michael would never have thought I would just go and find someone within five minutes of being back up here, and spend the night with them, just like that? Would he? Oh God! He does – he thinks I am some sort of loose woman after what happened with Richard. That's it, he is not finding out any more. I will not allow him to think that.

It doesn't matter, anyway, because last night was just a bit of fun for both Ed and me. It just happened and it won't happen again. For Christ sake, Ed is only a kid. *It was nice though* – perhaps I will just check if he would like to climb again tomorrow night?

CULMFIELD
FRIDAY 10 MARCH 2000

At weekends, Amir drives Michael and me between London and Culmfield. I don't need a car in the city and it's nice having time to talk through more work things. Michael always stops our discussions about the business at The Gatehouse and refuses to say anything more about O'Rowdes' until we leave on Monday morning.

The amount of work he has given me is astronomical but I now know a little bit more about the company. It started with just one small shop twenty-six years ago and now there all sorts of interests everywhere, and it's growing fastest in the Middle East at the moment.

It seems Michael has sought out every opportunity to make money using both gut feeling and meticulous research. 'There's been a bit of Lady Luck too,' he says. He has bought from the receivers, found sites whilst riding on trains, sold before downturns; he sticks his neck out while still keeping a wary eye, and he has loyal staff who like him. That's about it; a summary of what I now know of his business background.

So far, I have persuaded him to close a couple of offices and I have been all through the pros and cons of selling some properties and leasing them back to free up capital to give him less of a problem in a volatile property market. I still feel, however, that I haven't got a proper idea what O'Rowdes' is all about. Michael is right – it is a monstrous company, it makes me uneasy. I feel we could be missing something critical.

Amir has just spun the latest new Rolls Royce around the turning circle at the front of the main house and I can see Mary waving from the main window. It's good to be home.

Jessie is with baby Michael, who is nearly a year old, and as I say hello, I think how Mikey – as we call him – is likely to be another handful like his big sister.

Tea is ready, so in a moment, we will hear all about what Arthur and Mary have been doing all week. We are jetting off on the annual three-week skiing holiday in Klosters tomorrow, so I expect that will take up a lot of the conversation too.

We will leave Amir and his wife in charge while we are away. Nala is a vortex of energy, and when we get back she will have cleaned the main house from top to bottom. I suppose without the children around everything is easier for her to get on with. She will move in to her bigger, and much grander temporary accommodation at six o'clock tomorrow morning, while her husband drives the family, Charlotte, Grégoire and me to the airport in an old London bus Michael has bought.

Mary and Arthur love the eccentric bus and the family use it quite a lot. Michael drives it sometimes just to take the children to a birthday party on a Saturday afternoon, and often all the kids are dropped home in the vehicle too.

We finish every morsel of the mouth-watering cottage pie that Jessie made and chew through the teeth-cracking rock cakes that Arthur proudly crafted this afternoon.

I get up to go with the children to see their ponies.

'Hang on, Billy, can you stay for a minute?' Michael looks at Arthur and Mary. 'Carry on without Auntie Billy. She'll be with you in a moment.'

As the children go out, Charlotte walks in. 'Just to say, I've done all I need to do with the animals this evening,' she says. 'I've run through everything with Amir too. He is confident he knows what he needs to do while we are away.' Without being invited Charlotte sits down at the table next to me.

Michael ignores her, as he speaks to Jessie. 'Listen,' he says. 'I know how shocked you were when I organised for Billy to work in London with me, so I need to ask you something. I assure you, I haven't put anything in place, this is my first approach, nothing more.' Michael's eyes stay fixed on his wife. 'I know we agreed Billy would work with me for just a year, and Charlotte's time is nearly up, but Billy's work in London is *not* finished. I need her up there permanently–'

'If you want me to stay here longer that's fine by me,' Charlotte interrupts, 'in fact, I'm happy to stay here for good.'

I frown at her. 'I know you like it here, Charlotte, but I thought this was just a career break for you, are you sure?' To me, Tom's sister fits better in London than here. I always see her as the up and coming architect not the girl mucking out the horses. I thought she'd been stitched up when she came to Culmfield, I expected her to realise her mistake after a couple of weeks, anticipating phone calls from her complaining how dull it was and how the children nagged her to do things with them all the time.

'Yes, I am, Billy,' she smiles at me. I thought I knew Charlotte, but clearly I don't. 'Mary and Arthur are waiting for me,' I say, getting up to leave. I need more time to take this in. I love the job in London. I like working for Michael, but I always thought of it as 'just a year.' It's the whole basis of my relationship with Ed; we see each other on Mondays and Wednesdays and we agreed it would be for this finite amount of time, like a wonderful holiday romance, no commitment and no expectations.

'Will you carry on working for him?' Charlotte has followed me.

'I don't know, he is right. It is endless, the amount that needs sifting through. In a way, I have the best of both worlds now. I have this amazing place, this wonderful family at weekends and a truly fulfilling job during the week. It's not pointless drudgery, and I feel like I make a difference.'

'Stay then. There's nothing stopping you,' she says.

'Charlotte, there is, I miss Jessie. We were such a good team here before; it was as if we were one person moving in the same direction. Understanding each other, laughing and happy all the time. I miss her, do you see? Jessie and I, it worked. We had loads to do but we just got on with it. It was always fun somehow. The children too, I'm missing them growing up. They change so quickly. I miss them all.'

'Yes, I see,' Charlotte says. 'We are so mixed up, you and me. We have so many choices but we don't know what to do. Always struggling to find happiness, something we could have just taken for granted in Devon on the farm. No choice there, you just get on with it. That's what Tom does but he is definitely happy. My brother and Martha, they have it sorted, don't they?'

Mary runs up to me and grabs my hand. 'Come on, Auntie Billy,' she says, 'come and see what we've been doing.' The little girl looks so excited. Arthur and Mary have a new pony arriving when we get back from Switzerland, and they have cleaned out one of the old stables, ready for its arrival. Last weekend, the stable was filled with discarded horse rugs, bits of buckets, empty feedbags and other things that had rotted so much they would require a forensic investigation to identify them. Now, the walls are spotless. There is a filled hay net, a water bucket and a deep layer of wood shavings.

It will be Mary's new pony really, because she has grown too tall to ride the pony she has now. However, she keeps referring to the replacement as 'our new pony,' just to encourage Arthur to help her get its stable ready. I remember Tom and me at their age and I think how uncomplicated our lives were back then.

Maybe I am sixty per cent in favour of staying in London because I do have both lives. I can use my brain and I can still ride Prince around this beautiful place. Maybe I am seventy-five per cent sure, I just need to talk to Jessie.

'You must go, Billy,' she says. 'I'm worried about Michael.' So now I will phone Saffi to see if he will put up with me for a bit longer. I do love staying with him; his is a fantastical world.

THURSDAY 27 JULY 2000
BILLY

Skis crashing, helmets clattering and cackling as Charlotte, Grégoire, and the children get every item together.

Outside now, heavy boots in the snow. All heading and laughing to ski school. It's the last day in our snowy paradise. I never want it to end. Michael left yesterday; there was a meeting he couldn't miss. Breakfast has been cleared away. It's just Jessie, Mikey and me in the luxurious lodge. I put down the pocket-sized map, having checked where we will meet the others later. I look at Jessie, and I see she is reading my old book, Prince Sunshine. Her hair catches the morning sun, the rays highlight it orange. Suddenly, she is an angel floating upwards with my book held out like a song sheet. Jessie begins to sing quietly. Singing fades to words, 'Feels like old times,' she tells me.

I laugh. 'We wouldn't be lazing around back then. You must remember, Jess, we never stopped, always on the phone sorting out building materials or something, scooping up all the mess from the kids, ponies, spreadsheets, etcetera – I don't know how we did it all.'

'No, Billy, I mean being quiet together, the evenings when we used to collapse on our wrecked sofa.'

'The stillness, you mean?' I check.

'Yes,' Jessie sighs. 'We didn't have to tell each other what we'd been doing, or discuss anything, because we knew. We were always there together, you and me. Battle heroes. Musketeers, all for one. I miss it.'

I sit next to her. 'I miss you too, Jessie. I have never been so happy. It was like Mary and Arthur were mine too, wasn't it?'

I remember my miscarried baby and now the children of Columbine, their heartbroken parents and weeping friends. All of us crying for our lost children. Jessie sees my grief. She touches my hand. Our lips touch too. We are one angel floating. Now our angel has become Saffi and he has the Prince Sunshine book. He is writing something on the front page but I can't read his words. He starts to read aloud, 'the shadows fill you until their blackness overwhelms you–' I wake up, it's four o'clock in the morning. Ed has his arm around my hips. He is sound asleep.

This is how it always is, the night before my baby's birthday. My dream-filled sleep tortured with my loss and what might have been. Restlessness. Crying for the wondrous celebrations that never happened. Ross would have been eight years old today. I always mark the exact moment I decided he would have been born, five minutes to eight in the evening, it's the same time as Mum had me – I will light a candle tonight in Saffi's apartment. Only Jessie knows about my vigil because we used to watch the candle slowly burn together when I lived at Culmfield.

Saffi will not be there this evening, he is in London less these days. There must be someone more exciting in Paris, Ella perhaps? There is a sadness about Saffi, lately. I think he just wants to be with her all the time. He doesn't say, and just like I did when I lived with Simon, I don't ask him about his personal life. I don't want to tell him about Ed, so I avoid mentioning love or relationships. I think Saffi is wary of the subject too because of Richard, he guesses how I still think about him. He is so intuitive. Saffi sees my black dog arrive and he quickly finds some way to make me laugh.

Ed is unaware of my aching heart and my afflicted sleep. The lovely super-energetic boy knows only joy. We are in his basement flat now, just four hundred yards from Harrods. His place is cosy and it even has access up to a small private courtyard, crowded with flowers. There is still no routine with Ed except that we meet at the climbing wall at half past six on Mondays and Wednesdays, and I leave his flat at half past six the next morning to head for work. We may climb, or instead we could try out the newest restaurant, see the latest film or go to one of his friends' houses for a party, or we might just cook a meal in his flat and afterwards lie together on velvet cushions. I never know. I let him choose – it is always exciting.

I have a wardrobe of clothes in his flat and when he meets me, he brings me an outfit for whatever he has planned. Sometimes, he will just buy me something new. 'I just thought it would be perfect,' he says, and it will be just right. His friends know about me but I never tell anyone about Ed. I refer to him as Eddie, the girl who lived next door to me in Balham, we climb, we have a Chinese meal back at her flat and I stay over because it's just easier than trekking back to Saffi's.

Ed was an exhilarating secret at the start, and that is how I want him to stay. In my mind, there is no permanence with our relationship, no plans and no expectations either. Conversations are never about what we will do the next time we meet, or our future. It is safe and fun. I can't get hurt. Ed won't know about the candle tonight, he will be out with other friends enjoying every moment of his life, and I'm happy that is how it is.

I still smile about our game of draughts, I was embarrassed as I lost my clothes, but the way Ed treated the scar on my stomach was how he won the game that night. I hated my scar, it was faded and less than four inches long but a constant reminder of the loss of my babies. Yet that night, as I took off my tee-shirt, Ed asked me about it. Richard always ignored the corrugated mark just below my belly button but Ed kissed it and deep inside me a final remnant of ice dissolved. He suggested I could get a tattoo to cover it, not saying I should because it didn't bother him, but he appreciated how I felt.

His secretary had a breast removed because of cancer, and Ed had witnessed her distress from losing such an important part of her identity. He told me how she decided against reconstructive surgery. Instead an amazing tattooist in Tottenham Court Road created a beautiful rose design to cover her scars. I think Ed has seen it but I haven't asked him. This was how the idea of disguising my own painful mark was planted in my mind.

He calls me his 'Little Miss Fun.' It started as sarcasm because all Ed saw, at first, was how I was obsessed with my work. It took him ages to get me to relax. So, when I decided to get my wound painted out, I thought I would surprise Ed with a Little Miss Fun design. The tattooist offered me other intrinsic and beautiful options, but I knew what I wanted – but Little

Miss Fun is *not* tattooed on my stomach because, at the last moment, I changed my mind and instead 'Mr Tickle' lives on my body. One of his long wobbly arms meanders to my belly button and the other reaches downwards. I love it and Ed loves it too. I told Ed the tattoo artist had made a mistake and the image should have been Little Miss Fun but her arms started to get too long and he suggested the change. Ed said the man did it on purpose so it became more intimate. I won't admit Mr Tickle is a little bit of Richard hidden away. I still miss him, after all these years – a second tattoo of Little Miss Fun came later but she is high up on my leg, at the base of my bottom, I never see her and it is Mr Tickle who makes me feel better about my scar, Mr Tickle and Ed.

I try to think of anything but the missing birthday. An hour of undisturbed sleep would be good – I have a meeting later and I will need to concentrate.

Once a month, Saffi and I head for the Royal Opera House in Covent Garden. We go to whatever performance Saffi would like to see, and in between, I choose a musical in the West End. I love being out with him. Whenever he can, Saffi makes me laugh. He treats me like a princess. *No*, better than that, he still likes to pretend we are married, calling me his wife. When we are together, I wear the most beautiful opal and diamond ring he gave me. Sometimes I even forget we are not married, it's so comfortable being with him.

I don't have much time alone in Saffi's apartment but when I do, I spend it reading his books. It's an otherworldly place. A real escape. Grégoire had just finished it before he started work on the Culmfield chapel. Saffi's London home is a converted warehouse. On the outside, it has a galvanised roof and steel walls but inside you enter a Pharaoh's palace with magnificent gold and turquoise columns, ancient hieroglyphs and Egyptian kings and queens depicted in muted colours. There are golden masks and thrones. I feel like Cleopatra when I'm there. I think Saffi likes it as much as I do because he hasn't talked about making any changes when Grégoire finishes at Culmfield. He probably knows I love it.

Half past seven in the evening now. It's been a long day – worn out from my disturbed night. I open Saffi's front door, relieved to be home, but as I step inside waves of dread wash over me.

Chapter 26

SOUTH KENSINGTON, LONDON
THURSDAY 27 JULY 2000
MICHAEL

*C*rying. *Begging my mother not to leave me. 'Open your eyes, Mummy.' But she doesn't, so I shake her thin shoulders until I have no energy left to rattle her body anymore. I have shaken spatters of her blood from a chasm in her skull and there is appalling gore and holed flesh. No breath!* 'Ma, don't leave me.' I see my poor dead mother as clearly as I see Saffi lying there in the bath; Billy is pulling her heart out over his body, lit up by a solitary candle in the corner of the room.

Why, Saffi, why do this? Why, my darling mother? Why? You selfish bastard, Saffi – why choose tonight?

Billy begged me to come here. Terrified, speaking to my answerphone through sob-filled breaths. If only I hadn't been on the phone happily talking to Mrs M about the completion of their derelict barn into a holiday let. She has bookings from next week and I was happy she had allowed me to give her the money to pay for the building works – a wholesome chat, suddenly followed by Billy's horrific report.

She gave me directions but I kept ending up at a big shed. It took ages for me to realise this was where she meant. The door was open. Now I see her, bent over her friend's body, lost in what looks like Tutankhamen's tomb.

Saffi must have cut his wrists because the bathwater, and the splashes soaking into Billy's clothing, are red.

She won't leave him.

The emergency services are coming.

I prop myself up against the door watching her, thinking how this is too much for the poor girl to endure. His death will kill her.

BILLY

The policewoman has seen skin rucked up like his before – she believes he has been in the bath since the early hours.

I keep wishing I had spoken to Saffi. I knew he was unhappy. If we had talked, he might have told me about Grégoire and him -there was a photo here. Destroyed now. Bloodstained and crushed from my wrenching fury. A beautiful black and white photo, like the kind you see in the *National Geographic* magazine, the ones that are so atmospheric, carefully lit to add to the drama. It portrayed Grégoire and Saffi's naked and muscular upper bodies. The two beautiful men were facing each other, laughing hard, as though their joy had overtaken every other emotion. On the back, in neat black script. '*Prince Sunshine is dead. The sunshine has gone. Only rain – 27th July 2000 – Saffi.*' I smudged the words as I held the picture in my trembling hand. Saffi's last words – gone, just like him, bled and soaked away.

I lit my candle and I prayed for him and my baby, asking God to look after them both, then I left my dead friend alone for a moment, to phone Michael. I could not think what to do, horror was overwhelming me.

I feel like it is my blood in the scarlet water. I'm deflated. I am a barren void in a shell of skin and bone. Flashbacks to the bloodstained bathroom at Fox Halt Farm.

The policewoman says I have to move. They need more photos and they need to take Saffi away. I can't stand up because my legs are dead under me, the blood in them has gone and they are useless.

'Billy, darling, come on, sweetheart. You have to move.' Michael tries to lift me. I am too heavy. My body has fused with the cold sarcophagus. I am stone. Heavy. Just stone. A man helps Michael but I can't leave Saffi. I scream his name as they drag me to my feet.

When Michael tells someone to bring the candle, I quickly realise he knows its significance. I decide Jessie has told him. This explains why he wasn't at his club like he is every Thursday, and why he was at home in Richmond instead. Jessie must have asked him to be on hand just in case. Perhaps this was why he was easy on me today when I hadn't got all the information for our meeting. Poor man, he would never have imagined how much I would need him.

Michael and his helper put me in my bed with the candle next to me, and when the man leaves us, Michael climbs under my duvet wrapping his arms around me.

The candle has been placed on top of my Prince Sunshine book. *I haven't seen that book for ages.* Its flame is sputtering and now it dies.

'I'll stay with you, Billy.' Michael talks to the back of my head.

I turn my body around so I can look into his eyes. 'Thank you, Michael,' I whisper, 'you are rescuing me again.'

'Do you want me to stay?'

'Don't go.' I want him to kiss me, helping me forget all that has happened tonight. He holds me.

MICHAEL

I should be thinking how sorry I am for this destitute soul next to me, working out how to sort this out for her but I am not feeling pity, nor am I considering tomorrow. In this moment, my mind is filled completely with the wonder of her. Billy is seeping through my clothes. Her fragile frame against my clumsy limbs. Her bones, I can feel her bones. I want to be close. The scent of her. Her perfume and the salt from her tears, the salty residue around her eyes which I want to lick away. *Overwhelming desire.* I can't sleep. I will lie here in desperation all night.

FRIDAY 27 JULY 2000

As she opens her eyes, a fat tear runs down Billy's cheek. 'Why did he do it?' she asks.

'I don't know,' I shake my head. 'Billy, you can't stay here.'

'But…' She stares at me, with the same wide eyes she did last night when she asked me not to go. 'Where will I go?'

'Richmond, your old apartment,' I reply quickly.

Billy frowns. 'You still have it – it's empty?'

'Yes, I kept it in case you ever needed it. I never thought this would happen though. This is terrible. Poor bugger.'

'My apartment, in Richmond? I can go there?' It's as though she didn't hear my reply.

'Yes, missie, you can go back there. I'll get a cleaner in later, it's only dust, no-one's lived there since you left.'

I came to work, sending my personal assistant to shift Billy to the flat in Richmond. My PA said it was as though she was handling a mannequin, taking her out of a shop window, redressing and repositioning her in a new place in the store. Her only resistance was her determination to take that old book with her.

Amir is now, driving us both back to Culmfield for the weekend. There is an uneasy silence between us – I keep looking at Billy, but not at her face – like I see the woman she is for the first time, her neck, her breasts, her legs. *I want you, my lovely lost Billy. I need to look after you.*

RICHMOND
MONDAY 31 JULY 2000
BILLY

Remembering Culmfield this weekend is a fog. I can't stop crying. I slept with Prince each night, lying uncomfortably on his horse rugs in his stable. I couldn't be alone. Most of the daytime I sat in his field, watching him with the other horses and ponies.

Everyone was crying – all of us are guilty.

I had no idea Charlotte and Grégoire are lovers. Jessie knew; a guilty secret that both she and Charlotte kept from me, so I wouldn't tell Saffi. I so wish they'd trusted me, I could have spoken to Saffi about how sad he seemed. I could have shared his upset. We might have talked. *Surely, he wouldn't have killed himself then?*

Michael must have known too because he has been avoiding me. I see how tense he is. He said I shouldn't ride because I was too upset. He didn't want me galloping on a horse with my mind lost on my friend.

I feel guilty too. About Michael, feeling my heart quicken each time I am near him. I am so grateful he was there to help me when I found Saffi. He stayed with me all that dreadful night and my body has been aching for him to hold me ever since. I am so glad he didn't sell the apartment, and when my mind wanders – as it is doing now – I wonder if he would have preferred me living in the Richmond apartment all along. Does he want me like I have been wanting him ever since he climbed into my bed?

When I saw Jessie, I felt I was a lousy traitor who wanted to steal her husband. There were no accusations. No yelling, because we all hid in different corners of the vast estate.

Charlotte explained to me that as soon as Grégoire arrived at Culmfield there was an instant attraction between them, more because of their shared love of art and design than anything physical, but slowly they had come to adore each other. They are even talking about marriage. She never told me why she had wanted to extend her stay at Culmfield, but it's all clear now.

Saffi must have either guessed about the relationship, or just felt Grégoire was distant. That was why he hadn't been himself, lately. Grégoire talked to me too. 'I knew Saffi would be upset, so I wanted to see if Charlotte and I were really serious before I said anything to him. I never wanted to hurt my dearest friend.' He told me Saffi wasn't in Paris on Wednesday. He changed his plans so he could meet Grégoire. They went to the opera together. Afterwards, Grégoire told his friend about Charlotte. 'Saffi was happy for me. He was joking and he teased me. He was being Saff. He was *bon*.'

All alone, in the early hours of that following morning, Saffi had killed himself, wiped out by Grégoire's news.

I couldn't speak to Jessie. She is complicit in this cover-up. She always tells me everything but she has kept this from me. I am betrayed, and betrayer too – longing for her husband.

How I wish I had not suggested commissioning Grégoire to paint the chapel ceiling. If he and Charlotte hadn't met then Saffi would still be alive.

Michael refused to let me work today, he said I was too upset. I have been in my apartment for hours with only turmoil for company. I will go back to my office tomorrow. I have to do something, I can't just sit here crying. I need something to stop my mind thinking about Michael too; I know it's just a temporary madness, an infatuation because I feel so heartbroken. I just want darling Saffi to spin into my apartment and tell me that his death was all staged by one of his theatre friends; it was all a hilarious joke. The best acting he'd ever done. I want him here laughing. 'Wasn't I the best corpse? You couldn't see me breathing? Surely you could?' I imagine him laughing. 'All that fake blood. All that drama. I just wanted you all to realise you have to lose someone to appreciate how much you love them.' The relief as he tells me this is the best joke he has ever played, and how he has no feelings for Grégoire. I put Saffi's ring on my wedding finger. I will never take it off. I will love him forever, my marvellous friend.

Someone is letting themselves in. *Saffi?*

It's Michael. 'Hello, Billy, I brought a take-away.' It is Monday night, I am not with Ed climbing, and it seems Michael isn't playing squash with Richard either. That is usually what each of us do on Monday nights.

I sobbed at Ed until he understood I was too upset to see him. He said to come to his place and he'd comfort me all night but Ed fizzes with energy, I didn't want to burden him with me. I feel lifeless, I couldn't face his enthusiasm for everything. I told him I would see him on Wednesday and reluctantly, he agreed.

Richard has cancelled Michael, and even though that name is banned between us, Michael is using it now. 'Richard is as much in bits as you are. Saffi must have been a top bloke,' he says. I want to cry again. Michael puts the food on the side. He sits next to me. His legs press against mine. 'I love you, Billy,' he says.

I know he loves me like a lost orphan he needs to care for. I smile at him, a tiny pull of my cheeks to acknowledge what he has said. I don't know how to react; I am all over the place.

Michael strokes the back of my hand with his strong fingers. The fingers I watch in our meetings writing copious notes about what I am saying. Fingers he holds to his face when he considers a business opportunity. The fingers he uses to point out a small imperfection on his development plans. Those clever business fingers touching my hand are reassuring me.

He leans his head towards me and I look into his eyes. Eyes that sparkle when I provide a solution he hasn't considered. The eyes that carefully look over the spreadsheets I email him. Eyes that report to his incredible brain, which instantly remembers everything. His eyes with so much sorrow behind them that, sometimes, make me desperate to ask about his mother. The caring eyes that watched me in the bathroom with Saffi. I shut my eyes to hide that nightmare.

I sense his lips on mine, but it is only my imagination. He is standing up. The kind man is going to get the food sorted. He says I must eat something. I will try but my stomach is overfull with catastrophe. No hunger, nothing.

I ask him to stay, but he says he can't.

TUESDAY 1 AUGUST 2000

Michael won't be here until later. He is meeting a private investigator who's checking out one of his managers who Michael thinks is stealing. The investigation is in the early stages, so he didn't want to tell me any more about it. I don't care. I don't want to know anything about the company at the moment. I was useless today, I just sat in my office thinking about Saffi, wishing I had asked him what was wrong.

The private investigator was late and unhelpful, so Michael is in a bad mood when he arrives. 'I picked up fish and chips for us both,' he says, throwing them on the kitchen sink while he finds us plates.

'Lovely,' I tell him, trying to sound grateful enough to calm him down a little. I haven't had fish and chips since Grandad bought them for him and me, when Mum and Dad were helping her cousin move to a new house. They were horrible, nothing like Mum's cooking, so we fed them to the chickens. We were starving at breakfast and both of us asked for more helpings of everything. It was funny. A little shared moment with Grandad – *I wish God didn't take the best people away.*

Michael sits next to me on the sofa and hands me my dinner.

'Here,' he says. 'Have you eaten anything today?'

I think for a moment. 'No, I wasn't really hungry.'

'Billy.' I look at him but it is ages before he speaks again, and tension comes back into his voice. 'Where has your ring come from?'

'Saffi gave it to me, it was his mother's. I used to wear it whenever we were together. It was all part of his great pretence. He used to call me his darling wife. Can I show you something, Michael? It may help you to see what a special man he was.'

I fetch the Prince Sunshine book from my bedroom and sit down next to him again. 'Look, I'll read you Saffi's favourite bit, maybe it will help explain why I am so upset.'

As I open the book, two sheets of paper fall out. I pick them off the floor and stare at them.

'What's that?' Michael asks.

'It's a letter from Saffi,' I explain, as I realise now why the novel was beside my bed in his apartment, he must have put it there.

'Are you going to read it?'

'Do you mind?' I check.

'No, please go ahead, I need to find some sauce for these anyway, they're not very good, are they?'

'They're certainly not as good as Mum's,' I say, but really, I have no idea. I put the food in my mouth but I was unaware of its taste or texture. I am only eating because I thought Michael had been kind enough to bring something, and he would nag me if I didn't. As he gets up to go back to the kitchen, I start to read the note.

'*Dearest wifey,*

Sorry to do this to you. Forgive me. I didn't want to be found by Ella in Paris – she is my stepsister, I should have told you before, sorry again.

I know, I seem fine but losing the use of my legs has been so difficult. I always think what I could do before. I was Mr Action Man. There was no wall too high for me. I had no fear. My body and mind have been so badly affected by that bloody war.

Since Grégoire hasn't been around, I've been having terrible nightmares. They are gruesome, stemming from what happened in the Falklands to my mates and me. So many lives lost. So many who returned like me, suffering survivors' guilt. I've been considering this for some time, but G was a reason to live. I have no more strength left. I am sorry.

There are no words to say how much you mean to me, my lovely wife. I have loved you staying with me, but you must go too. Don't hide when there is happiness out there for you with Ed. I see how happy you are when you talk about your climbing adventures. I know 'Eddie' is male, Richard told me ages ago. He overheard chaps in the office talking about you and Ed. He was pleased to know you'd found someone. I know you aren't just climbing. See what you have there, young lady. Ed is my nominated Prince Sunshine replacement – see how good he is for you, before you lose him too.

I want to be buried at Culmfield with my memorial service in the chapel. I want to be close to G. No fuss please. No shiny happy requirements. I have already left everything to G. My will is in the Paris apartment. I would have changed the beneficiary if there was time because I want you to have half my books and Ella to have the rest, G never reads anything. My sister will probably sell hers, but it will be a bit of money for her.

Billy, you will get over this, you are stronger than you think. You are amazing; please remember that. Please don't live on regrets. My life should have ended in the explosion, but I'm glad I met you. I am so happy Richard and I were reunited. Live, laugh and love, my darling. Do it all for me. Come on, girl, no more blackness (the second page of this letter is for Richard – please post it for me.) Love always, your adoring Prince Sunshine.'

The letter for Richard is folded over. I won't read it. I will post it tomorrow. I place the papers back inside the book and shut it hard.

Michael is staring at me.

'I should have found that letter before,' I say. 'I knew it was odd, this book being in my bedroom.'

'Does he explain why he killed himself?'

'Yes. It wasn't just Grégoire and Charlotte, it was being paralysed too, and not being able to do all the things he could do before. He suffered terrible nightmares.'

Michael takes the book and then places it carefully on the floor. 'Billy, I can't bear you crying anymore. Please stop.' His eyes are filled with sorrow for me. *For him too?*

'I am sorry,' I say. 'Look, you are always helping me, can I help you too? Will you tell me about your mother please?'

'My mother?' he frowns at me.

I realise I have made a mistake, I will have to own up about Jessie. 'Jessie told me a little about what happened, she said your mother killed herself but you haven't told her any more.'

'I won't talk about my mother with you, or anyone. Jessie shouldn't have said anything.' His face is red. He is wound up, even more so than he was, when he first arrived tonight.

'I am sorry, Michael, I didn't mean–'

His voice softens a little. 'Billy, I will tell you one day, I promise, but not now. You are dealing with too much already.' He smiles at me, taking hold of my hand. 'Look, missie, I'm in Glasgow tomorrow. I won't be back till Thursday afternoon. Let's go out to dinner together that evening, it will do you good to get out.'

'Thursday evening?'

'Yes.'

'That would be nice,' I say, relieved he still wants to see me.

'Look, I need to go. You book somewhere, please.' As Michael leaves me alone again, I wish I hadn't asked about his mother.

Chapter 27
WEDNESDAY 2 AUGUST 2000
BILLY

*I*n my office, I answer the phone to Ed. We never call or text. We simply meet at the wall at pre-set times, it's all part of the adventure. I did ring Ed on Monday because I thought if we met, he'd persuade me to do something with him, when all I wanted to do was sit quietly in my apartment. Maybe he thinks arrangements have changed and we can call each other now?

'Billy, how are you?'

'Looking forward to seeing you *tonight*,' I say, trying to imply that calling me is not necessary. We can talk then.

'Sorry, I won't be climbing anymore. I have just heard I've been successful with a recent job application I made. They want me to go straight away. It's in Dubai.'

'What job application?'

'I know I didn't tell you, but we did agree not to talk about our future, didn't we?'

'Yes, we did, but still, this is a shock, Ed. I'll miss you,' I say, feeling lost. I didn't want to get hurt but this is upsetting me.

'Sorry, Billy, but I've been looking for a new venture for some time; it's one of MarcFenn's rivals so I hadn't even told Richard until just now. It's my dream job, it will be an amazing opportunity. Brilliant for my CV.'

'Well done, I am really pleased for you,' I lie.

'The job starts immediately – I will be setting up a new department. I get to recruit the whole team.'

'So, you'll be away some time?'

'A couple of years, at least.'

'I'd like to see you off, what time's your flight?'

'No, Billy, don't worry.'

'Are you sure?'

'Yes, I just wanted to ring to say goodbye. I am sorry about Saffi. This is really bad timing for you, isn't it? But you're strong. You'll be fine, I know you will.'

'Well, all I can do is wish you a safe flight, and lots of luck. Goodbye, Ed.'

'Bye, Billy.'

I put the phone down, staring blindly in front of me. I am thinking how our offbeat liaison is over, surprised he never mentioned anything before but then, that was how we were. All fun and no commitment. That is what we both wanted. Slowly, it sinks in that my gorgeous boy is no longer in my life.

Saffi's letter sinks in too, and I wonder if this is his doing. He was a head-hunter, maybe he organised for Ed to go away? Did Saffi think if he sent Ed off to Dubai, I'd see that I loved him? The more I think about it the more convinced I am, this is Prince Sunshine's final game. Another crafty plan to sort out my love life, just like he tried to do with Richard and me in Paris?

I wish I knew. If Ed loved me surely, he wouldn't have gone? Perhaps this is his way of finding out if I love him. Maybe what Ed said was true, he just wanted a new challenge. I was nothing more than a weekly entry in his manically busy diary. We only ever did what he wanted, and I was just his willing companion. This is so difficult, I have no idea how I feel about Ed or Michael, with the horror of Saffi, this is all too much.

I'm not going to get any work done today, my head is spinning. I will book the most expensive restaurant that Ed took me to for Thursday. *No, I won't.* I do not want those memories. I don't know where to go, so I decide I will cook for Michael in the apartment. It will give me something else to think about.

RICHMOND
THURSDAY 3 AUGUST 2000
MICHAEL

*I*n Billy's apartment, we discuss the work she has done to prepare the incredible meal she's made. She tells me how she got the new table and two dining chairs into the apartment. We chat about my journey to and from Scotland. I even mention the weather. It is as though we are talking on eggshells. *I am not sure what I am doing here.* That's not true, I *do* know. I can't get this woman out of my head.

'Michael.' Her eyes bore into me. I stare back, aware that this is the first time she has looked at me properly since I arrived this evening; until now she's been glancing away or stepping around me.

'What, Billy?'

'I don't want to be alone tonight.'

My insides are pumping. I am ravenous. *Starving hungry.* I try to sound calm. 'I will stay, Billy; if you are sure that is what you want?'

'I am sure.'

She doesn't need to pull me. She is magnetic, I am iron drawn towards her. Helpless filing. She pushes my jacket off my shoulders. Tantalising. I am lost. This should feel wrong, but I can't see it. All of me is overpowered.

Our heads rest on her pillows. Our noses are touching. 'Billy, in the morning,' I say, and she finishes my sentence. 'You need to leave very early.'

'Yes, I won't wake you but I need to ask you something.'

'What?'

'Do you want to go back to Culmfield this weekend?'

'No,' she replies.

'I thought you wouldn't. I'll tell Jessie you can't bear to see her. I'll explain you are devastated that she didn't tell you Grégoire and Charlotte's secret.'

'Yes, tell her that,' she says as she moves forward to kiss my mouth again.

RICHMOND
MONDAY 7 AUGUST 2000
BILLY

Michael phones to say he is not playing squash again tonight.
'Can I see you, Billy?' he asks.

'Now?'

'Yes, now.'

'Okay,' I reply. 'See you in a moment or two.'

The phone goes dead. I tremble. I have to tell him
Thursday was a mistake – it was wrong. He will understand –
he must be feeling guilty too.

I will explain how I was overwhelmed with grief – that
was all it was. I did not want him to leave me on my own. I was
desperate to get my mind off Saffi – I used him to make me feel
better. He will say we got carried away, it was stupid and then
we'll be like we were before.

Michael crashes into my apartment with so many roses
that they are almost impossible for him to hold. 'My gardener
left his secateurs by my front door so I thought I would bring
you a rose from my garden, but as I cut the one that I decided
was worthy of you, I saw another, equally lovely,' he says
earnestly, standing still and staring at me. 'I just kept collecting
them. All for you, my darling. I've left my gardener a note
saying there's been vandals and I've informed the police.'
There is no sadness in his eyes tonight, only belief that I want
him as much as he wants me.

The beautiful flowers spill out of his hands onto the
white rug. Michael kisses me, pushing me down hard. I am
with the roses on the carpet. He crushes me. His powerful
hands pull at the prim and proper shirt which I quickly pulled
on to look plain and boring. I did not want to be the seductress
tonight. I wanted this to stop and for us to see sense.

He bites my neck. My desire for him accelerates
upwards and I wriggle out of my shirt. Michael scoops my
breast into his hand. Stroking me with his tongue and watching
my reaction. I am willing, as he pushes my skirt up. Clever
educated fingers touch me. He tears into me, hammering my

back into the floor; I feel the thorns from the roses piercing my skin. He is rough. Pumping. Pushing. Harder. Until we explode and Michael rolls off me sweating and panting.

I turn towards him, easing the scratches on my back. We are coiled; cords twisted and melded together like rope.

'I love you, Billy.'

I don't reply.

'Sorry about the thorns,' he says gently – *Jessie, I need him.*

CULMFIELD

FRIDAY 18 AUGUST 2000

BILLY

*T*his is hell; Saffi's funeral hurts so much, watching Richard walk slowly to the front of the chapel with his head bent down. He reads his poem – I am sure he knows it by heart but he doesn't look up.

'Saffi hid his pain,
behind a bright charade.
I never saw his loneliness,
In all the jokes he made.
He made me laugh,
'til I thought my face would break.
He wore his top hat,
But the look he wore was fake.

'Hidden deep inside,
Deep inside my happy clown,
Was a breaking heart,
But I never saw him down.
'I cherished him,
I laughed with him,
I never saw his hell.
He made me smile and everything was well.

'Inside his head were terrors,

Of war. Of loneliness,
But Saffi was my joker,
I would never guess.
Prince Sunshine, was Saffi's only aim.
Everything to Saffi was just another game.
I miss my friend. He was the very best.
To have him in my heart, I am blessed.'

I listen to Grégoire and Charlotte sobbing, wishing I had written something too, wondering if I had the guts to stand up there like Richard. Ella is here and we hold each other up as Grégoire tries to give his own tribute to Saffi. He can't finish and everyone feels his heartbreak as he stares at his friend's coffin, motionless and silent.

I cannot go near Michael or Jessie because of the guilt coursing through me. How could I do this to Jessie? Her words on the mountain blast at me, icy words now. 'Three musketeers. We will look after each other, won't we?' Wanting Michael is so wrong. She is my friend, the best friend I have ever had.

I will head to Fox Halt after this and stay the whole weekend. I need my mother. I can hide in my bedroom if I need to. Michael will tell Jessie I want Prince back in Richmond. I won't move Kitten, she is happier at Culmfield than she would be cooped up in my apartment. I wonder if I would be too?

Goodbye forever, Culmfield. Goodbye, Jessie, Charlotte, and Mary – I am so sorry but I need Michael more than you.

Another quote from *The Three Musketeers* flashes into my mind. *'Love is the most selfish of all the passions.'* I am selfish like D'Artagnan, breaking my promise to my friend. Michael will be mine in London and Jessie's here. Three of us – but *not* all for one.

I twist the ring on my finger, whispering under my breath to Saffi, 'No regrets.'

Chapter 28

BEECHWOOD
SUNDAY 25 FEBRUARY 2001
RICHARD

As Janette comes downstairs, I realise I can't ask her straight away. I won't let her see how desperate I am to make a phone call.

She gets up from her breakfast and I try to sound casual. 'Were you listening to the news when you were upstairs? Did you hear that the foot and mouth outbreak is close to Okehampton?'

'Yes, I did.'

'Janette, I'd like to know if Daniella and Jack are okay, I think I would like to call Daniella. What do you think?' I smile, still trying to hide how scared I am for the farm.

'I was wondering about them too, it sounds awful,' she replies. 'Yes, Richard, you could ring her.'

'You don't mind?'

'It's fine, darling, call her.'

'I just want to find out if they're alright.'

'Listen, just give her a ring, if you want to; I am off to see your father now. Weeds are springing up in Sharpie's rose bed. He can't persuade any of his lady friends to do it for him, and he really isn't interested in the garden. I want to keep it nice; it meant so much to your mum.'

'Okay, love,' I say. 'I'll sort lunch for all of us when you get back. I just hope we can still cycle at Burnham Beeches this afternoon.'

'Why shouldn't we?'

'I just thought it might be closed because of the foot and mouth. There are so many rumours.'

'I hope not, it's always so nice us all going out together. Freddy and the girls, they love it there.'

'We'll just go and see, I suppose.' I kiss her on the cheek. 'Thanks for looking after Father, seeing him *every* Sunday morning.'

'I like him, he's always cheery, and there is always some nice cake around made by one of the Amersham ladies,' she smiles. 'I'll be back around twelve. Love you.'

'Love you too. Take care.' I watch her car drive away, and then I grab the phone.

I remember the last time I spoke to Daniella. Janette was pregnant with Freddy then. She was low again after he was born and we've had no more children. I never feel my wife is truly happy anymore, losing faith in me a bit. It's Jayne, our scatty next-door neighbour, who brings the most joy to Janette. She is a steam train of happiness; nothing gets that woman down. She and Janette have been friends since we first came to Jordans. I expect, as soon as my children get up, they will head to hers for breakfast. She'll be happy to have more chicks under her wings, cooking pancakes for them, and finding out everything they have been up to.

The news report explained foot and mouth is a contagious virus, mainly affecting sheep, cows and pigs. I can't stop thinking about the cows at Fox Halt Farm and all the work to carefully breed them. Surely, this epidemic can't wipe them out in a single swoop? The cows are the farm.

'Daniella. Hello, it's Richard MarcF...'

'Richard!'

'I wanted to know if you are okay?' I ask.

'It's great to hear from you, Richard. Are you okay?' she replies. 'How's Janette? How are the children? Harry and Sid must be what? Fourteen years old in April, my goodness time flies. Oh, it's so good to hear from you...'

BILLY

I planned to head to Fox Halt this weekend but with all the uncertainty, Mum asked me not to come. I never thought I would be kept away. My parents are always so happy to see me. Since Michael and I got together, I stay at the farm every other weekend. I spent two weeks there at Christmas. It's good for Mum and Dad, and it's good for me too. I am looked after like a child, I will never grow up in their eyes.

Mum is convinced I have a 'nice man' in London. Her certainty is fuelled by Saffi's ring which she noticed straight away. It was still too raw for me to talk about Saffi and it was useful to have Mum think I was engaged. I hoped she would worry less about me. It's good for her to think I am happy without having to tell her anything about my arrangement with Michael. If she knew I was his mistress it would break her heart.

She likes Michael, I know, but she went to his wedding and I am certain she wouldn't be pleased about what I might be doing to his marriage. She has never spoken about the situation I got myself into with Richard, but his name is banned at the farm, so that would be difficult for her, wouldn't it?

My mother keeps hinting about me bringing 'him' down to meet her and Dad, and I give her a vague impression that one day soon, I will. There isn't a day goes by when I don't think of Saffi. Even if it is just a sunray lighting up a tiled roof. I like to imagine Saffi looking down on me, checking I am alright – I am alright. Michael spoils me rotten. He didn't just bring Prince up to Richmond, he brought Sandringham too. He said the horses were too distressed when he tried to separate them. We ride during the week when the evenings are light enough. We go to the opera, the ballet, to concerts and to the cinema, and we have lovely meals out, never worrying if we are seen together. Michael just explains I am a friend of the family, and the outing was something to do in the week before he goes back to his gorgeous wife and family. He provides such a full account of his incredible Culmfield life that the listener is assured he is the most doting husband and father in the world, and sometimes even I believe him.

We have many business trips together, which are fun, flying in his private plane and staying in the best hotels – if Michael can justify me being with him, then I go. Always travelling in style. First class, everything laid on in spades, but I have also gotten used to having my weekends free. I savour the time to do just what I like. I have started sightseeing and doing things I have never done before, like rummaging around Camden Market, watching the street artists in Covent Garden, walking aimlessly in the parks and visiting galleries. It is a good life. *I am alright, Saffi.*

Going home every fortnight gives me a chance to help Mum and Dad physically, rather than just sending them money. I have been working my way around the farmhouse, giving it a good clean. Mum's eyesight is deteriorating and her standards have slipped. The guests who come don't seem to mind if she has missed a cobweb or two, but I like helping her. These days, Mum only has 'the regulars,' as she calls them and she treats them all like friends.

Mum is seventy-two years old now and I think the worry of me has aged her. Her hair is completely grey and her shoulders are slightly bent. She seems to have shrunk a foot in height too. Dad is nearly seventy but the years have been kinder to him, he could pass for sixty, and is as fit as any prize-winning sheepdog. They are a great couple. I love being home just to watch them together. They know what the other will say before it's said. Mum told me how they reconnected after she stopped writing to Richard. They are the parents from my childhood again but they are terrified of losing their cows. The farm gates are barricaded shut.

The relief-milker can't come because he has his own farm nearby so he could spread the virus. Mum and Dad will have to do it all themselves now. So, it's a good thing, in a way, that the holidaymakers are cancelled.

Mum is beside herself with worry. I ring her every day, when I can get through – she is on the phone constantly, talking to everyone she knows to ask what is happening. My parents watch their animals like hawks for any lameness, blisters on their nostrils or tongues, for milk yields to drop, or mastitis. Any tiny sign. Their life is on a knife-edge, while they hope this deadly plague won't reach Fox Halt Farm.

I have been stopped from riding in Richmond Park this morning. The park is closed to the public but that is so small a concern compared to the farm. I wish I was trapped there with them rather than being separated like this.

MICHAEL

This mad affair is not as hard as I expected. I thought I would feel like a dog when I saw Jessie. I don't. I love them both. I simply have two lives. My wife may know about Billy, she is far from stupid, but we have never talked about what I do in London. I am just 'away.' Weekends are all about Jessie and the children. The kids jump on me as I get in the door and Billy is wiped from my mind. On Mondays, as the car engine starts, I long for my London girl. We have a morning meeting and the circus starts again.

MARCH 2001 – BILLY

In London, I see my fellow commuters, and I wonder if they have any idea what farmers, and people in the countryside, are going through. *Cull,* a headline in their newspaper on their way to their comfortable workplaces. News today and tomorrow, but soon to be forgotten. The word somehow sanitises what is going on; there is nothing sanitary about it. They should put my parents' faces on the front pages and list the animals' names. Fill London cars, buses, and train carriages with the sounds of scared sheep bleating and the smell of rancid death. Then, everyone would understand the killing, in numbers that are unfathomable – *and feel it too.*

MAY 2001 – MICHAEL

Months now, and it still goes on. Billy is consumed by what the threat of the disease is doing to her parents. She might as well be at Fox Halt Farm for what little work she is doing for me.

In the evenings it is as though she is not with me, phoning her mum as soon as she gets into her apartment, mindlessly getting us something to eat. I watch something on the television while she pretends to read but I know it's just a cover for her anxiety. I know she doesn't want to go out because she won't enjoy it. Billy will be thinking about the farm, and if going out was enjoyable she would feel guilty about having fun when her family are in peril.

Sex is just a means of taking her mind off the farm. She tries like she tries at work, but her heart is not here. Billy can't go home because her parents are too scared, she will bring the virus with her, on her footwear, the car tyres, maybe even in the air she breathes out.

SEPTEMBER 2001 – BILLY

My money is running out, all invested in Fox Halt Farm; paying off the mortgage, converting two of the old farm buildings to holiday accommodation, building a brand-new barn and keeping the machinery running.

The ten years before the foot and mouth outbreak was hard for everyone, so this disease hitting now is desperate. Many of Mum and Dad's friends and family had already given up. Every six months or so, Mum would tell me of another farm sale. The people I grew up with, getting out of the only livelihood they knew, their farms had been in their families for generations too. Animals sold off one by one. The biggest heartbreak would be the sale of their sheepdog, no good as a pet; these dogs are workers and that's what they live for.

Tom and his parents must have had a small advantage over their neighbours because they have bought up surrounding farms as they have come on the market, feeling safer because they could diversify. Spreading the risk over different crops, making them less vulnerable to unpredictable weather and unstable markets. Tom and his father treat their farm as a business more than a way of life. They account for everything, managing all the costs as best they can. It's farmers like them who will survive difficult and economic changes, but now even these farms are on the danger list, the virus could hit them badly too.

I helped Dad last year because he wanted to diversify a bit too, worried about fluctuating milk prices. He rented extra land and bought beef cattle. They were expensive to buy but he predicted a decent return. The foot and mouth outbreak began just as his cattle were ready to go to market. They should have made good money but the government stopped all movement of animals, so none could be sold. The cattle had eaten all the grass in his rented fields but he couldn't move them to new grazing – he had to buy in forage for them, and he is thousands in debt now.

There is no money from the sheep and the lambs which he can't sell either. Mum and Dad have had to pay for all their food since. Many lambs died because they couldn't be moved into sheds to protect them from the bad weather.

The farmers who've had foot and mouth on their farms and had their precious animals killed should receive compensation, but it's those whose herds have escaped the cull who are in financial trouble now – their animals cannot be sold and they still have to be fed and cared for. Money out and none coming in.

There is a bit of a turning point, where farmers almost want the worst to happen just to survive. If they are compensated, they can restock when this is over. It is hard to imagine but my parents are contemplating this – that the best solution might be actually finding foot and mouth on Fox Halt Farm. They worry about slaughtering each cherished creature, digging the biggest grave imaginable and throwing their animals into it; tracking over their dead cows to get as many in as possible. Pouring on gallons of toxic fuel to ignite their bodies. They know from their friends who already have the disease on their farms, that the sad bulky carcasses probably won't burn completely and they will have charred partial remains left in their empty fields.

It is hell for them, but there could be a worse hell to come. Shooting. Dying. Burning and burying!

OCTOBER 2001

Armageddon. The army is helping as fifty new cases each day are reported. Ninety-thousand animals are slaughtered each week. The numbers are so big they lose meaning. There are questions about how so many animals can be killed so quickly, and maybe some are still alive as more animals are put on top; squashed to death.

NOVEMBER 2001

The cases are getting less. Mum and Dad think the outbreak in Devon has stopped. The news today is that six million animals have been slaughtered. *All those animals – all those farmers.*

Chapter 29
RICHMOND
THURSDAY 31 JANUARY 2002
BILLY

*I*t is considered that the epidemic is over but we are all still holding our breath. Michael insisted on paying off the final debt on the farm. He said it was a work bonus for me. I shouldn't, I know, but it makes me feel like it's payment for other services. Mind you – Michael hasn't got value for money there!

I am so relieved the farm, the cows and my poor parents have survived the nightmare disease. I can concentrate on Michael now, just as I should. He's been wonderful, while I pushed his patience to the limit. It is his birthday tomorrow but he will be heading back to Culmfield, so I have made him take a secret day off on Monday to be with me. I want to make a real fuss of him.

BEECHWOOD
SUNDAY 3 FEBRUARY 2002
RICHARD

I am up early as usual, walking Trixie and looking forward to ringing Daniella, once Janette leaves to see Father. I have phoned Fox Halt every Sunday morning since the outbreak began. I don't know who needed the calls more. Daniella, so worried about the farm, or me, so concerned about her and Jack. It was as if they were waiting for the sun to go down and never come up again. Years ago, Daniella's letters were wonderful, conjuring up romantic and funny scenes, but her recent phone conversations with me have been full of fear and funeral pyres. I am glad the outbreak appears to be over but ringing her every Sunday has become a habit. Daniella still takes me away to a faraway land, while Janette is not here. We haven't talked about Billy, both wary of discussing her behind her back.

The only information I have about her daughter is from Michael. She has been working for him for a long time now. He says she is engaged to someone but she won't tell him who he might be; typical Billy, always shrouded in secrets.

RICHMOND

BILLY

Michael asked me to check out his 'new little shop,' as he is calling it. This new store in Richmond only opened this week. It is a prototype, part of a new strategy for O'Rowdes'. Michael has decided it will be good for the business to have some representation back in town centres with smaller convenience type shops. I am here, buying a few bits and pieces so I can report back to him with my thoughts and feelings about it.

My eyes fix on a couple at the end of the shop. That is wrong, it's my hearing focusing my attention on the man and woman who are giggling about something. The man has his back to me but still I recognise him from his bubbly laugh. The familiar sound sends shivers down my spine.

'Hello, Ed,' I say, when the girl he is with moves away to find something.

'Billy,' he smiles and I feel my heart jump.

'Sorry, I don't want to get you into trouble,' I say, 'are you with your girlfriend?'

'No, that's my sister.' He points at the girl, who is talking to a shop assistant about whatever it is she wants to find. 'I am staying with her for the moment.'

I am not really listening, staring at him, remembering all the times we spent together.

'I've got to go now but how about we meet at the climbing wall later, half past six?'

'Yes.' I feel my insides jolt again.

'I'll see you later then.' He turns away to catch up with his sister.

Now as I walk out of the shop, I am in a hopeless quandary, wondering why I agreed to meet Ed, and why I feel so tense. Seeing him is stirring up uncomfortable questions about my true feelings for Michael. My pulse never races when I see Michael – I thought Richard, my miscarriage and Saffi's death had taken away all my ability to truly love anyone anymore, but the excitement I felt seeing Ed again makes me reconsider.

My relationship with Michael is built on me sharing him with Jessie. He can never be wholly mine, and perhaps that's why I never feel completely in love with him. I thought I was protecting myself by holding back, but the way I reacted to Ed makes me think that I just don't have those deeper feelings for Michael.

I wait outside the shop until I see Ed and his sister leave, and then, I go back inside, determined to focus on the place, its range of goods, and the service I receive – I will give Michael a precise account of what I think of his latest venture, but I won't be providing *all* the detail about the customers his *new little shop* is attracting.

BEECHWOOD
RICHARD

I have just put the phone down on Daniella. The house is empty so I pick up the Sunday newspaper, feeling quite content but now, our next-door neighbour comes into the kitchen uninvited.

'Morning, Richard,' Jayne says.

I ignore her, starting to read a report about how O'Rowdes' are trialling the creation of small supermarkets in town centres. I think about the extra work this new idea will generate for MarcFenn, finding Michael the appropriate locations and acquiring the premises he will need.

'Richard,' Jayne says again. I wonder why she wants my attention, and why she is here? Jayne should know her friend is at my father's, just like she is every Sunday morning.

I look up and see that she has made a pot of tea. 'Yes, Jayne,' I reply, still thinking more about Michael's newest venture than wondering why she is here, and why she has made tea for us both.

'How well do you think you know Janette?' She pushes a mug towards me. I am at a loss. I know my wife as well as I know myself, we have been together over twenty years. We have been married for sixteen of those. We are bringing up three fabulous children.

'Why?' I stare hard at Jayne and shake my head. *What an odd thing to ask? And why is she bothering me like this?*

'Look, Richard, I am sorry but I have to tell you something that you are not going to like.'

'Okay, go on,' I say, hoping she will hurry up and say whatever it is and leave me in peace again.

'I can't see you two living like this any longer,' she says, sipping her tea. 'It's just hell for me to watch.'

I am completely lost. I have no idea why this annoying woman is sitting in my kitchen. She is Janette's friend. Her children are my children's friends. I am her husband Jock's friend – he works in Brazil as a private security guard for some bigwig over there. Jayne can tell you to the hour when her husband is due home, even if it is four months away. When he does return for a few days, their five children seem to be encouraged to move into our house for a while. It's great, I love our home so full of noise – it comes alive. Jayne and Jock's eldest daughter and their youngest son are the same age as our twins and Freddy – so sometimes when Jock is away, our two families go on holiday, or days out together. Jock is ex-forces, like Saffi was. I get on well with him when he is home, it's nice to be able to discuss things with him, while our wives are chatting.

I have no real connection with Jayne, but maybe she's feeling a bit lonely, Jock having been away for a month.

'You've lost me,' I tell her politely, hoping she will quickly explain and that will be it. She can always talk to Janette at length when she gets back from Father's. I just want her to leave me alone.

'Your wife is not happy with you. She is unhappy being married to you, Richard,' she says. 'I can't bear her misery any longer.'

I have no idea how to answer. I just wish this insane woman would leave my kitchen.

'Richard, you're totally blind, aren't you? Listen, I'm going now, I said what I needed to say. At least, you now know how Janette feels.'

'I don't understand what you are talking about,' I tell her.

'Think about it, Richard. Tell Janette you worked it out for yourself. I won't say I told you.' She picks up her full mug of tea and heads back to her own home. I lift up my paper again, frowning.

What was that all about?

MILE END, LONDON
BILLY

I arrive at the wall at the same moment as Ed.

'Where's your kit?' I ask, noticing that he has nothing with him.

'Sorry, Billy, I haven't got much time, after all. Can we just have a drink here, and a bit of cake?'

'Okay,' I say, trying not to think about how long it took me to find my climbing gear, and the time I spent searching out something nice to wear. I feel let down too, I was looking forward to a climb.

In the next fifteen minutes he tells me bits about his job in Dubai and how he has decided to come back to London.

'I have to go,' he says, checking his watch. Sis is having a party – I promised her I'd be back to help get things set up.'

He sounds excited about the party, as he stands up. 'Same place, same time next week?' he asks. 'Are you up for another secret rendezvous, Billy?'

'To actually climb?' I check.

'Definitely, I'm sorry about today. It's good to see you again.'

'I am in Devon next weekend,' I say, feeling disappointed again. 'What about the following Saturday?'

'Yep, that sounds great. Look, I do have to go.'

And that is it, he leaves. I feel a little annoyed, he didn't once ask me how I am, or inquire about what I am doing now, but still, it was good to see him.

I head back to Richmond, utterly confused and feeling disloyal to Michael.

EXMOOR
MONDAY 4 FEBRUARY 2002
BILLY

Blackmore Gate on the edge of Exmoor was as far as I reckoned Amir could drive Michael's posh car without scarring it on the narrow stone-walled lanes. The chauffeur will take the Rolls Royce to London and Michael will drive my little car from here. It's nine o'clock in the morning and I am at the designated meeting point, determined to forget about my short encounters with Ed yesterday.

I feel a sense of relief as I see Amir with the car. Michael waves, looking so happy to see me, I think it will be easy to stay focused on him. I do feel excited, we have a whole day and a night alone together. This will be a magical birthday surprise for him.

'Right then, darling, where are we going, left or right?' Michael starts up my car and instantly, I remember us taking Kitten to the vet almost ten years ago. I grin at him. 'Left please,' I pause. 'Or you could go right?'

He looks at me. 'Not funny, Billy.'

'But it's true, Michael, you can go either way. If you turn left here it's about a mile longer but it will be prettier, we'll see the sea. It's quite narrow in places whichever way you choose.'

'Left then.' His eyes sparkle.

Snowdrifts of white Christmas roses line the mile-long private drive to our hotel hidden in a dense deciduous wooded valley. The setting might be first class but our accommodation is a little below Michael's usual standards, though as soon as the owners of the hotel come out to greet us, I see he adores the place. Years ago, the hotel was a comfortable home for a wealthy family, and today, it feels like we are their special guests. Inside all the decoration and furniture is a bit worn out, and what was once immaculate is now just comfortable.

We are the only people staying here, but it wouldn't have mattered anyway, because there are only ever two choices on the menu; delicious home-cooked food made by the Michelin-starred owner. Dinner is hours away so we leave our bags in our room and head off for a walk along a path that hugs the shoreline.

My overwhelming thought is that today it feels like Michael is entirely mine; we are a proper couple having a romantic break away. I feel closer to him than I have ever felt before.

We find a secluded beach, and perch on a rock. I am mesmerised by the clear water washing in and out. All my senses are engaged on the hypnotic waves, my mind focused on their rhythm. 'Billy, I want to tell you about my mother. Her name was Marilena Kenan.' I don't take in his words at first, distracted by the sound and motion of the tide but then I realise what he has just said. 'You don't need to,' I tell him.

'I want to, darling. It's important to me.' He launches into his story, without any further hesitation. 'My mother came to England as a baby after her parents were sent to a German concentration camp. She was adopted by a couple in London who treated her like their own. But they were strict. I think this because of the way they behaved when they found out she was pregnant.' His words are not fluid, seemingly rehearsed in a way. He stares out to sea and keeps talking.

'My parents were both just fourteen years old when my mother got pregnant. My mother's adopted parents gave her a choice; it was their comfortable home or the baby. My mother chose to keep me, so when I was born, she went to live with my father, staying with his family.' He gets up and picks up a pebble which he skims into the sea. He looks back at me still sitting on the rock.

'My father was Michael Connor O'Rowde, and he worked with his dad in the biggest pub in the area. I think he must have worked hard because eventually he saved enough money so the three of us, Mum, me and him could move into a room on the top floor of the pub. That was okay for a while, I think. My parents got married but gradually my father was drinking more than his wages would cover and they were asked to leave. There was a big family row and my father's parents washed their hands of their son, his young wife and their little grandson after that.'

'Michael, would you like to stop? Shall we have lunch in the pub we passed on the way here?' I ask. Now that Michael is telling me about his family, I am unsure I want to hear it. I know this story won't end well, and I do not want to spoil what seemed a perfect day.

'No, please let me finish,' he replies. 'What I am telling you is just what I have managed to piece together. I don't remember my father. I only have one photo of him, a faded picture of my parents on the day they were married.'

'Is that the picture in your office?' I ask. 'I saw it that first day when I started working for you, I wondered if it might be your mum and dad? You look like your father.'

'Yes.'

'Go on,' I say, staring into his eyes.

'What I told Jessie was not the truth. I know that now. It was a fog of false memories. I kept pushing the worst bits away. It wasn't until you asked about my mother that I decided to try and find out what *really* happened to my parents. I have been trying to separate reality from my nightmares ever since. Someone has researched this for me, but they found out very little. This is all I know and some of this is guesswork.' Michael comes and sits back down next to me.

'After the pub, my parents moved into a rough place. I remember Mum saying that everyone there was 'on the take.' You didn't steal from friends but everyone else was fair game. It was a place of felons and fighting. My father fought anyone when he was drunk, and one day, some men in a back alley

killed him. Mum didn't discover what had happened until
weeks afterwards, and she never found out where they
dumped his body.

'My clearest memory, I think, is when I was about nine
years old, Mum and I were living in a dismal flat high up in a
new high-rise block. We shared it with two other women, but
these women are vague to me, I was either with Mum or
outside on the street. I was not allowed back in the flat until
my mother's gentleman friends had left. I thought she had so
many friends and I didn't understand why she kept crying, or
why she was bruised sometimes.'

I put my hand on his, thinking how odd it is, that
Michael is opening up like this. I wonder if he is feeling a
deeper connection with me too? Trusting me at last. I clamp
my fingers tightly around his hand, trying to show him I care
about what he is saying. He continues.

'One day, I was on the landing when I heard shouting
inside our flat. As the argument stopped, a man ran out,
bulldozing past me, and shouting, 'You won't have to share
her now, son.' His evil words still wake me from my sleep
sometimes. When I ran inside our flat, I couldn't find my
mother and then I looked over the balcony and I saw her. Laid
out on the gravel at the back of the building, strewn amongst
the litter around the bins. I charged down to her and tried to
make her respond to me, but it was useless, so I lay down next
to her broken body, pretending we were in our bed sleeping.
When the police came, I scarpered back up to our flat, to hunt
out an envelope with all our personal papers inside. I grabbed
it and my mother's purse too, and ran away. Afterwards, I
lived wherever I could; hiding in the derelict buildings there,
which were awaiting demolition, so more high-rises could be
built. I was terrified someone would send me to an orphanage
or I'd be placed with a horrible adoptive family. I didn't go to
school, and stole everything I needed to survive.'

He has told me all this as if it was someone else's life. I
didn't sense any emotion. I am sure Michael has practised this
so he wouldn't get upset as he spoke. 'Is this why you helped
me?' I ask.

'Yes, sweetheart. My mother went through hell while I
just played outside. I saw that same haunted despair in you
when I saw you after you lost your baby.' Michael is about to

cry. I wonder if this man has cried since the day, he lost his mother. We sit in silence for a little while, both wrapped up in our thoughts.

'Come on, Billy,' he says eventually, standing up and pulling at my hand. 'Let's get to the pub.'

TUESDAY 5 FEBRUARY 2002
MICHAEL

I have been thinking this through for months. I wanted to tell Billy before, but I needed to work out which parts were true and what was terror. Billy puts her knife and fork together and leans forward to touch my hand. She asks gently, 'What happened to you after your mum died?'

'I can give you a bit of a summary,' I say, 'but do you mind not interrupting me for five or six minutes?' She nods. I take a slow breath in. I breathe out again so hard that the forced air seems to whistle through my teeth 'I spent nearly three years sleeping rough, stealing, scrapping and struggling to cope with the horror of it all but I always kept the envelope which contained the remnants of my parents in a plastic bag sweaty against my skin.

'I became obsessed with the people who had thrown my mother away. Their name and address were on a faded certificate. Mr and Mrs Michaelmas became my nemesis. When I broke into their large house in Streatham, I was shocked to find my mother's old bedroom had stayed as it was the day she left, as though she was expected home at any moment. I watched the house for weeks. I never saw the husband, but each evening, after the nine o'clock news, his wife went to the time-locked room and knelt by her daughter's empty bed and prayed. I watched her every night from behind a tree in her garden.

'It was my mother's birthday when I finally broke. Mrs Michaelmas cried so much that night. 'Mari, I am so sorry.' She said that over and over again. Witnessing her terrible remorse made me tap on the window. I should have frightened her to death, but she guessed who I was straight away, asking me to stay. I never called her grandmother; she was just Mrs M. She hugged me but never kissed me. I didn't kiss her either. It was just an understanding between us.

'School was hell to start with because I was so far behind but the good thing was that I only need to read something once to remember it. I caught up pretty quickly. However, I didn't take any exams because the night before they started, Mrs M died. I didn't go back to school; instead, I worked on her funeral, making sure it was just as she had specified in some papers I found. Mrs M had said no flowers, but still, I ordered two wreaths of red and white roses spelling out 'MUM' and 'GRANDMA.'

'After her funeral, I discovered how much money she had. We had lived so frugally, I had no idea she was rich. I inherited all her fortune. I was sixteen without a clue what to do with it all. And in an unbalanced moment, I bought a rundown shop on Streatham High Street, stocking it with anything I liked. I bought it all from the other shops on the high street. I purchased everything I'd dreamt of; all the things I had envied in the homes I'd stolen from. But what I loved the most was putting up the huge sign above my new shop, reading *O'Rowdes'* – to me, it was a memorial to my parents. My father's body disappeared, and I still haven't found out where Mum is buried, because when I ran off there was nothing left to identify her. Ever since, my life has been dedicated to growing my business just so I can display the O'Rowdes' name everywhere.'

'No more secrets,' I say, and Billy smiles at me and nods.

Chapter 30
BUCKINGHAM PALACE, LONDON
SUNDAY 13 APRIL 2003
BILLY

I cheer myself over the finish line of the twenty-third London Marathon. *Billy May, you did it! Three hours, twenty-one minutes and fifty-eight seconds. Three minutes faster than you thought you could. Saffi would be proud of you. You are a star. Okay, Paula Radcliffe did it in two hours fifteen, but she has been doing this a lot longer than me.* This all started over a year ago.

After my chance meeting with Ed, I stood outside the climbing wall on the prearranged Saturday and waited, wondering what the hell I was doing there. I think I wanted to climb and I wanted an explanation too, why he had left so suddenly and had never been in touch since.

He didn't turn up. I was curious because he had never let me down before, so I continued to wait. Two hours went by and he still didn't come. Two girls had acknowledged me as they went in to climb and they saw me still standing there when they finished. One of them asked if I was okay. I told her I was fine – I *was* fine because the no-show and Ed's previous lack of interest in me, answered a lingering question. My notion that he might have had any strong feelings towards me disappeared. If Ed had felt something, he would have come. He wouldn't have forgotten.

The girls came across to me, checking if I really was alright, saying I had a most unreliable climbing partner. Almost together, the pair asked if I wanted to climb with them the next time they were there. I explained about my commitment to the farm and they said I could join them every other Saturday. And that is what I did. Their ability put me to shame but they were always encouraging.

It was Abigail and Clarrie who suggested that running might help improve my climbing. They run together every Sunday morning around Hyde Park, and I started running with them too. They are fun to be with. The pair chatter away all the time. I have no idea how they do it. I will never find it that easy.

It was Clarrie who suggested we all entered this year's London Marathon but she was the only one, of the three of us, who got through the ballot. Abigail and I had to secure our places by raising money for a charity.

I chose to run for stroke victims and their families, quickly settling on this special charity because of Dad: after the foot and mouth, my parents decided to sell Fox Halt Farm. It wasn't too sad because they sold it to Tom. Dear Tom promised to keep on the cows and Dad planned to help him two days each week. My parents found a little two-bedroom cottage right in the centre of Hamsgate, next to the village shop. On the day they were due to move, Dad had a stroke. He was with my mum watching his beloved cows when the massive aneurysm struck; he died instantly. He had been complaining of headaches and Mum just thought he was unhappy about moving. He had high blood pressure too, but he didn't tell Mum, he never wanted her to worry.

My mother seems okay. She couldn't really bear dragging Dad from the farm; her husband had arrived there that fateful day they met and he never wanted to leave again. That's why I have run the marathon; it's for my dearest father.

There have been many changes since the virus, so many lives devastated. Tom and Martha are a casualty too. Their farm escaped the disease but since then, poor Martha has battled anxiety attacks. Having to deal with the farmers and their animals took its toll. The kind woman is finding everything really hard to cope with. She asked Tom to move out while she tries to sort herself out. She is living with his mum and the children now, while Tom has Fox Halt Farm to himself. Mum says it is tough for them at the moment.

RICHARD

I think I just saw Billy in front of me in the medal queue, but she has disappeared amongst the throngs. If it was, she looked fit and I am disappointed that she beat me.

This was Jayne's idea. She said her husband, Jock, always felt better after a run. I needed to feel better. It has been a rough road separating from Janette.

We have wrestled with our emotions through the whole thing. Janette felt guilty because she thought she had pushed me into marrying her when we were both too young, and she said she shouldn't have tried to mend things after my affair with Billy. She wanted us to be together for the sake of the children, and she saw how it had led to a long and unhappy pretence. I felt terrible because deep down I knew she wasn't truly happy. I had just gone along with it because it had seemed the right thing to do, when in truth Billy still lingers in my mind.

Janette made the divorce easy. She didn't want anything except to have the children half of the time. She has the house, and I have a cottage at the other end of the village. Our children stay with me every other week.

With all that has happened, I have decided to float MarcFenn on the stock market. There will be plenty of money for Janette, and our children won't be duty bound to carry on the business. I want Harry, Sid and Freddy to be able to choose what they want to do with their lives. I will have no expectations of them.

When I see my ex-wife now, she and I are better than we've ever been. It's as if I am discovering the real woman for the first time and it is good to see her content.

Jayne has taken me under her wing too and she spends loads of time in my new home. Finally, I have people around me, I can really talk to. To onlookers, Jayne and I are often mistaken for a couple because when I have the children, and Jock is away, we go out together as one big happy family. In truth though, Jayne has become the big sister I never had – we grumble and moan at each other just like proper siblings do. I am glad she is around, she never sugar-coats any of her advice and it is nice to have her honesty, even though it's brutal sometimes.

They are all here today, including Jock, because he didn't believe I could do this. He changed his leave dates to make sure he'd see me over the finish line. He is a good friend too. They are all great, Janette, Jayne, Jock and jogging. All getting me through this massive change in my life.

It will be satisfying getting my ten thousand pounds sponsorship money off Michael. I'll see if he knows if it was Billy. But it couldn't have been her, if it was, Michael would have said she was running the marathon too.

BILLY

Abigail and Clarrie have texted me because we agreed not to meet up straight away after our marathon run. I will cook them dinner tonight as a thank you for their support and their super-detailed training plan. Abigail said it would be best to go straight to our respective charity buildings so we can claim our free food and massage.

I am glad no-one is here waiting for me. I can take my time, soaking up the heady atmosphere.

I lie face down on the massage table. The lady who put me here has been doing this for an hour straight and she apologised when she said she needed a break. She is sending another masseur over to me. I am happy just to lie here. The euphoria of what I have achieved is coursing through me.

'Little Miss Fun.'

My all too short shorts must have exposed my tattoo. I bought the new shorts on Friday because they were the same deep purple as my charity shirt. They looked fine and I just put them in my rucksack to change into when I got to Greenwich. I broke one of the cardinal rules from Abigail's top tips: 'no new kit on the day,' she warned, 'new kit may chaff. Best to avoid chaffing for twenty-six miles.' Clarrie and Abigail screwed up their faces and laughed at the word 'chaffing.' The pair remind me of Jessie and me sometimes.

I turn my head to see who has commented on my tattoo. It's Ed and he is beaming at me, 'Hey. Well done, Billy. What time did you do?'

'Three hours something.' I can't remember my time, it was so important to me only seconds ago and it has now jumped out of my mind. 'Ed.' I frown at him. 'What are you doing here?'

'This is my big career change. I decided I had a chance, and I'd take it. I'm a fully qualified sports massage therapist now, I thought I'd get to see a lot of lovely bodies.' He laughs. 'Billy, I will have to get started, I'm not here to talk. Turn back over please.'

'Ed, I am sorry, can't you get someone else to do this for me? I am not comfortable with this.'

'We are working for free. You can't pick and choose, you know. You get who you are given. Now shut up. I am just trying to do my job. I'm good at this, you'll see.'

'No, Ed.' It is no good; I haven't said it loud enough he doesn't hear. Each muscle he irons out re-hardens with guilty pleasure.

'Billy, would you meet me at Box Hill in a couple of weeks? It would be nice to go for a walk together,' he asks casually, as he tries to wash massage oil off his hands.

'Okay,' I agree before I know what I am saying.

'Can I suggest the café at nine o'clock.'

'Will you remember this time?' I ask, wondering why I care so much. 'Look, do you have a business card and a pen, please?'

Ed quickly hands me both. I write the date and the time on the back of his card, before I hand it back to him.

'I'll be there, Billy,' he says as I leave.

Just an innocent walk, I tell myself. I try to remember if I have been to Box Hill before.

My mind is woozy. *He won't show up, Billy, you know he won't.*

PINEAPPLI 1
MONDAY 12 JANUARY 2004
RICHARD

*I*n the pile of mail on my desk, is an envelope marked 'STRICTLY PRIVATE – ADDRESSEE ONLY.' I recognise the writing even though I haven't had a letter like this for years and I tear it open.

'Dearest Richard,

I know you have been busy sorting out the company floatation but please phone again whenever you want. Thank you for your lovely Christmas card, I only got it today because your secretary sent it to Fox Halt Farm - please give her my new address - and remember, I still have a spare room here so you are always welcome to stay. It's been years since you came to the farm. I am sure dear Tom won't mind taking us around in one of his farm vehicles. Actually, William or Grace could probably drive us - they are eleven and ten years old now. Frightening isn't it, how time has gone by.

This was the second Christmas without my darling Jack, but to me, he is still here and I chat away to him all the time. I miss the farm but I am involved in many different things in Hamsgate, and I help out in the shop a bit. This year, I received over forty Christmas cards and letters from old guests; all remembering happy times staying at the farm.

Dear Tom is keeping the holiday cottages going but the farmhouse bed and breakfast is no more. Dear Tom is still on his own at Fox Halt Farm. (I so hope this is temporary, Martha and him always seemed so right together.) Tom has arranged it now, so the children can stay if they want to. William has Billy's old room and her old bedroom's walls are now covered in some of his rosettes.

Of course, Grace is only interested in her mountain bike, saying she can get just as dirty for a lot less effort and expense. She makes me laugh all the time.

She and William often come knocking on my door, looking for Battenberg cake - it's their favourite too!

Billy still comes down every other weekend, often helping Tom with the milking, though it takes twice as long because they don't stop talking, they have always got on so well those two. Billy loves being back with the animals too.

It is strange that this chap she has been engaged to for so long has never been here - why do I have such a secretive daughter? I feel closer to you sometimes. You tell me everything. Billy tells me nothing.

We do have a great time together when Billy is here. Most Saturdays, she drives us to Dawlish and we get fish and chips. We sit and watch the sunset, just like Jack and I used to. Sometimes, the two of us go away for the whole weekend on the Lizard, in Cornwall, staying in the same hotel that Jack and I stayed in on our honeymoon. Jack comes too, sitting with me on the hotel patio, or in the conservatory looking over the little cove below, and now and again, another guest or a member of the hotel staff, will find me chatting to his empty chair.

I am so glad you have Jayne keeping an eye on you. It must be difficult for her, when her husband is away. Please tell her that she and Jock are welcome here too. She does sound an amazing woman and I should love to meet her.

Sorry but it's my turn in the shop now. I will take this with me and post it.

Love Daniella x x x x'

Chapter 31
BOX HILL, SURREY
SATURDAY 22 MAY 2004
BILLY

*I*t is cold today at Box Hill. A little bit rainy too. I look up from my book and watch the misty drizzle slowly smear the windows of the café. I am waiting for Ed, and I start to think about how everything has worked out: It's odd, but I cherish routine now. I used to yearn for excitement; the thrill of charging my horse over scary fences, Tom and me racing our car around the fields and the anticipation of what Ed would plan each time I saw him, but now I just like things fixed and happy, and that is how it is.

Work is great. Michael and I always have something interesting to explore. We share the same passion and determination to keep his company successful.

The evenings with Michael are lovely too. We just fit together. There is no pretence, just love and trust in each other. Well, not complete honesty on my part because for the past year I've seen Ed nearly every other Saturday and I haven't told Michael. I don't talk about my weekends because I do not want to hear about his.

Michael mentions Jessie and their children occasionally, he can't help himself. He is proud of them all. They have four kids now and the youngest, Max, is four years old so it must be a madhouse at Culmfield.

My alternate weekends are spent in Devon, and I cherish them too. I still consider Hamsgate as home, I love Mum's new cottage in the middle of the village and I get to see a lot of my childhood friends and my relations. I help out at Fox Halt too and sometimes it feels like I never left.

During the weekends I am in London, I see Ed, often meeting at the café at Box Hill. It is completely platonic so I shouldn't feel guilty – just a few hours walking together. Always the same route, like my time at Culmfield with Michael, but Ed and I talk. Not about our work or our separate lives. It is all philosophy. It reminds me of past times with Saffi and Simon. I love being with Ed. The best way to describe him, is that he is *sparkly*, making me feel alive. I think he relishes my company too because twice, when I have been slightly late, he worried I wasn't going to make it, and he was terribly upset with me.

Saturday evenings are with Abigail and Clarrie, and on Sunday mornings I run with them in Hyde Park. There is time for me to keep the apartment nice, or ride Prince, or read one of Saffi's books in a single sitting. Once I have finished the book, I lend it to Ed, and that shared experience will be something else we will discuss on our walks. Ed never gives the books back. I imagine he keeps them but I don't mind if he passes them on to someone else who will appreciate them too. I don't like reading a book twice; dying to find out what will happen and loving the thrill of the plot's twists and turns.

When it's nice weather, Ed and I won't meet in the café because he prefers to find me at the stepping stones crossing the river Mole, underneath Box Hill. It is a special place, sometimes tranquil and other times overwhelmed by happy families and children splashing and shouting. I always take a book because Ed can be late, and sometimes he won't turn up at all. I have lunch in the café and then I go. It doesn't matter, I love it here.

Like we did before, we never text, phone, or discuss our future meetings, it is just set. I wonder if Ed wants to keep *us* a secret too. I don't know where he lives now, but something gives me the impression he is still at his sister's house. She may not even be his sister. It's intriguing, but I don't worry about it. I love his company and I feel that seeing me is an important part of his life too.

Actually, I do worry a little, becoming slightly more concerned each time I see him, a snail's pace of apprehension.

It started the first day we met here, after I asked him why he was at the stroke charity's headquarters. When I told him about Dad, he was sympathetic, and I expected him to talk about his family too, but he didn't. He said how much he enjoyed doing the massage work, and how much it meant to him, but then I saw his thumbs, all bent from kneading people's bodies so hard. He grumbled his wrists were hurting a bit too. I noticed then, how he wasn't the man I remembered; his body was not in the shape it was, the muscle I expected wasn't there anymore. He mentioned a girl friend who he used to run with. She had a stroke and died in a running race; a competition that he had been in too. He was so sad about losing her, he couldn't even tell me her name.

Then, the next few times he wasn't able to shift a cold. He said it was hay fever, but the bouts of the allergy seemed to get him down. He's been cagey and low occasionally. It maybe grief over the girl that makes his vibrancy come and go. I've asked him if he is okay but he snaps at me.

Most recently, I don't know what mood he will be in; bouncy and full of zeal for life like the old Ed always was, or a bit sulky and awkward to talk to. I am here today, for the fun of seeing him, but also because I think he needs me to be here – our fortnightly meet ups seem very important to my friend. Each time, we see each other, I wish he would tell me what's going on, but he hasn't yet.

BOX HILL
SATURDAY 15 OCTOBER 2005

Over the two and a half years I have been coming to Box Hill, the truth has slowly dawned on me. There is no longer a snail trail of unease. The snail is in the bill of a greedy thrush waiting to be hammered on a stone anvil. My dearest Ed is now someone I hardly recognise.

I have tried to help but he won't listen. I watch cocaine and heroin slowly steal him away from me but I haven't given up hope, still coming here at the appointed time waiting for the wreck who may, or may not, turn up. I have tried everything I could to help him, but it is as though his addiction is all he cares about.

At about eight o'clock last night icy rain started to fall in Richmond. I was soaked through by the time I got back from the livery where Prince and Sandringham are. The relentless rain was quite unexpected, and so different from the daytime – an autumnal day, crisp but bright and full of promise. It seems the furious rain hasn't let up since then. It's beating on and bouncing off the Box Hill café roof. I dash inside, and as I step through the door, I can hear my phone is ringing.

'Darling, come home.' Mum's tone is urgent, causing my brain to fly into overdrive, working out possible reasons why she sounds upset.

'What is it?' I ask quickly.

'I'll explain when you get here. Please. Billy.' She starts to cry. 'I can't explain because I'm scared that if I do, you won't be able to concentrate on driving.'

'Mum, you have to tell me. I won't be able to drive anyway – I'll just be worrying about what it might be. I'll catch the train and Tom ca–'

'He's dead.'

'What?'

'Dear Tom, it was a freak accident.' My legs buckle and I crash onto the first empty chair. '...a tractor and muck-spreader in our old yard. Late yesterday afternoon. I've only just managed to find out what happened, I couldn't believe it, not Tom – he is always so careful.'

'He died?'

'Yes, darling, he's dead. Straight away, they reckon.'

'Sorry, Mum. I can't take this in. You are right, he can't have had an accident. He's always cautious.'

'Somehow he wasn't yesterday. He was killed on the spinning shaft behind the tractor. William found him all wound around it, like a ball... Billy, it's so awful.' Mum is only just intelligible through her sobs. 'The police and health and safety people are still there. I have just been told all this, I don't know for sure, but I can't ring the family to find out the truth. I don't want to be bothering them. I don't know what to do? I want to help if I can...'

'Mum, I'll be home in four hours, probably sooner. Don't worry.' I get up and somehow stumble across the carpark. My mother screams at me, 'Billy you mustn't drive! I'll get someone to pick you up from the train station.'

As I slide into my car, the passenger door rips open and Ed falls inside with me, saturated, dripping wet and shivering. He throws himself backwards into the seat, staring at the rain-cloaked windscreen. I continue to talk to Mum, agreeing not to drive – even though I am about to. I say goodbye to her, turning to focus on my passenger. 'Sorry, Ed, I have to go home now. I'll drop you back at your sister's – you need to get out of those clothes. Get dry.'

'I will come with you. I mean to Devon... You can't leave me... You are mine this morning... you're mine on Saturday mornings... that's today.' He shivers so much that his words break up.

'No, Ed. I'll take you to *your* home – you need to get dry and warm. Look at you!' I pull off my coat, tucking it in around his stick thin body. When he starts crying, he breaks my heart.

He leans forward to touch my hand and sucks in a deep slow breath. 'No-one is going to stop me from being with you, Billy. No-one. I am coming with you, or you have to stay here with me.' I try to make him listen.

'Ed, I've got to go, I'll drop you off at your sister's, you need to get out of those clothes. You're soaked.' Ed usually catches a bus here but sometimes he walks. I don't know where he lives but I think it is fairly close by.

'No, Billy, I am coming with you... Please.' He is so fragile, I am desperate.

'Okay, you can come to Devon, but we must get you some dry clothes first.' I am thinking Mum will help me. Perhaps we can clean him up. *Perhaps I should have taken him to Devon before, getting him away from the drugs.*

I start my car, turning the heater up to full power.

'So, tell me how to get to your sister's,' I ask, thinking how after all this time, I don't know her name, let alone where she lives. He cocoons himself in my coat.

'Billy, she has thrown me out. She made me leave three days ago. I can't go back, I have let her down. I've let everyone down, stealing from my family and my friends too – everyone hates me.' I concentrate on his mouth to comprehend his trembling words.

'Where have you been since then?' I ask, trying to think where we can find him a change of clothes.

'By the river, near the stepping stones. I had a blanket–'

'Have you eaten?'

'Just coke.'

'Cocaine?' I check.

He nods and then shakes his head. 'I have none left, Billy.' His bloodshot eyes open wide. I am in turmoil, wondering if Ed needs more drugs, or a doctor; he might have pneumonia. 'What do you want me to do?' I ask, terrified by the way he looks, his almost translucent skin is deathly white.

I change my mind. 'I'm taking you to hospital,' I tell him, flicking on the windscreen wipers to see out.

'No, Billy.'

'Cocaine then? Is that what you need?' I say, my mind scrambling. 'We can go to your dealer. I've got money. I'll buy whatever you need.' I put my hands resolutely on the steering wheel, waiting for him to decide but he just stares at me. I have to help him. 'Dealer? Or doctor? Ed,' I ask sternly.

'No. No.'

'Ed, you are going to die – we have to do something. Shall I buy you more drugs? Will more cocaine stop you shaking? We need to go. Now!' I shout, hammering my hands on the dashboard.

'I won't go. Michael O'Rowde paid me to go. I don't want his money, Billy – I won't go. I am not going anywhere for anyone's money, no matter what threats you make. You and me, that's final.'

My heart thuds. 'Michael paid you? What do you mean?

'To not see you again. To go to Dubai. He made me go.'

I feel sick. *How could Michael have paid him? What is he saying? If anyone arranged for him to go to Dubai all those years ago then it was Saffi. Meddling Saffi. Michael didn't know about Ed.* I look into his frightened eyes and then I start to drive; heading for Epsom hospital. My car drowns in rain, I am drowning too. Ed is still talking.

'I told him, no… I told him I loved you. I said no money. No job opportunity was worth it.' Ed sputters like a dying flame. 'He raged, saying he wouldn't share you, but in the end, he accepted I could see you at weekends, when he was at home with his wife. He marched away seething but that was as much as I would give.'

Ed is desperate to tell me everything. I can't interrupt, it's so hard for him to speak. He sounds like he will cough his lungs up. 'The next morning Michael stormed into my office. He wasn't compromising this time, so angry I thought if he didn't kill me, he would find some henchman who would. I had no choice. He made it clear that I would never get another job anywhere else – I had to go to Dubai – he had connections everywhere and I was too weak to face up to him.' He chokes and cries. His crippling words beat down on me as I try to concentrate on driving as fast as I dare in the frenetic rain, but he doesn't stop, determined to expose what Michael has done.

'He stood over me while I phoned you, telling you I was going. He said I had to make it convincing. He told Richard MarcFenn that he needed me for an urgent project. He couldn't think of anyone else with my skills, lying that the chap he'd employed had been killed in a private plane crash and he needed me immediately, to replace him.' Ed's nose starts to bleed. He wipes the blood away and sniffs. 'O'Rowde took me to Heathrow. He said I must never see you again. He said he would know if I did and if I did, he'd kill us both. It's too late, Billy, my lungs or my heart will pack up soon. He's won.'

His voice is a whisper. 'The girl in the race, she was you. The chaps I used to climb with signed your sponsor form for the London Marathon. They told me you were running and that's why I volunteered with the charity.' He closes his eyes and his breathing falters. I can see the hospital entrance now. 'Ed, you'll be alright,' I tell him. 'Hold on – I love you… You can't leave me!'

EPSOM HOSPITAL

As I pull up in front of the hospital, I notice he is no longer shivering.

Ed is lifted onto a trolley. Rain spatters onto his face but he doesn't notice. I squeeze his bloodstained hand and he doesn't react to that either.

'I'm sorry,' the doctor says, 'but...'

'No!' I cry.

The man shakes his head. 'I'm so sorry.'

I can't help the hospital administrator with anything more than his name. It is all I know about Ed now. I give both Michael's and Richard's company addresses in the hope there is a personnel file somewhere with helpful information. The woman assures me they will find his family, and they will be able to notify them of his death.

My wonderful Ed is wheeled away to the mortuary and sometime soon, I hope, someone who loved him will claim him. His poor mother. *How could this have happened?* The young man with so many adventures unfulfilled is gone.

I leave my mobile number, asking if she will let me know when they find out anything. I want to say goodbye properly, I need to tell his family what a special man he was. I will stand up at his funeral. Ed and I won't be a secret anymore. I will shout his name from the rooftops – *Edward Mackintosh, you were amazing!*

When I get outside, my car has been towed away from the ambulance bay where I abandoned it. I pull my phone out of my pocket to make a call.

'Mum, I'm so sorry but I can't come home. Something terrible has just happened here too. I can't come back to Devon at the moment.'

'Darling, what is it?'

'I am sorry,' I tell her and then I lie, frightened how easily I lie to everyone. 'Ed, my fiancé. He has been in a serious car crash and I must stay with him – it doesn't look good, he is badly injured.'

'Ed? Ed Mackintosh, he's who you are engaged to?' I am surprised she has remembered his name from years ago. I am not sure she believes me.

'Yes, Mum. And he could die.' I start to cry. 'I have to go back to him, sorry.'

'Okay, darling, keep me informed please. I love you.'

'I love you too, I promise I'll be home as soon as I can.'

I am not ready to explain the truth to my mother, I have too much to sort out first.

THE OLD COTTAGE, JORDANS

RICHARD

As water starts to puddle on the kitchen sill, I decide I will have to invest in some new windows. The old wooden frames always seem to let in water when the rain comes from this direction but this time, the rain is so relentless that I keep finding new leaks.

The phone rings at the same moment as Jayne arrives. She is drenched through, and I laugh to myself, thinking that with all the water inside my home, she may want to keep her umbrella up. I pick the phone up but my mind is still focused on my visitor. It takes me a second to register that it is Daniella who is calling me.

'Hello, Richard, are you okay?'

'Yes, I am fine. Are you alright?' I ask, sensing she is not.

'There's been a terrible accident–' She stops.

'What? Tell me!'

'Tom, he has been killed on the farm.'

I try to grasp what she has just said. 'Is Billy with you?'

'No, Richard, she isn't. She is dealing with another crisis. Billy isn't here, I'll be okay though, Don't worry. I just wanted to tell you.'

'Daniella. You are not alright, are you? Do you want me to come down to Hamsgate?'

'Would you…?'

THE LIVERY, RICHMOND
SUNDAY 16 OCTOBER 2005
BILLY

I knock loudly on Annabelle Rossey-Jones' door; she owns the livery where Prince and Sandringham are stabled, and lives in the big house adjoining the yard. I expect she is in the kitchen sorting breakfast for herself and her young daughter.

While I wait for her to answer, I gnaw over the day when Ed told me he was going to Dubai. I keep thinking about it. Running over and over in my mind his unexpected phone call and my subsequent confusion over his shocking news. Flashes of detail whoosh through my head, like the meal I prepared for Michael afterwards. My desolation over Saffi's death and my desperate craving for my best friend's husband to hold me, as I awaited his return from Scotland. The stilted conversation as we ate the meal, which I prepared so carefully.

I go back over Michael's aggravated words about the unhelpful private investigator and the suspected thief, and realise how there was no investigation and no theft, he was meeting Ed that evening. Michael wasn't in Scotland either, instead he was fixing it so I would never see my darling man again.

Richard must have unwittingly talked to Michael about Ed, just like he told Saffi about us. Perhaps Richard wanted him to know that I was doing okay after the devastation of losing my baby, trying to ease his guilt about the awful aftermath of our affair.

I remember Michael probing me about Saffi's ring. I expect when he saw it, he jealously assumed it was from Ed. I do see why the scheming man didn't want to share me. His recurring nightmare about the evil man who shoved his poor mother to her death, *'You won't have to share her now, son.'* That terrible moment when he was left orphaned and afraid – but I have shared Michael for years, abandoning Jessie, Charlotte and little Mary, so I could.

The one person I thought was looking after me has contrived to manipulate so many lives. I know he is clever. I work with him and see how he gets what he wants but I didn't think him capable of using and abusing his friends, loved ones *and me* to this extreme. Ed is dead! Anger boils inside me, Michael won't get away with this.

'Hello, Billy, are you alright?' Annabelle asks as soon as she opens the door to me. I have got to know her well over the years. Sometimes, if she is short of a stable girl or boy, I help her. I like her and she likes me.

'Sorry, Annabelle,' I reply. 'I am sorry to trouble you but I have a bit of a problem.'

'So, how can I help you? I take it that's why you're here?'

'Yes, it's Michael's birthday today, and I hired a lorry to transport our horses up to Box Hill for the day. I had a special ride and a surprise picnic all planned, but the damn company I rented the horsebox from has let me down. Their lorry has broken down on the way here.'

'Oh, that's a shame.' She looks like she wants to go back indoors.

'You know that I don't usually see Michael at weekends,' I say quickly, 'I am *really* disappointed.'

'Take mine, Billy. That's no problem. I hope you both have a nice day. You know where the keys are kept, don't you?' I am not sure if Annabelle feels sorry for me, or she just wants to sort me out, so I'll leave her alone on her precious day off.

'Thank you, that's really kind of you,' I say, smiling happily.

'Well, you help me out sometimes, so it's nice to be able to do something for you for once – have a good day, Billy.' She goes back inside before I have a chance to say goodbye.

I am not going to drive the horses to Box Hill, I am planning a much bigger surprise for Michael. It's not his birthday and this will be no picnic for him.

CULMFIELD COURT

As Prince, Sandringham and I roll up to the front of Culmfield Court, I remember all the times Amir dropped Michael and me off here, and how happy I always felt to be back. I picture Mary waving as her father's Rolls Royce drew up.

This time, however, all I see through the front window is Michael charging towards the door. He must be shocked to see me arriving here, and he must be surprised too about the horsebox. I relish the uncertainty I ought to be causing him, I have so many things to say to my lover and I want to see Jessie too. I need to tell her about our affair. *One day, perhaps she will forgive me?*

As I jump out of the lorry, Michael is beside me. He is frowning, 'What the hell are you doing here?'

I ignore him as I make a step towards the house. He puts his hand on my shoulder and speaks gently. 'Is there some crisis? Why didn't you phone me instead of turning up here without warning?'

'Sorry, Michael, you should change the code on the gate more often if you don't want unexpected guests. I have come to see Jessie. I need to talk to her.' I feel confident as I move around him, still intent on heading indoors. He grabs my wrist.

'Billy, are you out of your mind? Why are you doing this? What's wrong with you?' The pressure he is putting on my arm hurts and he is stopping me from moving forward. I yank my arm to get away but he holds on to me, twisting my wrist around.

'Leave now, Billy. Whatever has upset you, we'll talk about it tomorrow. Get back in that vehicle and just go.'

He wrestles me back to the lorry. The pain of his tight grip on my wrist bubbles up rage. 'Ed Mackintosh is dead and you sent him away.'

Michael stops still. 'What in God's name are you talking about? Who's this Edward Mackintosh?' Michael is not yelling, but I can see he is seething.

'Stop pretending, Michael. I know what you did to Ed and now I am bringing your horse back and getting out of your seedy life. But first, I will tell Jessie what we have been doing these last five years.'

Michael's eyes are nearly closed as he breathes in hard through his nose. 'Believe me, girl, I don't know what you are talking about. I don't know this chap, Ed whatever his name is; alive or dead, as he may be. All that I do know is that you are going to leave here. Right now!' He pushes me hard, crashing my shoulder into the door of the lorry cab. I think he will hit me.

Jessie comes out of the house, shouting my name. Michael turns around to her.

'Jessie, sweetheart.' He is tender and calm now. 'Sandringham isn't well, Billy is worried about him and she thinks our vet is better than the one the livery use – so we need to unload him carefully and quietly. Could you go back inside, darling and call the vet?' He pauses and moves a little closer to Jessie before he continues lying to her. 'I know it's Sunday, so if Lana can just get here in the next couple of hours that will be fine.'

I can't believe how quickly he has made this up and how plausible it is. While he was explaining to Jessie I raced to the back of the horsebox and lowered the tail ramp. As quickly as I can, I open the back gates and step up inside. I think Michael and I cannot shout at one another now, it will upset the horses.

With a tethered animal each side of me I feel like the horses are my bodyguards. Prince nuzzles my coat pocket looking for a carrot or some other treat I might have.

Michael marches to the back of the lorry but I know that he won't climb up the wobbly ramp. Standing in the back of the tall horsebox, like I am now, would be too much for him. His terrible fear of heights will keep him on the ground. I could stay here all day and he won't be able to touch me.

'You sent Ed away.' I spit my words at him. 'You threatened to kill him if he didn't go, and now he is dead, and I hate you.' I cry and shout, both at once, wishing I could stop my tears and control my voice. 'You are a liar and a disgusting cheat!' I yell.

He puts a foot on the ramp and I think I may have misjudged him, he is going to throttle me, but he stops. 'Billy, please calm down. You don't know what you are saying.' His demeanour has changed in a split second, and I see now it's because Grégoire is approaching.

The artist smiles at me broadly. 'Hi, Billy, Jessie told me that you might need a hand. I am about to leave, but is there anything I can do to help before I go?'

Michael replies quickly. 'We need to get my horse into one of the stables. Would you mind seeing if there is an empty place for him?'

I don't want Grégoire to go. Michael's skilled improvisations scare me, he is managing everything too easily. While there is a witness, I think he won't hurt me, so I act quickly to keep Grégoire with us. 'Grégoire, did you know that Michael and I have been having an affair?' I ask, speaking to him as though I was talking about the weather. 'I have been his mistress for years. That's why I left Culmfield so suddenly, it wasn't because I couldn't forgive Charlotte for not telling me about you and her.'

The poor man looks shocked. 'I'll check the stables for you, Michael,' he says, not looking at me, 'and then I will be leaving to join Charlotte at her family's farm. They are having an awful time there.'

He turns away and I have no clue how to stop him. I can't delay him further, Charlotte needs him. Her brother's death will be dreadful for her too. But I have to forget Tom, I must deal with Michael first.

Michael waits for Grégoire to go. 'How dare you tell him that,' he hisses.

'I will also tell Jessie, when she comes back out here. I am sure she'll want to say hello to me too.' My temper suddenly explodes and I kick a plastic feed-bucket which wasn't secured properly in the lorry. The force I use splinters the container into pieces. Sandringham is frightened by both my frenzied strike towards him and the violent crack of the brittle plastic. Michael is shocked too. 'Stop this, Billy. You need to calm down. Let's talk about this properly.'

'You sent Ed away and now he is dead. Don't you care what you have done? You are evil, Michael. I trusted you and I finally see who you really are. You stop at nothing to get what you want.'

If he was within reach, I would scratch his eyes out. If there was something sharp available then I'd stab him, ignoring his superior strength, not caring about the consequences for me. I hate the man.

'Stop scaring the horses. Just look at them, Billy, they can't get away from you. They are terrified.'

He's right, both Sandringham and Prince have their heads up and their ears are back. They can't get any further away from me because they are tied up. I want to reassure them, but I also need to keep my eyes on Michael, to know where he is.

Michael sees me check the horses. 'Billy, bring Sandringham down here now and then you need to leave. We'll talk tomorrow, when you've had time to think about what you are doing. I warn you, girl. Don't cross me.'

I follow his instruction. As I reach the bottom of the ramp, Michael instinctively takes hold of Sandringham's lead rope. In the same instant, I release my grip on the horse's halter so the precious animal becomes solely under Michael's control. I have worked out that while he has to look after the flighty horse, he can't harm me.

'Now go, Billy, and don't think any more about telling Jessie anything. You have done enough damage already.'

Prince Sunshine whinnies for his missing friend and as I close up the lorry, I try to soothe him with a gentle word. I feel upset for my separated horse and for everything else that has happened in the last twenty-four hours. Wrath turns to overwhelming regret and my resolve to face up to Michael evaporates. All I want to do now is run away.

'I never want to see you again,' I say quietly as Michael steps back to let me get to the front of the lorry.

'Go, Billy, just go,' he replies.

I climb into the cab, turn the ignition key, and consider running Michael over. I don't.

Looking in my door mirror, I see the business mogul lead his striking black stallion across the courtyard of his beautiful mansion, and I know he is going to make me regret this.

HAMSGATE, DEVON
RICHARD

I woke up beside Jayne this morning. This was odd because I have never so much as kissed the woman. I like her, but she is just a big sister figure in my life, nothing more.

This situation began yesterday with Daniella's distressed phone call about Tom. I could hear how desperate she was and I wanted to help her. She has always been there for me, especially since Janette and I parted, letting me ring her whenever I needed to. Sometimes I feel she is *my* mother, not Billy's.

While Daniella was talking to me yesterday, Jayne pressed the phone's loudspeaker button. My nosey neighbour listened to my call. She is like that, there can be no secrets from Jayne. She pokes her long beak into everything. I let her listen, because I knew if I didn't, she would just keep on until she had all the information she wanted. It is really aggravating, but I know she just wants to help. Whoever she is with, she always seems to understand their point of view, giving her frank advice whether it's wanted or not.

She decided, there and then, she was going to come with me to see Daniella. She saw it as an escape from her kids and a chance to check out the Devon farm I am always harping on about.

Jayne telephoned Janette to organise for her to look after her children. My twins and her daughter, Amy, have just started university so Janette only had four to look after including Freddy. They are all good kids, so it wasn't hard for her to say yes. Jayne soon sorted my overnight bag too, and she happily drove me here.

Last night, Daniella and my neighbour didn't stop talking, and at bedtime, they were both adamant that it was fine for Jayne and me to sleep in the same bed. Nothing would happen, and it just wasn't fair to push old Barney off the settee. For all her annoying interference, I am grateful Jayne is with me. She is helping with Daniella. Tom's death has sucked out the happiness here, but my whirlwind of a neighbour is lightening things up a bit. I left Jayne this afternoon to help Daniella prepare a roast dinner, while I headed off to see Martha and Tom's mother.

I offered Tom's family some help, paying for a temporary farm manager while they sort out some of the terrible things they are facing, someone to help them for a few months, until they work out how they will cope. I am so glad they accepted. Having read all Daniella's letters, it feels like I knew Tom and his family, and I feel a special connection with Tom. I wonder if it is because we were both close to Billy. I am deeply upset by his sudden death. Maybe I am affected so much because it's bringing back the horror of Saffi's suicide. I feel I have to do something to help his family.

It's just before midnight, and Jayne and I are about to go to our bed, having been persuaded by Daniella to stay another day. Our bags were packed, so I am about to carry them back upstairs, but now Billy falls through the front door. She looks shattered.

She tells us that her fiancé has died, she is on the edge of madness about it. Billy doesn't question why I am here, she doesn't ask who Jayne is. 'I have given up my job at O'Rowdes', Mum, she says. 'I've arranged with Martha to stable Prince at Fox Halt Farm. I hope you don't mind but I am home for good.'

Daniella is lost for words, as her daughter heads upstairs to the spare room. We all hear the door slam shut. I imagine Billy lying on the bed I slept on last night. She is a wreck. Her poor Mum will have more pieces to pick up in the morning. 'Richard. Would you and Jayne mind leaving after all?' Daniella keeps her eyes fixed on the upstairs landing. 'I need to talk to her.'

'Of course, but, Daniella, ring me if you need anything,' I say.

'I will, don't worry,' she says, kissing me on the cheek. 'Jayne, it was lovely to meet you. Please come back and stay again soon, with Jock, or just your children, whatever, just come again, please.' Daniella kisses her too, and then she starts to climb the stairs.

Jayne drives us back to Buckinghamshire, while I try to get the images of poor Billy out of my head.

HAMSGATE
FRIDAY 28 OCTOBER 2005
RICHARD

Tom's funeral this afternoon is something I will never forget. Billy was so brave, driving the restored Fordson Major tractor with his coffin on the trailer behind.

It seemed that every farmer in the district came, all of them driving their tractors, and lots of them with restored and cherished machines like the one Billy drove. Families arrived in link-boxes and on trailers. The whole of Hamsgate was one big tractor jam until they parked up next to the village hall. We all walked in silence to the church. Everyone following the trailer draped in flowers. All of us bewildered. *How could this have happened?*

I arrived in Hamsgate this morning, having expected to be able to stay at Culmfield last night, but Michael has left on a surprise holiday with his family. His personal assistant told me Jessie organised it all without telling him, deciding that their thirteenth wedding anniversary wouldn't be unlucky for them. Apparently, Michael was thrilled, telling his assistant he would be uncontactable for five weeks, while they were on his private yacht somewhere in the Caribbean. He said his business was just going to have to manage without him. I am stunned, I never imagined that Michael would do something so rash but I suppose it shows how you never really know a person, do you?

It is now the wake, there are people crammed in everywhere in the village hall. The noise is deafening. There are so many stories of encounters and escapades with Tom. He meant a lot to so many people. I tell Daniella about Michael and his surprise holiday, and Billy stands beside us in a daze.

For once, Daniella isn't listening. Her reply is not linked to what I've just told her. 'All I want to do is to get Billy to talk to me,' she says, 'but she is avoiding me, spending every minute on Tom's farm instead. She is trying to do all the things her friend might have been doing, wearing herself out. Richard, will you tell her to stop, please? I am sure the new farm manager will be okay without her. The poor girl needs a break.'

Billy grabs her mother's hand. 'Mum, did you hear what Richard said about Michael?'

'Was it something about a holiday, dear?' Billy stares at her mother, mascara smudged around her eyes.

'Mum, I need to tell you something, I think Richard ought to know this too.' Billy looks at me. 'You believe Michael is your friend.'

She smooths down her black skirt and then takes a deep breath. 'I don't believe Jessie organised their holiday – it would have been Michael, he has a lot to sort out with his wife, and he needed to get her away from me.'

Daniella frowns at her daughter. 'Darling, I don't understand?'

Billy presses her hands onto her skirt again, but I don't think she is trying to smarten herself up, I think she is wiping sweat off her palms, she looks uncomfortable as she gazes into her mother's eyes.

'I was Michael's mistress. He lived with me in London and spent his weekends with his family.' She speaks quickly so we can't interrupt. 'But something awful happened so I ended it. I didn't know how to tell you this without hurting you, but I don't want to lie anymore. I am sure Michael took his wife away on this long holiday, so he can brainwash her with a stack of clever lies about our affair, making sure I can't tell Jessie what really happened. I was never engaged to Ed. Saffi gave me this ring.' She holds her hand up to her mother, still staring at her, waiting for the horrified response she knows is coming.

'How could you, Billy? Michael!' Daniella is nearly in tears. 'And you lied about you and Ed too, is he really dead?'

Billy pushes her shoulders back. 'Yes, Mum, Ed died.'

'In a car accident?' her mum checks.

'No, not in a car crash, it was cocaine and heroin that killed him, and his addiction was down to Michael.'

'Billy, you are not making sense, he didn't force Ed to take drugs–'

'Michael was jealous of my relationship with Ed and he made him leave London. He threatened him, saying he would kill him if we kept seeing each other. Ed was desperately unhappy in Dubai, and that's when he started using drugs – he was just trying to feel better, and he couldn't stop.'

It is as though Billy has kicked me in the stomach. I have seen Michael so often and he never gave the slightest hint of his relationship with her. He was the one who first told me Billy had a fiancé. *Michael, you underhand snake.* All I can think to do is to walk away. I need to find Martha anyway. I shiver, not wanting to believe what Billy has just said. I head outside to escape all the noise, and to get myself back together.

On a bench outside, I am joined by two boys. I suck in the smell of their cigarettes. I have never smoked, and never wanted to but I think I might like to now, maybe nicotine would calm me down a little. *Michael has really used me, hasn't he?* I don't feel mad at Billy, no doubt he used her too. Poor Ed, that young man was such a good member of my staff, so promising, and I let Michael employ him without a moment's thought. Ed working for O'Rowdes' left a big hole in my company – all just part of a scheming plan by that jealous bastard.

Billy has come outside too.

'I am sorry about Ed,' I tell her.

The two boys get up and she sits next to me. We haven't had a conversation for years, yet somehow it feels as though we are close friends 'Do you want to tell me what happened with Ed?' I ask.

'Do you mind?' she says. 'It would be good to talk to someone.' She is smiling. The first time I have seen her smile for a long time.

'Can't you talk to your mum, Billy?'

'I hate loading more grief onto her, she loved Tom so much and I have brought all my misery on myself. Don't you want me to talk to you about Ed?'

'Billy, tell me anything you want. I can listen – I won't judge you – I have made enough mistakes. I can't tell you what's right or wrong.'

'I should never have got involved with Michael – that was a big wrong. That was crazy and stupid, wasn't it?'

'Yes, it probably was, but I am not judging you,' I say again. 'I am shocked though. I can't believe he never let on to me he was seeing you. I thought we were close, especially after he helped you so much when you lost our baby.'

'I can't talk about our baby, Richard, not to you, not now. But do you mind if I tell you about Ed?'

'I am listening.' I nod.

'When Ed came back from Dubai, we started meeting up once a fortnight – just walking and talking, nothing else but I kept our meet ups secret from Michael. I suspected Ed was keeping me a secret too. We never discussed how we felt, but I know we both enjoyed each other's company very much. It was nice to start with but slowly Ed fell apart. I didn't realise he was terrified of Michael finding out. Looking back now, I think the drugs made him paranoid and then he used more drugs to conquer his fear. A vicious downward spiral until his heart couldn't take any more.

'After he died, I spoke to his sister, she told me how his family persuaded him to stay in a rehabilitation clinic a couple of times but it was always an uphill battle, which we all lost in the end. I can't believe he is dead – this is all so terrible, Ed and Tom – all of it. I feel so responsible about Ed, I tried not to get hurt by keeping everything between us temporary. I didn't want commitment but I couldn't hurt more than I do now, his death is all my fault.'

'You didn't threaten to kill him, and you didn't send him away,' I try to reassure her.

'I blamed Michael to start with too. I wanted to hurt him, so I went to Culmfield to confront him, and to tell Jessie about our affair. I messed that up as well, all I did was annoy him. I am scared Michael will come after me now, he warned me not to cross him. I keep worrying what he'll do.'

'Billy, I don't think Michael will hurt you. Please don't worry. He's not due back for a while anyway.'

'Listen, Richard, would you do me a favour? Later, when you're over some of the shock of all this, would you phone me, just so I can talk it all through again. Telling you this has made me feel calmer. I think putting my thoughts into words, makes it easier to bear.'

'I will,' I say, getting up. 'Take care of yourself, Billy – I need to find Martha and check something with her before I leave.'

'I'm heading back to the cottage,' she says, reaching to touch my hand for a second. 'Thank you, Richard. Bye for now.'

I watch her wander down the lane. She has come home, but Billy is completely lost.

Chapter 32

PINEAPPLE 1

SUNDAY 20 NOVEMBER 2005

BILLY

I am alone in Richard's office, he has just left and now I await the arrival of his next client. I hope Michael will be shocked to find me here. I try to ignore my nerves, and I start to reflect on all that has happened since Tom's funeral.

My poor mother, what I've put her through. She is a rock, I don't know how I would have withstood these last few weeks without her.

Both of us have been helping Martha as much as we can. Charlotte and Grégoire have been in Hamsgate a lot too, and the remorse and forgiveness has been heart-wrenching. Losing Ed and Tom has put everything in perspective. It's easier to see what's important now, and looking after each other is more helpful than apportioning blame.

I had a long chat with Grégoire about how Michael cajoled him into painting the chapel roof at Culmfield. He said Michael arrived uninvited at Saffi's apartment in Paris, while Saffi and he were having breakfast. They had already said Grégoire wouldn't work for him, the clever artist had just finished Saffi's London apartment and he wanted a break. They had been neglecting their Paris friends and Grégoire didn't want to be stuck in the country for months. Michael offered more and more money, he threatened Saffi that there would be no work from O'Rowdes' – Saffi didn't care, he had money and other work. But Michael had an ace hidden up his sleeve, telling Saffi how he would ensure that the Culmfield ceiling would get the same kind of acclaim that Michelangelo's Sistine Chapel receives, Michael described how everyone would rave about the wonderful work of art and its talented creator.

Saffi couldn't resist his friend being widely recognised and insisted Grégoire had to take on the commission. As a parting consolation, Michael told Saffi that I would lodge with him while his friend was away. Michael could see how close Saffi and Grégoire were, and planned on easing Grégoire's guilt about leaving his friend. Michael played us all.

Martha is selling Fox Halt Farm. William can't bear to be in the yard where he found his dad, and I am trying to decide if I should buy it back. Mum says she will sell her cottage to help me with the cost and she says how much she would love us to return there, but I don't want to be led by emotion and nostalgia – I need a sound business plan first.

I am considering ways to make the place profitable, researching making our own dairy products and selling them direct to customers. I have been talking to other people who are already doing this and I have read lots about making ice cream, clotted cream, yoghurt and artisan cheeses. I am even looking at different breeds of cows, and possibly sheep or goats, working out all the likely costs and how much we might market these farm-made goods for.

Martha has offered to let me buy one of her fields too, which is next to the main road, so I can start up a specialist farm shop selling our unique Fox Halt Farm products, as well as other locally made goods and crafts.

I am in London today because Richard insisted, he wanted to hear about all my ideas, offering to run through all the estimated figures with me. We discussed lots of options and some seem viable.

It feels strange to be back here, especially odd sitting on Richard's side of his desk. The door handle is being pushed down. Michael doesn't falter, he comes in and sits opposite me, saying nothing, just glaring, while I pretend not to be terrified.

I have to do this, Richard and I agreed that this seemed the safest place to meet up with my former lover. I hope surprise will give me an advantage for at least a moment or two.

'Hi, Michael,' I say. 'How was the Caribbean…'

'So, you came running back to Richard?' he sneers.

'No, you are wrong, I am looking at buying Fox Halt Farm from Martha and he's been helping me with my business plan.'

'Yes of course, he…'

I cut in. 'Michael, I need to speak to you. Please can we draw a line under everything that has happened? I can assure you I never want to see you again, and I am sure you don't want anything to do with me either.'

Michael leans forward, his face uncomfortably close to mine. 'You are not getting away so lightly, missie, you nearly wrecked my marriage. I had to drop everything to make sure I kept my family together. You will pay for turning up like that.'

I wanted to discuss this quietly, apologise for acting hastily. Rocking up, all guns blazing at Culmfield Court was ill-considered, I was not thinking clearly, but now, Michael's intimidation brings to mind all the times I have gone along with him, how manipulated I have been. Anger rises up from my feet into my mouth, and I can't help retaliating. 'I suppose you told Jessie a pack of lies just like you always do? I am deluded, I suppose? Or did I trap you in some way? The trouble is, Michael, I have told Mum, Richard, Tom's mother, Charlotte and Grégoire my version of events, and if I don't tell your wife the truth about our sordid affair, then I am sure one of them might. One of us will make Jessie see what a control freak you are. I think your month trying to convince your wonderful wife she has a perfect husband will prove to be in vain when she hears the truth.'

He grabs the collar of my shirt, twisting the fabric tight around my neck. I struggle to breathe.

Richard runs into the room and grips Michael's arm. 'Don't,' he says. Michael lets go of me, but as I gasp for air. I see his plan is to attack Richard instead – he is about to thump him with the hand that was choking me. Richard anticipates this move and traps both Michael's arms down by his side, forcing my assailant back into the chair.

'There are a few things we need to talk about,' Richard says. His adversary looks nonchalant. 'Firstly, Michael, I will never believe anything you say again, you have lost a valuable ally. From now on, I will be arguing against every one of your business proposals. I know your tricks so don't expect O'Rowdes' to have an easy time with any future property schemes.'

I wait for Michael to defend himself with a handful of spurious reasons for his deceit, but he doesn't. Richard looks directly into his eyes now and what he says next *does* upset Michael. It distresses me too because I can't believe what I hear. 'You murdered Tom Westcott, didn't you? Tom's death was no accident, was it?'

Michael's eyes narrow to slits. He is fuming, as he pauses between each individual word. 'Say – that – again, – what – do – you – mean?'

Richard doesn't repeat the terrible allegation, but he continues, 'Your car, your fancy Porsche Spyder was seen racing away from the yard at around the time of Tom's 'accident.' I know it was your car, Michael, and I have your distinctive little Porsche all safely locked away somewhere. The dung from Tom's muck-spreader is still on its wheels. There are splashes of Fox Halt Farm muck glued to its tyres, chassis and paintwork.'

Michael shakes his head. 'You don't have my car.'

'I do,' Richard tells him. 'I told Nala and Amir I had bought it from you, and they obligingly let me take it away. Shame Amir knows me so well, he believed me straight away when I explained I wanted it urgently for Harry, now that she has passed her driving test. He just wanted to help, even taking some photos of it, to record its condition. I warned them that you were a little reluctant to sell it to me but you knew how my daughter loved it, so I asked them not to mention the car to you again because it might upset you a little.'

Richard takes some pictures out of his desk drawer, placing them on the desk in front of Michael.

'This is ridiculous.' Michael doesn't look at the photographs, instead he laughs. 'You better give me my car back, Richard. There is no way you two are pinning some freak farm accident on me. Why on God's earth would I hurt Tom Westcott?'

I am sure the accusation is wrong too – there is no reason for him to have killed my childhood friend. It was an accident, it was starting to rain and Tom was rushing – he must have slipped. Michael had nothing to do with him dying, but Richard doesn't let up.

'You were jealous of Tom, weren't you? Just like you were jealous of Ed. You thought Billy was getting too close to him. He and Martha had split up and you reckoned your lover might leave you. That Billy might want to come back to Devon. Were you warning her friend off and he fell backwards onto the spinning shaft? Or did you shove him onto it?'

This can't be true. I shout at Richard now, 'Stop! There was no reason for him to be jealous of Tom.'

'He knew you were seeing him when you came down to Devon, he knew you were helping on the farm and he knew you were enjoying doing it because I stupidly showed him a letter from your mum.'

'What letter?'

'One your mother sent me a while ago. I thought Michael would like to know you were doing okay – this man would have taken in every word just like he does with every document, plan or spreadsheet I have ever presented him with. He knew how you were spending time with your old friend when you were in Devon. With Tom and Martha not getting back together, he was becoming more and more concerned he'd lose you to Tom.'

Richard turns back to Michael. 'Did you check up on the two of them? Did you see how happy Billy was, helping with the milking? Were they laughing together?'

Michael is motionless, and it seems to me as if Richard is taunting him, like a tiger trapped inside a paper cage. In a split second the fierce animal will shrug off his fragile prison and devour his captor. I think Richard should back off but he doesn't, he threatens him instead. 'Michael, I want you to leave this office, take all your business elsewhere and leave Billy alone. If you don't, I'll go to the police.'

I don't understand. *Why hasn't Richard spoken to me about any of this?*

'Richard,' I say, almost shouting at him, 'if you truly believe Tom's death wasn't an accident, then we must inform the police straight away.'

'No, Billy, I don't want to. Martha and the family don't need to endure a long police and forensic investigation, a trial and tons more upset on top of what they are already going through.'

Michael stands up, and speaks softly and slowly. 'I swear, I had nothing to do with Tom Westcott's death. I also assure you, I'll have nothing more to do with either of you. You two can rot in hell.'

I am too scared to stop him as he leaves the office, and Richard doesn't seem bothered that he is walking away. We both follow him to the end of the corridor, but then while he waits for the lift, he turns around. His face is red.

'If you, or anyone else, speaks to Jessie, or if I am arrested, then something could happen to one of Tom's kids, or maybe Daniella – an unfortunate drowning or a house fire perhaps – the old electrics in those ancient cottages are notoriously unsafe. Some horrible misfortune in the middle of the night.'

Michael steps into the lift and I stare at him in silence, taking in his terrible threats.

As the lift doors close behind him, I turn to Richard.

'Call the police now, we have to.'

I am sweating all over, Michael's warning about harming William, Grace or my mother has convinced me he caused Tom's death. My breath comes in short bursts as dismay about what Michael may have done takes over my body. He murdered Tom, and he might have killed me too if Richard hadn't stepped in.

Richard sits down on the floor of the corridor with his back against the wall. He looks up at me. 'Sorry, Billy, I can't phone them, there would be so little evidence. Tom used the muck-spreader for two days before he died, spilling dung onto all the local lanes transporting it to the fields. There was all that rain afterwards too. Michael's car is splattered with muck but it could be from anywhere nearby.

'William definitely saw a car like Michael's, and there may be other people who witnessed him driving it, but what would that prove? Only that he was in Hamsgate. I'm sure he'd buy a cast iron excuse for being there.'

'We know all the threats he made to Ed,' I say. 'And the threats he just made too.'

'Ed can't verify what happened to him, can he?' Richard sounds resigned to not taking this any further, he has obviously thought it all through carefully. He tries to explain some more. 'Amir told me Michael took the car out that evening but I am certain Michael's chauffeur won't be happy to testify this either; he and Nala have too much to lose, they are going to be in enough trouble, letting me take the Porsche. All the evidence is circumstantial, and Michael would get the best lawyers. He'd be out on bail in five minutes and free to hurt you. I don't want to take that risk. Do you?'

'So, we just leave it?' I ask. 'We have to hope that the fear of someone talking to Jessie, or getting the police involved is enough for him to leave us all alone. Is that what you are saying, Richard?'

'I am,' he says. 'Michael won't want his precious name and his private life dragged through the divorce or the criminal courts with all the tabloids ruining O'Rowdes' reputation. He could sue you for blighting his name, keeping his case going against you until he'd bankrupted the farm, with you paying massive legal fees to defend yourself. I'm sure he'd demand a compensation pay-out too. I'm sorry, Billy, he's going to win again. We have to believe the threat of Jessie finding out what a cruel husband she has, or the threat of us going to the police, is enough to keep him away.'

I feel exhausted, I hoped that talking to Michael would bring an end to my fears. I wanted to stop looking over my shoulder wondering if he was there. I see I have just one option left, I will have to put Michael out of my mind. I can only go forward if I stop looking back. I am so glad Richard is helping me. I wonder if he has saved my life yet again. I have to believe we will be fine.

'Okay, we'll leave it then, for now,' I say.

'We tell no-one this, Billy, is that agreed?'

'Yes, agreed,' I say, wishing I had another choice. 'Look, I've got to get back to Hamsgate, Mum is cooking a late supper. Thank you for looking through everything with me today.'

'Billy.' Richard stares up at me.

'Yes.'

He jumps to his feet and takes my hands in his. 'Would I be welcome there this weekend? Could I bring Freddy too, and show him around the farm?'

'Yes, that would be lovely, Richard, we could talk some more about what the future has in store for the place.'

'And for you?'

'Yes, and for me too. I know I will make Fox Halt Farm a huge success, and perhaps you will help me a little bit along the way?'

I kiss him on the cheek and he smiles at me. 'Let's get you back home,' he says.

Epilogue
FOX HALT FARM
FRIDAY 27 JUNE 2008
DANIELLA

*D*earest Richard

I hope you get this email in time for the wedding – please wish your daughter all my love, I am thinking of you all.

Billy's fortieth birthday today too, how can I have a child that old? But then I think back and realise an awful lot has happened in that time. Still happening too, the farm shop opens today – it's such a shame you won't be here.

I do forgive you, Richard, for missing Billy's big day, I mean, you couldn't help it that Harry has fallen in love with a New Zealander and chose today, of all days, to get married.

I hope New Zealand is as nice as you expected, have you all been skiing? Does your dad still ski? It does look fun, perhaps Harry could teach me one day – I am joking – I am far too old for that sort of caper.

The two weeks while you've been away have been manic, sorting out all the last-minute things for the grand opening. I can't believe Billy has managed to get a Royal to unveil a plaque to mark the occasion today – but then it is a pretty smart shop – it looks so impressive now everything is finished and all the shelves are full.

By the way, Grace is here, helping with all the preparations, and she is insisting that I have to say hello to Freddy. Please tell your son that I can't wait for him to be here permanently, so I don't have to deal with his moping girlfriend every time he is away.

Billy cleaned the holiday cottage from top to bottom ready for your furniture to come next week and your 'surprise' moving in party is all arranged. I am sorry it's not going to be a surprise. You know, I didn't mean to tell you, and I hope you and Freddy are good at acting when everyone turns up at your door. My daughter would be so upset if she discovered that you knew already. You have helped her so much and she wants the party to be a very special thank you. I wish you were moving into the farmhouse with us instead, but the cottage across the yard is going to be great for you and Freddy – my cakes won't be far away and I foresee a lot of chatting at the kitchen table.

I am attaching an article about yesterday's British Cheese Awards and I'll let you read it to find out how we got on – I do owe you a surprise, after all. The only thing I'll say about it, is that we can't really believe it, yet.

I assure you that I have not forgotten your birthday present for Billy, I will give the tickets to her when the shop opening is over. Until then, she won't be able to concentrate on anything else. I will make sure she understands that we have sorted out all the extra help we need for you two to go off to Paros for two whole weeks. You will both have such a fabulous time together – some proper time on your own, at last.

Please send me some photos later. I need to see you all poshed up. I wish I could be there. Harry is going to look stunning, and Sid will too, in that beautiful bridesmaid's dress she showed me when she came down to the farm last month. I hope the girls like the bracelets I bought them for today.

Love to you all. See you next week, Daniella xxxx

Dear Reader...

I hope you enjoyed this book, and if you did, please post a short review on Amazon and/or on Goodreads too. Reviews make a huge difference in helping others discover my books, and as I am sure you appreciate, they help a good deal with their success. Your review doesn't need to be long. Please take it from the heart, say how Fox Halt Farm made you feel, or what characters you liked – that's all. Please recommend my books to your friends too.

About Celia Moore
THE INSPIRATION FOR FOX HALT FARM

Fox Halt Farm includes a lot of things that have happened to me, but the events are all muddled up. The characters are made up and the outcomes are different – what I have written is more about trying to recognise feelings, and understanding the search for the elusive happiness we all seek. I can't say I wrote this book because it is more that I dreamt it. It came to me one night and it wouldn't go away.

I cried my heart out at times while I typed, believing before I started writing that I had my fabulous father's sudden death sussed, happy in the knowledge he was always looking over my shoulder watching me. I know now that I had a lot more grieving to do, and I needed to remember the incredible man he was and the things he did. I needed to cry over other losses too, and properly recognise the precious people and the extraordinary moments which have moulded my life so far.

I always thought you just get on with life and live for the day but I see now that we all have to take time to reflect and wonder at the past times too. Writing this book has given so much to me.

Happiness, I think, is recognising every gift. I have my wonderful husband, friends and family and the awe-inspiring wonder of what will happen tomorrow.

Other Books by Celia Moore

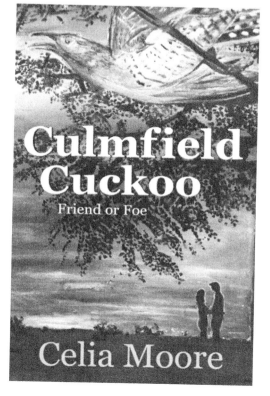

Culmfield Cuckoo (the sequel to Fox Halt Farm) published March 2019 – can also be read as standalone novel.

The final part in this trilogy is planned. If you would like to know when it will be available, or have questions about the author's writing or her talks about her writing, please contact Celia:

Website Celiascosmos.com
Facebook Celia Moore Books

Acknowledgements

I have to thank my husband, my mother and Tracey Lee for their endless support and encouragement.

Thank you too to Julie and Mark Heslington, Beth Webb, Melissa Eveleigh, Carol Noble-Smith, Jomie Gee, Celia and Marj Rundle, Jenny Ford, Graham Sercombe, Anne Williams, Debbie Johnson and Rachel Gilby.

I painted the picture on the front cover but the amazing Harrison Pidgeon put the design together.

Thank you to my editor, Amanda Horan, who is totally brilliant at what she does, opening my eyes to so many better ways to get my story across. Without her extraordinary help and knowledge, I could never have felt the delight I have for Fox Halt Farm.

Thank you, Julia Gibbs, for proof reading and finding all the mistakes I would never have seen.

And finally, thank *you* for reading my book. Without you, I couldn't have the joy of sharing my passion for telling my stories.

Printed in Great Britain
by Amazon

58814181R00159